BARRANCA AND BLOOD JUSTICE

Two Full Length Western Novels

GORDON D. SHIRREFFS

WOLFPACK
PUBLISHING
— EST 2013 —

Barranca and Blood Justice
Paperback Edition
Copyright © 2022 (As Revised) Gordon D. Shirreffs

Wolfpack Publishing
9850 S. Maryland Parkway, Suite A-5 #323
Las Vegas, Nevada 89183

wolfpackpublishing.com

Paperback ISBN 978-1-63977-695-5
eBook ISBN 978-1-63977-502-6

BARRANCA AND BLOOD JUSTICE

BARRANCA

CHAPTER ONE

The sun was almost gone beyond the softly rounded mountains. Long shadows moved down the leaden-hued slopes toward the smooth flow of rifted earth that buried the base of the range. The harsh light of the day had long been softened, but the sodden heat still hung heavily over mesa and mountain. It was too early for the desert to cool after the living hell of the summer day. The mountains and mesas seemed like islands rising from a dry sea-bed, waterless for countless ages. In all that burning land, still vague and indefinite from the heat haze of the day, there was no sign of man except for the faint wagon ruts that slanted across the desert and the thin thread of smoke that rose high in the windless air.

There was nothing friendly about that smoke. The thought haunted the heat-hazed mind of Sheldon Burnett. He raised his pounding head from his crossed forearms and stared stupidly at the smoke. His swollen tongue cautiously explored his cracked lips. His thirst had long passed from mouth and throat into his over-heated blood and now seemed to be penetrating his bones. He closed his burning eyes. The idle thought drifted through his mind that in other places and at other times he had looked eagerly for signs of smoke —the cheering symbol of hospitality in an otherwise barren land. He passed a dirty hand through his dusty, reddish beard, scrabbling in the stiff hair. He itched all over. It had been so long ago that he had stripped and bathed that he could not quite recall the incident.

He slowly opened his eyes again. The smoke was still there. The thread of it was a little thinner but it was still rising in the air as it had been doing for seemingly endless hours.

There was only one source for smoke in that country. No white man would dare betray his presence by kindling a fire. Neither would an Apache, unless he had left it *behind* him, and that fire had never been lighted to cook food. There was something evil about that smoke, something that haunted one's mind.

Matthew Dustin moved sluggishly in the shadows beyond Sheldon. "By God, Shell," he husked. "How much longer?"

Shell pressed a hand against his burning eyes. "Until we're sure, Dusty," he said patiently. For God's sake, he thought, I hope he keeps quiet this time.

"They won't be down there now," rasped Dusty.

The sear slipped on Shell's temper. He turned his head and looked at the dusty, bearded face of his companion. "Damn you!" he snapped. "Go on down and look then! Go on, you ornery sonofabitch! I'll bury what's left of you! *Go on down!*"

Dusty sat up and rubbed his right forearm across his eyes. "By Christ," he said, "it's either die up here or down there! I ain't about to sit here and wait for it! That ain't *my* way!"

Shell sat up too. "Haven't you got the guts to stick it out?" he said in a low voice.

Dusty lowered his arm, and his cold blue eyes flicked at Shell. Shell knew that look well enough. It had prophesied the quick and violent death of a number of men. In the hot thickness of the gathering shadows their minds seemed to reach out for each other for an opening hold in the death grapple. Flames of hate seemed to be fanned by the enervating heat and the destroying thirst. For a fraction of time, perhaps a few heartbeats, the hostility hung between them and then Dusty laughed. *"Compañero,"* he said, "I'll match you to see who goes down alone to the waterhole."

Shell turned away from Dusty. The sun was gone but there was still a great wash of rose and gold in the western sky stained with darker streamers. "We go down together, *compañero,"* he said quietly.

That was enough. Words like those, or the thought behind them, had held them together for more than five years. Through the blood and smoke of the war, from Wilson's Creek to the bitter end. It had held them together the night they had crossed the Rio Grande, riding with General Jo Shelby, the Confederate who had refused to accept Appomattox. Before the dripping horses had reached the Mexican shore, the stained and shot-riddled Stars and Bars had been reverently dropped into the dark waters, well weighted so that the battle flag should not rise again. To the south Maximilian had needed fighting men and was willing to pay in gold for veteran cavalrymen to help him win his fight against Juarez and his Republican forces. There had been no argument from Dusty and Shell.

"There'll be a new moon tonight," said Dusty.

Shell nodded. He tore his mind from the past.

"We oughta move down to the lower ground before then," said Dusty.

Shell nodded again. "While the Apaches are moving up," he said sarcastically.

"Yuh always have to be so damned knowing?" snapped Dusty.

Shell had the obvious answer but he was too dead beat to care.

"How much longer do we wait?" persisted Dusty.

The sun was fully gone and the western sky had

changed from rose and gold to fainter hues banded with streamers of light gray to a mottled grayness streaked with darker lines. The air was completely motionless. A foreboding silence hung over the dark desert between the eastern mesas of naked lava to the rounded mountains west of the great valley. Shell felt as though he and Dusty had strayed somehow from the Earth of the living into limbo, or perhaps to some unknown planet whirling through space, where the two of them were the only living creatures. It was eerie and uncanny, and despite the clinging heat a chill crept through him and raised his flesh.

"I asked a question," said Dusty.

He was like a canker worm gnawing at one's mind. It was his way. It was *always* his way. Dusty aimed directly for his immediate goal and went for it hell for leather and to the devil with the hindmost. It was his way and he was good at it. When he came unwound, *something* had to give.

Shell moved a little to ease his lean frame against the warm rock. The sour, acrid odor of his sweat-soaked clothing hung about him. The heat brought out an aura of odors. Sour sweat and sweat-damp leather, unwashed hair and flesh, and even the brassy odor of the cartridges in his gun belt. Shell reached out and placed a big hand on his Spencer repeating carbine. The wood and metal were almost hot to the touch.

Shell suddenly raised his head. Something had come to him from the darkness of the steep slopes below them. "Listen!" he said tersely.

It was deathly quiet. Somewhere in the darkness behind them something rustled. A sharp, pitiful squeaking arose and then died as suddenly as it had come. It was the death cry of some small creature caught by a nocturnal predator. Something else had alerted Shell. He wasn't even sure he had *heard* anything. Years of war and of traveling in hostile Indian country had honed some sixth sense within him. One either developed such a sense under such circumstances or died ... *fast*.

Shell sniffed the warm air. He slowly swung his shaggy head from side to side. He couldn't see anything but the darkness of the lower slopes and the thicker darkness of the thorned brush clumps, *yet there was something down there*.

Dusty moved softly. Shell mentally cursed him.

The two horses were well hidden in a deep draw a quarter of a mile away. No sensible man kept his animals near him when he stopped for the night in that country. One soft whinny could be picked up at almost unbeliev-able distances by the sharp ears of an Apache.

Shell hooked a thumb over the big hammer of the Spencer. It was already half-cocked. He touched his cracked lips with his tongue and almost stopped breathing to hear better, but his heart thudded so he was sure it could be heard twenty feet away. Shell put a curb rein on his emotions. *Apaches!* Despite his years of experi-ence in Indian country and in war he had never quite been able to govern the reaction that one word set off in his mind. He fought the faint, cloying sickness that rose in his lean gut and then hovered at the pit of his throat. The thought of dying wasn't so bad. One gets fatalistic after four years of war. It wasn't the thought of dying that unnerved him. *It was the thought of being caught alive by them*.

The darkness was full and thick by now, pressing down upon them, alive with the unseen. Dusty hissed softly. He had eyes like a cat.

Vaguely, as though seen through a misty waterfall, or a drifting, tenuous fog, there was a movement in the dark-ness. There were twin metallic clicks as Spencer hammers came back to full cock. Trigger fingers gently took up the slack. The clicking sound seem inordinately magnified.

A rounded object moved into view, faintly silhouetted against the skyline. There was no mistaking it. It wasn't a hat. It was a head, thickly maned. Only white men wore hats in that country. Higher and higher rose the head until the shoulders were seen, and the tossing head of a horse appeared. The warrior came higher along the dim trail as though manipulated by the strings of a master of marionettes. The Apache turned his head and looked directly toward the two breathless men lying belly flat on the rocks. The white bottom clay with which he had banded upper cheeks and the bridge of his nose could now be seen. There was a ghostliness about the appearance of this mounted buck. The soft thudding of the horse's hoofs came to them. The mount must be wearing rawhide boots.

The Apache was silhouetted fully now, an easy shot for the two expert marksmen who watched him. It looked so easy. The buck looked back down the unseen trail and then passed from view behind an upthrust boulder that seemed to raise an admonishing finger toward the sky. For a moment he was heard and seen and then he was gone. It seemed as though he had been unreal, a phantom conjured up in the thirst-ridden minds of the two white men.

It was quiet again, but something unseen still haunted the velvety darkness. Something that still pinned the two white men to the rock. Their thirst became aggravated to such an extent that both of them wanted to curse and to shout, to charge stiff-legged down the slope, slamming lead from side to side like a fireman playing a hose. It was a madness and it had to be fought down. Shell heard a sharp intake of breath and was about to curse Dusty when he realized it was his own unconscious action.

Dusty hissed again.

Sweat ran down Shell's face, cutting tiny furrows in the dust, crawling into his beard, setting up an intolerable itching. His sweat greased the stock of his repeater. It worked through his beard and mercilessly stung his cracked lips with a kiss of salt.

Another thickly maned head arose out of the darkness, followed by another and another, and still another, with the soft thudding of the hoofs beating steadily. A horse suddenly snorted.

Oh God, thought Shell, *he's scented our damned stink!*

One after another until fully a score of them were moving toward the upthrust pinnacle of rock. Lance shafts rose above their heads like single antennae. The heads of the warriors moved constantly, from side to side, then back, then ahead again, then from side to side again, in ceaseless vigilance, for an Apache hates surprise worse than anything.

The last warrior vanished behind the pinnacle. A thin cloud of bitter-smelling dust hung in the quiet air and drifted slowly down on the two white men, coating them, working into their eyes and nostrils, touching their cracked and burning lips.

"Now?" husked Dusty.

Shell fiercely shook his aching head.

Minutes ticked past, each tick feeling like a hammer blow to the gut.

Dusty moved restlessly. He winced in savage pain but did not cry out as Shell drove a boot toe into his side.

A horse blew in the darkness. Shell raised his carbine. The head of the buck and the head of his mount appeared as though rising from a pool of ink.

Dusty moved a little. His metal-shod carbine butt faintly tapped a rock. The Apache halted his horse. He sat his mount, looking directly at the two men. He couldn't possibly see them! It was physically impossible, and yet it seemed as though he *did* see them.

Shell pressed trigger finger against trigger. They'd have a few minutes' grace before the rest of them came back. A damned few minutes!

The buck touched his horse with his moccasined heels and rode on. The greasy loops of a swollen horse intestine hung across the withers of his horse. Just before he passed the rock pinnacle he glanced quickly back toward the two white men. It seemed to each of them that he was looking directly into their eyes with a prophecy of death. Then he was gone, as the others had gone, into the darkness of the upper slopes.

Shell released the trigger slack. His breath poured from his aching lungs. He rested his shaking head on his crossed forearms. He was too weak to move, to talk, to think. Too weak almost to get down to the life-giving water in the desert below the mesa. Half an hour passed. "Now?" said Dusty in a cracked voice. Shell raised his head a little. He nodded. "Now," he said.

They got stiffly to their feet and swayed a little like drunken men. They pushed their way through the brush, heedless of the catclaw and wait-a-bit thorns. Far to the east, beyond the ragged line of mountains, there was a faint, ever so faint, promise of the coming moonlight.

CHAPTER TWO

The lower slopes of the towering mesa were badly cut up, riven with crumbling draws filled with thorny brush. It was still dark on the western slopes, although the faint light of the rising moon had already touched the rounded tops of the mountains beyond the deep well of the lower land between mesa and mountains. Sweat trickled down the sun-ravaged faces of the two men as they led the stumbling horses toward the unseen lower ground. It seemed as though the clashing hoofs and the clattering of loose rock could be heard for miles. Time and time again they would halt to listen, impatient with the harsh breathing and blowing of the horses.

The eastern upper areas of the mountains were bathed in the light of the moon when at last Shell and Dusty reached the smoother land that flowed from the base of the mesa out onto the desert floor. They stopped for a breather, dying for a smoke, but knowing better than to show a pinpoint of light. Their red-rimmed eyes constantly scanned the heights above them, half expecting to see those bushy-headed devils in human form closing in on them, but there was no sign of life up there.

A faint breath of wind whispered softly through the still motionless masses of heated air that filled the great trough of the valley. It rustled the dry brush and dried the sweat on the men's taut faces. Slowly, almost imperceptibly, the moonlight crept down the eastern slopes of the mountains and touched the edge of the desert, but there was still a thick pool of darkness in the lower ground where the waterhole was located.

The smoke was still drifting upward, slanted a little by the wind. It either marked the site of the waterhole or was close to it. Shell tried to reconstruct the lay of the land in his tired mind. It had been a full seven years since he had passed that way.

"Supposin' there ain't any water?" said Dusty.

"The Apaches had water," said Shell.

"That ain't to say they got it here," said Dusty.

Shell turned his head. "You saw that horse-gut canteen that last buck had," he said slowly. "We've got to copper our bet that they got their water here. Because if they didn't. . ." His voice trailed off. It was better left unsaid.

Their worn boot soles husked on the warm sand as they slogged on. Shell sketched a picture of the place in his mind. A roughly oval area of upthrust rocks tip-tilted toward the south, with their bases buried deep in the ocher-colored sands. One who did not know that country would never suspect that there was water within that natural palisade of bone-dry rocks except possibly for the fact that the faint ruts of the long disused wagon road drove straight toward them from the western mountains and then slanted toward the northern end of the looming mesa to slant northeasterly toward Soldier Springs, thirty-five miles away. Soldier Springs had been almost bone-dry when Dusty and Shell had stopped there two days past.

"Yuh sure there's water out here?" said Dusty. "Don't look like it to me."

"Horno Tanks," said Shell.

Dusty glanced sideways. *"Horno? Oven* Tanks? They picked the right name for this damned suburb of hell!"

Shell touched his raw lips. "There's water all right. Holes worn in the rock inside the formation. A spring fills the holes. Tanks, the Mexes call them."

"Likely dry," said Dusty.

Shell shrugged. "What's the use?" he said to the sky. "They've never been dry in the history of this country. Not in the memory of the Indians, the Spaniards, the Mexicans and the Americans—and *he* doubts it."

Dusty wiped his face with his forearm and looked at Shell over the arm. "Jesus," he said softly. He winced as another crack split his raw lips. "Here we go with that gawddamned history again. I told you once, if not fifty times, that damned history don't mean a thing!"

"Then you'd better, by God, *hope* it's right! Don't you believe in anything except those guns of yours?"

Dusty grinned wickedly. "No," he said. "Do *you?"*

There was no answer from Shell. Dusty was right. Their lives and hopes were dependent on each other and their guns. It had been that way all during the war and later in Mexico. It had been that way since Maximilian had been executed at Queretaro and since Dusty and Shell had ridden and hidden through seven hundred miles of a hostile Mexico hunted by the Republican forces who had no use for gringo mercenaries. They had crossed the Rio Grande near Ojinago in the State of Chihuahua with Mexican slugs dimpling the moonlit waters of the river. The moonlight had glinted on something else too, on the Texas side of the river. The brass buttons of a patrol of Yankee cavalry. They hadn't been waiting for "unrecon-structed" Rebels, but any game was fair game to them. Shell and Dusty had no intention of taking the oath of allegiance. Dusty had killed two troopers and Shell had wounded one before they broke loose into the Sierra Vieja heading northwesterly along the Rio Grande for the El Paso del Norte area.

"There are the Tanks," said Dusty suddenly.

They halted. Dimly seen, for the full moonlight had not yet touched the area, were the upthrust rocks just as Shell had remembered them from years past. They hadn't changed. It was very quiet except for the breathing of the thirsty horses. Now and then the dry brush rustled. The Tanks looked peaceful enough except for one thing. The smoke was very thin, raveling out in the fitful wind, but it was still rising from beyond the Tanks.

Dusty grounded his carbine. "That damned smoke," he said quietly.

Shell nodded. That smoke stuck in his mind like a cholla needle, a nagging thrust of fear that he could not eliminate. Horno Tanks had been a swing station on the old Southern Overland Stage Line before the war. A branch line had been run through this area to service the mines. The war had swept everything away. Stagelines, mining camps, *placitas,* and forts had been abandoned or destroyed when the Federal troops had been pulled out to let Arizona survive by itself if it could. The Apaches had been barely kept in check up until that time. Without the soldiers there was nothing to stop them.

"Stay here," said Shell. He handed the reins to Dusty. Shell drew out his converted Navy Colt and checked the cylinder. The metallic whirring of the spinning cylinder sounded crisply in the quiet. Shell half-cocked the Spencer, pulled his faded military hat lower over his eyes and walked toward the dim outline of the Tanks. He glanced back as he reached the halfway mark. Dusty had already vanished into the thicker brush to cover Shell if need be.

The rocks seemed to rise higher and higher from the drifted sand as Shell approached the Tanks. Then he remembered how high they really were, rising thirty-five to forty-five feet from the desert floor like some ancient ruin. The entrance to the interior of the palisade of rocks was on the southern side. It was out of his view but the swing station structure and corrals should be there if they too had not been swept away by the Apaches. That mysterious smoke certainly could not be rising from the chimney of the station.

A faint, sweetish odor reached him on the invisible hands of the shifting wind. He stopped short. That smell was familiar enough to him. In some unnamed engagement in the war he remembered all too well that same odor drifting through the rifted battle smoke of the piney woods which had been set ablaze by shellfire. He halted as he rounded the corner of the rock formation. The skeletal ruins of the station were now lighted by the first rays of the rising moon. The roof had partially collapsed and the wall nearest him had collapsed within the structure in a diagonal fault from top to bottom corners of the eastern side. The heavy, bolt-studded door had fallen on the bare ground in front of the station. The smoke drifted thinly upward from beyond the building. The sickening, cloying odor was stronger now.

Shell wiped the cold sweat from his dirty face. He wondered where it came from, for it seemed that long ago all the juices had been drained from his lean body, leaving it like a piece of beef jerky. He glanced up at the ragged-looking top of the rock formation, half expecting to see white-banded faces peering down at him over rifle sights. There was no one there.

He touched his cracked lips with the tip of his tongue. He could not smell the water. The cloying odor overpowered everything else except the sour-sweat aura that hung about Shell like an old familiar cloak. He forced himself to go on, carbine muzzle swinging back and forth in an arc at hip level while his trigger finger took up the slack, ready to touch off seven rounds of bottle-necked .56.50. Tired and thirsty as he was, Shell was always the professional, ready to shake out instant death at the drop of a hat, or faster if need be. Shell suddenly realized he could see much better. The moonlight was beginning to fill the great desert valley. He saw a pile of horse droppings and bent down on one knee to rake his right hand through the manure, although he never took his eyes from the surroundings. The crust of the manure was stiff, but the interior was still slightly moist. Likely left by an Apache mount.

Shell stood up and saw the rounded, humped shape of a dead mule. His throat had been slashed wide open. The upper flank had been ravaged by keen-bladed knives, and fragments of the dusty hide littered the ground, while the dripping blood had stained the light soil in a black patch. The Apaches had been there, all right. There is nothing an Apache likes better than sweet mule meat.

Shell paused at the gaping doorway of the ruin. A foul stench drifted out to meet him. He stepped inside and flattened his back against the wall. The moonlight penetrated the half-collapsed wall and came into the room through the gaping roof hole. The stench sickened him, but it was not the same as the sweetish, cloying odor that haunted the outside air. This place had been recently used as a latrine. Shell took a lucifer from his shirt pocket and snapped it on a thumbnail as he walked about the darker area. The wavering light revealed a filthy shamble. Piles of excrement were mingled with shattered crockery, scattered book leaves, rags of clothing and other nondescript articles impossible to identify. The acrid odor of urine hung in the corners.

Shell blew an explosive breath to kill the match flame and to drive the foul aura from his lungs. He stepped outside and walked toward the corrals to the west of the station partially set within an arc of the rock formation and fenced across the front with peeled poles hauled from the mountains miles away. The fence had been destroyed. The poles had been shattered or chopped into short lengths, littering the ground within and without the corral. The corral was empty. Shell turned to look back the way he had come and realized the smoke was rising from the center of the corral, and the sickening odor hung more heavily there than elsewhere. He turned slowly. The corral was *not* empty.

Shell walked slowly toward the center of the corral.

Something lay in the middle of it. Something from which the smoke still arose. The moonlight gave enough illumination for him to identify the object when he was within ten feet of it. He stared, whirled, gripped his mouth with his right hand and took half a dozen stiff-legged strides before his outraged guts revolted and spewed out their contents. There wasn't much to spew, but Shell did a thorough job of it. His lips split with the strain and added blood to the greenish, dripping bile.

"Jesus God," slobbered Shell. Tears flooded his eyes and rolled down his dirty face. He shook his throbbing head to clear it. Now he knew why the corral poles had been chopped or broken into convenient lengths. There wasn't much else in the way of firewood around Horno Tanks.

Shell wiped his mouth and forced himself to walk back to what lay smoking in the center of the corral. The earth was gouged and trampled, and the object lay in the middle of it. He didn't quite know what to call it now. It had been human...*once*. The moonlight clearly revealed what it was. The naked body had been exquisitely mutilated. It was curiously mottled with a combination of dried blood, the soft yellowish-white of exposed bones and muscles, the charred areas of softer parts. The arms and legs were but blackened stubs with short pieces of charred wood radiating out from them, and from these arose the thin smoke. No surgeon could have operated with the deftness and delicacy of the Apaches who had worked on their helpless, screaming victim. They had kept him alive as long as possible before submitting his extremities to the slowly burning wood. They had kept the last flickering spark of life in him so that he might still feel the torture of the flames. The eyes and nose were gone, leaving thick black blood scabs to mark their former position on the caricature of a face. The white teeth, a fine and perfect set, were fully revealed in a wide lipless grin as though the dead man was laughing up at Shell for having played a ghastly prank on him.

Shell cinched his courage and kicked away the smoldering wood. God himself would have a hard time recognizing this victim of Apache torture. Shell walked away from the corpse. He reached the station and whistled sharply three times. The faint response sounded almost like an echo. There would be no fear of Apaches now. They would not return to that place of death. The restless soul of their murdered victim would haunt the darkness, disguising his voice to imitate Bii, the Owl, to lure his murderers into a trap.

Shell waited by the ruin. Hoofs thudded on the hard earth. Dusty appeared, leading the horses. "All clear?" he asked in a strained voice.

"All clear," said Shell.

"What about the water?"

"Inside," said Shell with a jerk of his head toward the rocks.

"Didn't you look?"

"It'll be there," said Shell laconically.

"What's that stink?"

Shell pointed toward the corral. "Go look," he invited.

Dusty dropped the reins, and Shell walked over to pick them up. Dusty walked into the corral toward the still-smoking object in the center of it. "What the hell!" he said. He walked a little closer to it. "Jesus God!" he spat out. He whirled, just as Shell had done, and ran a few awkward steps before he too spilled his guts.

Shell grinned evilly. Dusty wasn't quite as hardened as he always tried to appear. Shell led the horses into the entrance to the Tanks. He looked back at Dusty.

Dusty dashed away the strings of bile from his dripping mouth. "Yuh dirty bastard!" he spluttered.

Shell grinned again. He led the horses into the natural tunnel that gave entry to the tanks. His heart leaped as he smelled the water. The horses whinnied and pushed against him. The moonlight glinted from the shallow waters trapped in the natural rock tanks from a spring that welled from beneath a rock overhang.

The enclosed area was fully sixty yards across, roughly oval in shape, with the tanks close to the entrance and the remainder of the area covered with littered rock and drifted sand stippled with low scrub brush. The enclosure was shut off from the movement of the rising night wind, and the lifeless, heavy air still retained the heat of the day, bringing a fresh outpouring of sweat from Shell although he still wondered where it came from.

He watered the horses and dropped bellyflat beside them to drink a little himself. It was warm and a little gamey to the taste, but he had to force himself to stop drinking it as he felt his guts tighten again preparatory to retching.

Dusty dropped on the far side of the horses and drank as Shell had done. He raised his head and looked hard at Shell. "Yuh got a great sense of humor, *hombre,*" he said thinly.

Shell sat up and felt for the makings. He withdrew the sweat-damp sack of tobacco and fashioned a cigarette from them and the thin corn husks. He snapped a lucifer on a thumbnail and lighted up. He tossed the makings to Dusty. "You once asked me if the Apaches were worse than the Comanches," he said dryly. "Now you know."

Dusty deftly caught the makings. He formed a tube of the husks and tobacco and lighted it. He drew the sweet smoke gratefully into his lungs. "They won't be back then?"

Shell shook his head. "Not likely. Not for twenty-four hours at least. By that time, we'll be water-soaked and on our way again."

Dusty blew a smoke ring. "To where?" he said quietly.

Shell led the horses away from the water and tethered them. "To Sonora," he said over his shoulder. "You knew that."

"We got run out of Coahuila a little more than two months past," Dusty said.

Shell walked toward him. "And Texas," he said. "Because we fought those Yankees. And New Mexico because the Bluebellies were hunting us. If they know we're here in Arizona they'll track us down. We could have taken the oath of allegiance and avoided all this."

"Not likely," said Dusty. He spat to one side.

Shell squatted at the edge of the tank. He flipped a pebble into the water. "That leaves Sonora," he said quietly.

"What about California?"

"Same as Texas, New Mexico, and Arizona. There's no place for 'unreconstructed' Rebels in the United States, *compañero*. We take the oath or we get out. It's as simple as that."

Dusty lay flat on his back and studied the moonlit sky. "Maybe the word got down to Sonora from Juarez' boys that we might come this way," he said thoughtfully. "Them Mexicans won't take kindly to two men who fought for Maximilian."

"Sonora is a long way from Mexico City," said Shell.

"They got telegraphs in Mexico too," said Dusty. "And couriers. Word gets around fast and we've been on the way well over two months."

Shell had no ready answer. A cold feeling came over him. His temples tightened. A strange sort of fear settled in his gut. There really wasn't *any* place they could go. Four years of fighting a war that was doomed from the start. Six months of fighting for Maximilian, whose cause was also doomed when the French troops pulled out of Mexico. Two and a half months of running and hiding, first from the Mexican Republicans, then the Yankee soldiers in Texas and New Mexico. Too, they had had to avoid Comanche and Lipan, Mescalero Apache and now the Chiricahua Apache. If they went into Sonora the Mexicans would perhaps be waiting for them.

Dusty blew a smoke ring and idly watched it float up into the quiet air. "Maybe Colonel De Tassigny ain't even down in Sonora now," he said. "What then?"

"We've got to take a chance on that," said Shell.

Dusty turned his head and looked at him. "Yeh, but the colonel fought *for* Benito Juarez, not *against* him, like we done. Sure, Juarez granted him and his men the right to land in Sonora to start a *colonia*, but that was for ex-Rebels that fought on the Republican side. Yuh think De Tassigny's got enough pull with ol' Benito to keep us outta the hands of the Republicans? They got plenty of ammunition, *compañero*, and plenty of rifles, and all kinds of walls to stand a couple of *hombres* like us up against. You know what kind of trial we might get, Shell. *Ley del fuego!*"

Shell sipped a little water. *Ley del fuego*...the law of fire. Free a man and let him run for his freedom. If he outran the bullets he was free. It saved the time and bother of a trial and, besides, God would sort out the just and the unjust.

"You hear me?" said Dusty.

Shell nodded. "Maybe the colonel might be able to hide us out for a time. Maybe the heat will cool off. Maybe the Republicans will forget us."

"Maybe...maybe...maybe..." mimicked Dusty. "Yuh better, by all that's holy, hope so!" He rolled over on his belly and looked at Shell. His blue eyes narrowed. He took the cigarette butt from his lips. "What the hell is that?" he added in a low voice.

Shell turned his head. Sand had drifted in a slope from halfway up the full height of the rock wall at the northern end of the enclosure. The moonlight fell upon a cleared area in the center of the slope. It was clear and sharp. Something protruded from the sand, like some alien growth, for it was like nothing Shell had ever seen. It was rather oval in shape, but was not smoothly contoured like a rock shaped by wind and sand. It wasn't a rock. Of that he was sure.

Dusty stood up slowly, his leather creaking softly. "Shell?" he said in a low voice.

Shell stood up. He dropped the cigarette butt to the

ground and pressed a worn boot sole on it, slowly grinding it into the rock. He narrowed his eyes. The moonlight was bright enough now to read print with ease. He studied the object and then he knew what it was. *By God, he knew what it was!* He walked past the tanks and stopped for a fraction of a minute at the base of the slope. His boots grated as he walked on. They husked through the sand as he went up the slope. He knew without looking back that Dusty was not far behind him, drawn as irresistibly as Shell had been drawn.

Shell stopped twenty feet from the object. An eerie feeling came over him. The object had human features. The eyes were staring fixedly at him.

Dusty stopped beside Shell. He cleared his throat. "It's a head," he said huskily. *"A human head...."*

CHAPTER THREE

S hell moved forward as though in a dream, gazing at the head. The eyes were looking directly at him in a fixed, unwinking stare. It was the head of a dead man buried up to his neck in the hot sand. The Apaches had been at work, or rather at *play,* inside the rock enclosure as well as on the outside. They must have really *hated* this one. The long dirty gray hair had been gathered together and tied to a stake which had been driven deep into the sand thus drawing the head back so that it would stare upward a little toward the southern sky. The face was set and taut. How long had he been helpless there, staring at the burning sun until his mind had cracked and he had died a gibbering idiot?

"Jesus God," said Dusty. He passed a hand across his eyes.

One of the horses whinnied and the sound of it echoed around the rock enclosure and died quickly away. The wind whispered through the crevices and stirred the heavy air within Horno Tanks.

"There's an old shovel back there," said Shell. "Go get it so we can cover this thing."

Dusty turned on a heel and took three paces.

"Wait!" snapped Shell.

The head had moved a little. It had hardly been perceptible. Shell dropped to one knee. The head moved again and the swollen tongue was thrust between the cracked lips. The mouth worked. The man was trying to speak.

"Get that shovel!" yelled Shell. He began to dig at the warm sand with his bare hands as Dusty ran back up the slope. Shell cut loose the gray hair. Dusty shoved him aside and drew his Navy Colt in one fluid motion, hooking his thumb over the hammer spur to cock it. He leveled it at the head.

Shell jumped to his feet. "You loco!" he shouted. "You'll arouse every Apache within five miles of here!"

Dusty turned slowly, his eyes wide in his head. He let down the hammer of the Colt and sheathed the heavy weapon. He drew his thick-bladed bowie knife and stepped forward again. "*This* won't arouse them," he said quietly.

"He's still alive," said Shell.

Dusty looked at Shell. "For how long?" he said. "He can't live after that."

It wasn't mercy in the mind of Matt Dustin. They had no time to waste trying to bring this pitiful relic of humanity back to life. The man should have died hours ago. It was a miracle that he was still alive. Dusty was the practical one, the materialist.

"No," said Shell a fraction of a second before the razor-honed blade would leap toward that taut-corded throat. Dusty's eyes held Shell's for a fleeting moment. Dusty knew what he saw in those red-rimmed gray eyes. He looked away. "Christ!" he said disgustedly. That and nothing more. He sheathed the heavy knife and turned to plunge down the slope. Shell watched him for a moment and then resumed his digging. In a few moments Dusty was back with the old shovel. The moon was fully up by the time they were able to free the man from his sandy prison. He was partly clothed but his boots were gone. They carried him to the nearest tank and placed him gently atop a pair of blankets Dusty got from his cantle roll. Dusty plucked the makings from Shell's shirt pocket and teetered on his heels as he squatted beside the tank watching Shell with amused eyes as Shell worked on the limp body.

Shell washed the face and upper body. He bathed the swollen lips and allowed a little water to trickle into the dry mouth by inserting a wet rag between the lips.

"The Good Samaritan," said Dusty dryly as he lighted up.

The eyes puzzled Shell. They stared fixedly at the sky. The lids never lowered or raised. He placed his face close to that of the dying man. He touched the lids and turned away with a sickness in his soul. "Get my razor case," he said thickly.

"Yuh aimin' to shave him?" said Dusty sarcastically.

Shell looked at his partner. "They sewed his eyelids up with fine gut," he said quietly, "so that he'd be sure to get the full benefit of the sun tomorrow until he died."

Dusty got to his feet, casting a horrified glance at the fixed stare of the man. He hurried to Shell's horse and got the razor case.

"Make a small fire. Boil some water. Clean my best razor," said Shell.

"What about the smoke?" said Dusty.

"I said the Apaches wouldn't be back," said Shell patiently.

"They can wait on the trail," said Dusty.

Shell looked up at him. "God's blood!" he snapped. "Can't you make a fire *without* smoke?"

Shell looked down at the set face of the man. He was likely dying anyway. Dusty was right. The face moved a little. The lips worked. It was difficult to tell what he really looked like, but he was a man of spare build, perhaps in his middle or late fifties. "From the looks of him," he said thoughtfully, "he couldn't have been out in the sun very long. An hour or so. If it had been longer than that he'd likely have been dead by now. The devils wanted him to stay alive all night with the water right near him and then face the sun all day tomorrow."

"Beats me how he stayed alive at all," said Dusty as he lighted the fire he had built from scraps of dry brush. He scooped up some water in his old camp kettle and placed it near the fire. They sat and smoked until the water boiled. Dusty cleaned the razor and handed it to Shell. The light wasn't the best but there wasn't much Shell could do about it. He wet his cracked lips. "Hold his head firm," he said.

Carefully, delicately, he severed the fine gut that held back the lids. Blood flowed a little, but at last the lids could be lowered. Shell covered them with salve and bandaged the eyes. The moonlight was slanting from the west when he finished. He covered the spare body against the rising chill of the desert night.

Dusty had boiled some coffee. He handed a battered tin cup to Shell. "Bet you even-up he don't last until dawn," he said.

Shell did not answer. Dusty was probably right. He had seen enough men die in his time. Weariness swept through his body. He seemed to be more tired than he had been in many days.

"What about us?" said Dusty. "We can't stay here too long."

"We can stay until he dies," said Shell. "We owe him that much at least."

Dusty sipped at his coffee. "After Corinth I saw you walk away with half the company lying dead or dying on the battlefield. You never even looked back."

Shell did not answer. He placed his empty cup on the ground and studied the dying man. Somehow this was different. No soldier can remain efficient while breaking his heart over the many dead comrades and agonized wounded he has seen, for then his use as a soldier is gone.

The moon died. Darkness once again crept across the desert. It seemed to move in a little, crouch and listen, then advance a little further. The rocks began to crack and whisper as they cooled and contracted. Dusty took his carbine and patrolled outside of the rock enclosure. It was still difficult for him to accept the fact that the Apaches would not return.

Shell looked at the dying fire. The bed of ashes flared fitfully now and then, showing a glowing red eye like a ruby on velvet. He should have put it out but somehow he felt that if he did, the lingering soul of the dying man would drift off into the windy darkness of the desert. Now and then he would raise his head and listen. In a sense, Dusty was right. There was nothing to prevent the Apaches from waiting along the trail if they learned that two white men had reached Horno Tanks after they had left. It was just the immediate vicinity of the Tanks that would be haunted by the soul of the dead man, or men, for they would certainly believe the man they had buried to the neck could hardly survive. Nothing went on in that country they did not know about. They could move faster than white men. They could find water and food where a white man would die of starvation or thirst. They would never be seen but they would see everything. No man moved there without them knowing about it. Dusty and Shell had been the exception but that had been because Shell had out-Indianed them. It had likely been more luck than skill. A white man was a fool to think he could survive in that country in such times.

The wind began to die away as the hours passed. It became much quieter, but there was no peace in the quiet. The loneliness of the place moved in to settle over the Tanks. Shell could not sleep. He fashioned smoke after smoke and thanked God he had brought along a plentiful supply of the weed. Increasingly, in the past months, the intense feeling of loneliness seemed to move in on him out of the dark emptiness beyond the dying campfire. He had never mentioned it to Dusty. That rawhide-souled *hombre* would have laughed at Shell. There was no better man to stand beside one in a hard fight, or back to back if the odds got too great, but unless one talked in generalities Dusty was hardly the type for deep, soul-searching talk late at night about a bed of glowing coals when a man strives to reach his soul and learn the significance of his life.

"Barranca," the voice husked out of the darkness.

The flickering lucifer stopped an inch short of the cigarette tip. Shell narrowed his eyes. It was the wind. But the wind had almost died away. Shell shook his head. He was hearing things. He cupped the match about the tip of the cigarette.

"Barranca," said the low voice again.

Shell looked up. Dusty was moving through the darkness toward him. "What about barranca?" said Shell.

Dusty stopped and grounded his carbine. "What the hell are yuh talkin' about?" he said.

"You spoke, didn't you?"

Dusty shook his head. "Yuh been hearin' things. Quiet as the grave out there." He laughed shortly at the suggestive simile. "Toss me the makin's, *compañero.*"

"Haven't you any of your own?"

Dusty grinned crookedly. "Not as long as I can use yours." He caught the tossed makings out of the air. "Barranca? What's that?"

"A deep canyon. A river gorge."

Dusty digested that while he shaped a smoke. He lighted it and looked curiously at Shell over the flare of the lucifer.

"Barranca," repeated the voice.

They both turned and looked at the dim shape of the dying man. Shell got up and went to him. The ravaged lips moved and a faint sound came from them. *"Barranca. . ."*

"What does he mean?" said Dusty.

Shell shook his head. He drew the blanket about the stranger's shoulders. "Get some water," he said.

Dusty handed Shell a tin cup. Shell tenderly raised the gray head and dribbled a little water over the cracked lips. The tongue greedily licked at the moisture. The head sagged.

"Is he gone?" said Dusty.

"Not yet. Beats the hell out of me how he's still alive. How long can he live?"

Dusty blew a smoke ring. "Even-odds he don't make the dawn," he said.

"*Barranca,*" said the faraway-sounding voice. "*La Barranca Escondida.*"

Shell wet the lips again. Something touched his memory with a light finger and then was gone. "What is it, old-timer?" he said.

The lips moved but no sound came from them.

"He's delirious," said Shell.

The two of them sat smoking beside the tank. It was like a death watch. "Get some sleep," said Dusty at last.

Shell shook his head. "No use. Go ahead yourself."

Dusty yawned widely. He picked up a blanket. "Wake me when yuh want to sleep," he said. He looked about. "I believe yuh when yuh say *they* won't be back, but just the same I'll feel a helluva lot better with someone on watch." He walked to the sand slope and hollowed a place for hips and shoulders. He placed his Spencer at one side and his Colt at the other. He dropped to the sand, pulled the blanket over him, and was asleep almost the moment he lay still.

Time drifted on. The fire died. The ashes cooled. A faint puff of wind came through the entrance to the Tanks and scattered a fine film of ashes over the nearest tank. The darkness was now intense, like a living thing, filling the night with only the winking ice-chip stars as contrast.

"La Barranca Escondida," said Shell suddenly. He mulled the phrase over in his tired mind. Sometime, someplace he had heard it.

Shell started and his head snapped up. He shivered a little in the night chill. The wind had come again and was whispering over the rock palisade and rippling the water in the tanks. Shell had dropped off to sleep. He realized with a start that he could almost make out the ancient Indian pictographs that had been scratched in the rock wall on the far side of the tanks. It was the false dawn.

Shell stood up stiffly. He walked to the stranger and knelt beside him. Dusty's words came back to him. *"Even-odds he don't make the dawn."* Shell passed a hand beneath the blanket to feel for the heart. He waited a moment and then grinned. He should have taken up Dusty's bet.

Dusty moved. He sat up, threw back the blanket, and instinctively reached for his pistol.

Shell looked at Dusty. "You lose, *compañero,*" he said with a tired smile. "He's still alive."

CHAPTER FOUR

T he pungent odor of the cooking mule meat hung heavily in the rock enclosure. Already the heat of the day was beginning to be felt. Dusty had cut thin strips of mule meat and had broken up the tough tissues with his knife. He watched with an amused expression as Shell carried the spare-framed stranger into one of the shallow caves eroded in the rock wall beyond the Tanks.

Shell eased the stranger onto the bed he had prepared for him. "Barranca," whispered the man.

"Yes, yes," said Shell. "We know. Barranca."

Dusty grinned. "Probably the name of his horse. Maybe a woman."

Shell picked up his carbine and walked through the echoing tunnel to the bright light of the desert. The sun was already topping the mountains beyond the eastern mesa pouring a flood of light and heat across the great valley. There was no sign of life. No movement. No dust. Nothing except the windless desert and the stark, looming mountains. It was almost like being on the moon.

"La Barranca Escondida," said Shell aloud. "The hidden canyon. The hidden gorge." He rubbed bis shaggy beard. What did it mean? The stranger might die that day. His secret might very well die with him.

Shell walked into the stinking corral and fought back the green sickness. He found a rusted spade and dug a hole close to the edge of the rocks in the soft sandy earth that had drifted there. He cut loose the thongs that had not been burned through by the fire and dragged the pitiful relic of a man to the hole. He quickly filled it in, fighting back the sickness in his gut, but even so he had just mounded the grave when he whirled and ran, heaving out his gut. He stood there a long time, then returned to the grave and spoke a few words, then bowed his head and prayed. There was no way of telling who the man was. God would know. He picked up two pieces of wood, tied them into a cross shape, and thrust the cross into the head of the mound.

Shell walked back to the station and looked south across the bright desert. Already the heat waves were shimmering upward from the harsh surface. Far to the south, still distinguishable before the thicker heat haze arose, were two small ranges that formed a great V-shape pointing south. Somewhere roughly midway between Horno Tanks and the northern flanks of those ranges was the unmarked border between Arizona and Sonora. The country was waterless as far as he knew, until one reached the area beyond the tip of the V, and beyond that, at the northern end of the Sierra Madre Occidental, was the Mesa del Campanero—the Mesa of the Bellmaker. It was there that Colonel Marcus De Tassigny, who had commanded Shell's battalion of South Kansas-Texas Mounted Rifles until he had lost his left arm at Champion's Hill, had been given a huge grant of land to form a *colonia* composed of men whom he had led in battle during the war and also on the side of the Republican forces of Mexico in the fight against Maximilian. De Tassigny and his men were "unreconstructed" Rebels as were Dusty and Shell, but they had fought *for,* not *against,* Benito Juarez. It would make no difference, of course, to

De Tassigny that Shell and Dusty had fought on the opposite side in Mexico, for he'd likely welcome two fighting men. His *colonia* was on the frontier of Mexico, in Yaqui country, and two more guns would be more than welcome.

"Fighting men," said Shell. He slanted his faded campaign hat lower over his eyes against the glare of the desert. Two wars and sundry other fighting had etched one lesson into his mind. The wind was always blowing in his face; the battlegrounds were usually ill-chosen; the odds were always too great; the cause perhaps too insufficient to justify his death. "Above all," he said aloud, "no one seems to care whether I win or lose, live or die."

"Grub pile!" yelled Dusty from the mouth of the passageway.

Shell looked at him. Dusty likely had never considered the facts that had just been in Shell's mind. To Dusty a fight was a fight; a drink was a drink; one woman was the same as another. Likely he would have fought just as cheerfully on one side of the war in Mexico as he would have fought on the other. Maximilian had just paid more. Shell walked to the entrance of the tunnel. Once more he looked to the south. A bitter hopelessness descended upon him. It was something he could not eliminate, something he could not cope with in his mind. Guns, knives, fists, or boots had no effect on the unseen.

They ate silently, gnawing at the tough meat, the grease running down into their ragged beards. Now and then Shell would look at the still form of the stranger.

"We move today?" said Dusty.

Shell picked a stringy piece of meat from between his teeth with a dirty broken fingernail. "He's still alive, isn't he?"

Dusty picked up another piece of meat. "He won't last out the day."

"We can't move out of here during daylight."

The hard blue eyes looked at Shell over the dripping piece of meat. "We could have left last night."

Shell emptied the dregs of coffee from his cup. It was the last in the cup and about the last in their supplies. Supplies? They had nothing much left except tobacco and cartridges.

Dusty tore at the meat with his strong white teeth. "Now we've got to sit here for hours," he said thickly. "How long do they stay away from the dead?"

"Forty-eight hours."

"You said twenty-four before."

Shell leveled his gaze at Dusty. "You calling me a liar?" he said in a low voice.

"Don't get ringy," said Dusty. He wiped the grease from his mouth. He looked thoughtfully at the stranger. "What is this Barranca Escondida thing?"

"Beats the hell out of me," said Shell.

Dusty looked at Shell. "Does it mean anything to you?"

Shell shrugged. "Seems to me I've heard it somewhere before."

"Is it around here?"

"Not likely. Sounds Mex to me."

"Yeh. Yeh. But that don't mean a damned thing. It could be on this side of the border."

"Not likely. They call a gorge a gorge and a canyon a canyon on this side."

"What does it mean?"

"A hidden gorge. What else?"

Dusty emptied his coffee cup. "It must have more meaning than that. It's important to him, ain't it?"

"Ask *him* then." Shell stood up and rolled a cigarette. He dropped the makings into Dusty's greasy outstretched hand.

"How far to the border?" said Dusty.

"Twenty or thirty miles."

"Water?"

Shell nodded. He retrieved the makings after Dusty built his smoke. "Place called Papago Springs."

"That's Indian, ain't it?"

"Yeh. They're usually harmless. The Sand Papagos can get mean at times."

"What's beyond Papago Springs?"

"Sonora."

"And more Apaches," said Dusty dryly.

Shell blew a smoke ring. "Some," he said. "There are also Opatas, Tarahumares, and Yaquis."

Dusty looked up. "You sound like the Yaquis are something big, *compañero*."

"They are. Cousins to the Apaches. Some say they're *rougher* than the Apaches. The Mexes call them *La raza de bronce que sabe morir*."

Dusty inspected the glowing end of his cigarette. "The bronze race that knows how to die," he said thoughtfully. He looked up at Shell. "Great! From the frying pan into the fire. Salt, pepper, and gravel in the grease."

Shell spat. "You have any other ideas?"

Dusty slowly shook his head. "Man," he said reflectively, "we've got to go, whether we like it or not. But when?"

Shell sucked in lungfuls of smoke and blew it out. "We can take turns watching the desert today. We can't move during the day. If they do come back, we can't make a break for it. We'll have to hold them off here. At least *we'll* have the water. The horses are not fully rested yet. By tonight they should be all right."

"How long can we hold them off if they do come back?"

Shell ran a hand along the bright brass cartridges in his gun belt. His meaning was clear enough. "Save one for yourself, *compañero*. You saw what they did to the two men they caught here."

The heat came slowly, with insensate fury, pouring down inside the rock enclosure until it seemed the water in the tanks would rise in steam and the rock itself would melt and fuse with the burning sands. There was no escape from it. It weighted the body and burned into the lungs with every labored breath. There was nothing that could be done but to lie in the hot shade and try to live through it.

The motionless figure in the cave should have given up the ghost. It was impossible for him to live in the condition he was in, coupled with the hellish heat, *but he lived on and on.* All through that day of living hell, the very core of the summer's blasting heat, the man held on to life. It was hard to believe when at last the shadows grew on the western side of the enclosure and crept slowly across the burning rock and sand to touch the edge of the Tanks and then cover them as well. Minute after minute passed until at last the sun was gone behind the western range, painting the sky in rose and gold.

Dusty came through the passageway, his Mexican spurs chiming softly. Now that there was no fear of the Apaches he had put his silver spurs on again. They had been as much a part of him as his guns when he had fought with Maximilian. He had taken them from the corpse of an officer of the Republican cavalry after killing him. It was something Shell could not have done, but then Dusty was a materialist. He needed spurs. The man he had killed wore fine silver spurs. Therefore, the spurs were now Dusty's. It was as simple as that. They were indeed fine spurs.

The moon touched the tips of the eastern mountains as Dusty and Shell ate the last of the mule meat. There would be no more. The bloated carcass had given off foul gas all during that day until Dusty, in disgust, had gutted the putrefying flesh to let the gas escape. Even so, the stench of it still drifted about Horno Tanks.

The moon touched the Tanks. If they planned to move that night, they would have to wait until darkness came again. Both of them sat smoking, their backs against the warm rocks, their thoughts their own.

"La Barranca Escondida," said the voice clearly.

Dusty snapped his head around. "By God! I don't believe it!" he said. "He's still alive!"

Shell started a small fire and heated a container of broth he had made earlier that evening. He took it to the stranger and slowly fed him. By the time the moon slanted down toward the western range the man seemed to have regained some of his strength. He mumbled at intervals and then spoke clearly, and it was always the same. "La Barranca Escondida."

Shell went to get some water. He knelt beside the tank.

"Look!" said Dusty in an incredulous tone.

Shell turned. The stranger was sitting up. He pointed a gaunt hand at Shell, almost as though he could see him through the thick bandage he wore across his eyes. "La Barranca Escondida," he said clearly. *"Departamento de Camino a Las Minas de La Barranca Escondida y El Naranjal."*

"By Jesus!" yelled Shell. "That's it! That's it!"

"You gone loco?" cried Dusty.

Shell ran to Dusty and grabbed him by the arm. "He's talking about some of the biggest, richest, damnedest silver mines that ever existed! Some say they were richer than Tayopa!"

Dusty gripped Shell by the arm. "Are you in your right mind? What the hell *are* yuh talking about?"

Shell looked at the stranger. He had spoken in almost flawless Spanish and the accent was hardly perceptible, but Shell was almost sure he wasn't Mexican. "Those mines have been lost for over a hundred years," said Shell in a low voice so that the stranger might not hear. "I heard about them when I was out here before the war. I didn't pay much attention to the stories. Like all lost-mine legends they grow mightily with the telling."

"You still think he's out of his mind?"

"Can you blame him?"

They walked quietly over to the stranger. He had fallen back on his blankets again and was breathing harshly. Shell placed a hand on his forehead. He wasn't too feverish. "Who are you?" asked Shell.

The man moved a little. "We didn't know they were

here," he said. "My horse died in the mountains. Ignacio's horse died twenty miles from here. We took turns riding the mule. *We didn't know they were here!*" His voice rose almost to a scream and then broke.

Shell felt the cold sweat break out on his body.

"Jesus," said Dusty in a shaken voice. "Can you imagine what it must'a felt like to get here ready for a long drink and then see *them?*"

"They made me watch," said the stranger.

That was all he had to say. He didn't have to elaborate on it. They could imagine well enough.

"Your name?" said Shell.

The man moved. "Harley," he said. "Frank Harley."

"Where were you going?"

Harley threw an arm over his bandaged eyes. "La Barranca Escondida!" he said. "They shod the mules with silver. They didn't have enough iron for shoes. They had *metal* though. Silver! Silver in great chunks! They shod the mules with silver because the mine was so rich."

"Jesus God," breathed Dusty. He looked at Shell with wide eyes.

There was still enough moonlight to see Harley's bandaged face. Shell let him sip a little water, but not too much. He was afraid the man's stomach might revolt.

Harley lay still for a long time. "Tayopa?" he said, cocking his head as though someone had mentioned the name. "Tayopa?" He laughed. "Tayopa was great! But La Barranca Escondida and El Naranjal! They were the greatest. The records lie! The Jesuits were too clever to report how much they actually took out of La Barranca Escondida and El Naranjal. The Crown got one-fifth, *or so they thought.* But the Jesuits owed no allegiance to the King of Spain. Lip service perhaps, but not loyalty. They owed their loyalty to their order and to the Black Pope who was the head of their order!"

"What the hell is he jabberin' about?" demanded Dusty.

Harley was quiet now, breathing erratically. Shell felt

his pulse. Harley was hanging on to life. Something had kept him alive; *something* was still keeping him alive.

"Is there any truth in what he says?" said Dusty.

Shell squatted on his heels and rolled a cigarette. He nodded his head. "The Jesuits owned a great deal of land in Mexico. Ranches and mines. The Indians worked for them. There wasn't much control over the mine operators. The Indians were actually slaves and could be worked to death. I've heard reports that back in those days you could smell the mine workings a long distance off by the stench of rotting human flesh given off by the bodies of the Indians who had died working the mines and who had been dumped aside like offal. What puzzles me, though, is that Tayopa was always considered the greatest. I've heard vaguely of El Naranjal and the legend that it was greater than Tayopa. La Barranca Escondida is, or was, just a fairy tale, as far as I know." Shell lighted his cigarette and handed the makings to Dusty. "Don't get excited, *compañero*. These desert rats have more stories to tell than Shakespeare did. They weave 'em by the mile and cut 'em off by the yard."

Dusty fashioned his smoke. "But supposin' he *does* know something about those mines?"

Shell blew a leisurely smoke ring. "Sure, sure," he said soothingly. "Supposing he does? Hundreds of miles south of here through Apache and Yaqui country. Country that is trackless. Country that hasn't had a mine worked in a hundred years!"

Dusty wet his lips. "But the Indians would know about them mines, wouldn't they? Hell! Butter them up with a few beads on a string or a looking glass or something like that. They'd talk all right. Them tales are all handed down to them from father to son. They'd know where they were all right."

Shell took his cigarette from his mouth. "So? Supposing *your* great-grandfather had worked in those mines? Supposing he had seen his brother, his friends, and maybe even his own father die in them for silver that meant absolutely nothing to him. For wealth that poured out of Mexico in a silver flood to Spain. Was there profit of any kind in it for him and his people? You bet your life there wasn't! They couldn't even live the simple life of their forefathers. Every day in those damned mines away from the blessed air and sun until you dropped dead! So one day the Jesuits have to leave Mexico. They can't even go back to Spain! Would they leave those mines for anyone else? The hell they would! So they had the Indians conceal them and you know damned well when an Indian hides something no one else can ever find it."

"Then they *would* know where the mines were!" said Dusty triumphantly.

Shell shook his head in disgust. "Sure they would! But they wouldn't tell any white man where they were for fear the old ways would come back. Furthermore, my simple friend, *they aren't about to let any white man come poking around in that country looking for the mines himself.*"

Harley stirred. "They called them The Masters of Secrecy," he said.

"Who?" asked Shell quickly.

Harley looked directly at Shell although he could not see him. "Why, the Jesuits of course! They hoarded the silver, and when they left forever they could not take it with them. It is still there."

"Where?" said Shell.

Harley hesitated. He passed a hand over his bandage. "I... I...." His voice faltered and died.

"At La Barranca Escondida?" said Shell.

"Yes! Yes! That is it! The mines were of such wonderful richness, it is said, that blocks hewed from the veins had to be cut into pieces so that mules might carry them to the coast for shipment to Spain."

Dusty's cigarette dropped from his gaping mouth.

Harley moved restlessly. Shell wet his cracked lips and bathed his sweating face with a wet rag. "They were in bonanza since sixteen thirty-two," said Harley.

Dusty stared. He looked quickly at Shell. "When did these Jesuits leave Mexico?" he said.

Shell half closed his eyes. "About a hundred years ago. I think they were expelled in seventeen sixty-seven."

Harley nodded eagerly. "That is correct! A hundred years ago!"

"No one has been there since?" said Dusty incredulously.

Shell touched a finger to his lips. They sat there like two dusty ravens on a fence watching the tortured face of the older man. Shell bathed the face and allowed Harley more water. He thrashed about a bit in his fever. "The Jesuits had a control over the Indians that no other representatives of the Christian faith have ever been able to gain," Harley said quietly. "Therefore, when they left Mexico they charged the Indians, under penalty of a terrible curse, never to reveal the hidden treasures except to those of the Jesuit Order. They have kept their word."

Dusty stared at Shell's dim face. "By God," he said, "then that stuff must still be there!"

Shell quickly shook his head to silence Dusty. Shell leaned toward Harley. "You know where this place is?"

There was a long silence. For a moment or two Shell thought the older man had passed on, but then Harley spoke in a low voice, so very low that Shell had to place his ear directly over Harley's mouth. "Cerro de Huesos is the first key. Cerro de Huesos. For there, on a quiet night, one might hear the dogs of La Barranca Escondida barking." Harley shifted a little. "When the wind comes from the south, a bell may be heard at. . ." Shell did not catch the name. Harley gripped Shell by the arm. "That bell hangs in the bell tower of the church at El Naranjal." His voice died away.

Shell bathed Harley's face. He patted it. He felt Harley's heart and pulse. The man was still alive but he was in a deep sleep or a coma. There would be no more from him for a long time. Perhaps he would die before that time. Shell covered Harley with a blanket. Shell and

Dusty walked back to the tank and sat by the edge. It was cooler there.

Dusty sat quietly for a long time. "What do you think, *compañero?*" he said.

Shell shrugged. "He knows a lot, Dusty," he said quietly.

"Yuh think it's the truth?"

Shell blew a smoke ring and stabbed a dirty finger through it. He looked directly at Dusty. "Let's put it this way: he knows *something*. More than any other man I have heard talk about those lost mines."

Dusty looked back over his shoulder. "By God," he breathed. "Mules shod with silver! Mines in bonanza for a hundred years! Pieces of silver chopped into smaller pieces for easier transportation to the coast!"

"Maybe it's just delirium," said Shell.

Dusty wet his cracked lips. "Mebbe," he said in a low, hard voice. "But if it ain't. . ." He looked at Shell and the two of them agreed mentally. They knew each other well enough. There was no hope for them in the United States and Mexico, but with silver to pay the way...silver enough for Croesus...*silver enough to buy anything they wanted*.

CHAPTER FIVE

They should have pulled foot during the long night. They could have abandoned Harley or taken him along. They did neither. All night long, between dozing, they felt their minds teeming with the thoughts Harley had planted in them. Supposing he was completely mad? Supposing it had been sheer delirium? Supposing it was the senseless wanderings of a sick mind? *Supposing it was true?*

They had almost forgotten the Apache menace. A glittering sheen of silver stood between them and the bushy-headed devils. It almost completely blinded them except for the fact they still took turns standing guard. If the Apaches did come back that would be the end. If they did not, and Harley lived, it might be the beginning. The beginning of a life such as Dusty and Shell had never, in their wildest imaginings, dreamed about.

The dawn came again. The sun arose. The heat returned. Midday came. There was no sign of dust on the desert. There was no sign of life out there. Harley was still alive, but he did not speak. Late in the afternoon he stirred, and as the shadows crept down the slopes and into the rock enclosure, Shell kept a close watch on the older man. Shell's gut ached. He was a little faint from hunger and the enervating heat.

Harley moved. "Is there anyone here?" he said.

"Yes," said Shell. He beckoned quickly to Dusty. Spurs softly chimed as Dusty strode over to them.

"You have saved my life," said the older man.

"Por nada," said Shell carelessly.

"You speak Spanish?"

"Enough," said Shell. "But not as well as you."

Harley was quiet for a moment or two. "There are two of you," he said. "Who are you?"

"Call me Shell," said Shell. "My *compañero* is named Dusty."

"You have no other names?"

Dusty grinned. "Somewhere, someplace, old-timer," he said.

Harley smiled. "I understand."

"How do you feel?" said Shell.

"Weak, but lucid. I was in fever?"

"Very much so."

"I smell water," said Harley. "Are we at the Tanks?"

"Yes," said Shell.

"My eyes," said Harley. He pressed thin hands against the bandage.

"You'll be all right," said Shell.

"How did you get past the Apaches?" said Harley.

Dusty spat. "Shell knows their ways. I must admit I didn't like the way we had to do it, but ol' Shell was right. He says they won't be back because of the dead man out there."

"That would be Ignacio," said Harley quietly. He looked at Shell, although he could not see him. *"They made me watch."*

"We know," said Shell.

"They didn't kill me because I must have gone out of my mind."

"Mind-gone-far," said Shell.

"You know them very well," said the older man.

"They would not kill me then, but they made sure I would die. The sun would kill me, not them. You know them well, Shell."

"Well enough to stay as far away as possible from them," said Shell.

"So?" said Harley. "Then why are you here?"

A look sped between Dusty and Shell. "That doesn't matter," said Shell quickly.

"Let me have some water," said Harley.

Dusty rubbed his shaggy beard. "Is that all yuh got to tell us?" he said.

Harley touched his cracked lips. "A few hours of that sun," he said. He shivered.

"Yuh didn't answer me," said Dusty.

It was very quiet except for the whisper of the rising wind. Harley stopped exploring his ravaged lips. He could not see the two men, but he looked from one to the other of them.

"Well?" prompted Dusty.

Harley tilted his head to one side. "Can I please have some water?" he asked politely.

Shell reached for the water container but Dusty fiercely gripped Shell's wrist so that the water splashed over the side. Dusty shook his head. Dusty moved closer to Harley. "Yuh said something about La Barranca Escondida," he said.

"I did?" said Harley in surprise.

"You did," said Dusty.

It was quiet for a moment or two. The wind rippled the shallow water. It lapped against the side of the tank. "How about that water?" asked Harley.

"How about it?" repeated Dusty.

Shell placed the container to one side. It clinked faintly against the rock. "La Barranca Escondida," prompted Shell. Greed crawled in his mind like a canker worm. *"Departamento de Camino a Las Minas de La Barranca Escondida y El Naranjal"*

"What has that to do with me?" said Harley.

"You tell *us,"* said Shell.

A cold fear seemed to settle in the older man. He could not, of course, see those two fierce, bearded faces watching him, but he could *feel* them. Their greed seemed to reach overpoweringly out to him.

Shell tapped Harley's bony knee. "I'll refresh your memory, old-timer. Road to the Mines of the Hidden Gorge and Orange Grove. Come on, Harley! You know what we're talking about! You speak excellent Spanish but you're no Mexican. I don't know anything about Hidden Gorge, but I've heard of the Orange Grove and the Lost Tayopa as well."

"Who hasn't?" said Harley dryly.

Dusty gripped Harley by the shoulder. "Don't get cute!" he growled.

"You were heading south when the Apaches caught you and your friend," prompted Shell.

Harley shook his head. "East to the Santa Cruz."

"There's nothing along the Santa Cruz except the ruins of Tubac and Tumacacori," said Shell. "Nothing south of Tucson for white men but death with a painted face. You know the jingle...Tucson, Tubac, Tumacacori To-Hell! You were heading *south,* old-timer."

"What do you know about it? How do you know *where* we were going?"

Shell spread out a big left hand with the tips of fingers pointing south. "My left hand is before you," he said. "Tips of the fingers pointing south." He tapped the hand with a right forefinger. "The right edge of the palm are the mountains through which you came. The palm is the desert where we are now, with Horno Tanks in the center. The thumb is the great mesa east of here. My fingers are the parallel ranges of the Sierra Madre south of the border. If you have been heading for the Santa Cruz, as you claim, you would not have come from the west by way of the Tanks. You would have avoided them for two obvious reasons. The Apaches and the fact that you could find water north of here at Dripping Springs.

But, to go south, to Papago Springs, you would *have* to come to Horno Tanks. You aren't ignorant of the Apaches, but you took a hell of a risk coming here to Horno Tanks. Something made you take that deadly risk, Harley. *Something big!*"

"Like lost silver mines," said Dusty.

"Water," said Harley.

Dusty picked up the container and refilled it. He sloshed the water around within the container but did not offer it to the thirsty man. Harley held out a trembling hand. Dusty drank noisily and then poured out the rest of the water.

Shell rolled a smoke and lighted it. He passed the makings to Dusty. They sat there blowing smoke toward the bandaged face. Harley sniffed eagerly. He too was addicted to the weed. "Give me a cigarette at least," he pleaded.

Dusty grinned at Shell. Lack of tobacco might break Harley faster than the lack of water. "When did you say the Apaches would be back, Shell?" he asked.

"They won't come near the dead," said Harley.

"Not for a time," said Shell. "That time is running out."

"Especially if they know two white men are here with horses and guns," added Dusty.

"We can be out of here by then," said Harley.

"We can?" said Dusty politely.

Harley knew well enough what Dusty meant. A tremor ran through him.

"Can you imagine how surprised they'll be to find him still alive?" said Shell.

Dusty nodded. "It'll be quiet as the grave after we leave. So quiet he won't even hear them come in here. Then, all of a sudden he'll *know* they're here, standing watching him."

"I'd kill myself first!" said Harley.

"You wouldn't have a chance," said Shell. He eyed the older man speculatively. "Besides, you aren't the type to give up. You'll stick to the last cartridge, the last drop of water, the last drop of blood. Even if they don't come back there's no food here. All the water you want, but no food. Weak as you are, how long do you think you'd last? Three days? A week? That's hardly likely."

"You won't leave me here," said Harley. "You saved my life. You wouldn't throw it away again."

"Wouldn't we?" murmured Dusty.

Harley touched his lips with the tip of his tongue. "Look," he said desperately. "I'll pay you well to take me along. Anywhere!"

Dusty spat. "Yuh ain't got a centavo in your jeans," he said.

Shell glanced at Dusty. Shell hadn't gone through Harley's pockets when he had been helpless. He remembered now how in more than one scrap in the war Dusty had prowled out into the night after the shooting was over, armed with a rusted bayonet. It was handy to pry open jaws for gold fillings. His bowie had served to chop off swollen fingers that resisted having their rings pulled off. He should have known Dusty would have searched Harley when Shell wasn't around.

"Yuh can't dicker with us," said Dusty. "Not *that* way."

Shell almost felt sorry for the older man. He could smell the green fear emanating in Harley's cold sweat.

"La Barranca Escondida," said Dusty.

"They shod the mules with silver," said Shell.

"Tayopa was great," said Dusty, "but La Barranca and El Naranjal were the greatest. The records lie!"

"They hoarded the silver and when they left forever they could not take it with them," said Shell. *"It is still there."*

"Cerro de Huesos, the Hill of Bones, is the first key," murmured Dusty.

"When the wind comes from the south a bell may be heard at Cerro de Huesos," said Shell. "That bell hangs in the bell tower of the church at El Naranjal."

Harley sat still for a long time. "You win," he said. "May I have some water?"

Dusty looked at Shell. Shell nodded. Harley greedily sucked in the fluid. "A cigarette?" he said. Shell rolled one and thrust it between the cracked lips. He snapped a lucifer on his thumb and lighted the tip of the cigarette. Harley gratefully drew in the smoke. He smiled. "You have a persuasive way about you," he said quietly.

Shell grinned. Dusty laughed. "When do we leave?" said Dusty.

Shell blew out a puff of smoke. "As soon as possible," he said. "You feel well enough to ride, Harley?"

Harley raised his head. "God, yes!" he said. "I'd crawl on my hands and knees to get away from here before the Apaches return."

"Where's the treasure map?" said Dusty.

Harley tapped his head. "In here," he said.

Dusty narrowed his eyes. "What do you mean?"

"I memorized it."

Dusty looked at Shell. "Mebbe he's kidding us?"

"How could we know?" said Shell.

Harley inhaled the tobacco smoke. "You don't," he said quietly. "You put up your money and you take your chance."

Shell burst out laughing. "By God!" he said. "You've got us there, haven't you! Now we *have* to take you!"

Harley laughed with Shell, but Dusty's face tightened beneath the dust that masked it. "One thing, old-timer," he said. "This is a great joke. I'm splitting my sides. But you pull a fast one on us and you'd wish to God we *had* left you to the Apaches!"

Harley's laughter died away. A coldness seemed to settle about him. He ground out the cigarette. "Fair enough," he said.

Shell stood up. "Let's get moving," he said. "We've time before the moon rises."

"We'd better wait until the dark after the moon," said Harley.

"No," said Shell. He looked about. He had had enough of Horno Tanks. "If we move fast enough we can be at Papago Springs tomorrow morning."

They moved fast. Fear and greed were the spurs. They hid or wiped out all traces of their presence as best they could. Likely it wouldn't deceive the Apaches, but they'd have to chance that. The canteens were filled. Each of them drank as much water as he could hold. They mounted Harley on the rump of Dusty's rangy bay. Shell led the way with Dusty riding close behind. They did not look back as they rode south. The Apaches weren't there, but they had left something behind them, a brooding, malevolent feeling that would haunt Horno Tanks forever.

They rode steadily until the moon began to rise, making good time, reeling off the miles, until by the time the first light flowed into the valley, they were riding in a low, wide swale that cut off the view from either side. It wasn't Shell's desire to ride in the swale, for if the Apaches couldn't see them, neither could they see the Apaches, but there was little choice. Movement, or a thread of dust on that moonlit desert, would bring them down.

They halted ten minutes on the hour. Once Shell took his battered German field glasses, the only thing he had ever picked up from the enemy dead, and climbed to the lip of the swale to look back along the trail. It was almost as bright as day. Something hung in the quiet air between the mesa and the Tanks. Dust rose thinly. The dust of many horses. His guts contracted. They had just cleared the Tanks in time.

He did not mention the fact to Dusty or Harley, but Dusty knew. He had served too long with Shell not to know.

Hour after hour they kept on. Sometimes riding, sometimes walking, leading Dusty's bay, with Harley swaying weakly in the saddle, but he never complained.

He knew what would happen if he could not keep on. *Ride or die!*

The moon waned and died. There was no sound in the blackness of the night except the steady thudding of the hoofs. No one spoke. It wasn't a time for speaking. It wasn't a time for doing anything except to keep moving south, putting as many miles as possible between themselves and Horno Tanks. The danger was relative. They knew what was behind them, but they didn't know what was ahead of them except the promise of uncounted riches. Such a promise blotted out the fear of the unknown to the south.

Shell suddenly realized there were low mountain ranges on either hand. The ground was harder now and the worn hoofs rang like cracked bells as they struck rock. He could see the dim ranges more clearly now and knew the false dawn would soon be there. He didn't know if they had crossed the border or not. He really didn't care. One side of the line was as dangerous as the other, and the Apaches knew no such boundaries. It was all their country whether it be Arizona, Sonora, Chihuahua, and even as far south as Durango.

Dusty looked at the faintly graying sky and then up at Harley. "Papago Springs next," he said, like a train conductor. "Where to from there?"

"Cerro del Piloncillo," he said. "It can be seen when one is twenty miles south of Papago Springs."

Dusty looked at Shell. Shell shrugged as though to say: What else can we do?

The sun was slowly brightening the gray tones of the eastern sky when Shell called a halt. They led the tired horses into a draw and then climbed higher on a rugged slope to where a natural bastion was shaped amongst the tumbled rocks. They could hold off any number of Apaches here, providing their water held out, and they had no food at all.

Dusty made himself comfortable. It would be a long, hellish day amongst those rocks. Shell unbandaged

Harley's eyes and examined them. "How do you feel?" he asked.

Harley smiled and nodded his head. He kept his eyes closed while Shell bathed them, removing the sticky salve.

Dusty shifted, blowing up a puff of smoke. "Where to beyond Cerro del Piloncillo?" he asked.

Harley hesitated. He rubbed his sunbeaten face.

"Well?" said Dusty shortly.

"Mesa del Campanero," said the older man.

Shell looked quickly at Harley and then at Dusty. They did not speak, but they knew Mesa del Campanero —the Mesa of the Bellmaker—was where Colonel De Tassigny had his *colonia*.

"Then where?" said Dusty.

Harley smiled secretively. "I'll tell you when the time comes, Dusty."

"You'll tell us now!" snapped Dusty.

Harley did not answer. The sun had tipped the eastern mountains and now shone down into the valley. Shell eased off his gun belt and draped it over a rock. He checked both guns and placed them close at hand. He was dead tired and hungry. Maybe sleep would temporarily cancel out the hunger. The sun was warm on his bent back.

"It is a great country," said Harley. "Mountains a mile high and barrancas a mile deep. Sun-blasted mesas. The mountains are high, so very high. Gigantic and windswept, crossed only by the eagles. There are deer, bears, and jaguars in the lower country. On the heights there is no life except specks in the sky, like bits of charred paper, betraying the presence of the eagles."

The sun was hot on Shell's back. He eased off a boot to inspect a blistered heel.

"For miles there is no sign of the white man, and the Indian is seen only when he wants to be seen," said Harley. There was almost a dreamlike quality to his soft voice.

Shell eased off the other boot, wrinkling his nose at the stench. "Jesus," he said softly.

"You know that country well, eh, old-timer?" said Dusty as he rolled a cigarette.

"Yes," said Harley. "I've been there many times."

"But never found the silver."

"It takes time. This time I *know* where it is."

"You'd better," said Dusty as he lighted up.

"I do," said Harley. "I'll lead you there."

"Keno," said Shell. He straightened up and wiped his mouth with the back of a dirty hand. He reached for the makings and began to fashion a cigarette. He looked at Dusty. His companion sat with the cigarette pasted to his lower lip, his dusty hat slanted low over his blue eyes. He didn't move. He was watching Harley. "You're certain for sure you can lead us there?" said Dusty quietly.

"Positive," said Harley.

Dusty looked up at Shell. Shell turned. The blow of the intensely bright sun against his eyes made him wince. He slanted his hat over his eyes. Dusty jerked his head toward Harley. The older man sat hatless on a rock, thin hands resting on gaunt thighs, looking to the east with wide open eyes, *directly into the glare of the sun.*

Shell took the unlighted cigarette from his lips. He walked softly over to Harley and looked into his sun-ravaged face. The eyes were wide open. Shell passed a hand quickly up and down before those staring eyes and they did not blink. The man who was to lead them to La Barranca Escondida and El Naranjal, richer even than Tayopa, where mules were shod with silver, was completely, totally, absolutely blind!

CHAPTER SIX

The heat was a living thing, beating down from the pitiless sun and blasting the land. The dark rock absorbed the heat, and the lighter colored ground radiated it. Shimmering, dancing heat waves moved upward from everything and everywhere. Nothing could possibly live in that inferno, but three men and two horses did. There was no escape, no alleviation, nothing but to endure the endless blazing hours. The heat haze was like an enveloping fog until it seemed that the dividing line between earth and sky no longer existed. Everything was distorted, hidden, or partially obscured. The shade of the greater rocks meant nothing. The heat was the same, the only difference was that the sun did not burn itself into the skin in the shade. Water seemed sucked from the body, but they could not drink as much as they liked. The only thing to do was to rinse the dry, gummy mouth and squirt the gamey water back into the canteens. Shell allowed each of the suffering horses half a hatful of water, begrudging them every drop. His only solace was the temporary coolness of his battered campaign hat as he put it back on his burning head.

Surprisingly enough it was Frank Harley who stood the heat better than his two younger and stronger companions. He sat in the hot shade, his back against a rock, looking steadily at the rock face opposite him, thinking his own thoughts. Dusty lay flat on his belly, forearms crossed, bearded chin resting on his forearms, watching the peaceful, impassive face of the blind man. Taut lines etched themselves on Dusty's mahogany-hued skin. It was almost as though he was trying to worm the secret of La Barranca Escondida out of Frank Harley's mind.

Shell sat in the shade, knees up, forearms resting on his knees, hat slanted low over his burning eyes. There was no taste in him for the tobacco. At any given moment he would have traded his third share of the lost mines for a quart of ice-cold water. His third share? He grinned weakly to himself. All they had to go on was the delirious mumblings of a man who might be an utter dreamer or whose mind might have slipped from its hinges when the Apaches worked on Ignacio. Shell looked at the older man. "Who was Ignacio?" he asked in a cracked voice.

Dusty's red-rimmed eyes slanted toward Shell and then back at Harley.

Harley did not move. "My friend," he said.

"Sure, sure," said Shell patiently. "But what else was he to you?"

Harley smiled faintly. "What more would one want than true friendship?" he said.

"I'm not interested in your second-rate philosophy," said Shell coldly. "Who was he? What did he know? Why was he with you?"

Harley looked directly at Shell with his sightless eyes. "He was my friend. That was why he was with me."

Dusty shifted a little. "Mebbe it was Ignacio who knew the way to the mines. Mebbe it was *him,* not *you,* Harley."

Frank Harley looked in Dusty's direction. "But you don't know that, do you, Dusty?"

Dusty raised his head. "Mebbe I can find out," he said.

They did not speak for five minutes. The sun was directly overhead and the scant shade had fled. There was nothing to protect them now but their clothing. Shell fashioned a hat for Harley out of an extra shirt, a sort of a turban effect that gave the older man the air of a magi or a Hindu fakir.

Dusty grinned sardonically. "The Three Wise Men," he said. He laughed again. He looked about. "The Three Wise Men missed Bethlehem and ended up in hell!"

The long hours dragged past until it seemed that human flesh and blood could stand no more, and then the sun was gone behind the western ranges, dyeing the sky in an intense agony of rose and gold. The relief was almost instantaneous despite the fact that the motionless air was still thick and oppressive with heat.

Shell stood up. "Let's go," he said. "We can make Papago Springs before moonrise."

They carried the limp figure of Harley to Shell's horse. Despite his light weight the two big men staggered weakly. Dusty panted hard as he stood there in the darkness. "What about food?" he said.

Shell wiped the stinging sweat from his eyes. "Water first," he said. "We'll have to trust in luck for food."

"That's the story of our lives," said Dusty bitterly.

They led the horses down the slope of loose rock, clattering in the darkness. Shell struck out, heading due south. He had never been at Papago Springs but they'd have to chance it. It was somewhere at the southern end of the great V of naked mountains that seemed to move in closer in the darkness. Supposing the Apaches were there? Or maybe the Yaquis? One or the other, the results would be the same.

The moon had not yet arisen when both horses whinnied almost in unison. Shell stopped short. His dun pushed against him with his head. Shell turned. "What do you think?" he asked Dusty.

"We got to go ahead," said Dusty.

"Stay with the horses and Harley," said Shell.

Shell took his Spencer from the saddle scabbard and walked softly through the darkness. Each bush and rock looked as though it was alive, as though it was moving. A faint wind whispered through the valley. The southern slopes of the mountains angled slightly together. Shell was closer to the western side of the great V. He walked toward the humped shape of the lower slopes. He stopped often to look and listen. He moved on through the darkness like a great lean cat. He stopped to listen. There was a faint, fresh odor in the quiet air. He looked behind him. There was no movement and not a sound. He padded on and suddenly his worn boots splashed into shallow water. He had found Papago Springs.

Shell drank quickly. He started back for his two companions. Something moved in the brush near him. He whirled, thumbing back the hammer of the Spencer to full cock, but he didn't want to shoot. The soft thrashing noise continued. Shell peered toward the sound. He could see the brush swaying a little. There was something alive in the midst of the brush. Shell unsheathed his bowie knife. He could just make out a thick-shaped creature lying there. The tail thrashed out toward him and his knife came down with the full strength of his arm. The head fell from the thick body. Shell hoped to God it wasn't a gila monster. He knelt beside the quivering body. He grinned. It was a chuck-walla. The biggest one he had ever seen. He picked it up and walked toward his two companions, whistling softly three times. He halted. In a little while he heard the thudding of the hoofs.

Dusty staggered a little. "Yuh find it?" he gasped.

Shell nodded. He held up the chuckwalla. "Food *and* drink," he said with a grin.

"A damned lizard?" said Dusty.

"By God," said Shell. "The Indians can eat 'em and so can we. Beggars can't be choosers, *compañero!*"

They watered the horses, filled the canteens, then vanished over a rise as the first light of the moon appeared.

Dusty stood watch atop the rim of the great cup of black rock as Shell cooked the chuckwalla meat over a small fire. It had taken guts to make even a small fire, well shielded as it was, in the thick darkness before the rising of the moon, and the smell of the fire and the cooking meat would alert any Apache in the vicinity. Harley lay quietly, breathing erratically.

"Get it over with!" hissed Dusty from atop the rocks.

"Gawddammit!" snapped Shell. "I'm doing the best I can!"

The meat was done at last. Shell covered the fire with sand and carefully portioned out the meat. There wasn't a great deal of it, but there was enough to keep them going and that was all that mattered.

Shell awakened Harley and gave him his food. The three of them sat in a circle gnawing at the tender flesh. It was delicious, but there just wasn't enough of it.

Dusty laughed suddenly. The others stopped eating. "Roasted lizard and dirty water," said Dusty. "Helluva fare for three of the richest men in North America."

Shell grinned. He wiped his mouth. "Our time will come," he said, "eh, Harley?"

The blind man nodded. "You can have anything you want with that silver," he said quietly.

Dusty leaned back. "Wimmen," he said thoughtfully. "Big ones, little ones, redheads, brunettes, and blondes. Champagne by the bucket. Pheasant under glass. A pair of blooded horses to pull you around. Anything you want to eat, drink, or sleep with. What about you, Shell?"

Shell was dying for a smoke but they didn't dare light up. The smell of the tobacco smoke might carry too far on the night wind. He leaned back against the rock and picked the last scrap of meat from the bone he held. "Books," he said. "All the books I ever wanted to read and never got around to. Maybe a trip to Europe. China even."

"No fillies?" said Dusty in shocked surprise. "No champagne?"

"I can have them and the books too," said Shell.

Dusty shook his head in bewilderment.

Shell touched Harley's arm. "How about you, old-timer?" he asked.

Harley wiped his mouth. He looked at Shell. "I never thought much about that," he said.

"With the richest silver mines in Mexico waiting out there for us?" said Shell.

Dusty glanced at Harley. "It's a cinch *he* wouldn't go for the fillies and the champagne. Maybe he's a secret drinker. How about that, Frank, old boy?"

Harley shook his head. "I need no strong drink," he said.

"Women?" said Shell.

Harley shook his head. "I had one once," he said. "I didn't know what I had. That was long ago." His voice died away with a haunting note of bitterness and regret. An intense loneliness seemed to settle about the three men. Dusty cleared his throat, looked as though he was about to speak, and then remained quiet.

Shell studied the older man. Suddenly he knew what Harley wanted. To find La Barranca Escondida and El Naranjal. How many years had he lived with that dream? A vision that had led him almost to death and into blindness and which was now leading him into Mexico with two hardcase mercenaries as his eyes. It had already cost him Ignacio, whom he must have loved very much. Perhaps it had even cost him the woman of whom he had spoken in such bittersweet tones. Whatever led Frank Harley on was deep within him, so deep that no one, outside of God, could possibly ever know. Suddenly Shell felt uncomfortable as though he was trying to probe into something that did not concern him—and yet it *did* concern him. If it was the lost silver hoard that lured

Frank Harley on, the fever had passed from him into Dusty and Shell, enough for them to go with the blind man into the heart of a country virtually unknown to white men for a hundred years.

They took turns sleeping during the hours of moonlight and as soon as the moon was gone behind the western ranges they struck out again. Somewhere south of them was Cerro del Piloncillo. It could be seen when one was twenty miles south of Papago Springs. A sugarloaf-shaped hill, from the name.

At dawn they were far south of the waterhole. Dusty's bay was in bad shape. Harley rode the dun and Dusty led the bay, but the big horse was not taking it as well as the dun. Shell wondered at the wisdom of traveling at such a steady pace, and yet there was no place they could stop and rest. No water and no food. They must keep on.

Just before the sun came up Dusty spoke. "There it is!" he said.

The sugar-loaf hill stood out boldly from a flat plain with mountains ranges far to each side of it. "Describe it," said Harley.

"Rounded," said Dusty. "A sharper slope to the east."

"Is there a notch?"

"No," said Shell.

Dusty looked hard at the older man. "What's the notch got to do with it?"

"Cerro del Piloncillo has a notch," said Harley. Dusty wiped his mouth with a quick dash of the back of his right hand. "It ain't notched!" he snapped. His eyes grew hard.

"Keep on," said Harley.

Two miles passed and as the light grew and the angle of the hill changed, a sharp notch appeared. Shell looked at Dusty. He shrugged and spread out his hands, palms upward. Thus far Harley had been right.

"We will cross the Rio Magdalena seventy-five miles due south of here," said Harley quietly.

They halted. Shell rolled a cigarette for Harley and

one for himself, passing the last of the makings to Dusty. They were in a hard way now, without food and tobacco, one horse dying on its feet, and no prospect of getting food or other mounts for many miles.

Harley sucked in the good smoke. "Ten miles from here," he said, "there is a small *placita*, almost fully deserted. The Apaches have driven almost everyone from it, but there is a man there who is my friend. The Apaches do not bother him."

"Why not?" asked Dusty suspiciously. Harley looked down at Dusty almost as though he could see him. "His wife is full-blooded Chiricahua," he said.

"Great!" said Dusty.

Harley shook his head. "We will not be harmed," he said.

"As long as you're with us, eh, Frank?" said Shell. Harley nodded.

They moved on. Now and then Shell looked back at the impassive face of the blind man. What secrets did he know? An uneasiness came over Shell. He felt almost as though he was moving in a dream, but the blistered feet, the hungry gut, the gathering heat, and the haunting fear of Apache country were real enough. *Too* real.

The hill grew and changed shape and then Dusty motioned to Shell. On a slope of the western line of mountains could be seen something that looked as though a giant child had carelessly scattered his blocks, but they were too evenly spaced to be a natural feature of the land. Even as they looked, a thin thread of smoke arose from the blocks. It was the *placita* and someone was living there.

"There's the *placita*," said Shell. He looked up at Harley. "Are you sure it's all right?"

"As long as you are with me," said the older man.

"We haven't any choice," said Shell.

Within two miles of the *placita* the bay went down for good. Dusty impassively stripped him of his gear and loaded it on the dun. He pulled out his pistol, shook his head, and drew out his heavy bowie knife. He pulled back the bay's head, tightening the throat muscles. The blade sliced through the throat as though it was soft soap. The steaming blood gushed out and blackened the ground. They did not look back as they went on.

High, high in the sky was a speck. It grew larger. It was a Sonoran buzzard. A zopilote. By the time the trio reached the outskirts of the *placita* the intense blue sky was dotted with them, leisurely swinging around in great circles, lower and lower, over the still quivering body of the dead bay.

CHAPTER SEVEN

The one street of the little *placita* was empty of life except for a mangy-looking dog who eyed the approaching trio and then bared his teeth. He slinked away with his tail between his legs when Dusty scooped up a fist-sized rock from the ground. Most of the adobes and jacales were crumbling from long disuse. Earthen roofs had collapsed into interiors. Weeds and grass sprouted from the roofs of others like scrofulous hair. A sagging *carreta* leaned against an adobe wall. Somewhere behind the largest of the buildings a mule brayed hoarsely and horses whinnied.

Shell carried his Spencer in his right hand, leading the worn-out dun with his left. Dusty walked slowly on the far side of the street, Spencer at the ready, eyes darting here and there, watching for any overt movement. His spurs chimed softly. The smoke had thinned out but still drifted wispily from the chimney of the largest building. The faint odor of chile beans hung in the street. Shell felt his mouth water.

"Hola!" yelled Dusty. "Anybody here?"

There was no response. Down at the end of the street was a sagging *torreón* with a door that hung loose on its hinges. It had been built many years ago to protect the *placita,* but it had not stopped the Apaches. Northern Sonora and Chihuahua, as well as Southern Arizona and New Mexico, had many such *placitas,* each with its own *torreón,* but most of them had one thing in common; they were all abandoned, melting back into the earth from which they had been fashioned.

There was still no sign of life. Dusty looked at Shell. "What do you think, *compañero?*"

"We scared them," said Shell. "Frank is right though. I don't think the Apaches bother this place."

"How so?"

Shell jerked his head. "You hear that mule music? You think the Apaches would allow anyone to keep a mule in this country unless he was a friend of the Apaches?"

Dusty nodded. "If he's a friend of the Apaches, he likely won't be friendly to us."

They stopped in front of the largest building. Dusty tried the door. It was barred from within. He tapped on the thick, bolt-studded door with the metal-shod butt of his Spencer. There was no answer. Shell looked toward the *torreón.* Something had moved just within the open doorway. Shell dropped the reins and raised his carbine. "You there!" he called out. "Show yourself!"

"What is it you want?" asked a man with a deep voice.

"Food first."

"There is none to spare."

"We can take what we want."

The challenge hung in the thin air. There was no movement from the man in the *torreón* but Shell knew he had a gun.

"Anselmo Chacón, my friend!" called out Frank Harley.

Again the hesitation and then the man spoke. "Is it you, Frank, my old friend?"

"That is so and these are my friends. They will not harm you, Anselmo."

The man laughed. "I could kill both of them from here, and they are covered as well from across the street."

Shell looked quickly toward a tumbled ruin. There was someone in there.

A squat man with a thick, grizzled beard stepped out into the street from the *torreón*. The bright sunlight glinted from the heavy coin-silver ornamentation of his sombrero and from the well-polished Henry rifle he held in huge hands. He walked slowly toward them. Shell helped Frank down from the saddle. Anselmo looked curiously at Frank as he approached him. He gripped Frank in his arms, looking for all the world like a squat grizzly hugging an opponent.

Shell looked across the street. A figure stood there in the ruins. A woman dressed in Mexican fashion, but her face was that of a pure quill Indian, and Apache at that. But, by God, she was a damned sight younger than Anselmo, and she was actually pretty. Not a flat-faced squaw as so many of them were. Dusty whistled softly. Shell shot him a hard look.

"What is wrong, my friend?" asked Anselmo of Frank.

"I'm blind, Anselmo," said Harley quietly.

Anselmo crossed himself. "Body of God! How did this happen?"

Dusty leaned against the front of the house watching the Apache woman walk gracefully toward them, trailing a single-shot rifle. "Her relatives did it," said Dusty out of the side of his mouth. "Buried him up to the neck in sand at Horno Tanks, just long enough for him to lose his sight."

Anselmo stared at Frank. "And you have lived!"

"Thanks to my two friends here. If they had not come along...." His voice trailed off.

Shell looked at Anselmo. "My name is Shell," he said. "My partner is called Dusty. We need food and a couple of horses. Three, if you're willing to trade."

Anselmo shoved back his hat and looked at the dun. "Yes," he said. "I think I can trade a horse for this one."

"Two," said Shell.

Anselmo shrugged. "I have two horses and one mule for trading."

"A mule is good enough for me," said Frank.

"You ride with them, my old friend?" asked Anselmo. "I thought you would stay with me. It gets lonely at times, although Theresa is good company."

"Odd name for an Indian," said Dusty.

Anselmo looked at him. "Her real name is Pretty Hands, but I call her Theresa after my sainted mother."

"Cute," said Dusty. He shifted a little and looked at the side doorway into which Theresa had vanished. Smoke had thickened from the chimney.

The dark eyes of the Mexican studied Dusty thoughtfully. He took Frank by the arm and led him into the house. Shell led the dun to the watering trough, and as he drank, he stripped the horse of Dusty's gear and Shell's own saddle.

He rubbed the dun's neck. They had come a long way together but the dun could not go on. Maybe, on the way back... It was a long maybe.

"Cute little devil," said Dusty from behind Shell.

Shell turned. "Keep away from her," he said.

Dusty smiled in amusement. "Why? You got an eye on her?"

"No, but Anselmo has."

Dusty spat. "That old bastard?"

Shell looked beyond his companion. The heat haze was rising. Something flashed quickly and brightly across the wide valley. He turned quickly. An answering flash came from a pinnacle of rock thrust up from a gaunt ridge a mile from the *placita*. A cold feeling came over him. They had been followed. The Apaches knew exactly where they were. "You see that?" he said dryly to Dusty.

Dusty had stripped to his worn and dirty undershirt. He thrust his head into the water trough and came up dripping and spluttering. "Sure," he said. "I ain't blind like Harley."

"Harley can see a helluva lot better than you can. He didn't bring us here to hand us over to the Apaches."

Dusty wrung out his beard. "No? How do *we* know? He was never very keen on letting us in on his damned lost mine. Supposing he and ol' Anselmo are in there right now figgerin' on how to let the Apaches know how best to take us?"

Shell had never thought of that. The cold feeling crept over him again as he led the dun to the peeled pole corral and turned him loose with the other horses. He washed up at the trough as Dusty had done, reveling in the unlimited supply of water. He and Dusty walked back to the house. The odor of the rich chile and beans hung in the sunlit street. Shell tapped on the door and was bidden to enter by Anselmo.

The room was low-ceiled and huge, with a corbeled ceiling, with painted willow sticks set herring-bone fashion between the thick beams. The furniture was huge, dark, and ancient. A beehive fireplace was in the corner, and here and there along the walls were niches in which stood stolid-faced *santos,* plainly revealing the part-Indian ancestry of the wood carver. A candle guttered in front of one of the *santos,* and Shell was willing to bet it was that of Saint Theresa. The whitewashed walls were hung with skillfully woven rugs, and the beaten earth floor was also covered with the same style rugs. Dusty whistled softly. Always the materialist, he was impressed with such things, and Anselmo lived in the style of a *don*.

Frank was seated at the huge table beside an ancient bell, green with age. Places had been set for four. Dusty eyed a dark bottle that graced the center of the table.

Anselmo bowed a little. "Sit down, gentlemen," he said in courtly fashion.

Shell eyed the rich furnishings, seemingly so out of place in such a country, and the odd thought came to him that Anselmo must be a rich man. But where did he get his riches from?

The Mexican sat down and smiled at Shell. "Before the war," he said, "I was a *comanchero.*"

Then Shell knew. He was a man who had traded with the Indians, illegally perhaps, depending on the type of goods he had to offer. Most likely Anselmo had offered guns and ammunition, which was strictly against the law, but with the proper greasing of palms, nothing would have been said.

The Apache woman silently served the meal. Crisp tacos and rich chile beans were placed on the table. There was little talking while they ate. Anselmo had an amused look on his face as he watched Dusty and Shell stow away the food. Harley ate very little. Now and then his hand would touch the ancient bell beside him. Anselmo filled glasses with Bacanora brandy. Harley shook his head as the glass was placed in front of him. Dusty calmly appropriated Harley's full glass.

The woman cleared the table as silently as she had brought the food, and her liquid eyes never looked at the two companions, although now and then she glanced at Frank Harley. She vanished, leaving the men alone. Shell wondered uncomfortably where she had gone. He listened for the sound of hoofbeats but heard nothing. He glanced at their carbines leaning against the wall near the door and as he looked back at the table he saw the thoughtful eyes of Anselmo on him. Maybe Dusty had been right. The Apaches could come into the *placita* and be waiting outside for Dusty and Shell, for it was a certainty that they would not bother Frank Harley under the protection of Anselmo, even though they had left him to die a horrible death at Horno Tanks.

There wasn't much Dusty and Shell could do about it if Frank had led them into a trap. Dusty made the most of it. His eyes grew a little brighter as the good Bacanora caught hold. Frank Harley touched the bell and passed a hand over the molded surface of it.

"Yes," said Anselmo. "It is *the* bell, Frank."

"I thought as much," said the blind man.

Dusty eyed the old bell. "What's it doing in here?" he said.

Frank looked at him. "Let Anselmo tell you," he said.

Anselmo refilled his glass. "It is the Bell of Saint Joseph," he said. "For many years it rang in a mission far south of here. In seventeen sixty-seven that mission was abandoned. My ancestor was the sacristan of the church. There were four bells in the bell tower. One of them fell and was shattered when they attempted to lower it from the tower. Two had already been taken from the tower. The last of the four bells was left hanging in the tower."

"What's the deal?" said Dusty. He refilled his glass.

Anselmo continued as though he had not heard Dusty. "The two bells that had been taken from the tower were hauled from the barranca. One of them has been lost. The other one, the one you see here, was hung in a small church near the Rio Magdalena until Apache raids forced the abandonment of that church as well. My father was the sacristan there and the bell was in his charge as it had been in the charge of his father and his father's father. He brought the bell here. When this *placita* was at last abandoned, the first year of your Civil War, the bell was left behind. It is in my charge now."

Shell looked at him curiously and then at the bell. He leaned closer to it. The date 1750 had been molded above the flare of the bell mouth. He stood up and looked closer. He read the name Saint Joseph. He glanced around the side of the bell and his heart skipped a beat. He could make out the faint lettering. "El Naranjal," he said. He looked at Anselmo. "Then El Naranjal *does* exist?"

"It is not a tale made up by old men," said the Mexican. "It is a legend, but it is true. That is the bell brought from La Barranca Escondida in seventeen sixty-seven."

"When the Jesuits were forced to leave Mexico," said Shell.

"Exactly," said Anselmo. He looked at Frank Harley.

"He knows La Barranca Escondida and El Naranjal are real."

Dusty emptied his glass. "He had better," he said.

The dark eyes of the Mexican studied Dusty and then Shell. "No man knows more about La Barranca Escondida than my friend," said Anselmo. "But now that he cannot see, how can he possibly hunt for it?"

Harley leaned forward. "These two men are my eyes."

Anselmo nodded. "So?"

Shell sipped his brandy. "The idea doesn't appeal to you?"

"A blind man is helpless," said Anselmo.

"He still wants to go," said Dusty.

There was a tension in the room. Anselmo leaned back in his chair. "Let us speak plainly," he said. "Who are you two men? Who is to say what will happen to Frank if the treasure is found?"

"That is my risk," said the blind man. "I know the way without sight, Anselmo. They can't possibly find La Barranca Escondida without my guidance."

Anselmo looked quickly at him. "And if you do *not* find it? What then?" His meaning was plain enough. He did not like the looks of the two hard-bitten adventurers who had come out of the desert with his old friend.

Shell selected a cigar from the box on the table. He bit off the end and lighted it, eyeing Anselmo over the flare of the match. "Our risk is as great as his," he said. "How do we know he really knows where La Barranca Escondida is? You say he knows more about La Barranca Escondida than any other man, but he doesn't really know where it is. It has been lost for a hundred years, hasn't it? A man can go into that country and never find his way out again. The Indians do not want white men looking for lost mines in their country. He has a risk and we have a risk. We're willing to take a chance. Why shouldn't he?"

Harley nodded. "I am going with them, Anselmo."

Anselmo bowed his head. "It is the will of God," he

said quietly. "Come, Señor Shell, let us look at the horses."

They walked outside, leaving Dusty and Harley. Harley was passing a questing hand over the ancient bell while Dusty plied the brandy bottle.

The heat was intense after the coolness of the thick-walled house. Waves of it shimmered up from the lower ground and hazed the mountains on the east side of the valley. Shell saw no mirror flashes but he knew well enough the Apaches were still up there. The only thing that would keep them there would be their friendship with Anselmo. It gave Shell an eerie feeling.

Shell selected a blocky gray and a clean-limbed sorrel for the dun, taking a mule as well, and paying Anselmo fifty dollars besides. He hated to lose the dun, but there was nothing he could do about it. "We'll need supplies," he said.

"There is not much," said the Mexican. "I will see what I can do. When will you leave?"

"In a few days. Frank is not fully recovered. I haven't figured out yet how he survived."

Anselmo relighted his cigar. "A man with such a dream cannot die, my friend. It is what keeps him alive."

"Do you think he will realize that dream, Anselmo?"

Anselmo slanted his sombrero lower over his eyes and looked out across the burning landscape. "All men have dreams, my friend. I had a dream. It is gone now. Once I thought this *placita* would become a great place because of the mines in the hills behind us. I was content to live here as alcalde with my brothers and sisters and their wives and husbands. There would be many children." His voice died away.

Shell looked at him. "And so?"

Anselmo shrugged. He held out his hands palms upward. "I was gone to make money. The mines could not be worked because of the Apaches. There was plague. Those that did not die in the plague were killed by the Apaches. Those that survived the plague and the

Apaches fled to the south. They will not come back to this hostile land."

"Then why do you stay?"

Anselmo smiled. "Perhaps it is still my dream, my friend. A man must never give up his dream, his hopes, for if he does, he might as well be dead."

Shell looked curiously at the house. The smoke still drifted from the chimney but there was no sign of the woman.

Anselmo seemed to read his mind. "Her father and younger brother were captured by my people. They were to die. I saved them. In time they let me visit their camp. I was a lonely man. Kayitah, the man I had saved, was her father. Now she is my wife." He looked at Shell. "You do not like the idea of having an Apache woman for a wife?"

"I didn't say that," said Shell.

Anselmo nodded. "Here, in Mexico, perhaps we think differently, but then most of us have Indian blood in our veins." Anselmo studied Shell curiously. "I have my dream, or what is left of it. Frank has his dream of La Barranca Escondida. Your friend Dusty has a dream of great riches with which he thinks he can buy happiness. What is *your* dream, my friend?"

Shell laughed. "The same as Dusty's," he said.

Anselmo shook his head. "I do not think so," he said.

Shell looked angrily at the Mexican. "Why not?"

"There is something within you that tries to get out. If you do find all that silver it will not pay your way to happiness."

Shell hurled the cigar from his mouth. "What else is there?" he said harshly. "After five years of war we have nothing but our lives and our guns. How much longer can we keep on? What future is there for men such as us?"

Anselmo shrugged. He looked sideways at Shell. "I cannot answer those questions," he said quietly. "The answers are in *you*, my friend."

"You talk like a fool!" snapped Shell. He strode away.

Anselmo blew a puff of smoke. "Perhaps," he said

softly to himself. "But you know that I am right, my friend."

Far across the valley a small hand mirror caught the bright light of the sun and reflected it like a shard of silver. There was no sign of life. Then another mirror flashed from the sharp pinnacle of rock that stood on the gaunt ridge just north of the *placita*. Then there was nothing but the empty valley, with heat waves shimmering upward. A dust devil arose, whirled swiftly across the baking ground, and disappeared as mysteriously as it had appeared. It was the only movement aside from the shimmering heat waves. A feeling of watchful waiting hung over the empty country. Nothing could move out there without being seen from the hills. Nothing....

CHAPTER EIGHT

I n the week that had passed, Frank Harley regained his strength. For a time, he had hoped his sight, or at least part of it, would return, but at the end of the week he knew there was no hope left for that. For the rest of his life he would move in complete darkness. He knew Anselmo wanted him to stay at the *placita*. They were good friends and spent many hours talking together of many things. It was a strong temptation, but ever and again Frank's hands would touch the smooth metal of the bell and then trace the words molded about the flare of the mouth. 1750...Saint Joseph ... El Naranjal. He knew El Naranjal was no fantasy. *Cerro de Huesos is the first key. For there, on a quiet night, one might hear the dogs of La Barranca Escondida barking.* The dogs, of course, would no longer be there, but—*when the wind comes from the south, a bell may be heard. That bell hangs in the bell tower of the church at El Naranjal.*

Frank knew he had to go. He didn't trust his two companions, *but he had to go.* He needed their eyes and they needed his knowledge. If they found the silver, there would be more to each share than any of them could spend in a lifetime of prodigious spending. If they didn't find the silver it would not matter. The country would kill them one way or another. The Yaquis, or the lack of water, or the tangled, almost impenetrable country itself would finish them off. They were harsh odds, almost hopeless, but Frank Harley had to go.

Dusty stood at the barred window of the big, low-ceiled bedroom he shared with Shell. He blew a stream of smoke between the rusted bars. "We've got to do it my way," he said.

Shell raised his head from the pillow. "How far do you think we'd get?"

Dusty spoke over his shoulder. "I don't want to rot here. We're safe enough as long as Anselmo keeps his boys in the hills, but supposin' he changes his mind? I don't trust that smiling bastard."

"For that matter, he doesn't trust you either. He's seen you looking at that woman of his."

Dusty spat between the bars. "Maybe she needs a *real* man, not that bearded old goat."

"Like you?" said Shell dryly.

"Like me."

Shell sat up and dropped his feet to the floor, feeling for his boots. "I don't like it here any better than you do, but until Anselmo says we can leave, we stay."

Dusty whirled. "What's to prevent him from letting us go and having his bushy-headed buzzards waitin' out there for us?"

"We'd have Frank with us. He won't let anything happen to Frank, will he?"

"That don't mean they couldn't pick us off and then deliver Frank back to his *amigo* Anselmo. No, *my* plan is right. I know you don't like it, but by God you haven't come up with any other idea!"

Shell pulled on his seam-split boots. He rolled a cigarette and lighted it. Maybe Dusty was right at that. He wanted to force Anselmo and his woman along as hostages. It was risky, but Shell had no other plan. They'd never make it alone. Even if Anselmo believed the Apaches would not harm the trio if he asked them not to, there was nothing to prove that the Apaches would honor his request. Certainly, Anselmo and his beloved Pretty Hands were safe from them.

Pretty Hands was the daughter of a chief and Anselmo was his blood brother.

"The sun will be gone in an hour," said Dusty from the window.

Shell nodded. He swung his gun belt about his lean hips with practiced ease and buckled it, settling it down. He took the Colt from its holster and checked it. Anselmo had given them supplies enough for two days at least. Flour, beans, coffee, and a few cans of embalmed beef, greasy relic of the war. The three animals were handy. There were other horses in the corral. Enough for all five of them to ride south that night. How far would the Apaches follow them? What lay ahead? Those two questions harried Shell. The country south of Papago Springs was unknown to him and Dusty. Only Frank Harley knew it. Anselmo would never open his mouth.

Shell walked back and forth. They were damned if they stayed and damned if they moved. It was like being in limbo. But he had a feeling the Apaches could not be held off forever. They might not harm Frank, but Dusty and Shell would be another matter.

"Well?" said Dusty.

Shell stopped pacing and looked at him. "All right," he said. "When?"

Dusty came forward. "We eat at dusk. Anselmo doesn't carry a sidearm. His rifle is racked near the door. You sit in between him and the door. We'll have to take over when the woman comes into the room. If she breaks loose we'll never get her, short of killing her, and you know what would happen if we *did* kill her."

Shell nodded. He still didn't like the idea but, as Dusty had bluntly pointed out, Shell hadn't come up with any other solution.

"You cover Anselmo," said Dusty. "I'll take care of the woman."

Shell looked quickly at his companion.

Dusty grinned like a lobo. "I haven't got any loose ideas, if that's what's botherin' yuh."

Shell fashioned a cigarette. "How far will we take them?"

"How about the Rio Magdalena?"

"The Apaches will follow us all the way to Durango if they feel like it, Dusty."

Dusty shook his head. "I'll see to that," he said.

His meaning wasn't clear to Shell, but it didn't matter. They had to get out of the *placita*. They sat and smoked until the long shadows crept down the slopes behind the *placita*. Then the sun was fully gone. They could hear the woman setting the table in the big room. Anselmo had trained her well. Now and then the murmuring of voices drifted into them. Frank and Anselmo were off on one of their interminable discussions.

Shell took over now. "Go and saddle the horses," he said over his shoulder as he stood by the door that led into the big room. "Keep them in the corral. Make damned sure *she* doesn't see you."

"Yuh think I was born yesterday?"

"Sometimes you act like it. Fill the canteens. The food is packed and ready in the shed near the corral. Make it fast. I'll keep Frank and Anselmo occupied."

Dusty rubbed out his cigarette and spat into the beehive fireplace. "Yes suh, lootenant, suh! Yes suh!"

Shell looked back at him in the gathering darkness of the room. Shell had been commissioned second lieutenant from first sergeant during the Vicksburg Campaign by the old tried-and-true method of the South Kansas-Texas Mounted Rifles. A company election. Their company commander and first lieutenant had been killed in action. Shell's only opponent in the election had been Acting Color Sergeant Matt Dustin. No man fought better than Matt Dustin. The devil would have been hard put to keep up with him when the *Minie* balls played their strident, killing music. But Dusty could never lead other men. He was an individualist in battle. There was nothing inspiring about his fighting. He fought like a butcher slaughters beef. Kill, kill, and kill, like a Highlander who has gone fey and does not feel his own bloody wounds until the fighting is over.

"You'll never forget that, will you?" said Shell quietly.

"It was only a joke."

"The joke is *old,* Dusty. It's worn out. Retire it."

Their eyes held each other's in the darkness. "Keno," said Dusty at last. He quietly opened the side door, removed his spurs, and was gone like a hunting cat.

Shell opened the door into the big common room. Frank and Anselmo were already seated at the table, deep in conversation. Shell lighted a cigarette and walked about, ostensibly interested in the hangings and relics on the whitewashed walls. Anselmo's polished Henry rifle was in its rack near the wide door. The woman also had a rifle, but Shell had never been able to find out where she kept it. It was a cinch she wouldn't bring it into the big room while she served the evening meal. He could hear her working in the kitchen. She was making enough noise to cover anything Dusty was doing.

Shell usually sat near Anselmo, between him and the door, while Dusty sat opposite Shell and close to the kitchen door.

"Where is Dusty?" said Frank. Already he had begun to develop that uncanny sense of the blind wherein they can feel a presence.

"He'll be right along," said Shell.

A few minutes later Dusty opened the bedroom door and came into the big room, yawning a little as though he had just awakened. He winked to Shell over the head of Anselmo.

They sat down and the woman came in silently and began to serve the meal. Dusty looked at Shell and nodded. Shell stood up just as Dusty gripped the woman by her right wrist. Shell drew swiftly and covered the Mexican. "Don't move!" he said. Dusty yelled and cursed.

He jerked his hand away from the woman. She had driven her firm white teeth into his forearm. He staggered back, mouthing curses, then lunged for her. The knife came from somewhere, but from where only God and Pretty Hands knew. The hooked blade swept out at Dusty's face, and only his upflung right arm fended the blow, but even so the tip raked his right cheek from cheekbone to the very edge of his mouth. Bright red droplets sprayed from the wound as he gripped her knife wrist and fought her for the bloody blade. There was no outcry from the woman.

Dusty gripped at her dress with his left hand, and the fabric ripped from throat to waist exposing her swinging, dark-nippled breasts. She broke loose and slashed skillfully with the knife, falling halfway over the table as Dusty drew back. Crockery and cutlery clattered on the floor. The brandy bottle smashed against the bell of Saint Joseph and the rich fruity odor of the spirits mingled with that of the spilled food. Dusty stepped in close, his wild fighting blood heated to a killing pitch. He backhanded Pretty Hands, sending her staggering back against the wall. Her bloody knife tinkled on the earthen floor. Once again Dusty struck her. She had no defense for the white man's way of fighting. She sagged sideways and Dusty struck a third time. Her mouth flew open. Blood gushed from her nose and mouth, and she hit the floor in the corner.

Dusty stepped back, clapping a hand to his slashed face. His breathing was harsh. "The bitch!" he said. "The Indian bitch! I oughta kill her for that!"

Anselmo looked at Shell with cold eyes. He did not move but his eyes swiveled to Dusty. "I'll kill *you* for that," he said between his teeth.

Dusty dipped a bandanna into the spilled brandy and wiped the streaming wound, wincing as the alcohol bit deeply into it. He bandaged his face and walked to the cabinet in the corner where Anselmo kept his liquor. He ripped open one of the half-doors and gripped the neck of another brandy bottle. He jerked out the cork with his teeth and spat it into the fireplace. He tilted the bottle and gulped deeply.

"Sit still, Anselmo," said Shell. He half-cocked his Colt.

Anselmo looked up. "Is this how you repay my hospitality?" he murmured.

Dusty whirled. "Hospitality *shit!*" he snapped. "You planned all along to turn us over to the Apaches. You were fattening us for the slaughter!"

"That is a lie," said Frank Harley quietly. "Only an hour ago Anselmo told me he'd guide us to the Rio Magdalena."

"Bullshit!" said Dusty.

Shell looked at Frank. "We couldn't take a chance, Frank," he said.

"Get them out to the horses," said Dusty.

Shell stepped behind Anselmo and tapped him on the shoulder. The Mexican stood up, glanced at his wife, then walked to the door. Shell took Harley by the shoulder and guided him to the door. "Lead him to the corral, Anselmo," said Shell. "Don't try anything."

Dusty took a pair of bottles from the cabinet and placed them in a fiber morral. He looked at Shell. "Go on," he said.

Shell jerked his head toward the woman. "What about her?"

Dusty's eyes were enigmatical. "I'll take care of her," he said.

Shell raised his head a little. "By God," he said. "If you touch her I'll kill you myself!"

Dusty laughed. "With her family and friends out there waiting in the darkness? Don't be loco!"

Shell stepped outside, quickly closing the door. It was very dark. He marched Anselmo and Frank toward the corral. The horses whinnied a little. Shell talked quietly to them as he gave Frank a leg up into the saddle of the mule and then had Anselmo mount. He lashed the

Mexican to the saddle with a riata. He looked up at Anselmo. "Do I gag you or do you keep your mouth shut?" he asked.

"I will not cry out," said the Mexican.

Dusty had fashioned pommel and cantle packs with the supplies inside of them. Canteens hung like ripe fruit from the saddles. Shell led the four horses and the mule slowly up the dark street to the big house. He whistled softly.

Dusty came to the door of the house. "She's still unconscious," he said. "I tied her and gagged her. We can leave her here. I left the lamps on in the kitchen and living room."

There was no time to lose. They led the horses from the street, begrudging every hoofbeat on the hard caliche of the street. They mounted when they were a quarter of a mile from the *placita*. Now and then Anselmo looked back at the darker patch that indicated the *placita,* then his dark eyes would rest steadily on the broad back of Dusty.

Cold sweat worked down Shell's sides. He gripped his half-cocked Spencer in his right hand and swung his head from front to each side in turn and then to the rear. There was only one thing that kept hope alive in him. Apaches do not like to fight at night, for fear that if they die, their souls will wander forever in limbo. Still, perhaps if they had the chance, they might possibly attack. But the deadly time was in the cold gray light of the predawn, when a man's morale is at the lowest.

They could see the dark humped shapes of the hills on either hand, closing in on them as they rode further south. An hour passed uneventfully. Shell looked back. He could see the faintest of yellow specks off in the velvety darkness. Dusty had left the lamps on in the house in an attempt to convince the Apaches that the house was occupied. But if they came down to the house and found the woman....

They rode fifty minutes, rested the horses ten

minutes, on and on, all through the tension of that night, and when the faintest light appeared in the eastern sky they were almost sure they had fooled the Apaches.

When the sun came up they had taken cover in a shallow arroyo that meandered down from the broken hills. Shell helped Frank from his saddle. The blind man had not spoken all night. There was no telling what he was thinking. Anselmo was his good friend, but, on the other hand, Frank's consuming goal was La Barranca Escondida.

Dusty slowly worked the blood-soaked bandage from his face. The blood had coagulated. Shell examined the wound. "It'll be all right, but you're marked for life, *compañero.*"

Dusty nodded. He uncorked the bottle of brandy and took a deep slug. He had been nipping steadily all through the night. His bloodshot eyes flicked toward Anselmo.

"Take it easy on the brandy," said Shell.

Dusty spat. "It's me that got cut up," he said thinly. "You had the easy part."

"It was your idea to handle the woman," said Shell.

Dusty did not answer. He sat down on a rock with the bottle in his hand. "How far do we take him?" he said, jerking his head toward Anselmo.

Anselmo sat on a rock, with his bound hands resting in his lap. He never took his eyes from Dusty.

"Let him go," said Frank Harley.

"Hell no!" snapped Dusty. "He'd have every Apache between here and the border on our asses by noon!"

Shell shoved back his hat and wiped the sweat from his face. He looked curiously at Dusty. Something was riling Dusty; something deep inside. An uneasy feeling came over Shell. "The woman," he said. "She's still bound and gagged back there."

Dusty nipped at the bottle again. "She can work loose once she regains her senses," he said.

Anselmo moved swiftly. He reached for Shell's

Spencer that had been leaned against a rock not far from him. The loosened thongs fell from his swollen wrists. He moved swiftly but he had underestimated Dusty as many another man had done. Anselmo snatched up the heavy weapon and thumbed back the big hammer to full cock. Dusty dropped the bottle, rose into a half crouch, swung back his hand, swept the Colt up and forward, letting the weight of it cock the spur hammer under his thumb. He fired an instant before Anselmo did, and the roar of the Spencer sounded like an echo of the Colt. Anselmo went backward and fell heavily, the Spencer dropping from his nerveless hands. The Spencer slug struck the sorrel in the side of the head and he went down as though poleaxed.

Powder smoke swirled through the arroyo, and the twin echoes died away in the nearby hills. Dusty let down the hammer of the smoking Colt. There was no need for a second shot. A black hole between Anselmo's staring eyes leaked blood and matter.

"Anselmo!" cried Frank Harley.

There was no answer. There would never be an answer.

Shell whirled and ran up the crumbling side of the arroyo with short, digging steps. The sun had flooded the valley. How far had those shots been heard? There was no sign of life, but that didn't mean anything. An Apache is seen only when he *wants* to be seen. Shell slid down into the arroyo. "Let's go!" he snapped.

There was no argument from Dusty. The only thing that could save them now was speed. They led the three horses and the mule out of the arroyo, and Shell helped Harley up into the saddle of the third horse. There was no time to take care of Anselmo's body or to strip the dead sorrel. They spurred their horses and rode south toward the distant Rio Magdalena. Even Frank Harley had no other thought in his mind at that time despite the killing of his dear friend. His recent memory of his treatment by the Apaches crowded every other thought out of his mind.

They cleared the broken hills and struck open country that sloped gradually down toward the distant river. It would be dry, but there would be springs or waterholes nearby. But, supposing the Apaches had got ahead of them during the night?

Shell looked back. A thought had struck his mind. The woman might still be bound and gagged in that distant house. Supposing the Apaches did *not* come for her? Supposing she had not been able to free herself?

Dusty drained the bottle and hurled it to one side. It shattered on the hard ground. He wiped his mouth with the back of a dusty hand. "Don't worry," he said thickly. "Ain't nothing more can happen to her."

Shell stared unbelievingly at him.

Dusty nodded. "I hit her too damned hard, Shell. I didn't mean to."

Shell was sickened. He looked away from his friend. No, Dusty never *meant* to kill, it just happened. It had been that way in the past and it would be that way again. As Shell rode south, with the lurking fear of painted death in his soul, he could see the bearded face of Anselmo looking fondly at his young Apache wife. "Her name is Pretty Hands," he had said. "But I call her Theresa after my sainted mother."

CHAPTER NINE

Shell worked his way slowly down the mountain side. He winced as he scraped past a jumping cholla. The needles seemed to leap out at him. Not for nothing had the vicious plant been given its name. The sweat poured down his face although the sun was gone. He wiped it from his face as he reached the talus slope above the waterhole. He worked his way in through the thick brush to where they had made their simple camp.

Dusty looked up from the boot he was roughly cobbling. "Well?" he said coldly.

Shell looked at Frank Harley. The older man sat with his back against a rock, breathing harshly. "I covered the whole area southwest of here trying to see a twin peak with a white area on the north side."

"So?" said Dusty. He pulled on the worn-out boot.

Shell shook his head. "Nothing," he said.

"Are you sure?" said Frank.

"Positive," said Shell.

Dusty scratched in his ragged beard. "Now what?" he said to Harley.

The older man did not answer. He could feel the

menace emanating from Dusty although he could not see those icy blue eyes staring at him.

"Five gawddamned days in this hellhole," said Dusty, "and we ain't seen anything like twin peaks with a white area on the north side. Maybe we're lost, eh, Harley?"

Shell put down the field glasses. He rolled a cigarette and thrust it into Harley's mouth. He lighted it. "Maybe you're wrong, Frank," he suggested.

The blind man shook his head. Dusty spat to one side. He caught the makings out of the air as Shell tossed them over to him.

They had been on the way for over a week, and in the last five days Harley had insisted there was such a twin peak, but neither Shell nor Dusty had been able to spot it. They had crossed the dry Rio Magdalena and then the San Miguel and had reached the fork of another dry river, unknown to them. Harley himself had become a little dubious at that time.

"I'm sure it must be there. Ignacio said it would be there," said the blind man patiently.

"I'm sure it *must* be there," mimicked Dusty. He lighted his cigarette and hurled the match to one side. "Damn you! You blind bastard! You've led us on a wild goose chase! I got a damned good mind to leave you here!"

Harley looked toward him. "You won't," he said.

"Why not?"

"Your greed won't let you."

Dusty spat. "The hell it won't!"

Harley sucked in the smoke. He took the cigarette from his dry lips. "Then Shell won't let you."

Shell narrowed his eyes. He looked at Dusty. Dusty was ringy. He had been so ever since they had crossed the San Miguel. "Let's go over it once more, Frank," suggested Shell. "We crossed the Rio Magdalena, and then the San Miguel. We bore southeasterly for two days after crossing the river fork and followed the canyon for about twenty miles."

"To a dry waterhole," said Dusty.

"He didn't dry it up," said Shell.

"Who the hell asked you?" snapped Dusty.

Shell ignored him. "Are you sure this is the way, Frank?" he asked.

Harley nodded. "Ignacio would not lie to me."

"Look at him sitting there!" said Dusty. "Damn him! He doesn't know, I tell you, Shell! It was *Ignacio* who knew the way!"

Shell sat down on a rock. He studied the calm face of Frank Harley. There was no way they could tell whether Harley was lying to them or whether he just didn't know, and nothing seemed able to jolt him out of that complacency. There was a growing suspicion in Shell that Harley might just be playing with them. Perhaps he *did* know the way but was taking revenge for the death of his beloved friend Anselmo.

They ate the last of their food as they sat there in the gathering darkness. There would still be some moonlight that night, but not enough to reflect from the twin peaks' white area, as Harley had once suggested. If there was any such landmark in that part of Sonora, Shell was sure they weren't near it.

The moon arose, shedding a faint light over the tangled, trackless country. A lurking fear hung in Shell's mind. Maybe they were hopelessly lost. They hadn't seen a living person for four days, with the one exception of a Mexican who had fled from them as though they had the plague. There was no desire within Shell to backtrack. Somewhere between them and the border would be the Apaches, led by Kayitah, their chief, hunting for the white men who had killed Anselmo and Pretty Hands. "The Apaches will follow us all the way to Durango if they feel like it," Shell had said to Dusty back at the *placita*. They couldn't go back, and they didn't know what lay ahead.

Shell looked at the placid face of Frank Harley, and a spark of anger, fanned by fear, began to burn brighter within him. He looked at Dusty. The message seemed to leap between them.

Dusty got up and walked slowly to Frank, his spurs chiming softly. He stopped in front of Harley. "Once more," he said thinly. "Are you lost? Or are you bullshit-ting us?"

Harley did not answer. Dusty swung out a big hand, sweeping the cigarette from Harley's lips. A thin trickle of blood wormed from the blind man's mouth and worked down into his beard.

Dusty placed both hands on his hips. He leaned forward. "Once again," he said. "Are you lost? Maybe you're misleadin' us?"

Harley raised his head. The trickling blood looked black in the moonlight. "I am not lying to you," he said.

The open hand caught him alongside the head and he rocked with the vicious impact. Blood and spittle flew from his mouth. For a moment Shell almost felt compassion for the blind man, and then the lurking fear settled on his shoulders again.

Dusty's next blow drove Harley from the rock. He lay on his side, drawing up his legs. Dusty kicked him lightly. "Talk, you stubborn bastard," he said.

"For the love of God," the hoarse voice said in Spanish from the thick brush, "do not beat that old man, my son."

Two men whirled. Colts leaped from holsters and hammers were swept back. A bareheaded man stood in the brush looking sadly at them. "I am unarmed," he said. He held up his arms. He wore some kind of cowled robe. "I am Father Eusebio," he added.

"A padre?" said Shell.

"That's what *he* says," said Dusty. "Come on out here, you!"

The man pushed his way through the brush. He staggered a little. His brown Franciscan robe was torn and patched, filthy with dust and stippled with burrs and thorns. His feet were shod in sandals that looked paper thin. A cross hung from his roped belt. He touched his lips. "I can hardly speak," he said. "Do you have water to spare?" His brown eyes were as soft as those of a doe.

Shell nodded to Dusty. Dusty picked up a canteen. He looked at Shell. "Do we have enough for ourselves?"

"I can guide you to the next waterhole," said the padre.

"We've just about had enough of guides," said Dusty.

"Give him a drink," said Shell.

Dusty handed the padre the canteen. "Take it easy," he said.

Father Eusebio drank a little and rinsed it back and forth in his mouth. He sipped a little more after he had swallowed the first draught. He stoppered the canteen and handed it back to Dusty. "Bless you, my son," he said.

Frank Harley sat up and pulled himself up on a rock. His face was white and drawn in the pale moonlight. He wiped the dark blood from his face.

The padre looked from one to the other of the two tall Americans. "I can guide you to the next waterhole, as I have said, but where is it you wish to go from there?"

Dusty eyed the padre. "That's our business, ain't it?"

The padre raised a placating hand. "Certainly, my son, but it appears that you *are* lost, from the conversation I heard. I did not mean to eavesdrop."

"Yuh did a good job," said Dusty. "Just what are *you* doin' in this hell's hole?"

The padre sat down and pulled off his sandals. His feet were torn and bleeding. He poked a finger through a hole in one of the thin sandals. He looked so lugubrious that Shell couldn't help but smile. Shell walked to his horse and unbuckled a saddlebag. He withdrew a pair of worn but serviceable moccasins and tossed them to the padre.

"Bless you, bless you," said Father Eusebio. "I am penitent, but not quite penitent enough to walk bare-footed in this country."

"Jesus himself would have had a hard time in this

country," said Dusty. "Yuh didn't tell us what you were doin' around here."

The padre looked up. "The word of God has not been amongst the poor people of these mountains for many years. There are people living here in sin. The unmarried and the unbaptized, the dead who did not receive final absolution. I have been in these mountains for months and was working my way back to the mission when the Apaches cut me off. I had to flee this way."

"Apaches?" said Shell.

Father Eusebio nodded. "The band of Kayitah," he said. "A creature of Satan."

Dusty glanced at Shell. "How far was that from here, padre?" asked Dusty.

The padre waved a dirty hand. "Ten, perhaps fifteen miles."

"Which way were they headed?" asked Shell.

"This way," said the Mexican.

"When did you last see them?" asked Shell quickly.

The padre rubbed his unshaven face. "Just at dusk," he said.

"Jesus Christ!" said Dusty.

The padre quickly crossed himself.

Shell wearily shook his head. They'd have to move on.

Dusty raised his hand as though to strike Frank. "You and your damned twin peaks," he said.

"Wait!" said Father Eusebio. "Do not strike that man!"

Dusty turned slowly with the wolf look on his lean dirty face. "This is my business," he said.

The padre stood up. "You need water. There is none here. You are lost and do not know the way. I can lead you to water. I think I know of these twin peaks of which you speak."

"So?" said Dusty.

The padre looked at the blind man. "I have a price," he said.

Dusty grinned evilly. "I thought so! Even a man of

God has his price. Every man has his price, Shell. Yuh hear that?"

"Hear me out," said the padre. "Do not touch that old man, and I will guide you."

"You'll guide us with a pistol muzzle at your neck," said Dusty angrily.

Father Eusebio shook his head. "My guidance in exchange for the safety of the old man," he said firmly.

For a moment they stood there. The tall, lean American with the icy blue eyes and swift death in his holster. The short, squat padre with the soft brown eyes and the great cross hanging at his belt. Neither one of them moved. Neither one would give an inch.

"It's a deal," said Shell.

They both looked at him. "Get the horses, Dusty," said Shell. "We've got the extra one for the padre."

Dusty hesitated a moment longer. God how he hated to be told what to do!

Shell smiled a little. "Kayitah is on the way, *compañero,*" he said quietly.

That was enough for Dusty. He got the horses.

Father Eusebio led them in an easterly direction, rather than to the south to which they had been heading, according to Harley's directions. They passed through a tangle of thorny brush and riven rock and rounded a great gaunt shoulder of naked rock, and there before them was the dark mouth of a narrow canyon that trended southeasterly. The padre kicked his horse with his moccasined heels and plunged into the dark and uninviting mouth of the canyon without hesitation.

The walls were sheer, hung with masses of rock loosened by rain and frost. The uneven floor of the canyon was littered with detritus and the walls closed in as Father Eusebio pushed ever deeper into the canyon as though determined to enter the very bowels of the earth itself.

Now and then Shell looked up at the higher parts of the canyon walls faintly lighted by the rays of the moon.

Dried-out brush and driftwood hung in crevices and littered ledges high overhead. A flash flood would fill that canyon with a savage churning millrace of liquid death that would sweep before it and destroy any living or growing thing. Thank God the weather had been dry for months.

The moon was almost gone when at last Father Eusebio looked back at Shell and smiled. "It is but a little way," he said.

The dust swirled about them in the draft that flowed down the canyon, coating their faces and hands as well as their clothing. It seeped into nostrils and gritted between one's teeth. It burned the eyes and itched beneath the clothing.

Then suddenly it was lighter, and the ground sloped downward toward a thick line of brush and stunted trees denoting the line of a waterway. Father Eusebio slid easily from his sweating horse and led it forward. He pushed his way through the brush and was gone out of sight. They heard him cry out. "Water! Water! Water! Thank the Blessed Lord!"

Shell slid from the saddle and led his horse and Harley's mule into the thick, clinging brush. The horse whinnied and the mule brayed softly as they picked up the scent of the water. There was a clear area along the little stream. Father Eusebio raised a dripping face. *"Gracias a Dios!"* he said fervently. "By the grace of God it has not gone dry as it usually does at this time of the year."

"Lucky for you," said Dusty shortly.

Shell drank and then wiped his mouth. He rolled a cigarette and looked to the southwest. He lowered the cigarette. "Look," he said.

Clearly outlined against the sky were twin peaks, and on the side still lighted by the dying moon could be seen an irregularly shaped patch of white.

"Dos Cabezas," said Father Eusebio.

"That's it! That's it!" cried out Frank Harley.

Dusty raised his head from the water. "Yuh can thank

your God for that, Harley," he said. "If we *hadn't* found it..."

Harley wiped his wet mouth. "You could learn something from the padre here," he said quietly. "A man has to have faith in something else beside his guns."

"Don't preach to me!" snapped Dusty.

Harley looked toward Shell. "Cigarette, friend?" he said.

Shell handed him the makings. Harley rolled a cigarette. He was still a little clumsy at it but he was learning quickly. He placed the tube of tobacco in his mouth and snapped a lucifer on his thumbnail. The three men watched him raise the flickering match to the end of the cigarette and light it.

"Bueno!" said Shell.

Father Eusebio smiled. "The Good Lord makes allowances for those who are handicapped," he said.

Shell sat down on a rock and washed his face and hands. "You know this country well," he said. "Do you know where the Mesa del Campanero is?"

"I have been there," said the padre. He looked curiously at Shell. "There are other Americans there I have heard. Men who fought for Benito Juarez in his struggles for the freedom of our beloved Mexico. There is a *colonia* there now, although I have never seen it. My superior suggested that I might pass that way when I was through with God's work in these mountains. Perhaps some of these people are Catholics?"

Shell nodded. "Colonel De Tassigny, the leader of the *colonia,* is a Catholic. There may be others."

Father Eusebio nodded. He looked back at the tangled, almost impassable country through which they had come. "I do not wish to go back that way." He smiled wanly. "Nor would Kayitah let me. He has no use for the people of the Church. Why do you ask about the Mesa del Campanero?"

Shell and Dusty looked at each other. The padre looked puzzled for a moment. "But yes! You are Americans and quite likely Rebels, as De Tassigny is. What is it they call you? Unregenerated Rebels?"

Shell smiled. "Hardly, padre. *Unreconstructed* is the word."

The padre laughed heartily.

"You will guide us there, padre?" said Frank Harley.

The padre looked at the lean, scarred face of Dusty. "Yes," he said, "I think so. After all, it is my duty."

Dusty knew well enough what Father Eusebio meant. The padre's price to guide them was that Dusty must leave Frank Harley alone. Fair enough. After that, Frank would be on his own, and God help him if he went wrong again.

They moved away from the water after they and the animals had had their fill. The padre led them for several miles into broken country. Here they picketed the tired horses and slept, Dusty, Shell, and the padre taking turns on guard.

Shell lay awake for a time, staring up into the darkness, watching the winking ice-chip stars. Padre Eusebio had come along just at the right time. Shell had no idea in his mind as to what would have happened if the padre had *not* come along. Dusty had already killed two people in his quest for the lost silver mines. It wasn't likely he would have killed Frank Harley, for that would have scotched the whole deal, but the older man would have suffered. Shell felt a wave of shame creep through him. He had allowed his own greed to take over. He too had been bitter and angry at Frank because the man had become lost. Shell smiled wryly up into the darkness. A blind man becoming lost in a country where few men with sight could find their way. The shame in Shell was that he himself had not stopped Dusty beating the blind man. What had come over him?

He turned his head and looked toward Dusty, asleep a few feet away. They had been together a long time. Shell had forgotten how many times they had owed each other their lives. Shell narrowed his eyes. Was it possible that he was *afraid* of Dusty? He tried to cast the thought from his mind. He had never thought of it much before, but Dusty seemed to have changed for the worse since the sheen of silver riches had struck into his brain. The cold thought crept into Shell's mind and settled down comfortably, eyeing its new surroundings. Was it possible that the silver sheen had also outshone Shell's morals and principles as well as those of Dusty?

Frank Harley shifted in his sleep. "La Barranca Escondida," he said clearly. *"Departamento de Camino a Las Minas de La Barranca Escondida y El Naranjal."*

Father Eusebio moved a little in the darkness. He turned his face toward the supposedly sleeping trio. He padded closer on his moccasined feet and waited a long time as though to hear Frank speak in his sleep again. After a while he walked back to his post.

Shell looked toward the padre. How much had he heard? Surely he would know about the lost silver mines. What Mexican hadn't heard of Tayopa, La Barranca Escondida, and El Naranjal? To them it was the truth of God—not a myth, but a legend with a basis of truth. A wandering padre like Father Eusebio would know that country as well, or perhaps better, than most men. He would have learned a great deal from the simple people of those mountains. If nothing else the good padre would keep Dusty's hands from Frank Harley. It was better that way, for Shell felt as though he'd have to interfere the next time Dusty tried to beat the older man, and the results would be unpredictable. No one could stand in the way of Matt Dustin when he wanted something, at least not for long, and if Matt Dustin had ever really wanted anything in his life it was the lost riches of La Barranca Escondida.

CHAPTER TEN

T he sorrel had gone down thrashing with a snapped leg, hurling Padre Eusebio from the saddle. The padre had landed like a cat to clear the fallen horse. A canteen burst beneath the weight of the struggling animal, and the water darkened the light, powdery soil. It flowed into the hole into which the sorrel had stepped. Shell looked stupidly at the water as it vanished into the thirsty earth. It had been filled three days past somewhere in the unmapped country between the Rio Sonora and some unknown watercourse. It was the last of their water. They had run out of food two days past, existing on a pair of rabbits snared by Padre Eusebio. Now the sorrel was lost to them, and the gray Dusty had been riding limped badly from a punctured hoof that was now infected.

Padre Eusebio looked sorrowfully at the sorrel. *"Muy bravo,"* he said quietly. "A fine *caballo.*"

Dusty slid from the saddle. "You'll walk from now on," he said.

Shell dismounted. "We'll take turns riding." He looked up at Frank Harley. "How do you feel, Frank?"

"Muy bravo," said Frank weakly.

"Mesa del Campanero," said Dusty. He glanced toward the blind man and then at the padre.

"We'll get there," said Shell.

Dusty spat. He had become more silent in the past few days. More silent and gaunter, seemingly burning with an inner fever, and yet he was not sick. That is to say he was not physically sick. His sickness was of the mind.

"The silver will not run away," said Father Eusebio as he picked a cactus needle from his hand. For a moment he studied his hand, and then he looked up because of the sudden silence that had come over the three Americans. A weaker man than Padre Eusebio might have quailed before the hard eyes of the two tall Americans.

"What about silver?" said Dusty quietly.

The padre shrugged. "You are not in here to enjoy the scenery," he said. "There is an unholy haste within you to get to the Mesa del Campanero, and beyond that. . ."

"Beyond that?" prompted Shell.

The Mexican rubbed his dusty face. "La Barranca Escondida," he said.

Dusty's hand dropped to the butt of his Colt.

Eusebio shook his head. "I have taken the vow of poverty," he said. "Lost treasures mean nothing to me."

"They do to the Church," said Shell, "and to your order."

"I am not a Jesuit," said the padre.

"A fortune in silver can make even a Franciscan padre's head turn," said Dusty.

The padre smiled. "I will go as far as the Mesa del Campanero," he said. "That and no more."

"Yeh," said Dusty. He looked at the sorrel and at the water-soaked earth. His meaning was clear enough. No water, and short one horse.

"Where is the next waterhole?" said Shell.

"Tinajas Altas," said the padre.

"That's in Arizona," said Shell.

"There are many places with the same name," said the padre.

"How far?"

Father Eusebio shrugged. "Perhaps within ten miles. Perhaps closer. These mountains begin to look much alike after a time."

"Christ!" said Dusty. "You too? Harley gets his directions mixed up, that's bad enough, but you made a deal, Eusebio. Yuh mean to tell me yuh don't know where the water is?"

The padre stood up and looked to the south. "There are three canyons south of here," he said thoughtfully. "One them is a box canyon as you Americans call it. One leads deep into the mountains east of here. There is no water there. The third has the Tinajas Altas high on one flank. They are never dry, or so it is said."

"Or so it is said," repeated Dusty. "By God, people in this damned country always manage to cover up, don't they?"

The padre did not answer. He looked at the horse. "We cannot leave him here like this. He will be torn to pieces by tonight." The padre jerked with a startled expression on his face as the heavy bowie knife flashed past him and buried itself to the cross piece in the throat of the sorrel. The head dropped instantly and the dark blood gushed forth over the padre's worn moccasins. He leaped back and looked incredulously at Dusty. There was a faint smile on Dusty's face. A tinge of white showed beneath the brown patina of the padre's face. He hurriedly crossed himself.

Dusty walked over to the dead horse, his spurs softly chiming, and began to strip the saddle from him. He threw the saddle over the rump of Shell's horse, then jerked the bloody blade from the throat of the sorrel. He wiped it on the sorrel's dusty mane. He looked casually at Padre Eusebio, tested the edge of the knife with his thumb, feeling for nicks, then slid the bowie into its sheath. "Padre," he said softly, "you had better, by God, find the *right* canyon."

Padre Eusebio hurriedly set off afoot, glancing back now and then as Shell and Dusty led the animals behind him. He looked up at the sky. Already a speck hung there. The scout for the zopilotes. The padre shivered. These Americans dealt out death as casually as a monte dealer dealt out his cards.

The sun was slanting from the west when the faint sound of shooting echoed along the twisted canyon. The little party stopped in its tracks. There was no sound for a time except the dry wind, and then a shot flatted off to send its echo slamming back and forth between the canyon walls.

"Hunters?" said Father Eusebio.

Shell shook his head. He withdrew his Spencer from its saddle scabbard and levered a round into the chamber. He let the hammer down to half-cock. Dusty led the animals into the brush. He looked at the padre. "Stay here with Frank," he said. He also took his Spencer and followed Shell through the swaying brush. In a moment they were gone, hardly leaving a sign of their passage except a few faint boot marks.

Shell held Dusty back with a hand motion. He dropped to his knees and crawled through the tangled brush and broken rock to a point where he could look up the canyon. A shot cracked out and the echo died away. The right side of the great canyon was talus-sloped, a vast area of broken rock stippled with brush. The canyon wall above the talus slope was riven, with masses of rock looking as though the sound of the shot echoes would cause thousands of tons of rock to fall crashing to the slopes below. There was a place that was level, and here the rock had not fallen as thickly as on the talus slope. There was a rough oval of tumbled rock, head high, set on the level area. Even as Shell watched, a puff of smoke broke from between two of these rocks to be followed by the flat crack of a rifle.

Shell uncased his German-made field glasses. He took off his hat and placed the glasses to his eyes, focusing to bring in the ring of rock. The first thing he saw was a mule, laden with hide *aparejos* on each side. Beyond the mule he saw the rumps of two other animals, likely horses. A horse's head showed in a clump of brush. What interested him more were the shining pools of water held in the natural rock tanks within the oval. There was a lot of water in those tanks. The sight of it set his dry mouth and throat to aching.

A shot flatted off, closely followed by another, and the twin puffs of cottony smoke drifted downwind into the canyon. He could not see the riflemen—there must be at least two of them. What were they shooting at? He scanned the slopes. The powerful lens brought out a moccasined foot thrust out behind a clump of brush seventy-five yards from the waterhole. He slowly scanned the area on his side of the waterhole, then the lower slopes, and finally the rock wall behind the tanks. He counted nine men who showed little more than an arm, a leg, or a quick movement of a head. None of the heads had hats on them. He lowered the glasses. He touched his cracked lips with his tongue.

"Well?" demanded Dusty.

Shell looked back at him. "Waterhole," he said. "Two or three people holed up there. At least nine outside the water-hole."

"Mexicans?"

Shell shook his head. "Indians, *compañero.*"

Dusty hesitated. "Apaches?"

"Quién sabe?"

Shell did not look at Dusty again. He knew what his companion was thinking. If those were Apache, they could very well be the band of Kayitah. It was possible they had got ahead of Shell, Dusty, Frank, and Padre Eusebio.

"Maybe they're Yaquis?" said Dusty.

"What difference does it make?" said Shell.

There was a sudden outburst of gunfire, sending rolling echoes down the canyon. Powder smoke swirled about the waterhole and drifted up from the rifles of the besiegers.

Dusty bellied up beside Shell and took the glasses. He studied the situation and then the terrain. "Those people at the waterhole have horses, and it looks like they have food aplenty. They've got control of the waterhole, for a time at least. If we let those Apaches or Yaquis, or whatever the hell they are, get that waterhole, it's the end for us, *compañero.*"

Shell nodded. He looked along the canyon wall. There was an area there like a wide shelf with a natural rampart of rock ledges extending almost to above the waterhole. At the end of it were two of the besiegers, firing almost directly down into the oval of rocks. Whoever held that position had the key to the siege. He eyed the waterhole. Horses, food, and water, and they needed all three.

Dusty shifted. He looked at Shell. "We can take those Indians," he said. "After that we can take care of them Mexes at the waterhole."

Shell cased the glasses. He picked up his Spencer and led the way into the thick brush that covered the gentler slope that lay at the base of the rock shelf. The gunfire was sporadic and the Indians were so intense on their siege they'd hardly notice the approach of Dusty and Shell; at least Shell hoped so.

It took them the better part of an hour to reach the rock ledge and to lie bellyflat there, breathing harshly, their thirst a terrible thing, their sweat stinging the myriad cuts and scratches they had suffered in their stealthy approach. Shell rested his head on his forearms. His heart was thudding erratically and his lungs seemed to be on fire. It took all his discipline to crawl on, taking advantage of every scrap of cover. If they were seen they'd never get off that ledge alive.

Shell stopped fifty yards from the end of the rock shelf. Nothing could be seen of the pair of riflemen at the end of the shelf, but now and then a shot indicated they were still there. Shell placed his carbine between two rocks. He felt for his bowie and withdrew it. Foot by foot he wormed his way along. He stopped. Someone was crawling back from the end of the rock shelf. He quickly rolled into a clump of scraggly brush and behind a flat rock, cursing mentally as the hooked thorns ripped through worn clothing into flesh.

There was no sign of Dusty. Rocks clattered a little as the Indian came closer. Shell held his breath. The bare brown back of the Indian could be seen on the other side of the flat rock. As the Indian passed, Shell rolled over the rock. His bowie sank into the small of the back as Dusty's swiped clean across the throat of the buck. He fell without a sound.

The hot, sweet smell of blood filled the windless air along the rock shelf. Shell sat back resting against a rock. He looked at Dusty. Dusty grinned. He was in his element. Dusty casually wiped his bloody blade on the thick hair of the dead buck. "Apache?" he said to Shell.

"*Quién sabe?*" said Shell. He wasn't that much of an expert.

Dusty rifled the bloody corpse, cursing softly to himself.

He shoved the thing aside. "Let's get the other one," he said. "I can last about another hour without a drink."

Shell bellied along the ledge until he could see a pair of thick-soled moccasins protruding from the brush that fringed the end of the ledge. A rifle cracked. He heard the tinkle of the smoking brass hull on the rock. He moved swiftly in as the buck reloaded. The warrior was only ten feet from him, settling himself for another shot down into the waterhole area. As he squeezed off, Shell closed in, the noise of his approach covered by the roar of the shot. The buck never knew what hit him. He died even as he opened the breech of his single-shot rifle.

Dusty and Shell lay flat at the end of the ledge. Now and then, Dusty would fire a wild shot from the buck's rifle. Shell peered between two rocks. He counted seven places where gunsmoke appeared as the warriors fired at the water-hole. Even as he watched, a buck stood up, pitched forward, and fell heavily, dropping his smoking rifle. A good clean head shot at seventy-five yards, thought Shell. Whoever was handling that long gun was no amateur.

Shell touched Dusty on the shoulder. Silently he pointed out the positions of five of the Indians. None of them were concerned about who was behind them. They thought the shooting from the ledge was being done by their mates. Shell drew up his Spencer and full-cocked it. Dusty did the same. Together they sighted on brown backs not fifty yards below them. The two Spencers crashed together driving flame and smoke from the muzzles. One of the bucks leaped to his feet, whirled about and fell heavily. The other did not move. Shell and Dusty levered round after round into hot, smoking Spencers. The 385-grain slugs smashed into flesh and bone or ricocheted off into space screaming eerily. Startled brown faces, banded with white paint, looked up at the ledge. One face exploded into a mass of red jelly as two soft slugs tore into it.

The hell of the rattling repeater fire slammed back and forth in the canyon like rolling thunder. Shell rammed cartridges into the loading aperture in the repeater's metal-shod butt and dropped over the side of the ledge, plunging stiff-legged down the treacherous slope. From behind him came the piercing, thrilling rebel yell. A startled buck caught a slug in his chest and another in his back as he was spun about by the impact of the first bullet.

The two men plunged through the thorny brush, ripping clothing and flesh, firing from the hip at times until suddenly there was nothing to shoot at. The echoes died away. The smoke drifted thickly, then drifted out and slowly vanished. Then it was very quiet in the canyon except for the thrashing sound of a wounded buck who clawed for his knife, his pain-stricken eyes on the two hated white men. Dusty raised his smoking repeater and fired once, at twenty-foot range. The heavy slug ripped through the wounded buck's gaping mouth. The shot echo died away.

Shell reloaded the Spencer. He shoved back his hat and wiped the sweat and dirt from his face. His breathing was harsh and erratic, and all of a sudden, his legs grew weak beneath him and he almost sat down on the rocky ground. He leaned on his Spencer and looked toward the waterhole.

"Who is it?" someone called out in Spanish. The voice was surprisingly high pitched.

"Friends!" yelled Shell hoarsely.

Dusty looked about. "I thought yuh said there was nine of these bastards," he said. "I tally eleven."

"Mark it up to profit," Shell said dryly. "They're all *good* Indians now."

They plodded toward the ring of rocks that held the full tanks within them. A sombrero bobbed about. The barrel of a long rifle showed.

"Christ!" said Dusty. "Smell that water!"

Shell walked between two rocks that stood like a natural entrance way. A bareheaded man stood with a single-shot rifle in his hands. A band of dingy cloth held back his thick black hair. His great eyes studied the two white men.

Dusty dropped a hand to his Colt.

"No," said Shell. "He's likely a *mozo.*"

The other man stood with his back to them, bent to the waist, and there was no question about what he was doing. He was swiftly losing his last meal. He staggered a little as he held his hands to his face.

Dusty grinned. "Yuh don't like bloodlettin' even if it saves your life, eh, *amigo?*"

The man turned and withdrew his slim hands from his face. Shell whistled softly. A pair of great pain-wracked eyes looked at him. A slim hand took the heavy, silver-banded sombrero from the head, and a wealth of dark hair fell to the slim shoulders.

"My God," breathed Dusty. His eyes fell from the lovely oval face to the full, firm breasts that pushed out against the thin material of the shirt. The rounded hips beneath the rather tight charro trousers. The dusty figured boots on the small feet.

The Indian *mozo* moved quietly over beside the woman.

The rifle began to rise. Dusty walked forward, his Spencer at hip level. "Put down that rifle, you," he said coldly.

The *mozo* did not move. The woman looked at him. She spoke swiftly. "It is all right, Victor," she said. "These men are our friends. They have saved our lives." Slowly he lowered the rifle. She looked at Shell. "He cannot speak," she said.

Dusty knelt by the nearest tank and scooped water up in his free hand, but he never took his cold blue eyes from the mozo "Tell him to throw down that rifle," he said.

She spoke to the *mozo*. Obediently he threw down the rifle, but he did not move away from the woman.

"I am Rafaela Padilla of Hermosillo," she said. "This is our *mozo* Victor."

"Our?" said Shell. He looked quickly about.

Her lovely face changed. "My brother...Rodrigo...he. . ." Her voice died away and a stricken look came over her face. She looked beyond the water tanks. A slim hand crept up to her full-lipped mouth.

Shell scooped up some water to wet his mouth and throat. He skirted the tanks and walked among the scattered rocks to where a man lay face down, tightly clutching a Henry rifle in his slim brown hands. Shell hooked a boot toe under him and rolled him over. The great brown eyes stared unseeingly at Shell. The white shirt and soft leather charro jacket were darkly stained with blood. The resemblance to the young woman was unmistakable. They must have been twins.

Shell took the rifle from the stiffening hands. He walked back to the water tanks. Her eyes held his from across the tanks. He shook his head. She turned away and covered her face with her hands. Sobs racked her body.

Dusty drank again. He walked to the nearest horse, a fine, clean-limbed bay. He swung up into the saddle. "I'll get the others," he said. The dark eyes of the *mozo* followed Dusty as he rode down the slope.

Shell drank again. "We got into a water scrape," he said. "Horse broke a leg. We were on our way here when we heard the firing. My name is Shell."

She nodded. "We were on our way back to Hermosillo from the ranch of my uncle Teodoro who died last month. We had a strong party with us, but they became frightened when we heard that the Yaquis had arisen between the ranch and river. They split away from us during the night and rode further south. Rodrigo insisted that we come here to Tinajas Altas. Thanks to God we reached the water first. But Rodrigo is dead. It is a terrible price we paid."

Shell sipped a little more water. It seemed to revive him. He glanced at the animals. "What will you do now?" he asked.

She took her full lower lip between perfect white teeth. "I do not know," she said. She glanced at him. "Perhaps you will ride with us toward Hermosillo?"

"Hardly," said Shell.

Hoofs clattered on the slope below the water tanks. Dusty appeared, urging the bay up the slope. There was a grin on his scarred face. "By God!" he said. "What a horse!"

"It was Rodrigo's," said Rafaela.

The woman watched curiously as Shell helped Frank Harley down from the saddle. The worried look fled from her face as she saw Padre Eusebio. She ran to him.

The padre took her in his arms and comforted her. "It is the will of God, my child," he said soothingly.

Afterward, when the simple meal, furnished by the supplies of the Padillas, had been finished, they sat about the bed of coals in the gathering darkness. Father Eusebio spoke quietly and reassuringly to Rafaela. "You cannot ride toward Hermosillo with just a *mozo,* my child. It is said that the Yaquis are raiding between here and Hermosillo. This was just a small party of them. There may be many more of them west of here."

"With Kayitah and his Chiricahuas coming down from the north," said Shell.

Dusty had spoken very little. It was plain that he didn't want to burden his little party with a woman, but, on the other hand, his eyes would wander again and again to the body of Rafaela Padilla. He rarely looked at her lovely face. Always the body. To Dusty, one woman was like another. When he had his fill of one he would walk away from her and close her from his mind.

"I can pay you well to escort us to Soyopa, at least," she said.

Dusty's eyes flicked up at the mention of pay.

Rafaela flushed. "I have a little silver with me," she said.

"Where's the rest of it?" said Dusty.

"In Hermosillo," she said.

"We ain't goin' there," he said.

It was very quiet except for the moaning of the wind down the canyon. One of the horses blew.

Shell picked up a stone and tossed it from one hand to the other. He looked at the horses and at the filled *aparejos* lying near the sturdy mule. There was enough food in those packs to supply Shell, Dusty, Frank, and the padre for at least a week, on short rations. They needed that extra horse as well. Still, from what the padre had told him privately, it would take them only a few days to escort the woman and the *mozo* to the Rio Yaqui in the hope that she might be able to work her way safely back to Hermosillo.

"There will be soldiers at Soyopa," she said.

Dusty nicked his eyes at Shell. That was all *they* needed. Soldiers! Soldiers of the Republic of Mexico.

"No go," said Shell. He tossed the stone back and forth.

She bit her lip and looked uncertainly at the two tall Americans and then at the dust brown padre. Eusebio shrugged expressively. "There is our own safety to consider, my child," he said. "Who knows how many Yaquis are between us and Soyopa, or that there *are* soldiers there? We have no supplies and you have more than enough. Come, Rafaela Padilla! Ride south with us. I know this country as far south as Mesa del Campanero to which we are riding. There will be soldiers there, or at least one can stay there in safety until such time as it is safe to travel again."

There was no further argument from the young woman. She nodded. There was no expression on Victor's wooden-looking face.

Shell stood up, tossing the stone into the nearest tank. "We'll move as quickly as we can," he said.

"Tonight?" asked Rafaela in astonishment.

Shell looked at her. "We've wiped out about a dozen of them," he said. "They won't forget that. Ever! We have water and food, and the horses are in fair shape. We'll ride and walk this night."

"My brother," she said.

The padre looked at Shell. "There is time enough for that at least," he said.

"No!" snapped Dusty.

The padre looked steadily at him. "We do not leave," he said quietly, "until that boy is buried."

Dusty opened, then closed his mouth as he saw the look on Shell's face. "I'll saddle the horses. Come on, you!" he said to the *mozo*.

It was fully dark when they covered the slim body of

Rodrigo Padilla with earth, then piled rocks atop the grave. Father Eusebio spoke over the grave. Rafaela, between sobs, placed a gaily striated stone atop the lonely grave. She did not look back as Shell took her arm and guided her to her horse.

They rode down the slope past the scattered bodies of the Yaqui dead. In the coolness of the night the dead spoke restlessly as the expanded gases in their swollen bodies sought to escape, filling the clear night air with a foul and lingering stench. The zopilotes would take care of them in the morning. By dusk of the next day the picked yellowish skeletons would have begun to dry and bleach. In a few days the stench would have vanished as well, and Tinajas Altas would be the same as it had been for hundreds of years—with one exception. In the years to come it would be known as Tinajas de la Muerte—the Tanks of Death.

CHAPTER ELEVEN

The mesa was high, with riven sides, thickly covered with brush and scrub trees, but the backdrop of the towering mountains made it seem small in comparison. The approach to Mesa del Campanero was tortuous, crossing steep-sided arroyos and dropping down into shallow, rough-floored valleys. Smoke rose leisurely from the western end of the mesa which overlooked sloping country that carried down to a line of broken hills, and thence, by a week's travel on rough trails, to the Gulf of California.

The sky was bright and cottony puffs of clouds drifted lazily toward the unseen Gulf. The air was clear, with a sharper feeling to it, and the hellish heat of the lower land had become dissipated except during midday and in the middle of the long, sunny afternoons. The wind brought the pungent odor of the warm brush and trees with it.

Shell squatted on his heels looking up at the mesa. Dusty lay in the shade, his hat tilted down over his eyes and nose. Frank Harley sat with his back against a rock, hands lying in his lap, his sightless eyes looking to the south.

Somewhere between the mesa and the place where the trio of Americans were resting were Rafaela, Victor, and Padre Eusebio. The great mesa was Mesa del Campanero. The smoke might be rising from Colonel De Tassigny's *colonia*. There might be soldiers there. They would not bother Rafaela and Victor, and of course the padre could go anywhere he liked. He had guided them well in the past week, and when he had been in doubt it had been Victor who had gone ahead on foot to scout the lay of the land. The *mozo* was a Tarahumare, Rafaela had told Shell. An outcast from his tribe for some crime he had committed years ago. He had been found by Rafaela's father, close to death in the mountains, and Señor Padilla had taken him to his home in the vicinity of Hermosillo. The *mozo* had served him tirelessly until Señor Padilla's death and then had transferred his loyalty and his services to Rodrigo and Rafaela. He never rode, preferring to trot along at a tireless gait. His people lived in the great canyons to the east, in Las Gran Barrancas de las Tarahumaras. Twenty in number, at least, of formidable gorges, covering an estimated area of ten thousand square miles. These people spoke no Spanish and lived in stone-age style in their almost inaccessible country. The Tarahumares were great runners. Rafaela had told Shell that a pair of them would spend two or three days running down a deer until it fell from exhaustion.

Shell rolled a cigarette. There was something else that was noteworthy about Victor. He was never very far from Rafaela, and he did not seem to fear the two bearded Americanos, particularly the blue-eyed one who always covertly watched Victor's mistress. Shell knew well enough that if Dusty made a pass at Rafaela either Dusty would die himself at the hands of Victor or Dusty would have to kill Victor. It was as simple as that.

It was late afternoon when Rafaela returned, with Victor running tirelessly ahead of her. She slid from her saddle and took off her sombrero. "Padre Eusebio stayed there," she said. "Colonel De Tassigny told me to tell you that you must come up the side trail of the mesa and remain at the top of the trail until he comes. There are soldiers near the *colonia*, camped at the springs. Their officer, Capitan Hernán Galeras, has warned the colonel not to give aid or shelter to men such as you."

"He knows of us then?" said Shell.

"Not by name," she said. She glanced at Dusty. "He described both of you rather well to the colonel. He does not know that the colonel was once your commanding officer."

Dusty sat up. "All we want is supplies and fresh horses," he said. "He owes us that at least."

Shell looked up at the mesa. The riven sides were deepening in shadow. He didn't like the idea of going up there. If Captain Galeras had scouts out, as he should have, the presence of American strangers would have been noted.

Shell fashioned a cigarette and lighted it. He looked at the young woman over the flare of the match. "You did not have to return," he said. "Why did you?"

She shrugged. "I owed that much to you."

"You will leave for Hermosillo from the Mesa del Campanero?"

She hesitated. "The trails are not safe as yet," she said.

"Yuh can stay with the colonel," said Dusty. He looked slantways at her with his cold blue eyes.

Rafaela slapped the side of her charro trousers with her quirt. She studied Shell for a moment and then turned on a heel. She walked to Frank Harley. "Do you feel well enough for the climb up the mesa, Senor Harley?" she asked.

He looked up at her and smiled. "Yes," he said. "We can't go on without food and fresh horses."

"Must you go on?" she asked.

He nodded.

"It is a terrible country," she said. "Broken by great gorges and towering mountains. It is said that even the birds require a map and compass to pass over it."

"I know," he said. "I have been there."

She sat down beside him. "To La Barranca Escondida?"

Dusty and Shell turned slowly to look at her. None of them, including Frank, had once mentioned their goal to Rafaela. As far as she knew, they were heading for the *colonia* at Mesa del Campanero.

Rafaela looked calmly up at them. "The padre told me," she said simply.

"How did he know?" said Dusty.

Shell waved a hand. "Frank talked in his sleep one night while the padre was on guard. We can't hide it, Dusty. These people can easily guess why we are here."

"There is such a place," said Rafaela. "The stories of La Barranca Escondida and of El Naranjal are true. When I was a child my grandfather told me of them."

Frank Harley sat up straight. He reached out a gaunt hand and held her shoulder. "Go on," he said quietly.

"My grandfather was a man such as you men," she said. "Always he was in the mountains and the barrancas, looking for lost silver or gold mines. Much of his life was spent in treasure hunting. He had many maps and charts. He would listen eagerly to every tale that was told of Tayopa, of El Naranjal, of Scalp Hunter's Ledge, and of the Treasure of Moctezuma. But somehow, he always returned to his search for La Barranca Escondida and El Naranjal.

"Some years before I was born he was trapped by Yaquis in the mountains near a broken hill, not too far from Nayarit. His companions and servants were all killed, but he managed to escape. For two full days he hid from them, and on the third day he was forced south, into unknown country. He fled through waterless, tangled *chaparral*. When night came he was nearly dead of thirst and exhaustion. He slept that night on the brink of a barranca. It was so deep he could not hear dropped stones strike the bottom and he was afraid to move in the dark.

"In the morning he awoke to a deathly silence. There was no sign of life. No, not one! Not a bird, or a rabbit, or anything alive. He lay there until the rising sun warmed his body. The wind rose a little with the coming of the sun, and then he distinctly heard the faint, ever so faint, sound of a bell." Her voice died away as she saw the look on Frank Harley's face.

"Go on! Go on!" said Dusty hoarsely.

"He crawled to the very lip of the barranca and looked down," she continued. "He could see straight down for thousands of feet. The sun was already shining on the western wall of the great gorge. It sparkled on water. A running stream that passed through dark groves of trees. The floor of that great canyon was more than a mile across. As far as he could see, the walls of the huge canyon were sheer. He watched those dark trees as the sun crept to them and he saw what he swore—until the very day he died—were oranges, hanging thickly from those dark-foliaged trees."

Shell whistled softly. Frank gestured impatiently at him.

"Far back in the groves," said Rafaela in a low voice, "he saw patches of white and he was sure there were many buildings there. Something arose above the trees. It looked like a tower of some kind. Perhaps a bell tower. He never was sure about that. He sat there for hours looking down at the unattainable, for he knew he could never get to the bottom of the gorge, at least not in his condition. At noon he heard the bell again, or he *thought* he heard it. He could not remain there any longer. He walked to the west and late that night he found water. A week later he stumbled out onto the road that leads to Los Mochis. It was a month before he had the strength to travel. He was in delirium for days."

Dusty spat. "He *thought* he saw it."

She shrugged. "Perhaps," she said. She looked up at Shell. "He was a man of honor. A simple man. Many people doubted his story, but I never did. I never knew him to lie."

Frank Harley nodded. "It jibes," he said excitedly. "It jibes! You spoke of the broken hill not far from Nayarit. Do you remember if he had a name for it?"

She bit her lip for a moment and narrowed her eyes. "It had an odd name," she said thoughtfully.

"Go on!" snapped Dusty.

Shell hurled the cigarette from his lips and looked at her.

"Cerro de...." She shook her head.

"Rafaela!" said Shell.

She looked up at him, her lovely face taut with tension. "Cerro de...."

Frank Harley wet his cracked lips. "Cerro de Huesos, Rafaela?" he suggested softly.

She smiled. "Yes! Yes! That is it! The Hill of Bones!"

"Jesus God!" said Dusty. "He was right there! It was right in his dirty greaser hands and *he walked away from it!*"

Rafaela flushed at Dusty's description of her beloved grandfather. "There was nothing he could have done," she said. "There was no water. The Yaquis were hard on his trail. He had no food and no way to go except to walk toward the setting sun. If he had stayed there he would have died, one way or another. You dishonor the dead, *hombre!*"

Dusty grinned. "Take it easy," he said.

"For many years he tried to find that barranca again," she said, "but he never did. Time and time again he would journey for days to Nayarit and thence to the Hill of Bones. There were times when he thought he heard that mysterious bell, but he was never sure about that. He died without ever finding any treasure."

"Poor old bastard," said Dusty.

"No!" she said. "He was happy! It was the dream that made him happy. He always knew in his heart that someday he would find El Naranjal again."

"But he never did," said Dusty.

She stood up. "Perhaps it was best that way," she said. She walked to her horse and mounted it, touching it with her quirt, to ride back toward the mesa. Victor trotted ahead of her into the gathering darkness.

Shell gave Frank a foot up into the saddle. "What do you think, Frank?" he said.

The blind man looked to the south. "She knows a great deal more than she lets on, Shell," he said.

The two tall Americans looked at each other. The same thought had struck both of them.

"She might know more than I do," said Frank. "I have never met anyone who has seen El Naranjal or who has known anyone else who has seen it."

"Maybe she is lying?" said Dusty.

Shell shook his head. "No," he said.

The other two knew he was right. Rafaela might have the key to La Barranca Escondida and El Naranjal locked in her lovely head.

"Supposin' she decides to stay here at Mesa del Campanero?" said Dusty. He swung up into his saddle and looked down at Shell. "Supposin' she decides to return to Hermosillo?"

"She won't," said Frank Harley.

They looked back at him. "Why?" said Shell.

The blind man leaned forward in his saddle. "I think she is falling in love with you, Shell," he said. "So long as she feels that way, she'll go with us. It's up to you, Shell."

Dusty's cold eyes studied Shell. A tinge of jealousy swept through him. *He* wanted to sleep with her. On the other hand, she was just a woman. With all that silver he could have one like her each night in the week and perhaps matinees besides.

"What about it, Shell?" said Frank.

Shell mounted. He touched his horse with his spurs. "It's damned dirty," he said. He rode down the trail.

"Well?" said Dusty to Frank.

The blind man nodded. "He'll do it," he said. He touched the mule with his heels and rode forward. "God help her," he added softly.

CHAPTER TWELVE

The wind moaned softly over the top of the great mesa, swaying the brush and the scrub trees. On the wide slopes to the west there was a cluster of faint yellow light where the adobes and jacales of the *colonia* were situated. The faint odor of wood-smoke drifted across the top of the mesa.

Shell Burnett sat on a flat rock, looking down at the warm and friendly lights of the *colonia*. There would be men down there he had known. Men who had fought with him at Wilson's Creek, Pea Ridge, Corinth, and throughout the Vicksburg Campaign as well as the Red River Campaign. The South Kansas-Texas Mounted Rifles had virtually ceased to exist as a unit after the Vicksburg Campaign, but there had been plenty of fighting left for the remnants. There would be men down there who had fought beside Shell and Dusty throughout the war and who later had fought against them on the side of the forces of the Republic of Mexico.

Hoofs clattered on rock. Dusty was on his feet in an instant, Spencer cocked and ready. Shell stepped behind a tree and picked up his Spencer.

"Señor Shell?" came the hesitant voice of Padre Eusebio.

"Here, padre," said Shell.

"It is the colonel," said the Mexican.

A horseman appeared behind the mounted figure of the padre. "Burnett?" he said eagerly. "Is it really you?"

Shell smiled. "Yes, sir! It's good to hear your voice, Colonel De Tassigny."

The tall officer slid from his saddle. "We meet in a strange place, lieutenant. Dustin is with you, is he not?"

"Here, sir," said Dusty. He had always had a respect for De Tassigny, not so much for his gentlemanly manner and his background, but for his ability as a first-class fighting man.

De Tassigny strode to meet them. In the faint light Shell could see the narrow face, trimmed with a small, neat beard and the sweeping mustachios the officer affected. The colonel still wore his Confederate gray coat, the brass buttons showing clearly through the dimness. He thrust out his right hand and gripped Shell's hand hard. "By God," he said, "this is wonderful! I heard you both were executed at Queretaro."

Dusty laughed. "We moved a little too fast for you Republicans, sir."

The colonel smiled. "Maybe we didn't try very hard to catch you Royalists, Dustin."

Shell looked down the dark slope of the mesa side to the site of the *colonia* village. "How does it go, sir?" he asked.

De Tassigny felt inside his coat and took out a cigar case. He handed it to Shell. Shell helped himself and Dusty also selected a cigar. They lighted up along with the colonel. Padre Eusebio had vanished up the slope to where Frank Harley sat in the darkness with Rafaela and Victor.

De Tassigny sat down and puffed his cigar into life. His brown eyes looked across the flare of the cigar tip at Shell. "Not too well," he admitted. "Times are hard. Many of the Mexicans do not accept us. We have four times as many men as women. It is a hard country for men, let alone women. The country is alive with animal and human predators. Banditry is rife. The soldiers who have been sent to protect us and the other villagers are little more than bandits themselves, for they haven't been paid and have to live off the country. Only our unity and our skill with arms, coupled with the appreciation of Benito Juarez for what we did in his cause, have thus far saved us from greater trouble than we have already had."

"Do you plan to stay?" said Shell.

The colonel shrugged. "We plan to give it a fair trial," he said. "If it doesn't work out we'll have to leave."

"For where?" said Dusty.

"The United States," said the colonel.

Dusty spat. "To take the oath?"

The officer nodded. He puffed at his cigar. "It is a great country, Dustin. We fought for our cause and we lost. It might have been better that way. The Lord works in mysterious ways," he said quietly.

"I never thought I would hear you talk like that," said Dusty coldly.

The officer looked at him. "You are a single man, Dustin. An adventurer. A mercenary, if you'll pardon the expression, sir. Many of us have wives and children here at the *colonia*. In the short time we have been here our children have begun to speak Spanish more frequently than English. Some of my men have married Mexican women. In time we will cease to exist as a unit and will be absorbed into their culture, sir. In two generations nothing will exist of our *colonia* except for the Anglo-Saxon names and the light-colored eyes."

"That's better than crawling back to the United States to take the oath," said Dusty.

De Tassigny inspected the end of his cigar. "Is it?" he said thoughtfully. "I wonder."

Shell could see the colonel's point. The planting of the *colonia* had been idealistic; the results were factual. De Tassigny had likely predicted the future with accuracy.

The officer looked at Shell. "I can't give you shelter," he said. "The soldiers are always hanging around the *colonia*. You'd be seen and likely identified. You must return to the States, Burnett."

Shell shook his head. "Even if we wanted to," he said, "it is impossible. The Apaches and Yaquis are behind us, and following us, sir."

De Tassigny looked quickly at him. "Did you have anything to do with the death of Anselmo Chacon and his Indian wife?"

There was no answer from Shell. He had never found it easy to lie to his commanding officer.

"A runner came in a day ago to tell us of a fight at Tinajas Altas. Many Yaquis were slain. It is said the Yaquis have joined forces with the band of Kayitah the Chiricahua, to hunt down the slayers of Anselmo Chacon and his wife, as well as those men who killed the Yaquis at Tinajas Altas. By God! I would not want to be in the boots of those men!"

"Chacon tried to kill me," said Dusty.

"The Yaquis were in between us and the waterhole," said Shell. "It was them or us, colonel."

De Tassigny took the cigar from his mouth. "For the love of God!" he said. He looked quickly at them. "You must not stay here then."

"We need supplies and fresh horses," said Dusty.

The colonel stood up. "Agreed! As much as I want you to stay with me and work at the *colonia*, I can't risk the lives of my people by doing so. Do you understand?"

"Yes, sir," said Shell.

The colonel nodded. "Send the padre and the *mozo* down to the *colonia* for horses and supplies. They can bring the woman with them. I will let her stay with us until such time as she can be helped to Hermosillo."

"No," said the soft voice behind them.

They turned to see Rafaela Padilla. "But you cannot go with these hunted men, young lady," said the colonel.

"I am being hunted as much as they are," she said.

"The Yaquis know both myself and my *mozo*. They will track us down. If they find us in your *colonia*, Colonel De Tassigny, there will be no safety for anyone. The soldiers will run away as they usually do."

The officer wiped the sweat from his forehead. "As you will," he said. He gripped Shell's hand and then that of Dusty. "Go with God," he said in Spanish. He swung up into his saddle. "I had hoped you could stay," he said. He shook his head and touched his horse with his spurs, riding down the dark slope toward the distant lights of the *colonia*.

Dusty spat. "Take the oath? He makes me sick."

Shell leaned back against the tree and relighted his cigar. There was nothing to say. He knew, or at least felt, the way De Tassigny must feel. The colonel and his people were Americans, and in time, perhaps in one generation, they would no longer be Americans, and their only impress on this wild and lonely country would be what the colonel had said. Light-colored eyes and Anglo-Saxon names.

"There was nothing else he could do for us," said Rafaela. "Thank God he can give us fresh mounts and food."

In the long dark hours of the night, past midnight and on toward the dawn, the padre and the *mozo* went down to the *colonia* with the worn-out horses and mule. They brought back fresh mounts and a pair of burros laden with supplies. In the few hours until dawn they crossed the great Mesa of the Bellmaker to the southern side, and as they reached the dim trail that led deep down into a wide barranca, the false dawn began to tinge the eastern sky.

Shell looked at Padre Eusebio. "Is it good-bye here, padre?" he asked.

The padre shook his head. "There is no need for me at the *colonia*, and the soldiers are all godless men. There is no reason for me to stay here and I cannot go back the way I came. May I ride with you?"

Dusty tilted his head to one side and eyed the padre and Shell. There was a thoughtful look on his scarred face.

"Let him come along," said Frank Harley. "We will have need of someone who can perhaps communicate with God before we are through with this mission."

Shell looked at Rafaela. She nodded.

Dusty shrugged. He swung down from his mount. "Who knows this trail?" he said.

"I do," said the padre.

There was no argument from Dusty. Padre Eusebio slid agilely from his horse, gripped the reins, and led the animal down into the dimness below.

CHAPTER THIRTEEN

The bottom of the barranca was still in darkness although the sky was faintly gray from the coming dawn. A cold wind swept up the barranca scattering dried leaves and whirling dust before it. Padre Eusebio led the way to the south, following a trail that was hardly visible, but there seemed to be a confidence in the Franciscan.

Shell rode behind the padre while behind Shell was Frank Harley. Dusty was close behind Frank, and Rafaela rode a little way back from Dusty. Victor brought up the rear, leading the supply-laden burros.

The padre looked back at Shell. "We can make good time this day," he said. "The trail will be good and the horses are fresh."

His sentence was punctuated by a loud voice. "*Halte!* In the name of the Republic of Mexico! *Halte!*"

"Go on!" yelled Shell at Padre Eusebio.

The padre crouched like a monkey on the back of the horse and lashed it with his quirt. The horse buck-jumped down the trail hurling a big-hatted man aside into the brush.

"*Halte!* Halt or we shoot!" cried the voice from the darkness.

Shell spurred his horse, crouching low in the saddle. A man jumped back out of his way, raised a rifle, and fired. The slug plucked at the slack in Shell's jacket. He looked back, dragging at the reins of Frank's horse. "Lay low, Frank!" he yelled. The blind man dropped to the horse's neck and gripped his arms about it.

Dusty fired once from the saddle and then broke through the brush, crashing along the dry stream bed. The echo of the shot was followed by other shots. Orange-red flashes sparkled through the darkness, and the acrid smell of powder-smoke swirled along the barranca, borne by the freshening wind.

Shell tore into a clump of willows, digging in his spurs. The claybank took the slope in mighty surging jumps. Shell hoped to God that Frank could hold on. He looked back as the claybank cleared the rise. Gunfire rattled through the dimness. There was no sign of Dusty, Rafaela, or the *mozo* Victor. Shell galloped through the dimness, following the faintly defined trail. Somewhere ahead of him was Padre Eusebio. For a padre, the Franciscan could ride like a Comanche when he had to.

The sky was fully alight when Shell drew in the lathered claybank. "Are you all right, Frank?" he said.

The blind man raised his white face. "Yes," he said faintly. "Who were they?"

"Soldiers," said Padre Eusebio from the brush. He led out his horse. "I saw them plainly. Their leader was Capitan Galeras. It was he who ordered us to halt. I recognized his voice."

Hoofs clattered in the thicket. Shell raised his Spencer. He saw the faded and dusty hat of his *compañero*. Dusty rode out onto the trail. His scarred face was scratched and bloody. He wiped the blood from his face. "Gawddamn them greasers!" he said. "They got the supplies!"

"What about Rafaela and Victor?" asked the padre.

Dusty spat. "What about 'em?" he said. "Good riddance! It's them supplies I'm concerned about."

It was very quiet now in the barranca except for the sighing of the wind. Something Colonel De Tassigny had said came swiftly back to Shell. "Banditry is rife. The soldiers who have been sent to protect us and the other villagers are little more than bandits themselves, for they haven't been paid and have to live off the country."

Father Eusebio wiped the cold sweat from his face. "There were not too many of them," he said. "Perhaps a dozen. It was hard to tell in that light."

Shell looked down at him. "What are you hinting at, padre?"

The padre shrugged. "We need those supplies. Those soldiers are little better than the Yaquis or Apaches. Galeras himself has a foul reputation with drink and with women."

"There were at least a dozen bottles of brandy in the supplies," said Frank Harley.

There was nothing more to be said. Shell had a vivid picture of Rafaela Padilla as he had first seen her. The great eyes, the full red lips, and even white teeth, the firm breasts pushing out against the thin material of her shirt, the rounded fullness of her hips beneath the taut charro trousers. A dozen bottles of potent Bacanora and a captive woman in that lonely country. Who would ask questions? What was it Padre Eusebio had said? "Galeras himself has a foul reputation with drink and with women."

"No use sweatin' it out," said Dusty. "We'd best make tracks while we can."

There was no answer from any of the others.

Dusty dismounted and tightened his girth. "Sun'll be up soon enough," he said over his shoulder.

Shell shoved back his hat. "Give them a couple of hours with those brandy bottles," he said, "and a drummer boy could take them."

Dusty straightened up slowly. "What the hell yuh mean?" he said.

"We need those supplies ourselves," said Shell.

The icy blue eyes studied Shell, as though to penetrate into his mind for the *real* reason Shell was willing to
go back.

"Shell is right," said the padre.

"Nobody asked you, Eusebio!" snapped Dusty.

"There are no inhabited *placitas* south of here," said
Frank. "No place to get more supplies, and we can't go
back to the Mesa of the Bellmaker. Not now. They know
about us."

Dusty leaned against his horse and rolled a cigarette.
"All right," he said, "I'll go. But for the supplies! Not for
that woman and that gawddamned *mozol.*"

"They likely won't go back to the springs," said Shell.
"Galeras isn't fool enough to do that as yet. Likely he'll
find a place to camp out for a few days, giving the impression he was doing his duty in hunting us down. When the
brandy is gone, he'll go back."

"What about the woman?" said Frank.

Padre Eusebio crossed himself. "She could talk if they
took her back," he said. His meaning was plain enough.

The light grew brighter as they talked. Shell knew it
would be up to him and Dusty to go back. Father
Eusebio was not a fighting man, and of course Frank
Harley was of no value because of his blindness. There
was no sound from the direction of the ambush. They
might be at the bottles and at the woman already.
Somehow the supplies seemed of no importance to Shell,
but the thought of that lithe, full-breasted body being
torn at by greasy, dirty hands made him sick within his
soul.

"We can't go on without those supplies," said Dusty.
He wiped the blood from his face with the back of a
hand. "If we can save the woman *after* we get the supplies,
it's all right with me." Maybe Dusty was also thinking of
that lovely body, but not in the same sense as Shell
thought.

Father Eusebio looked up at Shell. "Twenty miles south of here," he said, "there are springs. One follows the barranca to them. The way is not hard. I will take Señor Harley with me in a roundabout way and wait for you near those springs."

Shell nodded. He was tired. They had had no sleep during the night and little enough in the preceding nights. The thought of going back to tackle at least a dozen Mexican soldiers was pure hell in his mind, but it had to be done. Didn't anything come easy in this damned world?

Dusty swung up into his saddle. "Come on," he said. "No use wasting time."

They rode down the wooded slope and when they neared the dry stream bed Dusty scouted ahead. He came back through the shadows. "Nothing," he said. "Empty brass hulls and foot and hoof marks. Tracks heading *up,* instead of *down* the canyon."

They both knew what that meant. Galeras wasn't returning to the springs at the base of Mesa del Campanero. Not with two burro-loads of supplies and brandy, and with a lush-bodied woman to occupy his time when he should have been chasing Shell and Dusty.

It was almost noon before they caught up with Galeras' party of big-hatted, somewhat undersized *solda-dos.* Some of them rode horses and others rode mules. In the middle of the party were Rafaela Padilla and the *mozo* Victor. Victor had his wrists lashed with the cords crossing his deep chest. A stick had been thrust through the crooks of his elbows and against his back. A noosed lariat was about his corded neck and he was half dragged, half pulled behind the horse of one of the soldiers. The dust veiled the party as it rode slowly up the canyon.

Dusty wiped the sweat from his face and looked at Shell. "Well, they ain't touched the supplies, *or* the woman, from the looks of things."

Shell rested his chin on his crossed forearms and

looked down the steep slope at the soldiers. "They're riding to water," he said. "Likely to the same springs the padre told us about. All set for a real fiesta. Wine, women and song."

"On *our* damned supplies," said Dusty bitterly.

Shell looked up the canyon. "We can't pass them," he said. He looked up at the canyon rim. "If we got up there, we could cut across the higher land and maybe get ahead of them."

"Maybe," said Dusty. He rolled a cigarette. "We might get lost too, *compañero*."

"We'll have to take a chance on that. You game?"

Dusty nodded. "Keno," he said as he lighted up.

They led the horses up the crumbling side of the canyon. The soldiers and their captives were almost out of sight by the time Dusty and Shell reached the top of the canyon wall and stopped for a blow. The dust trailed up from the canyon and was dissipated by the dry wind. The mesa top on which they stood was badly broken up, stippled with dry brush and scrub trees. There didn't seem to be any sign of habitation up there, or water either.

Shell led the way. The barranca curved far to their left and then curved back to the south. Shell reasoned that by cutting across the curve, like following the string of a bow, instead of the curved bow itself, they might come out ahead of the soldiers and get to the springs first.

"I hope to God the padre has enough sense to camp away from the springs," said Dusty.

"He will," said Shell. "He's a damned capable man, for a padre."

"Yeh," said Dusty. He fashioned another cigarette. "Almost too damned capable in things a padre shouldn't ought to know."

Shell shrugged. "They are trained to live in this country," he said. "They could hardly survive otherwise. Some of the old padres founded the main trails running through this country and up into the States. They had to be capable beyond most men to do that."

"Jesus," said Dusty dryly. "We're off on the history again."

Shell clammed up. He should have known better. Just keep the subject on horses, weapons, gambling, booze, and women, and Dusty was a good conversationalist—but digress in the least, and Dusty was completely lost

Shell led the way, orienting himself by landmarks. He checked his battered brass compass again and again. If they missed the canyon, and the springs, it wouldn't make much difference about the supplies *or* the woman.

The sun lanced down upon the mesa top and reflected from the mounds of naked black rock, setting up a shimmering heat haze that bored into the eyes as though trying to reach the brain and destroy the reason within. They ran out of water by the middle of the afternoon. By early dusk they were completely lost.

Dusty looked at Shell with red-rimmed eyes. His tongue explored his cracked lips. "To hell with the supplies," he said. "What about water?"

Shell shoved back his hat and wiped the sweat from his forehead. He looked toward what he thought was the dim line of the barranca far ahead of them. It would be dark soon enough, and if they kept on through the darkness there would be no telling where they would end up. It would be easy enough to keep on until one found the barranca by simply stepping off into it. The bottom would be a long way down.

"Well?" said Dusty.

He was depending on Shell as he always did in such situations—the situations that required reasoning powers.

Shell checked the compass.

"What the hell good is that thing?" demanded Dusty.

Shell checked the landmarks. Far to the south was an irregular line of mountains, like a saw set edge-up. A peak stood out. A peak shaped like a thick-bladed knife. He had been using that as a landmark for hours.

Dusty leaned against his horse and shaped a cigarette. He lighted it and flipped away the match. "Christ," he said in sheer disgust.

"You said you were game," said Shell. "You losing your guts now that the going is getting tough, *hombre?*"

Their eyes locked. The tiny seed of hate that had sprouted in the past weeks was growing every day.

Shell looked beyond the icy eyes of his companion. He narrowed his eyes. "Look!" he said.

Dusty turned. A faint streamer of smoke arose from a darker area, not more than a thousand yards from where they stood. "Come on," he said.

They led the tired horses toward the smoke. They tethered them to scrub trees not far from the edge of the barranca and walked ahead, trailing their carbines. They went down fifty feet from the edge and worked their way forward, with the smell of smoke and cooking food rising to meet them.

The shadows had already filled the barranca. Firelight leaped and postured on the rough canyon walls. Here the canyon had widened out and branched and at the junction of the branch canyon was a cluster of tumbledown buildings, seemingly long abandoned. Some of the roofs had fallen in. Several of the buildings had collapsed completely. Beyond the buildings the firelight reflected from a shallow pool of water. Horses and a pair of burros were in a makeshift corral. The odor of cooking meat drifted up to the two hungry, thirsty Americans who peered like lobo wolves over the canyon rim.

Some of the soldiers sat about the roaring fire. Now and then one of them would raise a bottle to his lips, then pass it on to the man next to him. Already two of them lay in the shadows, perhaps asleep, but more likely dead drunk. There was no sign of an officer. A squat, broad-shouldered man with sergeant's insignia sat on a rock, his shoulders hunched forward, staring into the fire.

Now and then he would look toward one of the smaller buildings, then back into the fire.

Shell could only locate seven of the soldiers, and two of them seemed helpless. Maybe Galeras had sent some of his men back.

Dusty wet his lips. "We can take 'em," he said.

Shell did not answer. It went against his grain to attack them. Bad enough that they had been hunted by Yankee soldiers for the killings at Ojinago, and by the Apaches and Yaquis for a little more killing. If they killed Mexican soldiers on Mexican soil they would eventually be hunted down. There would be no going back after that.

Dusty was ready for more killing, but, as usual, he was waiting for orders. Trust him to carry them out to the letter if there was killing to be done.

The sergeant looked back at the building. He drank deeply from a bottle he kept between his feet. He did not pass *his* bottle to the others. Their bottle had been emptied. It crashed in the shadows and another bottle was opened.

"Quite a party," said Dusty dryly. "We wait up here long enough and we can walk in and take 'em *without* shooting."

Shell looked back at the horses. There was no way of getting them down into the canyon. "Come on," he said to Dusty.

They stripped off the saddles and took whatever they needed. Shell cut their tethers almost all the way through. In time they would break loose. They'd have to find water on their own.

Shell led the way across the dark mesa top. He dropped his long legs over the brink of the canyon and felt for a hold. He struck a ledge. Slowly he worked his way along the ledge. He stopped and fashioned a sling for his carbine and slung the heavy weapon over his back. Drunken laughter echoed through the canyon. The fire-light flared up and died down sporadically. The smoke drifted along the canyon wall, partially concealing the two men who worked their way down that treacherous, crumbling wall of rock.

Halfway down the wall the fire flared brightly as more wood was thrown on it, and the light leaped up, fully illuminating the two men who clung to the rock face like insect specimens pinned to a board. The Mexicans were tearing into the cooked meat. The sergeant was not eating. He raised his head to drink, and his eyes looked directly at the two Americans just as the fire died down, leaving them in partial shadow. For a moment he stared at the rock wall. He shook his head and took another drink, wiping his mouth on the back of a hand, staring at that darker patch on the shadowed wall. If he saw them, all he had to do was have more wood thrown on the fire, and drunk as his men were, they could hardly miss their living targets.

One of the soldiers handed the sergeant a full plate of food. He looked down at it and picked up a dripping piece of meat in his thick hand. He gnawed at it, the grease dripping down his chin.

Shell moved as quickly as he could. He worked along a ledge, passed behind a rock that tilted outward, seemingly held in place by magnetism, and then he lay bellyflat on a rock shelf not twenty feet above the talus slope at the base of the cliff. Dusty inched up behind him, breathing harshly.

It took half an hour to belly down the ledge. Shell crawled down the talus slope and dropped flat behind a clump of brush. He could smell the water, and his throat seemed to close up.

"Christ," said Dusty hoarsely, "can't we get a drink before we start the evenin's killin'?"

Shell nodded. There seemed to be no one near the water-hole, but the animals might scent them and make a fuss. He wormed his way across the open flat ground, hoping to God the fire would not flare up. He kept his face turned away so that the firelight would not reflect from it, but it likely was so filthy that it couldn't reflect anything.

He crouched behind a pile of rock fifteen feet from the edge of the waterhole. There was no one in sight. He crawled over the rocks and bellied to the edge of the tank, feeling his way with his free hand until it struck the water. He thrust his face into the water and drank a little. He raised his head and looked toward the fire. The sergeant was on his feet, swaying a little, the bottle again at his mouth. He hurled the bottle aside, wiped his mouth, pulled up his slack trousers, and staggered toward the building he had been watching ever since Shell had first seen him.

The soldiers about the fire were laughing as they watched the staggering sergeant. "Watch her, my *sargento!*" one of them yelled. "She is a wildcat!"

Shell quickly skirted the tank and paused next to the canyon wall. Something moved at his feet. He leaped back and full-cocked the Spencer. A man lay at his feet, mumbling in a low voice. Shell stared at him. It was Victor. His contorted face looked at Shell. They had not unbound the *mozo*. Dusty came up behind Shell. "Cut him loose," he said. "We can use him."

Dusty covered Shell while Shell cut loose the *mozo*. The thongs had cut deeply into his flesh. He could not move his arms. He looked at the water, so close at hand. Shell picked up a battered tin cup and filled it for him, holding it to his lips. Victor slobbered at the water and Shell realized with horror that the Tarahumare did not have a tongue.

"Get movin'!" snapped Dusty.

Shell pulled the *mozo* to his feet and handed him the Colt. The *mozo* shook his head. He touched the handle of the heavy bowie knife. Shell sheathed the Colt and handed Victor the bowie. Something crashed at the front of the buildings. A woman screamed like frightened mare. Shell snatched up his Spencer and ran behind the buildings. He rounded the end building. The woman screamed from within it. Shell kicked open the partially closed door and ran in, Spencer at hip level. The sergeant's broad, sweaty back was in front of him. Rafaela stood with her back against the dingy wall, her hands covering her naked breasts. The tattered ruins of her thin shirt hung about her hips. The charro trousers had been ripped down to her shapely knees. Her dark unbound hair fell over her white shoulders. Her eyes were wide with terror, and a trickle of blood wormed down from the corners of her mouth. The sergeant lurched forward, muttering drunkenly. Shell struck once with the metal-shod butt of the Spencer. The sergeant staggered sideways. He stared at Shell, then ran for the door. A dark figure stood there, bowie knife in hand, staring at the Mexican with unblinking eyes. The Mexican screamed once. He drove past the *mozo*. The blade flicked out and blood flowed.

A Spencer cracked once, then again. A man yelled. The Spencer barked again. Shell ran to the door. A Mexican was raising a rifle, aiming it at Dusty. Shell fired from the hip and the Mexican whirled and fell into the fire. Shell looked back. The sergeant was making the biggest and probably the last mistake he would ever make in his suddenly shortened life. *He was trying to outrun a Tarahumare!* Already his life was leaking out as the bowie sliced skillfully at his fat rump or at his churning legs. Blood splattered as he ran as fast as he could. He vanished, screaming, into the velvety darkness, with silent death close behind him, almost like his shadow.

The shooting died away, letting the echoes slam back and forth in the canyon. They too died away. Dusty and Shell faced each other across the fire. The Mexicans had died where they had been drinking. The fire was licking hungrily at the clothing of the Mexican Shell had dropped into it. He gripped him by the ankles and pulled him free. The choking smoke from the burning cloth mingled with the acrid powder-smoke.

There was one final despairing scream like that of a

mortally wounded animal. It echoed down the canyon and died away. In a little while Victor appeared, walking slowly, with the bloody knife in his right hand.

Shell looked at the two Mexicans who had been asleep or dead drunk. They'd never awaken again. Dusty was thorough, if nothing else.

"We get all of them?" said Dusty.

"You ought to know," said Shell.

The woman came to the doorway. She had wrapped herself in a serape. Her eyes were wide in her pale face. Shell walked to her and supported her. "Are you all right?" he said.

She nodded. There was a sickness deep within her. She looked at the bloody dead and then buried her face against Shell's chest with muffled sobbing rising and falling from her.

Dusty walked to the biggest building. He kicked open the door and walked in. A moment passed. "Hey, Shell!" he called out. "Look who's here!"

Shell helped Rafaela to a seat and walked to the building. He entered. A man sat at a rickety table. A candle guttered in the neck of a brandy bottle. His head lay on the table amidst the liquor slops. The candlelight reflected from his tarnished epaulets.

"Capitan Galeras, no doubt," said Dusty with ironic politeness. He raised his Spencer.

Shell knocked the Spencer aside. "You've done enough killing," he said.

Dusty eyed Shell. Slowly he lowered the repeater. "What are yuh goin' to do with him?" he said, jerking his head toward the officer.

Someone called from outside. They walked to the door. Padre Eusebio was leading two horses from up the barranca. Frank Harley swayed in the saddle of one of them. The padre stared at the dead. He crossed himself. "Mother of God," he said in a hoarse voice.

The quietness of the canyon was in direct contrast to the hell that had broken loose twenty minutes earlier.

They had their supplies back and the woman as well. Shell shoved back his hat. There was no place for them to go but ever southward to hunt for La Barranca Escondida. If they found the silver, what could they do with it? They'd be hunted down in time. Shell shook his head. He cursed the day he and Dusty had found Frank Harley at Horno Tanks. It might have been better to let him die.

CHAPTER FOURTEEN

The canyon was filled with a cold searching wind as the sky lightened with the dawn. The fire had died down during the night but now and then a cat's-paw of wind would stir the thick bed of ashes and fan a red eye of life into them. A film of ashes drifted on the waterhole and furred the blankets of the sleeping men.

Shell Burnett came down from his perch above the waterhole where he had stood last guard. He walked to the blanketed forms. "Rise and shine," he said. "Get up! Get up!"

Padre Eusebio was on his feet almost right away. He dressed simply by pulling on his moccasins and dropping the faded cowl of his robe. He quickly rolled his blankets and placed them near his saddle. Dusty thrust out a shaggy head and yawned. "Jee-sus," he said. "Killin' sure takes the starch out of a man." He grinned as the padre hurriedly crossed himself.

Frank Harley got up quietly. He shivered in the cold wind. "It will be cold up in those mountains," he said. "The fall will soon be here."

Victor appeared from where he had slept alone, near the door of the shack where his mistress had slept, and close to the barred door of the building that held Capitan Galeras prisoner. Actually, he was more a prisoner of the brandy than of the men who had wiped out his little command.

Padre Eusebio busied himself about the fire, preparing breakfast. The smoke from the revived fire drifted down the canyon and wreathed itself over the piled Mexican dead who had been dragged by the horses away from the waterhole. Shell looked thoughtfully at the tumbled, dirty corpses. Once the rest of the Mexican soldiers saw those bodies, there would be no rest for the ill-assorted little band of treasure seekers.

Rafaela appeared in her doorway. Somehow, she had contrived to patch up some of her clothing. Shell had given her one of his shirts, and she had managed to drape it fetchingly about herself. She had tied the serape about her slim waist to cover the ruins of the upper part of her charro trousers. Dusty looked up from his first cup of coffee and studied her as she spoke to Victor. He wet his lips, saw Shell looking at him, then slowly looked away. Shell himself remembered all too vividly how she had looked the night before, with her full breasts hardly covered by her slim hands, her lovely thighs and the cleft between them. He drove the thought from his mind.

They ate silently. It wasn't quite a festive mood, not with those blue-faced dead not fifty yards away. When they were done, Father Eusebio and Dusty gathered up the gear, saddled the horses, and filled the many canteens they had inherited. There were horses to spare now.

"What about Galeras?" said Dusty at last, jerking his head toward Galeras' prison.

"No more killing," said Frank Harley quietly.

"He is one of God's children," said Padre Eusebio.

Shell looked at Rafaela. She shook her head. "You cannot do it," she said quickly.

Dusty laughed. "All of a sudden we got mercy," he jeered. "What difference does it make?" He looked at Shell. "Yuh gettin' soft, *compañero?*"

Shell walked to the building and pulled away the bars. He placed his hand on the butt of his Colt and opened the door. Galeras sat at the table with his head supported in his hands. His body was shaking.

"Capitan Galeras?" said Shell.

The head slowly raised. "For the love of God," said the Mexican, "give me a drink, *amigo!*"

Shell rubbed his shaggy beard. "Victor!" he said. "Get a bottle."

The *mozo* brought a half-full bottle of the Bacanora. Shell placed it on the table in front of the officer. He gripped it as though it was liquid gold and took a deep draught. He wiped his mouth and took another drink. His body shook spasmodically and for a moment Shell thought he'd spew the whole mess out over the filthy table, but Hernán Galeras was a first-class drinker. He knew his ability, if not his limitations.

Shell studied the flushed face of the officer. Galeras was handsome enough, in a rather evil-looking way. His rather narrow face did not detract from the handsomeness of it. Despite his heavy drinking there were not too many traces of the vice apparent in his features.

Galeras looked up at Shell. "You're one of the Americans, eh? I saw you in the barranca when we tried to halt you."

Shell nodded.

Galeras felt in his coat and came out with a tobacco pouch. He shakily began to fashion a cigarette. "You have captured my men, eh?"

Shell did not answer. He watched Galeras light the cigarette and draw the smoke deep into his lungs. Galeras looked at Shell. "You did not answer," he said.

Shell leaned against the side of the doorway. "You let them get out of control, *capitán,*" he said. "If we had not arrived the woman might have been dead from a mass raping."

"I know nothing of that."

"That's no excuse," said Shell. "As an officer of the

Army of the Republic of Mexico it was your duty to control your men."

"I . . ." said the Mexican. He gestured at the bottle and shrugged.

"You got stinking drunk," said Shell.

Galeras shrugged again. He looked up at Shell. "What is to become of me?" He looked down at Shell's holstered revolver.

Spurs chimed softly behind Shell. "We're all set to go," said Dusty. "What about them bodies?"

Galeras paled. He drank deeply again.

"Help yourself," said Dusty dryly.

The Mexican looked up at those two lean, sunbrowned faces, and at the cold Yanqui eyes, and he knew well enough what was going to happen to him. "You ride to the south?" he said.

"We do," said Shell.

Galeras wiped his mouth and puffed thoughtfully at his cigarette. "The man Frank Harley is with you, is he not?"

"He is," said Shell.

Galeras tilted his head a little. "To La Barranca Escondida, no?"

"To La Barranca Escondida, yes," said Dusty. He looked at Shell. "The whole damned country knows where we're goin'. Well, it won't matter to the *capitán* here."

Galeras raised his head. "Listen, *amigos,*" he said. "Let me make you a proposition. I do not want to die and you do not want me to die either."

Dusty grinned. "We *don't?*"

"Keep talking," said Shell. He had to admire the Mexican for his cool nerve despite the bitch of a hangover he was carrying.

Galeras held up a lean finger. "*Escuche!*" he said. "I planned to trap you at the bottom of the mesa. That was only partially successful, as you well know."

"Hear, hear," said Dusty.

Galeras ignored him. "Some of my men went back to Mesa del Campanero, with a message for my commanding officer at Hermosillo. In that message, I heroically stated that I, Capitan Hernán Antonio Federico Adolfo Bartolome Panfilo Galeras y Castaneda, would stay on the trail of the Americanos until death stopped my quest."

"*Viva, viva!*" said Shell.

Galeras nodded. He sipped at the brandy and flipped his cigarette butt into the filthy fireplace. Quickly he rolled another.

"Get it over with," said Dusty. "It's a good day to die, greaser."

Galeras looked up. "So, my commanding officer thinks I am pursuing you. As long as he doesn't have to leave his women and his brandy in Hermosillo, why should he concern himself about Capitan Hernán Galeras and his brave men?"

Shell nodded. The Mexican was downright amusing, if nothing else.

"So," said the Mexican, "if the bodies of my men and myself are found it will be understood that we *did* die in our heroic quest, and therefore you Americanos managed to escape. But, if those bodies are not found, it would be assumed we are still on the quest."

Shell took the tobacco pouch from the table and began to shape a cigarette. "Get to the point," he said.

Galeras wiped the icy sweat from his pale face. Looking at those two pairs of cold Yanqui eyes was enough to unnerve any man, especially when he was pleading for his life. "Let me go with you," he said. "If I cannot be of value to you, you can kill me. I know this country. I am a fighting man as you are. You will need every gun you can get to fight off the Yaquis."

"What's your price?" said Shell.

"A share in the treasure if you find it. My life if you do not."

Dusty laughed. "A share in the treasure? What's your life to us?"

Shell lighted his cigarette and automatically handed the makings to Dusty. Galeras had made some sense. As long as his superiors thought he was hunting down the Americanos, they wouldn't bother to send out any more troops. It might just give them enough time to get the treasure and escape. It was a long shot. Everything they had done in this mad quest had been a long shot. Galeras knew well enough if he went back to Hermosillo with the story of the massacre of his men that he would not live to see the next day. His life would be forfeit to his superiors and he would be living on borrowed time while he was with the treasure hunters.

Galeras eyed Shell. "Well, *amigo?*" he said quietly.

Shell nodded. "It's a deal," he said.

"What the hell!" blurted Dusty.

Galeras grinned. He reached for the bottle and raised it to his lips. Shell drew and fired. The soft slug smashed the bottle, driving fragments of it against the wall. The strong odor of the spirits hung in the air. Hernán Galeras slowly and shakily wiped the brandy and blood from his face. There was green fear on his features as he glanced at Shell and Dusty.

Shell sheathed the smoking Colt. "You've had enough liquor," he said. "That was just a warning, Galeras. Remember it." He turned on a heel and walked into the growing light of the day.

It was almost noon by the time they had concealed the swelling bodies of the dead. Shell had sent Victor to get the body of the sergeant. His guts moiled when he saw what the Tarahumare had done to the man. They had tumbled the bodies into a hole a quarter of a mile up the canyon and heaved rocks in atop them. It had been Galeras who had thought of the idea of climbing a ledge just above the charnel pit to pry loose the scaling rock. Tons of it fell with a dusty crash into the pit to hide the bodies forever from the sight of men.

They rode south along the barranca as the heat of the day began to fill it. There was no sign left behind to indicate what had happened there except for a few dark stains upon the rocks. By late afternoon they climbed out of the barranca to the higher ground.

Frank Harley called to Shell. "There should be a landmark in sight, Shell," he said. "A knife-shaped peak almost due south."

All heads turned to look south. Sharp against the cloud-dotted sky stood the dark outline of a great peak shaped like the blade of a heavy knife. It was the one Shell had seen the day before.

"Cuchillo Peak," said Hernán Galeras as he bent his head to light a cigarette.

"That is it!" said Frank. "Head directly toward it."

"That won't be easy," said Shell. "This country is broken up into a hell's puzzle. Padre, can you get us there?"

The padre shrugged dubiously. "In time, perhaps," he said.

Galeras blew a smoke ring. "Already I am of value, *amigos,*" he said casually. "I know the way. We can be there in two days. Otherwise it would take a week, *if you got there at all.*"

Before the darkness came down Shell studied the country to the south. Those were huge mountains, towering thousands of feet into the dark sky, and between them were immense barrancas, thousands of feet deep. In all that vast, trackless country there was not one sign of human life. Not a building, a road, a trail, or a thin thread of smoke. Misgivings came over Shell. He did not trust Galeras. Padre Eusebio was already beyond the country he really knew. Rafaela Padilla had never been in there, although the story her grandfather had often told her had given her landmarks and signs that might help to lead to La Barranca Escondida. Dusty and Shell, of course, were utterly out of their element. Victor might know the country better than any of them, but if he did, there was no sign of it on his impassive face, and of course he could not speak.

Dusty looked at Shell. He was thinking the same as Shell. A man could get lost in that country and spend the rest of his life trying to find his way out of it, if he lived to do so. If once they entered that country they would be dependent on Hernán Galeras, whom they could not really trust, and on the memory of a blind man who might or might not know the location of the lost silver mines.

Minutes ticked past. It was rapidly getting darker.

"We must ride the trail to the lower ground now," said the officer, "while there is still enough light."

Shell rubbed bis dirty beard. He looked at the shapely woman and her silent *mozo*. He looked at the patient, rather simple face of the padre. He looked at the hard lean face of his partner Dusty. Last of all he looked at the calm, patient face of Frank Harley. Harley seemed so sure of himself.

Now or never, thought Shell. *"Adelante!"* he said.

Galeras grinned. He flipped away the cigarette and set spurs to his horse, clattering over the loose rock into the thick brush to the south.

They would soon be committed. But there was no going back in any case. This time the die was surely cast.

CHAPTER FIFTEEN

Hernán Galeras had been as good as his word. They had reached the base of Cuchillo Peak in two days as he had said. Beyond that the route plunged deep into a barranca that almost made one faint of heart to look down into it and to see the vague trail that seemed to hang on the side of the barranca wall. From a sun-blasted mesa, heat shimmering in the late summer sun, they slowly descended the faint trace of the trail. To look down was to lose all courage, but there could be no going back. Halfway down, one of the riderless horses missed his footing and went over the side, turning end over end like a wooden replica of a hobbyhorse, to strike far, far below. So far below, the sound of the heavy body striking the hard ground could not be heard by those who stood white-faced on the crumbling trail.

It took the better part of a day to reach the bottom and here the world had changed. Instead of the sun-ravaged heights, swept by the dry wind, they saw a dense, lush tropical forest. Birds of many varieties flew through the woods and above them. Raucous guacamayo parrots greeted them fearlessly with outlandish noises. Water raced through deep-cut channels. Halfway across the bottom of the huge gash Padre Eusebio kicked his mare in the sides and raced ahead. In a few minutes he was back clutching two oranges in his hands. They rode ahead to find a small grove of the fruit trees beside a clear stream whose gravelly bottom was plain to be seen in the dying light. The bright fruit dropped from the overhanging trees and swirled in the furious current. Wild cotton trees thrust out thorn-studded trunks. *Urraca* jays screamed furiously at the strange intruders. High, high above the three-thousand-foot south wall of the incredibly huge barranca rose towering heights with drifting clouds swirling about them, hiding the tips of the mountains.

It was almost impossible to believe that such an area could exist in those mountains, after the days of travel through barren, almost waterless country, where sere vegetation could hardly survive. The air was quiet and heavy amidst the trees. It was a place where a man could idle many days away occupied with his thoughts.

Shell picked a campsite in a clearing not far from the edge of the stream. There was no sign of human life in the area, and yet he always had the uncanny feeling that they were being watched by someone who was never seen. This was the edge of the Tarahumare country. Those shy, wild people were seen only when they wanted to be seen. Rafaela had told Shell that they did not live in villages, but were nomadic, ranging through the pine-clad mountains in the summer, seeking refuge from the winter in the tropical canyon bottoms. It was not a country for the Yaquis. Their domain was farther west, and the quest for La Barranca Escondida would lead the little party in that direction once they passed the looming heights of Cuchillo Peak.

Shell looked thoughtfully at Victor. Rafaela had said he had been outlawed from his tribe and left to die. Had his own people cut out his tongue?

Hernán Galeras strolled up to Shell, sucking on an orange. "We will be safe here for a time," he said. "The

Yaquis do not come here and the Tarahumares will not bother us. We know, of course, that there will be no soldiers following us."

"You did a good job guiding us here, Galeras," said Shell.

The officer shrugged. "I had to," he said. He smiled. "One always does a good job when he seems to feel a pistol muzzle against his neck."

Rafaela disappeared into the lush growth. Victor sat down on a fallen tree between the place where she had disappeared and the camp. His dark eyes studied Dusty. Dusty sat down and pulled off his worn boots. He rolled a cigarette and glanced at the woods where she had gone. In a little while the sound of splashing came to them.

Shell and Hernán walked into the woods in the opposite direction, then stripped and went into the cold water of the swift stream, gasping and shuddering as they bathed. In a little while the padre came to watch them. His churchman's modesty would not permit him to strip in front of these two godless men.

A fire crackled in the clearing when Shell and Hernán returned to the campsite. Rafaela was seated on a log, combing out her thick, lustrous hair. Victor was nowhere to be seen.

It was the first time in many weeks that Shell had felt at ease, but he knew it was for only a little while. Somewhere south of them in that tangled, forbidding country was La Barranca Escondida and El Naranjal. It drew him and the others. There could be no denying its powerful attraction for them.

Victor came out of the woods. He had something in his hand. It was a stone and it had been shaped by nature or man into the shape of a tablet. The Tarahumare held it to the firelight and looked toward the blind man. Hernán jumped to his feet and hurriedly scanned the stone. "*Ojaldl*" he said. "See? Here is an inscription!"

Dusty stood up and walked quickly to them. He gripped the stone in his big hands and turned it closer to the fire. *"Departamento de Camino a Las. . ."* His voice died away. "Part of the lettering has been worn away," he said.

"Wait," said Hernán. He scooped up a handful of ashes and wet them in the stream. He rubbed them into the weathered face of the rock until at last the ashes had penetrated into the inscription. He wiped the remainder of the stone clean. *"Departamento de Camino a Las Minas de La Barr. . ."* He wiped the sweat from his face and peered at the lettering. *"Escondida y. . . .* That is all I can read, *amigos."*

It was very quiet around the camp. They all looked at Frank Harley. "Is it as close as that, Frank?" Shell said at last.

The blind man shook his head. "I don't understand it," he said quietly. "There was no *camino* to the mines through here."

"Maybe yuh just don't know," said Dusty.

Harley shook his head again. "Impossible," he said.

Hernán studied the stone. "I have seen stones like this elsewhere," he said. "Many years ago all the highways through the lower country were marked with such stones."

"There was no such highway in this area," insisted Frank.

"Mebbe you're just tellin' us that," said Dusty. He looked quickly about. "Maybe this is La Barranca Escondida."

"That is foolish," said Rafaela. "It is many leagues south of here. That I know."

"Then how is it this marker is here?" said Hernán.

Padre Eusebio pointed to the rushing stream. "In flood, such a stream could carry a stone like that for many miles. In the passage of many years the floods could carry it still further. The stream itself originates southeast of here. In a hundred years that stone could have been brought down here. See how worn it is?"

They all looked at the stone. There was little question but that the padre was right. "It proves one thing," said

Shell. "If they put up highway markers in those days, they put them up to mark the route to real places, not myths or legends."

Dusty looked up into the darkness toward the towering peaks. "Yeh," he said slowly, "but how far did the stream carry it and where did it originally come from?"

No one had an answer. The stone was only a teaser. It could have been swept for miles and miles over a period of a hundred years or more, as the padre had so wisely said. But it whetted their appetites. Somewhere, in the velvety darkness to the south of them, beyond Cuchillo Peak, there must be an immense, hidden barranca holding a treasure in silver that would stagger the imagination.

"We'd better get some sleep," said Shell. "We climb up out of here tomorrow, and it should take us the best part of the day. We ride before dawn. We can reach the south wall of the barranca by first light."

Padre Eusebio extinguished the fire. In the darkness they all sought their blankets. Dusty had first guard that night. But there was little sleep at first for any of them with the exception of Victor. To him, the silver meant nothing; to the others, it meant everything.

Before the dawn they were up. A fire was built and a hurried meal was made and eaten. The horses and burros were rounded up, and Victor led the way through the darkness of the woods with the sure knowledge of the Indian.

By first dawn light they sat their horses at the bottom of the three-thousand-foot wall and eyed the thin thread of trail that seemed lightly tacked onto the sheer side of the barranca. None of them spoke, but each of them remembered all too well the sight of the horse that had fallen from the trail on the north side of the barranca the day before. It was not a pleasant thought.

It was Victor who made the choice. He walked up the trail with sure-footed skill. Rafaela Padilla glanced at the taut faces of the others, then touched the flanks of her horse with the small spurs she wore. The horse started up the trail.

"Ladies first," said Hernán Galeras with a rueful smile. He followed Rafaela.

Padre Eusebio took the halter of Frank Harley's horse. He looked at Shell. "Perhaps it would be best if I followed with Señor Harley," he said. "Do you lead the burros, Señor Shell."

Dusty spurred his horse up after Galeras. Broken rock was cast aside from the hoofs. "He is in a hurry, that one," said the padre.

Shell followed Dusty. Now and then he glanced back and down to see the padre patiently leading Frank's horse. The burros trotted placidly along. They were used to this sort of thing and were as sure-footed as cats. Now and then a rock would tumble over the edge of the trail and the sound of it striking would come faintly from below, but as the sun rose and the party struggled higher and higher up the face of the barranca wall, the falling stones and rocks could not be heard when they struck.

Halfway up the trail everyone who was riding, with the exception of Frank Harley, dismounted. The horses were nervous, unsure of themselves. They shied in terror at the worst spots on the trail. It was all the party could do to keep on, dragging on the reins, gripping unsure handholds, ready at an instant to release the reins of a horse if the animal should make that last fatal step.

By noon they had reached three-quarters of the way up the barranca wall. They stopped for a rest and to regain control of their nerves. Far, far below them they could see the sunlight flashing from the ripples of the watercourse where it debouched from the cover of the semitropical trees. The bottom of the barranca was thickly covered with the trees, but the far side of the barranca stood naked in the bright sunlight. No one spoke. The sweat from near exhaustion and from the clinging fear of the terrible trail they had ascended ran down their dusty faces.

Victor was looking across the giddy depths of the barranca. He looked at Rafaela and then pointed across the canyon. Everyone looked in the direction to which he had pointed. Only Dusty, whose eyesight was excellent, saw anything. "Get the glasses, Shell," he said over his shoulder.

Shell got the field glasses. He raised them to his eyes and focused them on the far side of the barranca, about where the trail should be. For a long time he saw nothing but the cracked and riven rock of the barranca wall, and then he caught a movement. He refocused the glasses. Something was moving down the trail, although he could hardly distinguish the trail itself. Gradually he could make out what it was. A long file of hatless men leading horses. They were halfway down to the bottom of the barranca. Shell handed the glasses to Dusty. Dusty whistled softly as he saw what Shell had seen.

"What is it, Shell?" asked Rafaela.

"Yaquis, most likely," said Shell.

It was very quiet except for the sighing of the warm wind and the occasional blowing of a horse or burro. Rafaela looked up toward the top of the barranca wall, then down into the depths, and then toward the distant wall.

"It will take them hours," said Shell. "We can be long gone by then." He knew well enough they'd outdistance them that day, and perhaps the next, but in time they'd catch up. There was one other thing he was quite sure of, and that was the fact that the Yaquis would not quit. Too many of their kinsmen had died back at Tinajas Altas. They could not return to their people without having exacted vengeance. They were just as committed to their quest as were the people of the party watching them from across the huge barranca.

They started up the trail and none of them looked now across the barranca. Their full attention had to be on the crumbling trail. It was late afternoon when at last they reached the top of the trail and stopped again to rest. Shell scanned the far side of the canyon with the glasses. There was no sign of life on the other trail. He scanned the bottom of the barranca but nothing moved down there except the rushing stream and the wind-blown treetops. A hawk hung in the air midway between both sides of the canyon and level with the tops of the walls.

Shell lay bellyflat on the lip of the barranca. Dusty sat on Shell's legs as Shell hung the glasses over the crumbling brink and studied the bottom of the trail. He wasn't sure, but there seemed to be some movement down there. He spoke over his shoulder. "Pull me back, *amigo*." Shell stood up and cased the glasses. "Padre, Galeras, Victor, Dusty, give me a hand." Shell gripped a bushel-basket-sized rock and rolled it over the edge. It struck the trail and bounded out into space, dropping far down into the wooded depths below. Rock crumbled from the trail. Rock after rock was rolled over the edge. They worked together to heave over a huge boulder. The roaring of the falling rock thundered from one side of the huge barranca to the other, and a veil of yellowish dust hung in the now windless air.

They sat back from the edge, with sweat running from every pore. Their action had driven some of the fear from their minds. Whether or not they had killed or injured some of their pursuers was of secondary importance. What mattered most was that the trail be ruined for anyone following them, but there was no way of knowing that.

Dusty wiped the sweat from his face. "Maybe it'll make 'em cautious, if nothing else," he said.

Galeras nodded. "Even so, *amigos*," he said, "it would be best to push on. A Yaqui can go where a cat can go. Of this I assure you."

They rode to the south through the gathering shadows. Beyond them loomed the mountains, with their towering peaks still illuminated by the sinking sun. A chill wind swept the heights. Shell, Dusty, and Hernán rode ahead of the others, fanning out to keep track of the faint trail that crossed the mesa. The sun was nearly gone when the trace ran out. They sat their horses. Shell shaped a cigarette and passed the makings to Dusty.

"It is hopeless," said Hernán. "This is the wrong way, *amigos*."

Shell nodded. He turned in his saddle to look back toward the others. The wind shifted and blew from the south. Dusty slowly took the cigarette from his mouth. "Listen!" he said. Faintly, ever so faintly, came the sound of a bell.

"By God!" said Shell. He looked at Dusty. "We've run into it by dumb luck!"

Hernán lighted his cigarette. "Impossible," he said. Dusty shot him a hard glance. "Don't try to sidetrack us, Galeras, just as we're right on top of it!"

The rest of the party came up slowly. Padre Eusebio crossed himself when he heard the bell. There was a puzzled look on Frank Harley's face. They rode on through the gathering darkness. A mound showed ahead of them, with a tilted wooden cross, silvered by time, thrust into the top of it. Padre Eusebio, Hernán, and Rafaela tossed stones to add to the mound. It was the custom, in memory of the dead who were buried beneath the mound. The others? If Victor had a religion it was his secret. Frank Harley's religion was La Barranca Escondida. The two others? The tall, bearded Americans? Their only religion hung at their belts, sheathed in shaped leather, ready always to deal out sudden death.

"Look!" said Hernán. He pointed out rounded floors of paved rock. "*Arrastres!* To crush the ore from the mines!"

"Yes," said Frank Harley. "But *not* the mines of La Barranca Escondida. There were ancient workings in this area. *Minos reales.* A group of mines. El Refugio, El Santo Nino, El Yaqui, La Barbayena, La Urraca, and Los Dulces

Nombres. All were once of good assay. I repeat! This is *not* La Barranca Escondida."

As though to give the lie to his words the bell rang softly.

Rafaela kneed her horse close to that of Frank. "It is possible that this is Guadalupe de Santa Ana," she said. "My grandfather spoke of it. At one time it was populous, but that was long ago."

They rode on. Ruins appeared on either hand. A large building stood at the end of the street, and the last of the light caught the outline of a cross atop a crumbling tile roof. A tall pole leaned away from the prevailing wind, and from the top of it hung a small bell with a frayed rope hanging a few feet below it. The wind blew harder. The pole swayed. The bell rang softly. It was as simple as that.

Hernán grinned. "The ghost bell," he said. "The sacristan has not rung that bell for a long time."

"He'd have to have damned long arms to reach *that* rope," said Dusty.

Hernán looked about. "Is this indeed Guadalupe de Santa Ana?"

"The bell might be marked," suggested the padre.

"There's one sure way of finding out," said Dusty. He kneed his horse close to the pole. Three good blows of his bowie knife severed the pole. The bell clanged dismally as it shattered against a rock. Padre Eusebio crossed himself and squatted in front of the bell, fitting the pieces together. Shell lighted a match. The padre traced the worn letters with a finger. "The Church of Guadalupe de Santa Ana," said the padre quietly. He crossed himself again.

"We'll stay here tonight," said Shell. "Hernán! Find the water. Let's get these animals watered."

Father Eusebio carefully picked up the pieces of the bell and carried them into the dusty, echoing interior of the old church. In a little while the nickering light of a fire came from within the old church as the padre kindled a fire. The church afforded the best protection from the searching night wind which became a little more chill every night. Besides, the walls were thick and bulletproof. Padre Eusebio, as well as being devout, was also very practical.

Later, as Shell stood guard, he listened to the wind moaning across the mesa, whining about the old buildings and driving rolling brush through the empty streets. The wind did not like the return of humans to its playground.

Something howled out of the night. It was a long way off. Shell raised his head. There wouldn't be any coyotes at this altitude. Perhaps it was a wolf. The long-drawn-out howling came again. Shell shivered but it wasn't from the penetrating night wind. There was enough of his Celtic ancestry still in his veins to make him wonder if the howling came from a creature of flesh and blood.

CHAPTER SIXTEEN

The mesa top was still shrouded in the cold gray light of the early dawn. The great barranca south of the mesa was like the blow of an immense ax that had cut deeply into the earth. Rafaela sat her horse, muffled in her serape. "If that is truly Guadalupe de Santa Ana," she said to Shell, "then there is a trail at the bottom of this barranca. The Arisciachi Trail. Is that not so, Frank?"

"Yes," said the blind man. "The trail branches three ways. West to the Rio Mayo. East to the Rio de Haros."

"And the third way?" said Hernán Galeras.

"To the vicinity of Nayarit," said Rafaela, "and the Cerro de Huesos. Beyond that? Perhaps La Barranca Escondida. *Quién sabe?*"

The sky was lightening. Padre Eusebio looked back toward the empty village. "Look," he said quietly.

Twin streamers of smoke, perhaps two miles apart, stained the gray sky. "Those are not Tarahumares cooking their breakfast," said Hernán dryly. "I suggest we do not wait. We cannot go back. We must chance the trail that leads to the bottom of this barranca."

Victor led the way into the thick brush, searching for the trail. In a few minutes he halted, pointing wordlessly down into the dark depths. A wisp of a trail clung to the face of the wall.

"*Santa Madre de Dios!*" said Hernán. "Is that the only way?"

The Franciscan crossed himself. "We will make it with the favor of God, my son." He quirted his horse forward and then slid to the ground to lead the animal and one of the burros down into the barranca. The others followed him. Hernán and Dusty led the extra horses and the burro. Rafaela led her horse and that of Frank Harley. One blessing Frank had; he couldn't see that horror of a trail.

Two hundred yards from the bottom something struck the trail behind Shell. A rock bounced off into space. Rock after rock began to fall as the Yaquis pushed them over. Shell's horse whinnied pitifully as a rock struck his rump. A great rock fell with smashing force on the back of the bay. He fell sideways, dragging the reins through Shell's left hand. Shell opened his hand, nicking out bright droplets of blood from the furrow gouged by the reins. He heard the horse strike far below.

They led the horses and burros toward the far side of the canyon. Rifle fire crackled from the canyon brim, but the Yaquis were only wasting good cartridges. Dusty looked back. "They're starting down the trail, *compañero,*" he said. He ground-reined his horse and drew his Spencer from its scabbard. Casually he rested the heavy repeater on a boulder and looked at Shell. Shell joined him. Hernán smiled. These Yanquis and their conceit! Body of God! How did they expect to hit anything at *that* range?

The Yaquis were working their way down the trail. Dusty let them get two-thirds of the way down. "Bet a drink I get a hit, *amigo,*" he said out of the side of his mouth.

Shell nodded. He took up the slack in his trigger. "Take the lead man, *amigo,*" he said. "I'll take the last one."

There was no wind. The light was still vague. There

was a moment's pause and then the two repeaters cracked almost at once. The lead Yaqui dropped on the trail. Dusty grinned at Shell. "Yuh owe me a drink, *amigo*," he said.

Shell ejected the empty hull. It tinkled on the hard ground.

"Por Dios!" exclaimed Hernán. "Look!"

The last Yaqui swayed on the trail, pawing at the air with his hands, and then he fell from the trail, turning end over end to strike heavily far below.

"Even-up," said Shell. He levered a fresh round into the chamber. "Scratch one free drink, *amigo*."

It was almost noon when they called a halt to rest the animals. They had long ago passed the place where the Arisciachi Trail had branched three ways. "We turn to the left here," said Frank, "following the barranca wall for a mile or so. There should be what looks like a box canyon right there. We follow that. The floor of it rises, and several miles from the mouth of the canyon we should reach the level of the mesa. Somewhere near there is a thicket of trees, eh, Rafaela?"

"Yes," she said. "Madrono trees."

"And beyond that?" said Shell.

Frank wet his lips. *"Cerritos chapos.* Three hills, or runt mountains. They are capped with red *topueste* dirt. One of them stands apart from the others."

"Cerro de Huesos?" said Rafaela.

"It should be," said Frank quietly.

"It better be," said Dusty meaningfully.

The afternoon came and began to wane as they forced their way through the choked canyon. It was indeed like a box canyon. Several miles from the barranca, as Frank had said, the floor of the canyon began to rise, and in the light of late afternoon they rode out upon the mesa top near a thick grove of madrono trees. Southwest of them, standing out boldly in the slanting rays of the sun, were two rugged-looking hills, or runt mountains. *They were capped with red topueste dirt!*

Dusty stood up in his stirrups. "There are only two of them," he said coldly.

"Impossible!" said Frank.

"Yuh can't see 'em!" snapped Dusty. "But *we* can! Damn you!"

Frank's face was dewed with sweat. He wiped it off.

Shell took out his field glasses and swept the terrain. Far to the left, crowning the flattened side of a ridge, he could pick out tumbled ruins. "Ruins to the left," he said. "Perhaps two miles off. Deep ravine between them and us."

"Nayarit?" said Rafaela.

"Don't you know?" said Dusty harshly.

"Be patient, my son," said the Franciscan.

"Shut that canting mouth of yours!" said Dusty angrily.

"If that is truly Nayarit," said Frank, "then there must be *three* hills."

"Damn you!" snarled Dusty. "There are only two of them!"

Shell spurred his horse and rode toward the hills. He did not look back. Let them come on or stay back, it didn't matter to him. He was getting sick of the whole business and especially of Dusty's constant carping.

The light was almost gone when he passed between the two hills. He looked to the right. A third hill stood there, capped with *topueste* dirt as the others were. It had been hidden from view by the two other hills. Some time in its past there had been a great landslide from the eastern face of the hill, revealing the naked subrock. It was shaped in broken ridges that looked exactly like a huge pile of gigantic bones! "The Hill of Bones," said Shell. He rode toward the lower slopes, looking back to see the others riding between the first two hills.

There would be a moon that night, but it had not arisen as yet. Shell reached the top of the hill and swung down from the horse. He took off his hat to feel the dry wind on his heated face. He could hear the others riding up the slopes below him. The wind shifted. He felt for the makings, and as he did so, the wind blew strongly, and he could have sworn he heard the faint sound of a bell. He slowly fashioned a smoke and was about to light it when he remembered that the Yaquis were somewhere behind them, pushing on, likely traveling faster than the party they were relentlessly pursuing.

They all dismounted at the top of the hills to look south into the clinging darkness. "My grandfather stood here many times," said Rafaela quietly. "To listen for the bell of El Naranjal."

Dusty laughed. "That's only a legend," he said. "How about that, Shell? Did you hear anything?"

Shell hesitated. "No," he said.

Frank Harley looked toward Shell with that uncanny sense of his. Shell knew Frank couldn't see him, but even so he turned his face away. "Let's get off this damned hill," said Shell. "It makes me uneasy."

They rode south of the three hills. The hoofbeats echoed hollowly in the thick darkness. "There is no water up here," said Hernán.

"We keep on," said Dusty.

"If we keep on much farther," said Hernán, "we will not be able to make it back to the last waterhole, with the little water we have left. Who knows? Perhaps the Yaquis are already there."

"Is there any water up here?" asked Padre Eusebio.

Frank looked toward the sound of the padre's voice. "Only at La Barranca Escondida," he said. His meaning was plain enough. They either found La Barranca Escondida, or they would die of thirst—if the Yaquis did not catch them first.

Shell looked back into the mysterious darkness. "I'll scout ahead. I'll be back by daylight."

"Alone?" said Dusty.

"Why?" said Shell. "Are you afraid I'll find the silver and run off with it?" He looked at Frank. "Any landmarks or any signs to show the way, Frank?"

"On a quiet night you're supposed to be able to hear the dogs barking at La Barranca Escondida. Yuh got a damned quiet night," said Dusty.

"There haven't been any dogs at La Barranca Escondida for a hundred years," said Frank.

"The bell then!" said Hernán.

Frank shrugged. "A legend. A myth. There is one landmark, Shell, that you might find. A thick grove of trees. The scientific name is *Populus wislizeni*. They are very rare. It is said that they grow only in two places in this country and few other places in Mexico. Here they are supposed to grow near Nayarit and La Barranca Escondida. The trail down into the barranca is masked by a grove of such trees."

"What do they look like?" said Shell.

"I don't know," said Frank.

Dusty spat viciously. "Great!" he snapped.

Padre Eusebio raised his head. "I know them," he said. "They are known in this country as *guerigo* trees. Furniture is made from them because the wood is tough and long lasting."

"Ride with me then," said Shell.

The padre mounted his horse. "There is said to be water at La Barranca Escondida. It will be of far greater value than silver."

"If you find it," said Hernán.

"It will be God's will," said the padre. They rode off into the darkness. Hernán leaned against his horse. "Maybe they won't come back," he suggested.

"The padre is a servant of God," said Rafaela hotly.

"That is very true," said the *capitán*. "But Shell is not"

"Keep your thoughts to yourself, greaser," said Dusty thinly.

Hernán shrugged and smiled to himself m the darkness.

They rode for well over two hours through the darkness. There was a faint trace of moonlight in the eastern sky. "Wait!" said the padre. "My horse has picked up a stone in a hoof."

Shell dismounted. "We'd better lead them for a while," he said. It was much darker ahead of them. Shell looked back at the dim figure of the padre as he walked on. "Hurry up," said Shell. His right foot struck out into emptiness. He fell, grabbing onto the ground with his left hand while his right hand clung to the reins. He shouted once and the echo sounded far away. Strong hands gripped him and pulled him up. He let go of the reins. The horse reared and blew in terror. Shell crawled weakly onto solid ground.

Padre Eusebio tethered the horses to a scrub tree. "Wait here," he said.

Shell looked up weakly. "I wasn't thinking of going anywhere right now," he said with a sickly smile.

Father Eusebio padded off into the darkness, feeling his way with a long stick. In half an hour he was back. He pointed his stick at the scrub tree to which the horses were tethered. "That tree is *not* a *guerigo* tree," he said conversationally.

"I didn't expect it to be," said Shell dryly. "Did you?"

Padre Eusebio shook his head, "No. The grove of *guerigo* trees is a hundred yards beyond us."

Shell stared unbelievingly at him. "You're sure?"

"Positive," said the padre.

The light grew. Twenty feet from them was a great swath of darkness, seemingly stretching on into infinity. Shell gingerly crawled forward. He stopped at the lip of an immense barranca. He dropped some rocks. He could not hear the sound of them striking far below. Padre Eusebio crawled up beside him.

The light grew. Gradually they realized they were looking down into the biggest barranca they had ever seen, so deep that the moonlight did not fully penetrate the darkness at the bottom. It was so vague and illusive they could not definitely make out any of the features.

They slept fitfully while the moon died and the darkness came again. The morning sun warmed their backs as they lay there. The morning wind whispered over the mesa top. "Listen!" said the padre. Faintly, ever so faintly, came the sound of a bell from the depths of the barranca.

When the sun filled the barranca, Shell focused his glasses on the bottom. The sunlight sparkled from the waters of a running stream and shone on great groves of dark-leaved trees. Shell could just pick out globules of orange against the dark foliage. Beyond the stream, surrounded by the orange trees, he could make out white walls. A tower rose above the trees. Shell handed the glasses to the Franciscan.

"There is no question about it, my son," said the padre, after a few minutes. "This is La Barranca Escondida and El Naranjal."

"We'd better find the trail down into it," said Shell.

"I wonder," said the padre, almost as though to himself.

"What do you mean?" demanded Shell.

The soft brown eyes probed into Shell's hard gray eyes. "Is it a good thing?" said the Franciscan. "What will happen to you people when that silver is found?"

"That's why we fought to get here! It means *nothing* to you. It means *everything* to us!"

The padre looked down into the barranca. "Perhaps," he said reflectively. "Perhaps Satan himself placed that silver there as a trap for men. It is haunted, my son. Haunted by greed, sin, and possible murder."

"You sound almost like you wish it would happen."

The padre quickly crossed himself. "God forbid!" he said in horror.

The padre led the way to the grove of *guerigo* trees. Beyond the grove the trail appeared, tracing a faint line down the wall of the barranca. Shell felt a little sick as he looked down it. "Go back and bring up the others," he said to the padre. "I'll scout the trail."

Shell worked his way down on foot. The trail was crumbling, seemingly held to the side of the barranca by magnetism. Halfway down he found a place where the trail ended, to continue on fifteen feet further. A row of deep holes indicated that at one time poles had been inserted, to form supports for a crude bridge. He plodded wearily up the trail to the grove of trees. By the time the rest of the party arrived he had hacked enough poles and shorter pieces to use as supports and stringers.

It was late afternoon by the time they had bridged the gap. They carried the supplies across and then crossed the animals one by one. Just as Shell crossed the bridge he looked back up the trail. His blood ran cold as he saw a hatless figure move quickly into cover. *"Adelante!"* he called out. "Our friends are at the top of the trail! Get the horses and burros down! Dusty and Hernán! Drop behind to give me a hand holding them off!"

Frank Harley turned his blind eyes toward Shell. "No need for that," he said. "No Yaqui would ever come down here. To them the place is haunted. Remember the curse of the Jesuits."

"What about Victor?" said Shell.

"Look at him," Father Eusebio said.

The *mozo's* face was a mask, but fear showed in his dark eyes. Only his loyalty and devotion to his mistress would get him to go down into the barranca.

Dusty looked up the trail. "Supposin' this *ain't* La Barranca Escondida?"

Frank smiled. "Then we'll find out soon enough, won't we, Dusty?"

Dusty stared at him, then spat over the side of the trail. "Stop," he said, "you're killin' me!"

It was dark by the time they reached the foot of the trail. They rode to the rushing stream and watered the animals and themselves. The night wind moaned softly through the great barranca. Every head was raised when the faint sound of the bell came through the darkness. Then it was quiet again.

CHAPTER SEVENTEEN

The moonlight was flooding down into La Barranca Escondida. It glinted from the rushing stream and reflected from the white surfaces of the buildings. It shone fully on the ancient road that passed through the dark-leaved orange trees. At the far end of the road were the mysterious buildings. Shell glanced behind him as he walked the road. Dusty was fifty feet behind, followed by Hernán at an equal interval. Rafaela, Victor, and the padre followed, leading the animals. As Shell looked back he could clearly make out Frank Harley who was riding one of the lead horses. What was going on in Frank's mind now that he had found his dream? Would it crack if there were no buried treasure in the barranca?

The Yaquis had not appeared. Frank had been right. There was nothing to fear from them as long as one stayed in the haunted barranca. The Spaniards had left it a hundred years ago. Yet it seemed to Shell that someone, or *something*, was still there. There were times when he could have sworn he had seen a quick movement just out of the corner of an eye, but when he looked, there had been nothing there. Imagination of course. Or was it imagination?

He stopped in awe at the edge of the square. The old padres had built for the future, not realizing perhaps, that their handiwork would stand empty and echoing, lost for a hundred years. Facing Shell from across the empty square was a solid-looking church with a bell tower rising from the left-hand side of it. A cross, still showing traces of giltwork, shone in the moonlight. A rounded dome covered with white cement rose at the rear of the church. To the right of the church stood an L-shaped building, the long leg of the L forming the side of the square. A colonnaded arcade extended the full length of the building. To Shell's left there were other smaller buildings and several narrow side streets faced by more buildings. A *carreta* leaned drunkenly in the center of one of the narrow streets as though waiting for its owner to come and hitch the oxen to it. All of the buildings were shuttered and lifeless-looking.

Shell waved an arm and walked across the square. Midway he stopped and picked up a little bundle of faded, rotting cloth. The stolid wooden face of a doll looked unblinkingly up at him, showing traces of the Indian ancestry of the woodcarver. The child who had dropped it had likely died as an old lady, years past.

Shell walked to the raised flagstoned *pave* in front of the church. The shattered pieces of a bell were scattered beneath the bell tower. He looked up and saw that only one bell still hung in the tower. Anselmo's words came back to him. *"There were four bells in the church tower. One of them fell and was shattered when they attempted to lower it from the tower. Two had already been taken from the tower. The last of the four bells was left hanging in the tower."*

"So Anselmo was right after all," said Dusty from behind Shell.

Shell nodded, "So much for legend," he said. He stepped up onto the *pave* and walked to the carved double doors of the church. He tried the wrought-iron handles. The doors creaked open. A musty odor drifted from the dark interior of the church.

"Go on in!" said Dusty eagerly. "Some of them church ornaments and stuff were made of solid gold or silver!"

Shell shook his head. "Let the padre go in first," he said.

Dusty walked toward the entrance, spurs climbing.

Shell stepped in front of his companion. "I said: *Let the padre go in first!*"

For a moment their eyes locked. Dusty shrugged. He smiled. "Have it your way, *amigo,*" he said carelessly. "There ought to be enough for all of us, even that stupid padre."

Hernán stood at the foot of the steps. He fashioned a cigarette. Someday, perhaps soon, those two cold-eyed gringos would have at each other, and with a little bit of luck they might just kill each other. He lighted his cigarette. That would leave all the more silver for Hernán Galeras, and the woman too, of course. With a little more luck, he might stumble onto the stores of wine that the Jesuits were sure to have left. He half-closed his eyes and smiled. It was such a beautiful thought!

Shell looked back across the square. There was a dreamlike quality about the place, as though it had a spell upon it. As though time no longer existed. It was so quiet and peaceful he almost felt as though the legendary and fabulous wealth of La Barranca Escondida was of little value compared to the peacefulness of the place.

The rest of the party came up. Rafaela was describing the place to the blind man. He kept nodding his head. "Yes! Yes! I can truly see it, Rafaela!"

The padre crossed himself as he came up the three wide steps to the *pave*. He hesitated at the door. He looked at Shell. Shell nodded. "Go on in," he said. He handed Father Eusebio a block of lucifers. The padre threw back his cowl and walked in. A moment later a flicker of light came from within the cavernous interior. "Shell," said the padre in an awed tone, "they even left the candles!"

They walked in behind the padre. Rafaela held Frank

by the arm, but the *mozo* stopped at the doorway and would not enter. He returned to the horses and burros.

The flaring light of the ancient candles revealed the untouched interior of the nave with the stations of the cross on either side. The adobe brick flooring was covered with dust which arose in a thin cloud and drifted toward the open doorway. The padre advanced to the sanctuary and lighted more candles and then he went down upon his knees before the bare altar.

Shell looked about. The flickering light revealed the intricate painted decorations on the walls and ceiling, done in black, red, green, yellow, orange, and indigo blue. Pictures of the Twelve Apostles still hung on the walls. Over the sanctuary altar was a dusty statue of the Madonna, and above it, close to the domed ceiling, was a statue of a saint with outspread arms as though in blessing. Under the white dome, seemingly suspended in space, were the crossed palms of martyrdom.

Rafaela walked forward and went down upon her knees behind the padre. Hernán looked back at Shell and Dusty with a faint, self-conscious grin, then trod out his cigarette, took off his hat, and went down upon his knees beside the woman. Dusty prowled about the nave looking for gold or silver ornaments, but the Jesuits had not left any, at least in the church. He snapped a lucifer on a thumbnail and lighted a cigarette, eyeing Shell as Shell took off his faded campaign hat. Dusty walked from the church, his spurs chiming softly. The echo came down from the vaulted roof of the nave.

"No one has been here in one hundred years," said the soft voice beside Shell. He looked at the calm face of Frank Harley. "One hundred years of peace and quiet, Shell," added the blind man. "Do you feel it, Shell?"

"No," lied Shell. Frank had an uncanny way of probing into a man's innermost thoughts.

The Franciscan stood up. He looked down on Rafaela and Hernán, placed a hand on each of their heads, then walked to Shell and Frank. There had always been a calm, reflective look on the padre's brown face, but if it was possible it seemed as though now it was even more so, as though a great weight had been lifted from him. "It is time to leave, my children," he said.

"Where is Dusty?" said Hernán.

They walked out onto the *pave*. Father Eusebio had extinguished all the candles except one, which he left guttering in a red glass receptacle on the altar.

There was no sign of Dusty in the square. Victor pointed toward the massive L-shaped building that dominated one whole side of the square. A door hung open, and from within a faint flickering of light could be seen. Dusty wasn't wasting any time.

Shell walked to the building and into the colonnaded arcade that ran for many feet on either hand. He followed the sound that came from a room whose door hung open. A pale wash of light came from within. Shell stopped at the door. The room had dark, massive furniture to it, typical of many missions he had seen. Dusty had thrown back the lid of a heavy, iron-strapped chest. He was tossing out articles of clothing and cursing softly. "A lot of useless crap," he said over his shoulder.

"You're in one helluva hurry," said Shell.

Dusty looked at him. "*I* didn't come here for the good of *my* soul," he said.

"You might consider it, *amigo*."

Dusty laughed. He stood up and rubbed his dusty beard, watching Shell with amused eyes. "Yuh think you'll make time with the filly by actin' religious?"

"You've got a warped mind," said Shell coldly.

They could hear the others in the corridor. Shell walked to meet them. "This is evidently the old mission," he said.

Hernán nodded. "The old padres had the Indians digging for silver with one hand and lighting holy candles with the other."

"They left the candles," said Dusty from the doorway, "Let's hope, by God, they left some of the silver."

"They did," said Frank. "There was no possible way they could have removed it *all* before their expulsion. The padres here in La Barranca Escondida had more time to hide their bullion than most of the Jesuits did."

"There is a lovely old room here," said Rafaela from down the corridor. She beckoned to them with the lighted candle in her hand.

The room was low-ceiled, but very wide and quite long. A large beehive fireplace was in one corner, and a thick bed of ashes still coated the hearth. Dusty hangings were on the peeling whitewashed walls. Candle sconces of wrought iron were fastened to the walls, and a pair of solid-looking iron candelabra still stood on the massive table that dominated the center of the room. Hernán lighted more candles. As he touched the tablecloth, a thin film of dust arose from it and drifted toward the open door.

Dusty dropped into a chair and thrust his long legs up onto the table. One of his spurs caught in the ancient cloth and ripped it. "Where do we start looking, Frank?" he said as he formed a cigarette. His eyes were as hard as flint.

Shell made a cigarette and placed it between the blind man's lips. Rafaela took a candle from its holder and leaned over to light the cigarette. As she did so her full breasts swung against the thin material of her patched-up shirt. Dusty flicked a glance at her breasts. Shell watched her lovely face, ivory in the soft candlelight. She looked at him with her dark, lustrous eyes, and something caught at his heart.

"What about it, Frank?" repeated Dusty.

"He's very tired," said Rafaela. "Cannot we get some rest?"

"He ain't *that* tired," said Dusty.

Frank drew in the smoke and blew it out. The smoke wavered in the musty air, drifted toward the candles, then toward the door. "It's all right," he said. "I can't sleep right now. It's taken me twenty years of research and hunting to get here. Twenty years of death and defeat, of blood and sweat. *Twenty years....*"

"Cut out the history crap," said Dusty. "We ain't interested."

Frank rested his thin hands on the table. "It is said that the bullion and other items were placed in one of the mines, the entrance of which is supposedly twenty-two hundred *varas* west of, and seven hundred *varas* south of the door of the church. A *vara* is thirty-three and one-third inches. This mine was then protected with a *patrón* and the entrance closed and carefully concealed."

"*Patrón?*" said Shell.

Frank nodded. "An Indian most likely. Killed on the spot and left there so that his ghost would always guard the mine until the true owners returned."

Father Eusebio crossed himself. "I have heard of such things," he said.

Dusty laughed. "What's supposed to be hidden there?"

Frank leaned back in his chair and blew a cloud of smoke. "I have read a copy of the inventory. Don't ask me how I found it. The man who I bribed to let me see it died quite mysteriously shortly thereafter. I memorized many of the items. *Item:* a baptismal font of carved cedar inlaid with silver. *Item:* a small cut-stone box filled with jewels. *Items:* a pair of processional candleholders, six golden incensories, three large golden communion plates, a pair of silver chalices, a shrine made of solid silver, and three candelabras of solid silver. *Item:* seventy-five *cargas,* or packloads of silver, each *carga* packed in cowhide bags, two bags to a wooden chest, each chest containing one-half of an *arroba.* These are from divers mines located in La Barranca Escondida. *Item:* ten *cargas* of gold, wrapped in cloth and cowhide, and stored in wooden chests. These from the placers of El Naranjal. *Item:* five *arrobas* of Castilla ore, twenty-two carats assay, clean and without mercury, from El Naranjal." Frank's voice died away.

There was a long pause. Tobacco smoke rose in rifted

layers above the candles. Dusty leaned forward. His lean, scarred face reminded Shell of Mephistopheles. "How big is an *arroba?*" he asked in a hoarse voice.

"Two hundred and twelve pounds," said Frank calmly.

Dusty clapped a hard hand on the table. "Jesus God!" he said.

Father Eusebio hurriedly crossed himself. "The church items will be returned, in good faith, to the Church, of course."

Dusty flipped his cigarette butt into the fireplace. "Of course," he said. He grinned. "When do we start searching?"

"The moon will soon be gone," said Hernán. "It would be best to wait for daylight. The silver and gold do not have the legs. They cannot run away in fright from us."

Later, Shell lay in his room, hands locked behind his neck, staring up at the dim ceiling, blowing smoke rings up at it. He could not sleep. Here they were, as ill-assorted a bunch of adventurers as one might dream up, sitting on top of a fabulous fortune in silver and gold, and yet they could not leave the barranca. The Yaquis would wait. They had all the time and patience in the world.

Something moved near the open doorway. He raised his head. He sensed, rather than saw, who it was. "Rafaela?" he said.

She came quickly to him as he sat up. "I am afraid of this place, Shell," she said.

He drew her close to him. "It's only a legend," he said. "There is nothing to fear here."

She shook her head. "It isn't that," she said. "It's haunted by greed and by death. I feel it, Shell. I can't help it."

He slipped an arm about her slim waist. "Nothing will happen to you, Rafaela."

"It isn't me, Shell. It's you I'm thinking of. When Dusty and Hernán look at you I can see the greed and hate on their faces. Shell, don't ever turn your back on them!"

Something moved near the doorway. Shell placed his hand on the Colt lying on the small table beside the bed. He could see the dim outline of Victor. The dull sheen of a knife showed against the dark of his clothing. "Your watchdog, Rafaela," said Shell.

She turned her head. For a moment or two she looked at the Tarahumare. Shell could feel her heart beating against his chest. "Go, Victor," she said at last. "Get some sleep. I will be all right here with Shell. Go, I tell you!"

The Tarahumare hesitated. Slowly he sheathed the knife. They could hear his dragging footsteps as he walked away.

She looked at him in the darkness. "I am not afraid to be alone with you," she whispered.

"Are you sure?" he asked. "Perhaps it would be better for you to leave with Victor."

Her cool hands touched his flushed face. "I am not afraid, Shell. I want to be with you. I can't stand to be alone any longer."

He drew her back to him and dropped his head to the pillow, drawing her closer. There would be no going back now or ever. The wind whispered through the trees. The bell rang softly, just once, but neither of them heard it.

CHAPTER EIGHTEEN

T he steady ringing of the heavy bowie knives and the camp ax against the trees echoed from the towering barranca wall behind the church and mission buildings. A narrow path had been cut through the tangled growth of thorned brush and tough scrub trees that extended beyond the untended orange groves. Dusty, Hernán, Shell, and the padre had been at it since dawn. Nothing could force the *mozo* to come anywhere near the area. Perhaps he saw or felt something that they did not, but not even the threat of a bullet between the eyes from Dusty's cocked Colt had been able to move him. At last Shell had given him a rifle and told him to go hunting. The immense barranca abounded in deer and bear. The gobbling of wild turkeys had come to them on the dawn wind, and once during the night Shell had been aroused by what he thought was the screaming of a panther. But Rafaela had sleepily drawn him to her again. Shell wiped the dripping sweat from his face. He looked back toward the white buildings. She had gone before the dawn while he was still asleep.

Hernán again drove a stake into the ground they had so laboriously cleared and then stretched the knotted measuring-rope from it. He looked up at Shell. "Five hundred *varas* south of the east-west line of the church door," he said. "Two hundred to go."

Dusty leaned against a tree. He had stripped off his shirt and his corded body was wet with sweat. He looked up at the sky. "Damned near midday," he said.

"We've got plenty of time," said Shell.

The padre worked his way into the brush. *"Dulce Madre de Dios!"* he exclaimed. He reappeared holding something up in the air. "It is a *zurrón,"* he said excitedly. "A rawhide bag that was fastened to the head to carry ore from the mines!"

No further time was wasted. The bowies and the ax cut steadily into the brush and trees. The padre hauled the cut material back to a clearing. Another hundred *varas* and Hernán found another *zurrón*. Dusty stumbled over a rusted miner's pick. Then the way seemed easier. Shell realized that they were now cutting growth that had come up in the past hundred years in what had once been the road to the mines. They broke through at last into a wide cleared space in the shape of a great crescent. Towering above them was the barranca wall, and at the foot of it a great talus slope. There was no sign of a mine entrance.

Dusty slammed his bowie into a tree, then made a cigarette as his eyes darted up and down the slope and to either side. "Jesus God," he said. "There's tons and tons of rock there."

"It would take months to dig into that," said Hernán.

Father Eusebio nodded. "I will get Señor Frank," he said.

Dusty watched the padre vanish down the laboriously cut trail. He lighted his cigarette. "Seems to me the ol' padre is sure interested in worldly goods," he said. "I thought he had taken vows of poverty, chastity, and obedience."

Hernán laughed. "They're all alike," he said cynically. "The old Jesuits were smarter than any of them. The Indians believe that the mountains are the masters of all riches. They think they can bargain with a mountain for something the mountain is master of, but they cannot bargain with a stranger to show him that something. The Indians likely began to believe this after the Conquest. The Jesuits took advantage of this. When Christianizing the Indians, they taught them that if they showed precious metal to anybody but the representatives of God—the Jesuits themselves— that God would be wrathful and take vengeance." Hernán laughed. "The profane must not steal gold out of God's pocket. The fools believed the Jesuits."

The Franciscan reappeared leading Frank by the hand. Rapidly he explained the terrain to the blind man. There was a tense look on the blind man's face. "Look about on the rocks or trees," he said. "Look for strange markings. Anything!"

In twenty minutes Hernán raised a cry of triumph. "Here is a cross marked plainly on this rock!" he said exultantly. "What does it mean?"

Frank took his cigarette from his mouth. His hand trembled. "A cross can mean a number of things," he said. "Perhaps it means rich objects of the Church buried nearby. It might simply mean a Christian has passed this way."

"It is horizontal," said Hernán.

Frank's head snapped up. "Then the long part of the upright points toward the treasure!"

Four pairs of eyes swung quickly in the direction to which the upright pointed. It was a hopeless pile of tumbled rock, riven and shattered, thickly overgrown with thorny brush. Dusty led the way through the bright sunlight. In an hour Shell found another chiseled marking, partly obliterated by time. It was an arrow without heft inclining upward. Frank translated this into meaning that there would be other signs in the direction to which the arrow pointed.

There was no wind penetration of the jumble of rock and thorned growth. Sweat dripped from the four men as they worked their way through the tangle. It was midafternoon when Dusty stumbled over a rock and fell bellyflat atop another symbol carved into the flat rock upon which he had fallen. "The letter A!" he called out.

Frank was led to the spot by the padre. "It's a triangle," said the blind man. He raised his head, although he could not see. "Treasure is to be found within a triangle formed by trees or rocks."

"There are no trees," said Hernán. He looked at the piled-up masses of fallen rock and then up at the sheer barranca wall, golden-yellow in the sunlight. "Perhaps the rockfalls have covered everything."

Shell climbed atop a huge boulder. He scanned the area. Within a hundred yards to the east and to the west were boulders quite similar to the one upon which he stood. He was about to descend when he noticed part of a mark beneath a loose rock. He kicked the rock aside and saw yet another chiseled symbol. "There's a mark up here," he called down. "A triangle with a curved line projecting from the top."

Frank wiped the sweat from his face. "Wait a minute," he said. "Wait ... ah, I have it! The treasure deposit is around a bend or curve formed by the rocks or trees."

"No trees," said Shell. "We'll have to settle for the rocks."

They pushed their way through the tangle, hacking with their knives and the ax. It was the padre who stumbled into the deep arroyo that was not apparent until one was almost on top of it. He crashed down through the growths with a clattering of rock and a rising cloud of thin and bitter yellow dust. His muffled voice came up to them. *"Gracias a Dios!* There is a mark here, Señor Frank It is the numeral three, but it is backward. . ."

"Change direction," said the blind man.

"But there is no place to go!"

Shell slid down the slope. The concentrated heat of the windless arroyo nearly felled him. He saw the padre standing by the marked boulder. Beyond the padre was a thicket. Shell slashed into it. There was a natural passageway penetrating into the thicket of shattered rock and brush. "There's another mark here," he called out. "Like a U lying on its side."

"U hell!" said Frank excitedly. He laughed. "That's a *mule shoe!* It means that we're en route to the treasure! Keep on, Shell! Keep on!"

Shell led the way down the stifling passageway with the padre close behind him. The padre's brown robe was in sad shape, torn and dirty, seemingly held together by the rope girdle from which was suspended the cross. Shell had to hand it to the padre; he was as hard a worker as any of them. The others followed them, and once when Shell looked back at them, he saw Rafaela. There was no shame on her face for what had passed between her and Shell. There was almost a look of pride, perhaps of possessiveness. She was no *puta,* who'd leap into the feathers with any man. It had troubled Shell at first as to why she had come to him, and then the realization had entered his mind that she must feel that they'd never leave the barranca except by the last trail out for any living soul. That was why she had come to him. She was grasping at what little life and love were left to her. For that surely God could not and would not condemn her!

It was Hernán who found the rusted mule shoe. Dusty looked at Frank. "I thought yuh said the mules were shod with silver?" he said.

"Part of the legend, Dusty," said Frank.

Dusty hurled the rusted shoe into the rocks. "The loot better not be part of the legend," he said truculently.

Rafaela stood beside Shell. She raised her eyes to look at his lean, sweat-glistening face. "Look!" she said. She pointed to the rock face above the piled talus. Faintly seen, and likely not visible if the sun was at any other angle, was a carved sunburst.

"What is it?" said Frank eagerly.

"A sunburst, Señor Frank," said Padre Eusebio.

For a moment the blind man did not speak, and then

he smiled. "There are mines close by, my friends. Any symbol of the sun indicates the proximity of mineral wealth."

All eyes scanned the hopeless-looking tangle. Then the searchers plowed through the brush, stumbling over loose rock. Even as they searched, the sun moved on and the symbol seemed to fade away. Rafaela, by what seemed a miracle, had seen the sunburst at exactly the right time, during the few minutes the sun brought it out.

"Shadow writing," said Frank as he felt his way along the passageway. His blind face stared unseeingly up at the rock wall. "Only visible at the right time of day, perhaps even the month of the year. Look closely, my friends! It might be only a fraction of time!"

Shell wiped the sweat from his face and scanned the wall. Dusty ran a few feet along the passageway and stared at the wall. "Jesus! Oh Jesus!" he yelled. "I see somethin'! A bracket!"

"It means a tunnel is nearby!" cried Frank.

Padre Eusebio scrambled up on a rock. His robe split along the side, revealing his sweating flesh. He hurriedly drew it together and pinned it with a thorn. "There is something, my friends!" he said excitedly. "I am not sure. Yes! Yes! *Con el favor de Dios!* I see it!"

"Damn yuh!" roared Dusty. "Stop gibbering What *do* yuh see?"

The padre pointed. "Look there," he said. A mark showed clearly as the sun struck it. An arc with a dot beneath it. Even as they watched, it seemed to be fading back into the rock face. They all looked at Frank, who was shaping a cigarette with trembling hands. *"Treasure directly beneath this sign,"* he said. He closed his eyes. Sweat dripped from his face, and at last the trembling of his thin hands caused him to drop the tobacco and thin corn husk. Rafaela took the makings from Shell's shirt pocket and expertly fashioned a cigarette which she thrust into Frank's mouth and then lighted it.

"Look at it," said Dusty in disgust. "Tons of rock!"

Shell worked into a twisted offshoot of the main passage, with Rafaela close behind him. His bowie cut a way through the brush that choked the way. He broke into a comparatively clear area and looked up at the barranca wall. "Nothing," he said in disgust.

She touched his arm. "You are looking too high for your treasure."

He looked down at her. "You meant that *you* are truly my treasure?"

She stood on her toes and kissed him. "That is true, but I did not mean that, Shell. Look at that smooth-faced boulder behind you."

There was something cut into the surface, but it was partially covered by overhanging brush. Shell cut the tough stems of the brush to reveal another symbol. "Looks like a vertical mule shoe with three dots inside of it," he said. He could hear the others working their way into the clearing.

Frank Harley was led up to Shell by the padre. Frank took the cigarette from his mouth. "It means a flight of steps down into a mine or shaft, perhaps a cave," he said quietly.

"*Where,* damn yuh!" yelled Dusty. His harsh voice echoed loudly.

Frank looked toward him. "You loudmouthed jackass," he said pleasantly. "*You're likely standing right on top of it!*"

Dusty stared down at the hard earth beneath his feet, then dropped to his knees as though to tear at it with his big bare hands.

Shell looked about. "We'll need tools," he said. "We'll need the burros to help free the rocks that are piled here." He touched Frank on the shoulder. "You're sure of this, Frank?"

The blind man nodded. "I've kept my word. I've brought you to the place."

Dusty stood up and brushed his hands. "We ain't found any loot yet, mister," he said coldly.

Hernán rolled a cigarette. "It would be better to come back in daylight tomorrow," he said.

Dusty whirled on him. "Tonight!" he snapped. "There'll be enough light by the moon, *hombre!* We dig *tonight!*"

Hernán shrugged. "As you say, *amigo*."

They cleared more of the brush out of the way as they worked their way back to the passageway and then out of the deep arroyo. The sun was already gone and deep shadows filled the barranca. A cool wind blew through it. The church bell rang softly.

As they neared the mission they could smell roasting meat. Victor evidently had been successful in his hunt.

Padre Eusebio looked up at the dark towering walls. "A man could find anything he needed here," he said reflectively. "There is water and fruit. Bear, deer, and turkeys. There is fine shelter from the winter winds and the cold. Above all, there is peace, wherein a man can examine his soul."

Dusty laughed. He took the cigarette from his lips and ground it beneath a heel. "For *you,* Eusebio," he said. "But not for *us!* There's enough loot buried back there to make us kings in the outside world, eh, *amigos?*"

No one answered. Each of them had their own thoughts. Who was right? The padre or Dusty? *Quién sabe?*

CHAPTER NINETEEN

A drifting cloud of thin yellow dust hung in the deep arroyo. Ancient picks and spades tore at the loose rock near the boulder marked as the site of the shaft or tunnel. The bigger rocks were hauled off by the dusty burros and dumped to one side. There was no conversation as the four sweating men tried to rip their way into the tons of fallen rock behind the huge boulder. They had started to work by the light of sotol torches fashioned by Victor, but the *mozo* still would not come near the arroyo.

The moon was well up when at last Dusty's pick struck something that was not rock. He dropped the heavy pick and tore at the loose rock with his bare hands, heedless of the blood that dripped from the torn flesh. It was as though the man was possessed by a demon. The others stood back and let him work. To stand near him was to get struck by a flying rock. The rock clattered behind him until the moonlight shone on a heavy wooden door, well-strapped and studded with metal, which was set into a cleanly cut opening in the living rock. Dusty tried the door. The padres had not forgotten to lock it. Dusty snatched up the ax and slammed blow after blow near the thick bottom hinge until at last the blade broke through the door. It was a matter of minutes to hitch up the burros as a team. Meanwhile the ax broke through at the upper hinge and the door leaned outward a little. The ropes were made fast by Shell, and at a signal the burros were lashed by Hernán. The door sagged further and then fell with a resounding crash that echoed hollowly in the arroyo and then slammed back and forth between the canyon walls to die slowly away. Dusty leaped over the door to meet an onrush of bitter-smelling dust and something else that was mingled with it.

"Wait!" yelled Hernán. "The air might be poisonous!" Dusty waved a hand back at Hernán. "To hell with that!" he yelled. He disappeared into the darkness of the tunnel. His boots thudded on the rock floor. "Wait!" cried out Frank. "Don't go in!" Shell started forward. The smell sickened him. "Dusty, you damned fool!" he yelled. His voice sounded hollowly in the tunnel.

"Shell! Shell!" said Dusty. Something fell heavily within the tunnel. Shell ran in, his guts heaving at the stench, and he stumbled over Dusty. He gripped him under the arms and dragged him back, over the fallen door. The padre and Hernán hauled Dusty into the fresh air beyond the tunnel. Shell swayed as he walked. He got violently sick in the brush. The moon climbed higher as they waited. In an hour the air had cleared sufficiently enough to enter. Shell lighted a torch and walked in. Twenty feet from the entrance he stopped short. A skeleton sagged against a wall, the ghastly skull looking directly at him.

"The *patron!*" said Padre Eusebio. He quickly crossed himself.

Shell grinned. He looked back at Dusty. "Is that what scared you, *amigo?*" he said. "Get on!" snapped Dusty.

"Wait!" said Frank. Rafaela guided him to the three men. Frank sniffed the air. "Fresh enough," he said. "Watch for pitfalls, or traps of any kind. This has been a little too easy to suit me."

They lighted more torches and progressed slowly,

finding more crumpled *zurrones* mingled with rusted picks and spades. Shell eyed the walls, ceiling, and floor. There was no sign of any sort of trap.

"Stop!" said Padre Eusebio. "Look down, Shell!" The floor was studded with what looked like long dried shoots of some kind, with dark-colored thorny tips. Shell knelt and looked at them. The tips were as sharp as needles. He reached out a hand to touch one, and his hand was pulled back by Hernán. *"Madre de Dios!"* he said. "No! It is the maguey, tipped with poison. One prick from one of those and you die within the hour!"

The floor was studded with them for twenty feet. Hernán moved slowly along, burning the long dried plants with the flame from his sotol torch. The thick smoke drifted slowly from the tunnel past the coughing people. At last they could walk forward over the crackling and now harmless magueys. "Look here," said Hernán. To one side a dark tunnel slanted steeply down into the depths. The Mexican held his torch over the mouth of it. A heavy log had been placed in the hole, and it had been notched like a gigantic chicken ladder. The wood was as smooth as glass and the notches had been deeply worn. "For the miners," said Hernán. "They carried the heavy ore in *zurrones* up these ladders from great depths."

"Only God knows how many of them died in these noisome holes," said Padre Eusebio, "for the glory of the Spanish Crown."

Dusty spat down into the hole. "For the glory of the Jesuits, you mean." He laughed. "God goes out the window when you padres smell gold or silver. Ain't that so, Eusebio?"

The padre did not answer Dusty. "There is more to be searched," he said.

The tunnel twisted and turned and at times was partially blocked by rockfalls. The old miners had not tunneled on a straight line or cut in cross drifts, but had evidently gophered in, following the rich vein in its meanderings. In an hour they reached an impassable rockfall. Dusty cursed as he tore at the loose rock.

"What do you think, Frank?" said Shell. "The mine may be empty, Shell. They may have hidden the treasure elsewhere."

Hernán threw up his hands. "This is the end!" he said. "Mother of the Devil! It would take days to get through this, and to what end? Perhaps there is nothing after all."

"Have faith, my son," said the padre. "I urinate on my faith!" spat out the *capitán*. Frank raised his head. "There is still a draft in here," he said quietly. He placed his hand on the wall behind him and felt it. He struck it with his fist. Shell came beside the older man and worked his hands up and down on the solid wall. He stepped up on a rock and felt the cool draft work over his hands. Shell stepped back and raised his pick. He drove it hard at the wall. The sound seemed hollow. Again and again, he struck. There was a cracking noise. A piece of rock fell. The inner side had traces of mortar on it. Shell drove the pick once more. A large piece of the wall fell heavily. Rock clattered on the dusty floor. The pick smashed hard into the rock, and there was a grating and crashing as the wall fell outward toward Shell. He had just time to clear it by a wild jump, bumping against the padre and driving him down.

The dust swirled through the passageway, half blinding them and causing them to choke. "Drop flat!" yelled Shell. They dropped to the floor below the thickest of the dust. Dusty alone did not drop. He jumped over the prostrate body of Hernán and clambered over the rockfall. He held a torch in each hand. He hurled one ahead of him. Shell raised his head to see the torchlight reflect from something that glittered. He saw something else. A heavy vertical beam was moving slowly toward Dusty. "Get back!" yelled Shell hoarsely. Dusty jumped. The beam fell heavily exactly where Dusty had been standing. The crashing sound reverberated through the tunnel. As the beam was falling, Shell saw a triple row of murderous six-inch-long spikes protruding from it. If it had fallen on Dusty....

The thickest of dust drifted down the tunnel. Dusty lighted more torches. Shell, the padre, and Hernán crowded behind him as he walked into a large, squared-off room. "Jesus God!" said Dusty.

"By the nails of Christ!" said Hernán breathlessly. The padre crossed himself.

"Gracias a Dios!" he said. Shell was speechless. The rear wall of the room was completely concealed by the masses of material piled in front of it. Heavy wooden boxes, strapped with rust-scaled iron, were piled one atop the other. To one side was a pile of rawhide bags. One of them had split, and a pile of small silver ingots had fallen out onto the rock floor. There was a double tier of the wooden boxes in front of the back row, and atop them glittered a wealth of gold and silver objects.

"Look!" said the padre. He went to his knees even as he pointed out the ranked silver and gold vessels and other items of the church. There was, indeed, the baptismal font of carved cedar inlaid with silver. Two great silver candleholders were placed in front of six golden incensories. The torchlight shone brilliantly from the polished surfaces of three large communion plates. The display was dazzling.

Dusty strode forward and slammed his pick into one of the wooden chests. Half a dozen blows stove in the side, and a flow of small silver ingots fell to the floor in a tinkling cascade. Shell picked one up. It weighed about half a pound and was about four inches long, crudely cast. A cross was embossed on the surface as well as the name Carlos and the date 1766. He handed the ingot to Frank. Frank traced the embossing with his sensitive fingers. "Yes," he said, "Carlos the Third of Spain. It was he who in seventeen sixty-seven banished the Jesuits from all Spanish dominions."

Shell looked curiously at him. "But why would they mark the ingots with *his* name?"

Frank smiled. "They likely never intended for him to get his Royal Fifth, but if, by any chance, his officers *had* come into the barranca to check on the Jesuits, they would have showed them such ingots as evidence of their good intentions."

Dusty was smashing into other chests. Silver ingots clattered to the floor.

"Take it easy, Dusty!" said Shell. "It's all there!"

Dusty shot a wild glance at him. His face was so transfigured it was hard for Shell to recognize it. "I want to make sure those cheatin' bastards haven't cheated *us!*" he said.

"The chests can easily be opened," said the padre. He started back and stood behind Shell as Dusty moved toward him with the murderous point of the ancient pick aimed at his throat. For a moment, Dusty stared murderously at Shell, and then he slowly lowered the pick. He laughed, but there seemed to be no mirth in his eyes.

Shell slid an arm about Frank's thin shoulders. "You were as good as your word, Frank," he said.

The blind man shrugged. "It was you who got us here," he said.

Dusty turned quickly. "What about *me*, Harley?" he demanded.

"I meant that," said Frank. He smiled. "I meant all of you."

"There is plenty for all of us," said Hernán quickly. *"Madre mia!* I am rich! Rich beyond all my imaginings!"

"Yuh got no real right to any of this," said Dusty.

It was very quiet for a moment. An ingot slipped from the pile and clattered to the floor.

"But surely there is enough for all!" protested Hernán.

Dusty pointed a finger at Hernán. "We promised you nothin' but your life! Yuh want to lose *that* too, greaser?"

"Son of a whore!" yelled Hernán. He dropped his hand to his pistol. Dusty swung with the pick, but Shell drove it up with his right hand while he clamped a hand on Hernán's gun wrist. He slammed a shoulder against

Dusty, driving him back over the tumbled pile of ingots. Dusty fell heavily, striking his mouth against one of the chests. He dropped onto his side and rolled over, shaking his head. Shell pulled up on Hernán's wrist and twisted hard. The pistol clattered to the floor. A backhander drove the Mexican against the wall.

He reached back for his knife. "You dung in human form!" he said between clenched teeth.

Shell stepped back and drew swiftly, cocking the heavy Colt. "Listen," he said in a flat voice. "Listen, all of you! By God, we haven't even got the damned loot out of here and already you're fighting about who gets what! No one is taking his share until we vote on what he gets! No one leaves here unless we all leave together! Agreed?" He looked at Hernán.

Hernán slowly dropped his hand. He smiled. "I agree, *amigo.*"

"Dusty?"

Dusty raised his head. He wiped a thin trickle of blood from his mouth. He nodded, but his eyes were as hard and cold as sapphires.

"Frank?" said Shell.

The blind man shrugged. "I have felt that way all along," he said.

"Rafaela?"

She looked quickly at him. "Is not your share between us, *mi corazon?*"

"We share alike," said Shell.

Dusty stood up. "Great," he said dryly. "Two shares for the pair of you." He laughed. "Are you not *one* in soul, *compañero?*"

"Padre?" said Shell.

Father Eusebio nodded.

"What share does *he* get?" said Hernán quickly. "He has taken the vow of poverty."

The padre raised his head and looked at the glittering treasure. "Let my share be that of the sacred vessels of the Church," he said. "That and no more."

Dusty laughed. "Listen to *him!* Poverty, eh? He asks for a fortune in gold and silver."

"We'll discuss that later," said Shell. "Let's get the sacred vessels out of here."

"Wait," said Dusty dryly. He dabbled at the blood that leaked from his mouth. His hard eyes flicked at Shell. "Yuh forgot the *mozo, compañero.* Don't he get a share as long as *all* of us are in on it? It ain't hardly fair to leave *him* out. Then you and the woman can have *three* shares."

It was very quiet for a moment. Shell slowly lowered his Colt. He let down the hammer and then sheathed the revolver. "Sometimes you try me, *compañero,*" he said quietly. Their eyes locked, and the hatred that had begun to sprout between them grew just a little bit more. "Don't try me too far, Dusty," added Shell. "You're wearing me a little too thin."

Dusty smiled. He picked up the two great processional candlesticks. "Let's get this stuff up to the church," he said. "Maybe God will let us get past the Yaquis if we return this to the church."

The padre crossed himself, bent his head in prayer, then reverently picked up the exquisite baptismal font. Each of them took some of the sacred objects and carried them through the echoing tunnel to the outside. They breathed deeply of the fresh night air.

Shell looked back at the tunnel. "This is almost too easy," he said. "There must be a joker somewhere in the deck."

Hernán silently pointed to the northern rim of the barranca. A thread of smoke rose high in the moonlit sky. To the east and west it was the same. Shell looked over his shoulder at the towering southern rim. Something warned him. "Run!" he yelled. He gripped Rafaela and half-pulled and half-dragged her toward the passageway. Hernán passed him, running like a goat. The padre dropped the baptismal font and grabbed Frank to drag him behind a boulder. Dusty jumped to one side, looked up, cursed savagely, and leaped across a rock ledge. The huge rock struck just above the mouth of the tunnel, shattering into bits that hurtled through the moonlit air like canister shot. A fragment struck Hernán between the shoulder blades driving him face-downward against the harsh ground.

The echo thundered through the canyon and died away. Dust drifted through the quiet air. Shell looked up at the rim. There was nothing to see. Had the rock dropped by itself or had the Yaquis pushed it over the edge?

Hernán sat up and felt between his shoulder blades. "Body of God!" he said lugubriously. "No mule ever kicked me *that* hard."

They walked back to where the sacred objects had been dropped. No one spoke. The baptismal font had been ruthlessly shattered. Several of the golden incensories had been dented. One of the large golden communion plates had bent almost double by the blow of a large rock fragment. The solid silver shrine had been damaged by being dropped to the hard ground.

Hernán wet his lips. He looked up at the barranca rim. "God in Heaven," he said, "this is an omen! We are cursed!"

Padre Eusebio went down on his knees and reverently touched the damaged articles. He bowed his head and prayed.

"A lot of superstitious crap!" said Dusty. They gathered up the sacred objects and carried them from the arroyo to the mission. The moon was almost gone. Faintly seen along the barranca rim, near the top of the only known trail down into and *out* of the barranca, the glow of a fire was seen, while the thin smoke rose straight up into the darkening night.

CHAPTER TWENTY

Weeks had passed during which the days were a medley of sweat, labor, and tension. Hour after hour they hauled the heavy chests from the mine and loaded them onto the patient burros. One of the burros almost died from exhaustion, and despite the protests of Dusty and Hernán, Shell turned the weakened little beast loose in the hopes that it would recover. The very night it was turned loose they heard the eerie screaming of a mountain lion, and the next day Victor found the horribly mangled remains of the burro. Somehow or other—it was impossible to figure out how—a zopilote appeared, the first one they had seen anywhere near the barranca, and by noon of that day, the pitiful little bones were already bleaching in the sun.

They stored the chests within a windowless room of the mission. There was no reason to guard it. The Yaquis would not come down into the barranca, but even if they had come down, they would not have bothered with the gold and silver. Padre Eusebio saw to it that the sacred objects were placed in the dusty, echoing church, and then patiently began to piece together the baptismal font. To replace the objects and see to it that they at least were partially repaired became almost an obsession with the Franciscan.

Only the *mozo* Victor and Frank Harley did not work to take the treasure from the mine. When the *mozo* was not hunting, as he usually did every day, he would sit with Frank, and in time, although the *mozo* could not speak, there seemed to be a communion between the two of them. Frank would talk in his quiet voice, telling the *mozo* of the wonders of the world, of history and philosophy, of science, and of religion. It must have been to Victor more like a fanciful tale than the truth, but even so, he seemed content. The treasure meant nothing to him. Now and then his dark eyes would raise to the barranca rim. He knew what the Yaquis would do to him if they caught him. The loss of his tongue would be as nothing compared to what they would do to him.

Once the treasure was secure in the mission, Shell saddled one of the horses and explored the huge chasm. The place was self-contained. An inexhaustible source of water flowed from one end to the other, appearing from beneath the barranca wall and flowing under the opposite wall. Deer, bear, and turkeys abounded and there were many birds. The orange trees bore heavily and there was grass in abundance for the horses and the lone burro. There was, indeed, just about everything a man could wish, except for a safe way out to the rest of the world. As long as the Yaquis held the top of the trail, there was no possible way to escape from La Barranca Escondida.

It was not uncomfortable. The mission was well built and roomy. There was plenty of firewood for the many fireplaces, and there was a plentiful supply of bedding and other articles stored within the mission.

"It is almost as though they fully intended to come back, Shell," Rafaela said one evening as she worked in the kitchen.

Shell rolled a cigarette and lighted it. "They likely did," he said. "They certainly didn't plan to leave their treasure for people like us. Somehow, they must have believed they would be allowed to come back. Frank says the Tarahumares, Opatas, and Yaquis firmly believe they will come back. That is why they still guard this country."

She nodded. "They knew no one could take the silver and gold from here without a great deal of trouble." She laughed. "I would have been content with the little cut-stone box of jewels."

Shell slowly took the cigarette from his mouth. He had no recollection of seeing such a box. It certainly wasn't in the church or in the mission storeroom. "Did you see the box?" he said.

She looked quickly at him. "Yes. It was behind the silver shrine. I distinctly saw it. Why do you ask?"

Shell rubbed his beard. He looked toward the open door. "I don't remember seeing it in the mine or on the way here," he said. "Nor is it here, Rafaela."

"But I saw it, Shell!"

He placed a finger to his lips. "I believe you," he said softly. "But whoever took it from the mine didn't place it with the rest of the treasure or in the church."

She looked toward the door. "Padre Eusebio?" she said.

Shell nodded. "He evidently thinks they were part of the church property. Dusty would kill him if he found out."

"You had better warn the padre," she said.

Shell nodded. He kissed her and left the kitchen. The moon was not up as yet. There was no sign of the others. He walked softly across to the church. It was where the padre spent most of his time now that the beloved sacred objects had been replaced in the church. The front door was closed. Shell eased it open and looked back across his shoulder. No one was in sight. Dusty and Hernán had begun to spend a great deal of time together. Hernán had rooted out some ancient bottles of brandy from one of the outbuildings, and they would suffice until his thirst grew again and he'd have to find more. Shell softly closed the door behind him. He glanced into the baptistry as he walked up the nave toward the sanctuary. The magnificent ornaments and sacred objects had been placed in the church by the padre after he had done his best to repair them. A candle guttered in a red glass on the altar, and several other candles flickered and guttered in the draft. There was no sign of the padre.

Shell walked to the altar and looked up at the figure of the Madonna and the saint. He was not a Catholic. In fact, he had no religion, but something made him remove his hat and put out his cigarette. Where was that blasted padre? He walked into the dim sacristy. A candle had burned almost to nothingness in a dish. The light flickered, forming grotesque shadows on the stained walls.

Shell crossed the sacristy. Beyond it was a row of rooms, formerly used as storage places and workshops in the ancient days. Here it was that Padre Eusebio stayed, rather than in the mission. He had become silent and withdrawn since the treasure had been discovered and brought out of the mine. A chink of light showed between the heavy shutter of one of the smaller buildings. Shell looked about It was very quiet. No one was within sight or hearing. Metal struck against wood within the building. Shell tried the door but it was barred from within. He peered in through the chink but could see nothing. He walked to the rear of the building and tried one of the shutters. It swung open easily. He thrust a long leg into the room and closed the shutter behind him. He walked into the main room. His boots grated on the dirty floor. The padre was bent over something on his cot, hammering steadily. He had stripped to the waist, and across bis muscular, bare back were healed welts, many of them, crossing and recrossing each other. Shell narrowed his eyes.

Those welts had been administered with the full force of the lash. Those were more than penitential stripes. He moved closer and accidentally kicked aside a tin cup that lay on the floor. The padre whirled. His eyes narrowed as he saw Shell. He snatched up a long-bladed knife and crouched a little as he came toward Shell. His face had utterly changed. As he moved, Shell saw something else. There was a letter branded on his left shoulder. The letter M. Deeply burned into the flesh so that it could never be eradicated. He knew well enough what that was. He had seen such brands before on Mexican prisoners. *M stood for murderer.*

The candlelight glittered from a pile of jewels that lay on the coarse bedding of the cot, and beside them was the small cut-stone box, and beyond that was the heavy wooden cross always carried at the Franciscan's belt. A hole had been bored into the upright of the cross.

Shell dropped his hand to draw his Colt and then realized he had left his gun belt in the mission kitchen.

Padre Eusebio, if he was *Padre* Eusebio, hefted the knife. "I can have this in your throat or belly before you can pull a stingy gun on me," he said in a low, threatening voice. "Keep quiet!" he warned.

"What's the game, padre?" said Shell quietly.

"Padre?" The man laughed. "I carried it off pretty well, but I didn't think I'd keep on getting away with it."

"An escaped criminal, a murderer," said Shell. "Is that it?"

Eusebio nodded. "I would have made my way to Mazatlán if it hadn't been for the Yaquis. I was in a bad way when I ran into you. I could hardly resist keeping on with the Franciscan role once you accepted me as such."

"You did very well," said Shell dryly.

Eusebio smiled, revealing his fine white teeth. "As a boy I served at the altar. My father was sacristan of the church. I wanted to be an actor and ran away from home." He shrugged. "As you see, other things came up. Thanks to the revolution I managed to escape. It was easy to don the robe. Who would suspect a humble Franciscan of being an escaped murderer?"

"Who indeed, padre?" murmured Shell. "And now what?"

Eusebio gestured toward the cot. "The jewels are

enough for me. I planned to secrete them in the cross. Now you have found out." His voice died away. He smiled apologetically. "I had grown to admire and like you, *amigo*."

"And now you must kill me," said Shell.

"That is so," said the Mexican.

"And when the others find I am gone?"

Eusebio laughed. "You think that drunken officer would care? You mean nothing to Victor."

"There is my *compañero*," said Shell.

Eusebio laughed again. "Him? Even now he and Galeras are plotting to take everything for themselves. I have overheard them. They would leave the *mozo* and the blind man here. They would kill you and me. The woman?" Eusebio shrugged. "She would be shared between them until such time as they found their way out of these accursed mountains with a fortune in treasure."

"If they don't kill each other," said Shell.

Eusebio tested the edge of his knife against his thumb. "Exactly," he said. "I am not an unkind man. It will be swift, *amigo*."

Shell shook his head. "You'd never get away with it. Besides, what will happen to you? As a supposed man of God you might give them away to the authorities. They'd never let you live to get out of these mountains, Eusebio."

The Mexican narrowed his eyes. "So?"

"Keep the jewels in the cross. I'll keep my mouth shut. The others need never know you are a fake."

"You want me to side with you, eh?"

Shell looked down at the glittering knife. "For a while, at least. I'm not sure you can be trusted."

"That is mutual, my friend." Eusebio smiled. "But then we have no choice, do we?"

"Put on that robe. I would have never known about you if you hadn't taken it off. You could have killed me easily if you had kept up the act, *amigo*."

Voices sounded outside of the building. Eusebio hastily pulled on his robe. He scooped up the jewels and dropped them into the cut-stone box. "Take the bar off the door," he said over his shoulder. When Shell turned from removing the bar, the cut-stone box had vanished. The heavy cross hung from the rope belt. The padre smiled and made the sign of blessing to Shell. It was amazing how the man could take on the role of the humble Franciscan.

"Shell! Shell! Where the hell are yuh?" yelled Dusty.

Shell opened the door. "In here," he said dryly. "Making a confession."

Hernán laughed. His dark eyes scanned the room. "It might be good for me as well."

Dusty looked quickly about the room. "What's going on here?"

Shell leaned against the wall and shaped a cigarette. "We were discussing the prospect of getting out of here," he said.

"That's why we came to see yuh. We'd better have a council of war. The sooner we make a break out of the barranca the better."

"Hopeless," said Shell. "You can't get up that trail."

Dusty grinned. "The *mozo* found another way."

Shell shrugged. "That's more than I could do. Let's go."

They met in the big room within the mission. A fire crackled on the hearth against the chill of the evening. Frank Harley sat in a chair beside the fire with Rafaela standing beside him, while Victor sat at his feet.

Dusty had the floor. Heretofore, whether he liked it or not, he had let Shell do the leading. But now, with the treasure in their hands, and the world waiting for it to be dispensed by Dusty, he had taken over the leadership. "The *mozo* can show us the way," he said. "We can take enough of the silver or gold with us to keep us in style for a long time. When we can arrange an expedition, we can come back here and get the rest of it."

"How much do you figure on taking out?" said Shell.

"We can load the extra horses and the burro. I'd say an *arroba* apiece for them, and we can carry more with us."

"Too much," said Shell. "If the Yaquis chase us, provided we can get clear of them at the barranca top, you'd never get away loaded down like that."

"It's a chance we've got to take," said Hernán.

Shell looked at Frank. "What about him and Rafaela?"

Frank raised his head. "Forget about me," he said. "I'm staying here."

"We might not get back to the barranca," said Shell. "You know the odds, Frank."

"I'll take that chance," said the blind man.

"You loco?" said Dusty. "Yuh got the wealth of Mexico in your hands!"

Frank turned toward the fire. "Somehow," he said quietly, "it just doesn't matter anymore. A man could find a worse place to live out his life. Besides, I'd only hold you back. No, I am not going with you."

"You can't stay here alone, blind as you are," said Shell.

"I will not be alone," said Frank.

Shell looked quickly at Rafaela. She shook her lovely head. "It is Victor," she said. "He will lead us out of the barranca and then return. It is what he wants, Shell."

"Supposing he doesn't return?" said Shell.

Frank raised his head. "He will return, if he can. If not, there is food for a long time. At that, I'll probably live longer down here than you will up there."

It was very quiet after his words. A log snapped in the fireplace. Dusty lighted a cigarette and eyed Shell.

"Why don't you stay with me, Shell?" said Frank.

Dusty laughed. "With the main part of the loot still here? No chance, Frank. Shell goes with us. We need every gun we can get."

"And if I decide not to?" said Shell.

There was no answer, but the intent was plain enough on the faces of Dusty and Hernán.

"When do we leave?" said Shell.

"Tonight," said Dusty. "The moon will give us light. We've got enough time to reach the top of the barranca and be well on our way by dawn."

Shell felt for the makings. He began to fashion a cigarette. He looked at Rafaela. "And you?" he said.

"I go with you, Shell."

"Very touching," said Dusty. He grinned. "If Shell doesn't make it, lady, you'll still have ol' Dusty here."

She looked at him. *"Bazofia!"* she said with all the venom she could muster. "I'd kill myself first."

Hernán spat into the fireplace. "The Yaquis might take care of that for you," he said. He grinned evilly. "After they have had their pleasure of you, of course, *querida.*"

"We're wasting time," said Shell. "Hernán, Dusty, get the loot ready." He walked from the room. He had no choice. The padre trotted after him and stopped him near the corral. "What do you think?" he said.

Shell shrugged. "If we ever mean to get out of here we'll have to do it before the winter comes on."

"And the Yaquis?"

Shell looked up at the barranca rim. "They'll be waiting, padre. *They'll always be waiting.*"

Eusebio plucked the makings from Shell's pocket and expertly fashioned a cigarette. Shell grinned as he lighted the cigarette. Eusebio drew the smoke in deeply. *"Madre de Dios!"* he said. "I needed that!"

"You don't seem enthusiastic about leaving, padre."

The Mexican shook his head. He looked down at the heavy cross. "Within the holy cross I have a fortune. Enough to take me anywhere I wish to go. But, *amigo,* it cannot take me away from my conscience."

"A conscience is not a good thing for a thief and a murderer."

Eusebio waved his cigarette. "That is so." He looked about. "I like it here," he said simply. "I have acted the part of a padre for so long I am accustomed to it. Perhaps, when I escape from this great natural prison, I could turn over the jewels to the Church and take holy orders, eh, my friend?"

Shell touched the Mexican's branded shoulder. "With *that* on your hide? And the stripes on your back? No, Eusebio."

The Mexican nodded. The weight of his crimes and his conscience weighed heavily upon him. He looked up at the barranca rim. "I will go with you," he said quietly. He looked at Shell. "Perhaps I can help you to escape."

"And then?"

Eusebio held out his hands, palms upward. "Señor Frank is right. If Victor dies, the blind man will need help. I realize now there is no place in the outside world for me. Here I will have peace and the care of the old church. I do not need a woman. They mean nothing to me. To live outside of Mexico would be too hard to bear. Here, at least, deep in this forgotten barranca, I will live in Sweet Mother Mexico."

"You don't have to go with us, Eusebio," said Shell.

The Mexican raised his head. "It is my duty to help you," he said quietly. "Say no more about it."

"And the jewels?" said Shell quietly.

Eusebio looked down at the belted cross. "They will be of no value to me here. If anything happens to me, take the cross with my blessing."

Shell did not speak. There was an irony in the words of the criminal turned pseudo-padre. Shell walked to the corral and began saddling the horses they would need. Now that Eusebio did not intend to escape with them, they would have another horse to load with the treasure, but Shell decided not to say anything about it. They might desperately need an unloaded horse with which to aid their escape. Shell had no illusions. All the gold and silver in La Barranca Escondida could not pay their way past those vengeful and grim-faced Yaquis, but a fast horse might save someone's life.

Hernán and Dusty dragged out the heavy cowhide bags that had been packed in the wooden chests. They were lashed onto the spare horses and the patient burro. The moon began to rise as they finished. They led the animals into the shelter of the trees and got their gear. Each rifle and pistol was checked and rechecked. Anything that would make a noise was either discarded or silenced by being wrapped in rags.

Shell and Rafaela said good-by to Frank and left him alone in the great room of the mission. Shell had looked back at the calm and patient face of the man who had spent twenty years of his life dreaming about La Barranca Escondida, prowling through the back country of Mexico gathering bits of information here and there. He had haunted the old missions and churches to read the dusty, crackling records of the Jesuits, until at last, no man knew better than he where La Barranca Escondida was hidden. But, when he had reached his dream, it no longer seemed to matter to him. Of what use was the fabulous wealth to a blind man who had committed himself to life imprisonment in the great barranca? Strange thoughts raced through Shell's mind as he walked with Rafaela to meet the others. The barranca had cast a spell upon Frank Harley and the *mozo* and Eusebio as well. None of them wanted to leave.

CHAPTER TWENTY-ONE

The silent *mozo* had led them through the thick orange groves and then through a bosque that grew from the edge of the stream, right where it vanished beneath the forbidding western wall of the barranca. He followed the barranca wall within the shelter of the trees and pushed his way through a thicket of brush to stop before a place where great shards of rock hung against the wall, seemingly ready to drop at the sound of an echo. Victor pointed toward the rock wall illuminated by the moonlight.

"He's loco," said Dusty. "There ain't no trail there."

The *mozo* walked ahead and seemed to vanish into the solid rock. Shell walked after him and then saw what appeared to be a darker line against the pale yellowish rock. A draft played about his face. Victor stood above him, perhaps twenty feet, looking up the narrow, precipitous cleft that seemed to sheer deep into the barranca wall. There was just about enough room for the laden horses to pass through. Victor looked down at Shell and motioned him to come on.

Shell went back to get his horse. He fastened the lead rope from a loaded horse to the saddle of his own mount and then led it up the steep passageway, followed by

Rafaela who led her horse. "Padre" Eusebio led his horse and the burro. Behind him came Hernán and Dusty, each leading his riding horse and one of the laden horses. Dust arose from the crumbling rock as they pushed their way up the narrow, twisting slot. If the Yaquis heard them, they could fill that trail with tons of rock, sealing the whole party, their animals, and a fortune in treasure forever from the sight of man.

Now and then a shaft of pale moonlight struck into the cleft when the angle of it was right, but most of the time they felt their way up in the dimness. Now and then a loose rock would slither and clatter down the cleft, and the progress would be halted while every ear strained to hear any alien sound from above. It seemed to Shell that they'd never reach the top. The horses were blowing heavily. If one of them slipped and broke a leg they'd never get the others past him.

Victor turned a shoulder of rock, and as Shell came up behind him, dripping sweat despite the coolness of the night and the steady draft down the cleft, he saw that the *mozo* had stopped. There was no telling how far they were from the top of the cleft, but Victor held a hand to his mouth and pointed upward. It was close, then.

Shell withdrew his Spencer from its sheath and carried it in his left hand as he pulled on the reins of his horse. The sorrel's eyes were wide in his head and Shell could swear that the harsh sound of his breathing and blowing would carry for hundreds of yards.

Victor stopped again. Shell worked his way up behind him. Just beyond the *mozo* was the top of the cleft, shrouded with thorned brush. Victor motioned Shell on. Together they bellied up the cruel rock surface and lay flat in the brush. There was plenty of moonlight now. The *mozo* vanished silently into the brush without stirring any of it. He was like a snake.

Shell lay flat, cuddling his Spencer, wetting his dry lips and wishing to God his heart would stop pounding so that he could hear better.

Victor came back as silently as he had vanished. He nodded to Shell. Shell brought up his horse and the lead horse. The brush was thick enough to conceal them. One by one the others reached the top of the trail and halted for a breather. Shell padded after Victor. Beyond the brush there was a naked, saw-edged ridge of rock that ran east-west, paralleling the edge of the barranca. Victor pointed to the west. There was a notch in the ridge. He held Shell by the shoulder and indicated the notch. That was evidently the way.

Shell went back for the others. He felt as though he was leading them into a deadly trap, but there was no going back now. If the Yaquis spotted them, they'd never let the *yori* escape down that deathtrap of a cleft. Victor led the way to the base of the notch. He looked at Shell and then at Rafaela, as though to say goodbye. He walked past them. Dusty casually raised his pistol and placed the muzzle against the *mozo's* broad chest. "Yuh ain't goin' anywhere," he said. "Don't play dumb. Yuh understand me, all right."

"But he must go back!" said Rafaela. "Frank depends on him!"

Dusty looked at her. "To hell with Frank," he said thinly. "We need every man we can get, and this clod can help us. He knows this country. He knows the water-holes. It's us or Frank, and right now Frank is strictly on his own."

"You're pronouncing a death sentence on him, my son," said the padre.

Dusty laughed. "Listen to him," he said.

"I will go back," said the padre.

The pistol swung to cover him. "I said we need every man we can get, Eusebio, and that even includes *you*," said Dusty. His eyes flicked at Shell. "Don't get noble, *compañero*," he added.

Victor led the way up through the echoing notch. Shell looked back as they reached the crest of the ridge. Far across the great void of the barranca he saw a faint glow of fire. To his left, a quarter of a mile beyond the notch, he was almost sure he could see a faint light as well. Perhaps Victor had truly found the way.

The moon was almost gone when they passed beyond the western end of the ridge. The way was clear enough. The ground was as hard and clear as pavement. The muffled hoofbeats echoed faintly. When the moon at "last was gone they could not continue because of the dense, velvety blackness that surrounded them; but they must be well clear of the barranca. They halted in a great bowl of rock. Shell stood first guard. He looked back through the darkness. Frank's words came back to him on the faint night breeze. *"He will return, if he can. If not, there is food here for a long time. At that, I'll probably live longer down here than you will up there."*

There was little sleep for Shell that night. Rafaela lay close to him for warmth, but there was no comfort in it for Shell. The thought of what might possibly happen to her if the Yaquis found them was too sickening to consider. At last he fell asleep with her snuggled up against him, and his last thought was of the first time she had come to him that night in the mission when she had been afraid. *"I am not afraid now, Shell,"* she said. *"I want to be with you. I can't stand to be alone any longer."*

A hard hand gripped Shell by the shoulder and another hard hand was clamped over his mouth. He awoke with a wild start to look up into the shadowy bearded face of Dusty. "That sonofabitch Galeras pulled out when he was on guard," said Dusty. "Took two of the loaded horses with him. Come on! He can't get far!"

"Let him have the damned stuff," said Shell. "There's still more than enough for us."

"Come on, damn you!" Dusty's voice sounded like that of a stranger.

Shell got up and picked up his Spencer. Rafaela had awakened and stood up. She clung to him. "Don't go with him," she said. "I am afraid!"

"He hasn't gone far," said Eusebio from the darkness at the lip of the bowl.

"That damned *mozo* here?" said Dusty.

"Yes," said the padre. "He will not leave Rafaela."

They climbed up to the lip of the bowl. "Stay here," said Shell to Eusebio. "Dusty and I will go after Hernán."

It was almost dawn. The faintest of gray light showed in the eastern sky. Shell thanked God that they had managed to get away from the barranca before daylight. The Yaquis would still be there looking down into the barranca, where a blind man sat all alone, patiently waiting for a tongueless Tarahumare to return.

Dusty trotted along with his carbine at the trail. "I'll kill that Mex sonofabitch," he'd say every now and then.

Shell was higher on the slope than Dusty. "There he is," he said. He could see the Mexican riding one of the horses and leading the other two. Dusty sprinted ahead. The Mexican did not see the two Americans closing in on him until Dusty was within fifty feet of the last horse. Hernán ripped his Henry rifle from its sheath. Dusty darted to one side and raised his Spencer for a lolling shot. As he did so he tripped heavily and went down on his hands and knees, dropping the Spencer, butt first. The Spencer reacted with its main weakness. Nestled in the butt stock were six rounds of .56.50, bullet-tip to primer, with spring tension holding them against each other. As Dusty fell, the buttplate struck the hard ground and the shock set off one of the cartridges. There was a shattering explosion as the other five rounds let go, splintering the stock. A shard of wood struck Dusty on the left cheek, and the spurt of blood blinded him. Hernán grinned. He swung the Henry rifle to fire on the helpless American.

Shell fired through the swirling smoke raised by the explosion of the Spencer. Hernán set spurs to his horse. The horse reared and plunged and tried to run, but Hernán hung onto the lead rope of the pack horses. Shell could hardly see the Mexican through the swirling smoke. Hernán aimed at Dusty again but Shell fired first. Hernán shook spasmodically. He dragged on the lead rope, and the first pack horse plunged sideways as the rope cut his mouth. Hernán was dragged from the saddle. He dropped heavily and tried to raise his repeater, but Shell fired first again. The Mexican jerked as the heavy slug ripped into his chest. His head dropped and he lay still.

Shell walked slowly through the rifted smoke. The crashing explosion of the Spencer and the other shooting could have been heard a long way off. Dusty got to his feet and wiped the blood from his face. "The sonofabitch," he said. He grinned. "He could have got away easily enough if he had let go of that lead rope."

Shell nodded. He picked up Hernán's Henry rifle and handed it to Dusty. He hooked a boot toe under the dead man and rolled him over. He unbuckled the cartridge belt and handed it to Dusty. "You'll need this," he said.

"Get the horses," said Dusty.

"To hell with the horses!" said Shell. "The Yaquis are sure to have heard that shooting. I'm going back for Rafaela."

Dusty spat. He looked at the loaded horses. "A load apiece," he said in disgust, "and you want to go back for a filly who can be bought for a handful of pesos."

Shell turned. "I ought to kill you for that," he said coldly.

Dusty spat again. "Go get her," he said. "I should'a knowed better."

Shell loaded several fresh rounds into the butt plate opening of the Spencer to replace those he had expended. He started back to where the others waited.

"Shell!" said Dusty.

Shell turned and looked at his *compañero*. "Yes?" he said.

Dusty grinned. "Thanks for just savin' my life, *amigo*."

"*De nada*," said Shell. He resumed his swift walking. He heard Dusty laughing to himself.

Eusebio waved him on. "We heard the shooting," he called. "Where are the others?"

"Hernán is dead. Dusty is with the horses. Have you seen any Yaquis?"

"Not as yet. Perhaps we are too far from the barranca."

"Let's hope so," said Shell fervently.

They mounted and led the pack horses and the burro to where Dusty waited for them. Dusty spurred Hernán's horse and dragged on the lead rope of the pack horses, riding into a broken-up area of shattered rock stippled heavily with brush. "Come on, gawddammit!" he yelled.

They could see no Yaquis, but the very thought of those predatory bronze humans was enough to spur them on. Victor trotted on foot beside Rafaela's horse. "Is this the right way?" asked Shell. The *mozo* nodded.

The sky was much lighter now. Every now and then one or the other of them would look back over his shoulder, half expecting to see those fearsome humans in pursuit. The packs bounced about on the backs of the horses and the burro. One of them broke loose and fell, scattering silver ingots on the ground. "Forget it!" said Shell. "It isn't worth our lives!"

The sky was lightening rapidly. Dusty suddenly reined in his horse. "Jesus God!" he yelled. "This can't be the way! I can see the barranca!"

Shell's blood ran cold. He spurred his horse and rode up behind Dusty. Sure enough, the western end of the barranca was ahead of them.

"It's that damned *mozo!*" yelled Dusty. He looked wild-eyed at Rafaela. "You put him up to this!" He swung down from his horse and ran toward the edge of the barranca. He looked back at Shell. "There's still time for me and you to get out of here, *compañero!* What do you say?"

Shell shook his head. He slid from his horse. They could not go back the way they had come. There was only one way to go, and that was west, and they had already lost too much precious time.

"It's that damned woman!" yelled Dusty.

Shell whirled. "Damn you! Enough!" he spat out. He dropped his hand to his Colt. Shell had always been fast on the draw, as fast or perhaps faster than Dusty, or so he always thought, but Dusty's gun seemed to leap into his hand. Just as it cracked, Victor's knife hurtled end over end through the air and struck deeply into Dusty's corded neck. The Colt slung whipped past Shell's face. Dusty staggered, dropping the smoking pistol. He reached up to grip the knife. He looked at Shell with staring eyes.

"Compañero! Compañero! Help me!" he said pitifully. He walked unseeingly toward the brink of the barranca.

"Dusty!" yelled Shell.

Dusty did not turn. He hesitated for a moment at the very lip of the barranca. "Done in by a damned Indian," he grunted. A spate of thick blood poured from his slack mouth. He stepped off the rim and fell end over end. They did not hear his body strike far below.

"We must run!" said Eusebio. "There is no time to save the treasure! Look!"

Shadowy figures were moving in swiftly on foot. There was no question about who *they* were.

"Too late," said Shell. He raised his Spencer.

Eusebio looked back at Shell. "You can't hold them off, *amigo,"* he said. "Let me try and stop them. They might be Christians."

"Don't take a chance!" said Shell.

Eusebio turned. "Once they listened to the robed men of this country," he said quietly. "Perhaps they have not forgotten."

"No!" said Rafaela.

Eusebio did not seem to hear her. He walked toward the approaching Yaquis. He held up his heavy wooden cross. "My children," he called out in Spanish. "Stop! Listen to me!"

It was very quiet as the pseudo-padre walked toward the Yaquis. The sun was tipping the giant peaks of the eastern ranges and flooding down onto the western slopes.

"They'll kill him!" said Rafaela.

"Perhaps not," said Shell. "There was a time, as the padre said, when they would listen to the robed men."

Victor pointed urgently to the very edge of the barranca.

"What does he want?" said Shell.

"He wants us to take advantage of what little time we have," she said.

Shell looked at Eusebio. "I can't leave him," he said.

"We can't hold them off here!" said Rafaela. "Shell, we need every second we can get!"

"I can't desert him," said Shell.

The Yaquis had halted. They stood there motionless, watching Eusebio as he approached them, holding high his cross and making the sign of blessing toward them. It was very quiet. Victor took Rafaela by the arm and led her to the very lip of the barranca. "Shell!" she cried.

"Go on," he said. He slowly raised his Spencer. The wind shifted and blew the padre's ragged robe about his bare legs.

"Shell!" she screamed hysterically. "Don't waste time!"

"Go on, dammit!" he snapped.

Victor pulled her to the very edge of the barranca and lowered her to a ledge. The last thing Shell saw was her great agonized eyes looking at him.

Eusebio halted twenty feet from the silent Yaquis. Shell could hear him speaking, but the words were not distinguishable. The pseudo-padre moved closer to the Yaquis. A burly-chested buck walked forward to meet him. Eusebio spoke to him. For a moment they stood there facing each other like figures in a tableau. The Yaqui's hand suddenly dropped to his knife. The heavy blade whipped up, glittering in the sun. The wooden cross was cleanly severed, scattering jewels about like brilliant droplets of colored liquid. Eusebio did not move. The blade swept up and then down, driving deeply into the Mexican's flesh. Blood flew as brightly as the scattered jewels. There was no sound from the pseudo-padre as he went down on his knees. The rest of the Yaquis moved in with unsheathed knives.

Shell wasted no more time. Eusebio was far beyond any mortal help. Shell sprinted to the edge of the barranca. For a moment he sickened as he looked down into that vast void. He saw Victor's brown face below him. Shell sat down and dropped his legs over the edge. Strong hands gripped his thighs, and Victor guided Shell down to a narrow ledge.

Victor led the way, at times with his face close to the wall and his outstretched hands digging into hardly discernible crevices, while his moccasined heels protruded over the edge. Shell had to follow him. It was that or face the Yaquis, and it would be better to fall cleanly to his death than to face their bloody knives.

Rafaela crouched beneath a rock overhang a quarter of the way down the face of the barranca wall. Shell drew her into his arms. A rock fell past them, a foot or so away. One after another, rocks fell, some of them rebounding from protuberances of the wall to soar out into the bright sunlight and then drop far, far below. The low thunder of their striking echoed from one side of the great barranca to the other. After a time, the rocks stopped falling. There was a pause, and then something else dropped. The headless body of Eusebio turned end over end as it fell.

"He saved our lives," said Rafaela. She crossed herself. "He was indeed a true son of the Church."

Shell nodded. There was no need to tell her about Eusebio. Whatever else he had been in his life, he had redeemed himself at the very end. *Greater love hath no man....*

Victor guided them until at last they reached the cleft by which they had ascended the barranca wall the night before. They had just reached the bottom when the first rock fell. Rock after rock crashed down into the cleft. Overhanging masses of loosened rock poured down into the cleft until it was completely impassable.

They walked through the woods in the dappled sunlight. The clear waters of the stream glinted sharply. Somewhere in the shadows turkeys gobbled. A deer bounded out of sight. A bear waddled slowly away. Victor trotted ahead to the mission and to Frank Harley.

Shell looked up at the barranca rim. "There is no way out of here now," he said. "Perhaps never, Rafaela."

She rested her head against his shoulder and then looked up into his face. "We came looking for treasure," she said. "Have we not found it in each other?"

"Yes," he said. He bent and kissed her. They walked toward the mission.

Perhaps someday they could escape from La Barranca Escondida, but would it really be an escape? Perhaps they had really escaped from the outer world. There was a spell in the barranca that had captivated them far more than the towering, impassable walls. Perhaps they never would leave La Barranca Escondida. *Quién sabe?*

BLOOD JUSTICE

CHAPTER ONE

I t was almost time for the first snow of the year. The first cold light of the dawn fingered the dark reaches of the eastern sky, but it was still dark in the valley of the Ute, while the river itself was a dull pewter ribbon against the shadows of the valley floor. The dawn wind had shifted and was driving up the valley, whipping the willows and thrashing the great limbs of the giant cottonwoods of the bottoms. Not a light showed in the sprawling town across the river. It was as though Ute Crossing were as dead as the Indian summer that had just fled to warmer climes. Beyond the sleeping town rose the low approaches to the tumbled, naked foothills, while beyond them, towering over the valley, dominating it while concealing the vast country westward, rose the grim saw-toothed mountains.

Jim Murdock shivered in the searching wind as he rode down the eastward slope of the valley floor toward the bridge that had long spanned the ford that had given the town its name. He hunched the collar of his sheep-skin coat up under the brim of his faded Stetson, and thrust a cold hand inside the coat to feel for the makings. It had been a long and lonely ride that dark night from the railhead to the east and he should have stayed the night there, but for some reason, unknown even to himself, he had wanted to get back to Ute Crossing as quickly as possible. To some of the people who lived there the name of Jim Murdock was still a bitter thing, almost an epithet, or so he had learned from his brother Ben's long, informative letters. But while there were a few who might remember him with warmer feelings, it was really the country that had brought him back.

He fashioned a quirly, protecting the loose tobacco from the boisterous wind with his broad back, then placed the cigarette between his lips. He snapped a match on a thumbnail and lighted the cigarette, the quick spurt of flame from the match revealing his gray eyes, the mahogany hue of his face, a product of too many border suns, the tiny sun wrinkles at the corners of his eyes, and the thin scar that traced a course from his left cheekbone down to the point of his hard jaw. Looking at Jim Murdock one would instinctively lower his voice and avoid looking for trouble, for here indeed was a lobo of a man.

He drew rein at the edge of the river and looked down at the swirling waters. He eyed the bridge, creaking, in the strong liquid grip of the current, and then looked beyond the bridge toward the wide main street of Ute Crossing. It was almost as dark as the inside of a boot. He sat there for a few minutes, drawing in on the cigarette, and when he did so the flare of the burning tobacco made the hard planes of his face almost like a death mask. He would not look up at the gaunt saddle-backed ridge that rose just south of the town and bordered the tumbling waters of the Ute. Something kept him from looking up at that accursed hill that knobbed the near end of the ridge, and yet he knew that if he was made welcome in Ute Crossing and decided to live in that area, he would have to look at that damned hill many, many times in the long years to come.

The eastern sky was faintly lighted by the false dawn when Jim Murdock looked up at the hill, and the sight of the three great trees still standing there struck him like a blow across the face. They, at least, had not changed much in the seven years since he had left the valley of the Ute, saved by the grace of God and a fast buckskin horse. It was almost as though nature had placed those three trees there for some special purpose, for the rest of the hill and the gaunt ridge beyond it were as naked of growth as a suburb of hell itself.

He flipped the butt into the river and slowly rolled another smoke to drive the grinding hunger from his guts. From the looks of Ute Crossing he'd get no breakfast for quite some time. He lighted the fresh smoke and shoved back his hat. Crossing the Ute might be something like crossing the Styx, for there might never be a return. Many people had not forgotten Jim Murdock and his record in Ute Crossing, despite the fact that he had long been cleared of the charges that had sent him pounding through Wind Pass with a posse not too far behind him. There were still hard-eyed men who did not believe that Jim was innocent of the death of Curt Crowley, only son of Big Cass Crowley, the man who had run that part of the country as far back as most people could remember.

He looked up the dark street, and as he did so he saw a quick spurt of yellow light beyond the slab-sided double-decker building that served as the county seat as well as the calabozo. Maybe somebody was opening up early. Someone who could feed a man who had ridden almost thirty miles that night through the windy darkness.

He touched the sorrel with his heels and crossed the bridge to the far side. The horse's hoofs rang clearly on the hard-packed earth of the street. There was another flare-up of yellow light near the building, and for the first time Jim saw what looked like a group of men walking toward the entrance of the jail. He drew rein, narrowing his eyes. A cold feeling of hostility seemed to flow from that group of men, and yet none of them was looking toward the lone horseman near the bridge. They were intent on other business. A thudding noise came from the wide double door.

Jim dismounted and led the tired sorrel into an alleyway beside Slade's Livery Stable. He ground-reined the horse and walked to the dark mouth of the alleyway to look obliquely toward the jail. There wasn't a light on anywhere in the ugly yellow structure. A shift in the wind brought voices to him.

"Get a-goin', Barney," said one man.

"I'm doin' the best I can, Van," said the man at the door. Something snapped and one side of the door opened. "There! Slick as goose grease!"

The men crowded into the building. There were at least fifteen of them, sheepskin or mackinaw-coated, hats pulled low, hard heels punching into the sagging wooden flooring, spurs chiming softly now and then. Three men stood outside the door, looking up and down the deserted street, Winchesters in hand.

A cold feeling flowed through Jim, turning his blood into what felt like icy red crystals, for there was something altogether too familiar about the scene spread out before him. It was almost as though part of his past were being played out. For an eerie moment the strange thought played through his mind that Ute Crossing was indeed a ghost town, haunted by the ghosts of the men who had broken into the jail one winter morning just before dawn and had hauled Jim Murdock from his cell while there was neither sight nor sound of the sheriff and his deputies.

He could hear them now within the building. A yellow rectangle of light showed where one of the windows was located on the east side of the building, and its bars cast a gridiron shadow on the dirty alleyway that bordered the structure. A cat scurried silently for cover from the revealing light. Something crashed hollowly within the jail, and a man shouted hoarsely. A door slammed.

They were making enough noise to awaken the whole town, thought Jim. But the dark street remained empty, except for the three men who stood outside the jail with rifles in their hands, looking up and down the street and talking in low voices.

There was a clanging of metal against metal within the jail. Once more a man shouted, and then it was very quiet. The light winked out in the cell window.

Jim padded to the mouth of the alleyway. Through the dirty windows of the jail he saw occasional flashes of wavering light, as though a lantern was being carried through the echoing halls. He looked up and down the street. Not another light showed. Not a man moved. The bitter wind picked up dust and gravel and rattled it against windows and walls like a boy playing tic-tac-toe on a Halloween night. A tattered newspaper rose from the street, glided upward, and then sailed off to vanish in the windy darkness.

There was a brief struggle at the jail door, and then a man's voice boomed out, "We've got 'em, boys! Jules, you get the horses! Get the three extra ones too, Webb! We can't expect our friends here to ride to the top of the hill!" He laughed loudly.

Jim wet his dry lips. Three men stood among the group. It was easy to spot them in the half-darkness for they did not wear hats. The wind blew the long dark hair of one of them down over his white face.

Two men hurried around the side of the jail and came back with some horses, followed by a third man with more horses. He held a rifle in his free hand.

Jim watched while the three hatless men were hoisted up into the saddles. They could not use their hands for they had been bound behind their backs. The lantern guttered on the jail steps. "Should we take the lantern along, Van?" called out a tall man.

"What for? We don't need any light for this job. Besides, it's almost dawn, Slim."

A boot heel drove against the lantern, smashing it

against the side of the doorway, and it winked out. The smell of coal oil drifted across the wide street.

An intolerable crawling feeling came over Jim. Violence and blood were not strangers to him, for a man could hardly be raised in this country, or have spent as much time along the border as Jim had, without being accustomed to it, but there was something utterly alien about the activities across the street, as though these were not men of flesh and blood at all, but rather chimeras conjured up from the depths by some unseen sorcerer who chuckled evilly in the whining voice of the cold, bitter wind that scoured the valley of the Ute. The very evil of their actions and thoughts flowed outward from the group and enveloped Jim Murdock, and for a moment he was almost tempted to turn back, away from Ute Crossing, never to return, for he knew as sure as fate that the evil which had driven him from Ute Crossing was still extant.

There was enough light now to see more clearly. A horse nickered. Another danced sideways as his cursing owner, left foot thrust into stirrup, right hand gripping Winchester, hopped on his right foot trying to make the saddle. "Damn you, Spade!" he said to the skittish horse. "Stand still or we'll miss the hanging!"

What Jim had already realized was now fully proved by the man's statement. These *were* the preliminaries for a lynching; a *hanging at dawn*. The strange thought fled through his mind that such activity might indeed have become the sole occupation of the men of Ute Crossing and its environs. He had left to escape such a lynching, with himself as the victim, and had returned by some Devil's trick, to see another lynching. How many others had happened in his absence? His brother Ben had never written of such activities, but then Ben wouldn't. All he had ever written about was his teaching job, the future of Ute Crossing, the future of its young citizens entrusted to his care to learn to become good citizens. *Good citizens!* By the gods, it seemed to Jim as though lynchers were the only ultimate product of Ute Crossing's citizenry!

Horses were kneed aside to let the cursing man on foot mount his horse. "Stick with him, Lyss!" jeered one of the mounted men. "By God, he'll have his comeuppance when and *if* you straddle him. Hawww!"

There was a sudden movement from one of the bound, hatless men who had been brought from the jail. He raised a leg and slid agilely from the saddle, then ran like a spooked deer across the broad street, his chin outthrust and his eyes wide with fear and panic, expecting at any moment a soft-nosed slug between his shoulder blades. His booted feet slammed against the hard earth. For a moment it looked as though he'd make it from the street although his chances of ever getting away were impossible.

Two horsemen broke loose from the group. One of them snatched his reata free and fashioned a loop as he rode toward the fleeing man, while the other raised his rifle.

"Christ's sake, Barney, don't shoot!" roared a man from the group. "We want him to swing!"

The fugitive veered, almost as though he expected a loop to drop about his shoulders. He raced toward the alleyway where Jim Murdock stood watching expressionlessly. For a moment he did not see Jim, and then his mouth squared, almost in agony. "For God's sake, mister! Stop them! We haven't done anything! We're innocent, I tell you!" There was a Mexican quality to his voice.

"Trip the bastard up!" yelled the man with the poised loop.

Jim stood aside, pressing back against the worn clapboard of the livery stable. All he had to do was thrust out a foot and the frightened man would drive his face cruelly against the flinty ground, but he could not bring himself to do it.

"Son of a bitch!" yelled the man with the rifle.

The man with the reata reached the alleyway first and

threw a neat *peal,* catching the fugitive's feet in a figure-eight loop, as skillful an exhibition of roping as Jim had ever seen. Jim darted forward and dropped to a knee, catching the lassoed man across the chest with his left arm, saving his face from the hard-packed earth. The roper dropped from his saddle and came hand over hand down the rope as though he had roped a calf. "Who the hell are you?" he asked in a brittle voice of Jim.

Jim stood up and saw the man named Barney drop from his horse and plunge forward, stiff-legged, rifle at hip level, lever slamming down and up to load. The metallic sound grated like the creaking of the rusty gates of hell. Jim's .44 was holstered beneath his buttoned sheepskin, and he was twenty feet from his saddle-scabbarded Winchester. The rifleman stopped as Jim rose to his feet. The muzzle of his rifle touched one of the buttons of the sheepskin right over Jim's shrinking navel, and Jim found himself looking into pale gray eyes that were somehow disconcertingly familiar.

The roper coiled his reata and pulled the fugitive to his feet by twisting his free hand down under the man's collar, half choking him. He manhandled him toward the mouth of the alleyway. "Bring that bastard along, Barney," he said over his shoulder.

Jim wet his lips. He stared at the rifleman. "Barney Kessier," he said quietly.

Kessler stared back at Jim. "You know me?" he demanded.

"Ought to. We went to school together at the crossroads," said Jim dryly. "You've come a long way, Barney."

Barney's face looked even more ill-adjusted than it had in the old days. It had always seemed to Jim that Barney was really two different people, each one struggling to get the upper hand and neither ever succeeding, but managing to raise a pocket-sized edition of hell between them in the struggle.

Barney let down the rifle hammer to half cock. "By ginger," he said quietly. "Jim! Jim Murdock!"

Jim smiled thinly. "Now take that gun outa my gut, Barney, like a good boy. This coat is old and too thin to stop a .44/40 at this range."

Barney grounded the rifle. He smiled; then the smile vanished, then reappeared again, while his loose mouth worked a little. "You shouldn't ought to have done that, Jim," he said reproachfully.

"What?" asked Jim.

The smile came and fled. The eyes widened and narrowed. Barney Kessler's face had a way of looking like a picture coming into focus and then as rapidly slipping out of it, so one was never quite sure what he was seeing. "Been in the way," said Barney a little stupidly. The rich, fruity odor of spirits drifted to Jim.

"Come on, Barney!" yelled a man from across the street. "Bring that hombre with you!"

"You got to come along, Jim," said Barney.

"Where?"

"To the hill, of course."

"What for, Barney?" Jim knew well enough why they were going to the hill.

Barney jerked his head. "You're a witness," he said.

"To what?"

"You seen us take them men from the calabozo, didn't' you, Jim?"

Jim nodded.

"We don't want no witnesses," repeated Barney.

The picture came clearly to Jim. They'd *invite* him along. He'd be under gun surveillance of course. He'd thus be considered one of the lynchers, unable to bear witness against them. He knew now why the streets of Ute Crossing were so empty, why no early riser's lights were showing.

"Get your hoss," said Barney. "Keep your hands away from that saddle gun."

Jim picked up the reins. He led the sorrel as Barney walked beside him toward the waiting group of men.

"Who is he?" called out a hard-voiced man.

"Jim Murdock," said Barney.

There was a moment's silence, and then a broad-shouldered, meaty-bellied man, kneed his horse toward them. "You're drunker than I thought you was," he said.

"You think I'm bullcrapping you, Lassen?" said Barney in an aggrieved tone. "I went to school with ol' Jim here and we was amigos in the old days, working for Cass Crowley, wasn't we?"

"I hope he didn't come back lookin' for his job with Cass," said another of the men. He laughed shortly. "He sure as hell made a long trip for nothing."

"Shut up, Jules," said Lassen. He peered at Jim. "By God! It's Murdock, all right!"

Jim looked up at the big man. "I see you haven't changed much, Lassen," he said quietly and coldly.

Lassen's eyes, hard as amber, studied Jim. "You always were loose with your lip, Murdock," he said.

"Let's get on with this, Van," said one of the men to Lassen. He looked nervously up and down the street. "We're making enough noise to wake the whole town."

Barney laughed. "Ain't no one going to come out and ask us what we're doing, Webb. You ascairt?"

Webb flushed. "One of these days, Barney," he warned.

"You tough, Webb?" sneered Barney. "You wanta make something out of it?"

"Oh, my God," said another man. "The booze is making a fighting man outa Barney again."

Lassen slapped a hard hand down on his thigh. "You men think this is a damned church social? Shut up, I tell you! Maybe Webb is right at that! Look at the dawn!"

The eastern sky was strangely figured in dark and light grays, interwoven with a cold, pearly luminescence.

"Get up on that sorrel, Murdock," said Lassen.

Jim obediently mounted under the cold, hard eyes of the mob. Lassen jerked his head. Jim kneed the sorrel close beside the nearest of the prisoners, the one who had hopelessly tried to escape.

"All right, boys," said Van Lassen. "We all know the way, don't we?"

They clattered toward the eastern end of town where the ridge road ran at right angles to the main stem of Ute Crossing, a tight bunch of horsemen with the three prisoners, and Jim Murdock in the center of the group.

The man who had tried to escape looked at Jim. *"Gracias,"* he said.

"Por rarcto," said Jim politely. He eyed the man. He was Mexican, all right. "You're a long way from home, amigo," he added quietly in his cowpen Spanish.

The dark eyes were sad. "This is a cold country and cold people. I might have expected something like this, amigo. A thousand Jesuses! I am not ready to die!"

"Cut out that spic talk!" snapped Barney Kessler. He slapped a hand on the breech of his rifle.

Jim reached inside his coat for the makings.

"Don't you pull no hideout gun on me!" roared Barney pugnaciously.

Jim withdrew the makings. He looked at Barney. "What kind of red-eye you been drinking, Barney?" he asked mildly. "You're almost talking like a real man."

Lassen laughed dryly.

Jim rolled a cigarette, lighted it, and placed it between the lips of the Mexican. He looked at the other two men. One of them was young, hardly out of his teens, maybe not even twenty yet, and his frightened blue eyes met Jim's with a sick look that almost repelled him. "Smoke?" said Jim.

The kid shook his head. His blond hair fell down over his forehead, and he impatiently threw it back with a toss of his head. The third man was older, plain of appearance, nondescript, looking ahead with no expression on his grizzled face. He looked to Jim like a man who had expected nothing better out of life than to die with a rope around his neck.

"Who's that?" said the man called Webb. He was still nervous.

Jim looked ahead. A slim man stood in the center of the street. His neat black hat was creased fore and aft. His dark coat was set off by a pure white shirt and string tie. His neat boots glistened with polish, and a badge of some sort shone on his coat lapel.

"By God," said Van Lassen. "It's Brady Short!"

Jim leaned forward in his saddle. He had not seen Brady Short for seven long years, and had often thought of him. Brady had been Jim's chief rival for the favor of Ann Whitcomb, only daughter of Judge Enos Whitcomb, chief legal light of that country. Ann had been head and shoulders the best-looking belle in Ute Crossing, if not in the whole valley of the Ute.

"You think he means to stop us, Van?" asked Webb.

Lassen turned in his saddle, and the look on his face seemed to lash Webb across the face like a quirt. "Ain't nobody goin' to stop us, Webb," he said harshly. "Not even Brady Short!"

The riders drew to a halt as Brady Short raised a slim hand.

CHAPTER TWO

"Do you men realize what you are doing?" asked Short.

"We got a pretty good idea," said Barney Kessler brightly.

"Don't give us none of your pretty lawyer talk, Brady," said the man named Lyss.

"I didn't plan to," said the lawyer. He touched the badge on his lapel. "As a deputy sheriff of this county, I advise you to return those men at once to the jail."

Barney guffawed. "Hell's fire, Brady!" he said. "Where'd you get that tin badge? In a box of taffy candy from Gamble's Drugstore?"

The lawyer flushed. "Certainly it's only an honorary title given to me by Sheriff Cullin, and if it doesn't mean anything to you, I then appeal to you as law-abiding citizens not to take the law into your own hands. Take those men back."

"After you've seen who we are?" asked Lassen.

"You didn't expect to get away with it, did you, Van?" asked Short.

"Was you planning to give us away, Mr. Short?" asked Lassen in return.

Lassen's implication was plain enough.

Short swallowed. He was scared, but he stood his ground. "That wasn't my point," he said.

"His point is that he'd make a lot of ground in his chasin' of the judge's position if he managed, single-handed, so to speak, to stop a mob," said a gray-haired man. He shifted in his saddle. "By God, Short, you get to hell outa our way or you'll never get no vote from me, and I been in your party before you was born!"

Jim studied the lawyer. Brady hadn't lost any of his good looks. He was older than Jim by at least eight years, and the touch of gray at his temples and in his neat moustache had added dignity to the clear freshness the "boy wonder" of the bar in that county had always had, coupled with a sharp, precise legal mind.

"Then you won't listen to me?" said the lawyer.

There was no answer. Hoofs thudded against the ground as though the horses too were anxious to get the business over with.

Lassen jerked his head. The lawyer walked toward his black horse, tethered, to a hitching rack in front of the general store. As the group passed he mounted and rode behind them. Jim turned in his saddle. "Hello, Brady," he said.

Brady's dark eyes narrowed. "Jim Murdock!" he said. "What are you doing here?"

Jim shrugged. "Come home to roost," he said with a faint, bitter smile. "Find myself *invited* to this lynching. You follow me?"

Short nodded. "You picked a great time to come home," he said quietly.

"I have a habit of doing such things," said Jim.

"When this is over you must come and see us, Jim. Ann will be glad to see you, I'm sure."

Jim's eyes narrowed. "Ann Whitcomb?"

Brady smiled proudly. "Ann Short," he said. "Mrs. Brady Short, Jim."

Jim felt sick deep within his guts. He had known that Ann must be married by now. He had never asked Ben in his letters about her, for a man's stubborn pride is a hard thing to defeat, particularly in the case of women. It was logical enough she would have married Brady Short. Her father had been the best lawyer in that part of the country. She would have cottoned to one as good as Brady Short. It was in the cards, and the deck had not been stacked.

Jim turned again. He let his horse drift back toward Brady and no one stopped him. Their eyes were on the naked ridge and the ugly hill at the end of it, crowned with its three horrifying trees.

Brady held out a slim hand to meet the hard grasp of Jim's hand. "I did the best I could," he said. "You witnessed that."

"What did they do?" asked Jim.

Brady's eyes narrowed. "You don't know?"

"They never bothered to tell me," said Jim dryly.

"They murdered Cass Crowley," said the lawyer.

Jim stared at him. "Cass Crowley? Old Indestructible?"

"Yes. Cass had been negotiating to sell out his holdings.

There was supposed to be a lot of money at his place. Most of his men had been paid off. He was alone at the ranch house. He never had a chance, Jim. Three bullet holes in the back of his head. When Sheriff Cullin caught up with these three each of them had an empty chamber in his gun. Murray Cullin thinks each of them placed a bullet in Cass' head so that each of them would share the guilt. They're sharing the guilt all right."

"Cass Crowley," said Jim in wonderment. "He was like Warrior Peak around here." He looked back toward the saw-toothed mountains. The first light of the dawn was silvering the snow-capped tip of Warrior Peak, the great up-thrust ringer of stone that had always seemed to admonish the valley of the Ute and the people who lived there. Nothing would ever destroy or bring down Warrior Peak.

The wind was sweeping along the river road, driving dust, papers and tumbleweeds ahead of it into the fence corners and against the trees that bordered the road in between it and the brawling Ute.

Van Lassen turned toward the faintly rutted, almost indistinguishable road that led vaguely up the side of the ridge. It was then that a buckboard was seen in the middle of the road. Its driver was standing up, reins in his left hand, right hand upraised, as Brady Short's hand had been raised back in town.

"It's 'Deacon' Hitchins," said Webb.

The group came to a halt, sitting their horses on the narrow road, hemmed in by the swaying bushes. Van Lassen rode forward. "You aimin' to stop us too, Deacon?" he said.

Jim stood up in his stirrups. It had been seven years since he had seen Alfred Hitchins, local businessman, city father, staunch pillar of the church, a man widely known for his sanctity and honesty, called "Deacon" with respect by one and all, although he had never served in such a capacity. It was Al Hitchins who had helped Ben Murdock get his education after he had been crippled, and who had damned well seen to it that Ben was installed as teacher in Ute Crossing Elementary School despite the stigma of the name Murdock at that time.

The businessman dropped the reins. "Think of what you are doing, men," he said softly. His round face worked a little. "For the love of the God whom we all cherish and obey, do not do this thing."

Lassen touched the brim of his hat. "We're seeing that justice is done, Mr. Hitchins," he said, not without respect.

"This is not justice, Vanderbilt," said Hitchins quietly.

Alfred Hitchins was the only man Ute Crossing knew who could use Van Lassen's first name with impunity. "You'd better get out of the way, sir," said Lassen.

"I have no way of stopping you. God give me the faith and the strength to do so. Think, men! Think of what you are doing! These men are God's lambs. It is not up to us to destroy them because we believe they have done wrong."

"Some lambs," said Barney Kessler. He looked about, expecting a laugh.

"Shut up, Barney," said Van Lassen shortly. There was a long pause. The dawn light had almost tipped the eastern range far beyond the valley of the Ute. Slowly Al Hitchins drove his buckboard aside to an opening in the waving brush. The group jingled past up the slope of the hill, and not one of them looked at the man of God; no one except the kid looked at him. His face seemed to plead for help, but there was no help. Hitchins' eyes were moist. He raised a hand. "Jesus wept," he said. No one seemed to hear him except Jim Murdock.

Jim looked up at the three trees. They had a perpetual slant from the cruel battering winds that swept wildly up the valley of the Ute in the late fall, winter, and early spring. Maybe the wind should have felled them long ago, but for some reason they had resisted all efforts of the wind to do so. Battered and gnarled, twisted and ugly, they seemed to reek with an insensate evil. Jim looked away. One of them had almost borne his lifeless body, swinging stiff-legged in the constant wind, tongue protruding, seven long years ago. The sickness returned to his guts and his mind. There was nothing he could do for these three doomed men. Not a single blessed thing!

The horses were reined in. All dismounted except the three prisoners. The Mexican was stony-faced; only his great eyes were alive. The older man bowed his head and stared unseeingly at his saddle horn. Now and then his bottom lip quivered. The kid looked about him with unbelieving eyes. Once he looked quickly down at his trousers, and when he looked up again his face was deeply flushed. No one seemed to notice his embarrassment, but the wind, in its insensitivity to all human feeling, brought the odor of his embarrassment to the hard-faced men who stood there.

The roper stepped out into the open, coiled reata in his hand. He eyed the first of the trees, then smoothly cast the reata, uncoiling like a snake, up over a great limb, while the weight of the loop and honda brought the end down to his feet. Three times he made a perfect cast. He did not look up at the three shivering prisoners as he quickly fashioned a hangman's noose at the end of each of the three reatas.

Barney Kessler swung up on his mare and picked up the first of the loops, widening it quickly, to drop it over the shoulders of the older man. He tightened and placed the knot in professional fashion under the man's left ear. The second loop went about the Mexican's slim neck. The kid bent his head, pressing his chin down against his thin chest to prevent the loop going about his neck. "Come on, kid," said Barney. "We ain't got all day."

The kid turned his head away, pressing down hard on his chin. Barney swung a big hand, catching the kid cruelly over the ear, so hard he must have broken an eardrum. The kid screamed in terror but did not raise his head. Barney drew back his hand once more.

"You hit that kid again, Barney," said Jim coldly, "and I'll break your dirty neck!"

Barney turned quickly. He had left his rifle leaning against one of the trees. There was pure hell in his pale, washed-out eyes. Then his eyes met those of Jim Murdock and his face seemed to slide, dissolve, go in and out of focus.

"He's right," said Webb.

"You keep outa this!" said Barney.

Webb turned a little and moved his rifle. "You heard me, you drunken son of a bitch," he said thinly.

The kid raised his head. "Go on," he said in a choked voice. "I ain't afraid."

Barney saw his out. He wanted no part of Webb and much less of Jim Murdock. "You ain't, kid?" he said in a kindly voice. He smiled benignly, almost like Alfred Hitchins.

"No!" said the kid desperately.

"Then how come you shit your drawers?" demanded Barney. He guffawed. He looked about at the others.

His cruelty struck even hard-faced Van Lassen. "Get on with it, Barney," he said. "Shoulda knowed better than to let you do anything around here."

"Aw, hell, Van," said Barney sheepishly. "I was only joshing."

"This ain't no time for joshing!" snapped Lassen.

But Barney Kessler, no man himself, had effectively stripped the last tatters of manhood from the kid. The boy was completely broken now, a sobbing, retching thing that made even Van Lassen look away.

The Mexican spat to one side. *"Cobarde!"* he said in a low voice to Barney. "Give me a knife, *bazofia,* and we will see the color of your guts! A month's pay they are yellow!"

Barney grinned loosely. "No bets," he said. "This is a serious occasion, spiel. Besides, where would you get a month's pay? Shovelin' cinders in hell with the Devil ramroddin' you?"

Silence came, except for the whining of the wind and the snuffling of some of the horses.

Van Lassen looked up. "You men got anything to say?" he said, not unkindly.

The Mexican shrugged. "One day is as good as the next to die. It is not the thought of dying, hombres, that is painful, only the way of it." He bent his head and mouthed silent prayers.

"You?" said Lassen to the older man.

The man shook his head without raising it.

"Kid?" said Lassen.

"I got a sister," said the kid. His voice broke.

"He's got a sister," jeered Barney.

"Go on, kid," said Van Lassen.

"I got a sister," repeated the kid slowly. "Lives in Three Forks, over the mountains west of here. Name of Jessica. You'll tell her I died?"

Lassen nodded. He looked at Barney. Barney deftly

tightened the nooses. Oh, he was good at *that,* thought Jim Murdock. The loose-mouthed polecat couldn't shoot, rope or ride, but he was good at anything like that.

There was a long pause, and then Lassen raised his hand. Three men, one of them Barney, of course, stepped behind the three horses. Barney grinned as he fingered his quirt. Lassen's hand was steady. All eyes were on it. Lassen dropped his hand with a sharp downward stroke. Three quirts struck the rumps of the three horses, and they buck-jumped forward in sudden pain and fear. The Mexican's neck snapped cleanly. The older man raised his head, shrieked hoarsely, fought the rope for a moment, and then hung still. The kid fought like a tiger, kicking his legs upward as he fought the killing noose, thrashing and turning, until Barney ran forward and gripped his legs and pulled down on them.

There was a long silence as the three bodies swayed, twisting and turning in the wind, the tree limbs creaking beneath the unaccustomed weight. Although they should have been used to it by now, thought Jim. They had served this purpose before and might do it again...

"Well," said Van Lassen. "There ain't no use in standin' around here freezin' our butts. Come on, boys! We'll drag Baldy outa his sack and get a few rounds of drinks. We earned it, I think."

Jim watched the men mount. Some of them took the riderless horses in tow as they started down the narrow, winding road. No one spoke to him. He was a dead issue now. He had participated in the merciless lynching just as much as most of them had, for he had stood there and had done nothing to save the three doomed men. It was then he noticed that Brady Short had not come up to the hill. Hoofs clattered on the hard earth, leather squeaked, a horse blew. In a few minutes they were all gone, leaving nothing behind but the acrid odor of fresh horse droppings and the cold, almost imperceptible odor of fresh death.

Jim rubbed his bristly jaws and looked up at the three

men, and for the first time he realized he did not even know their names, nor had any of the others mentioned their names. The only thing Jim knew was that the kid had a sister named Jessica whom he had wanted to be notified about his death.

Jim slowly rolled a smoke and lighted it, looking up at the three dead men twisting in the wind, swinging stiffly back and forth in the gallows' dance. "Jessica," he said quietly. "How does a man tell a girl named Jessica her kid brother crapped in his drawers just before he was lynched for murder in Ute Crossing?"

There was no answer in the whining wind. It was getting colder and had an edge to its invisible teeth.

Jim felt in his pocket for his clasp knife and then shook his head. No use in him cutting them down, and besides he did not want to touch them, or have any part in their lynching, before or after. Dead men had relatives someplace, who might just come looking for the men who had lynched their kin.

He flipped his cigarette butt away and rolled another. The sun had peeked up above the eastern range, a cold, watery sun that would bring little heat, if any at all, to the valley of the Ute. The growing light had crept across the hills and worked its way down into the valley before Jim mounted his sorrel and rode him down the twisting road toward the river road.

There was a different feeling in the wind. A driving gust of it struck Jim's face like stinging, sharp-edged grit, and it wasn't until he reached the bottom of the slope that he realized that it wasn't grit at all, but the harsh reality of the first snowfall of the year.

CHAPTER THREE

A knot of men sat their horses near the bridge as Jim Murdock rode into the teeth of the wind and the stinging snowflakes. It wasn't until he reached the first building at the southeastern corner of the main street and the river road that he realized the men were what was left of the posse, if one could call it a posse. More like a lynching bee, thought Jim. Some of them were there, Van Lassen, Barney, and the men named Webb, Slim, and Lyss. Brady Short stood to one side, holding the reins of his black, and beyond him Alfred Hitchins sat in his buckboard listening to the words of the tall, broad-shouldered man who sat his gray squarely in front of the hard-faced men who had just hanged three people. Jim recognized the tall man as Sheriff Murray Cullin, one of the best lawmen in the territory.

Cullin held a legal-looking paper in his left hand, the biting wind flapping it about. "I got clear to Benedict Junction late yesterday afternoon," said Cullin, "and sent a wire to the governor for a change of venue for those three men up on that hill there. The wires were down south of town and there was no time to waste. I took the freight train to Parthia and caught a fast passenger run to the capital. Caught the governor ten minutes before he was to leave for Washington and got the change of venue. Took the train back to Parthia, got a fast horse, the fastest horse I could get, and came over Wolf Pass in the dark, pushing that horse all the way, and got here twenty minutes too late! Well, you've had your way, men." He ripped up the paper and let the scraps drift from his big hand. They flew southward with the tiny flakes of snow. "You know what you've done. Brady Short and Mr. Hitchins did their duty as law-abiding citizens to stop you from this crime. You'd listen to no one, would you?"

"You sayin' they weren't guilty, Sheriff Cullin?" asked Slim.

The sheriff's face tightened and he tugged at his dragoon moustache. "Cass Crowley and I were raised together," he said fiercely. "By God, he was like a brother to me! I could have killed those three men when I caught them and no one would have been the wiser, nor would they have cared. But I had the law to uphold. If I break it, then there is no restraint on men like you. The law would have dealt fairly with them, and there is no doubt in my mind that any jury would have found them guilty!"

"Then what's the beef about?" said Van Lassen. "We just saved the county a bill they can't afford right now. Ain't we citizens? Ain't we got rights? Well, we took those rights. We hung 'em, and you can do what you damned well like about it, Sheriff, but let me tell *you* something. You said there wasn't any doubt but what any jury would have found them guilty. Well, you bring us to trial and you won't find any jury that will find us guilty. Not here in Ute Crossing. Not in this county! Not in this whole damned state!"

Cullin shrugged. He knew these men. He also knew Van Lassen was right, and there wasn't anything Cullin could do about it now. He kneed his gray aside and watched the group ride toward the Grape Arbor, not the biggest but certainly the roughest saloon in Ute Crossing, if not in the county, if not in the whole damned state, as Van Lassen had just put it concerning juries.

"An eye for an eye," said Hitchins. "'Vengeance is mine; I will repay, saith the Lord.'"

Cullin nodded. His eyes caught sight of Jim Murdock. "You," he said coldly.

"I didn't have any choice, Sheriff," said Jim. "They made me go along because I might be a witness against them— as though that mattered."

"I wasn't thinking of that, Murdock," said the lawman.

Jim rolled a cigarette. He looked at the tall man as he wet the edge with his tongue and folded over the paper. "I was cleared of those charges, Cullin," he said quietly.

"Not in my book you weren't, Murdock."

"Are you the sole judge of law around here?"

Cullin leaned forward in his saddle. "I keep two books," he said thinly. "One for those who have not been caught for committing crimes. One for those who have broken the law and gotten away with it."

"And no book for those who have been cleared?"

Cullin smiled without any light in his eyes. "I don't bother with them, mister," he said.

"So you still consider me guilty of killing Curt Crowley?"

There was no answer from the lawman. He turned his horse and rode toward the jail. It was answer enough for Jim Murdock. He might have expected it from Murray Cullin.

Brady Short led his black toward Jim. "He doesn't mean that," he said.

"Thanks," said Jim dryly. "He sounded convincing enough to me."

Brady studied Jim. "You've changed," he said. "For a moment, when you first spoke to me, I didn't recognize you at all."

"I've been around a bit, Brady," said Jim.

"Where?"

Jim held out the makings to Brady. The lawyer shook his head. "Where, Jim?" he repeated.

"Along the border. Arizona. New Mexico. Texas. Mexico."

"You did all right for yourself?"

Jim smiled. "I worked most of the time," he said. "Made a small strike in the Guadalupes and have an Apache bullet scar on my left thigh to prove it."

"What kind of work, Jim?"

Jim rolled a cigarette. "Stock detective. Texas Rangers for a hitch. Scouted for the Army. You know the usual run of such things. It's been a long time, Brady."

The snow swirled high over the street. Alfred Hitchins had driven silently away, and his buckboard stood in front of the Ute Valley Mercantile Company. He was nowhere in sight.

Jim jerked a thumb over his shoulder, toward the hill and its grisly fruit. "What about them?" he said. "You surely don't want the kids, the future citizens of Ute Crossing, to see these products of justice, do you, Brady?"

"Murray Cullin will take care of it."

Jim drew in on his cigarette. "Who were they, Brady?"

"Drifters. Saddle tramps. Bums. No one really knows who they are or where they came from."

"Figures," said Jim.

"Where are you staying, Jim? With your brother?"

Jim shook his head. "Ben might not like my habits, Brady."

"You are welcome to stay with us. Ann and I have taken over the old Whitcomb place. The old judge passed away last year." The lawyer laughed. "You know how big that place is. We have help, of course. It's quite too much for Ann, you know."

"Any kids, Brady?"

The lawyer flushed. "Well, no. You see ... I—Well, hang it all, Jim, it's a personal matter really, isn't it?"

"Sure, Brady. Clumsy of me to ask that way."

"You'll come, then?"

Jim shook his head. "Thanks just the same. I said Ben might not like my habits. I'm sure Ann and you wouldn't like them either."

"You'll come for dinner, then, sometime?"

"Be delighted," said Jim. He touched his sorrel with his heels and rode a few feet. He reined in and looked back at the lawyer. "The kid has a sister named Jessica," he said. "Lives in Three Forks. West of here, over the mountains."

Brady had a puzzled look on his handsome face. He nodded. He watched Jim ride toward the livery stable, shrugged, then mounted his horse and rode out on the river road, north of town, toward the big house that he called home.

Jim swung down in front of Slade's Livery Stable. Yellow light showed through a dusty, cracked window where Old Man Slade had had his office in the old days. Jim opened the door. An incredibly tall and incredibly thin man, all knobs and angles and no meat, turned quickly from a stove where he was brewing coffee. "Jesus God," he said. "Shut that damned door! We ain't open for business yet, mister."

"Meany Gillis," said Jim. "I thought you had withered away to all bones by now."

Meanwell Gillis eyed Jim with watery green eyes; then he grinned, revealing a gap-toothed mouth. "Jim," he said with genuine pleasure. He thrust out an incredibly thin hand. "Set and have some joe, amigo! Barney Kessler said you was in town."

"He ought to know," said Jim. "Let me put my sorrel up. He needs feed and rest."

"Sure thing, Jim. Lemme open the big door."

Jim went outside as Meany withdrew the bars and opened one of the front doors to let Jim in. Jim led the sorrel into a stall, unsaddled him, rubbed him down, and then gave him feed. He could hear Meany puttering around in the office, and the tantalizing smell of Arbuckle's best brew drifted out to him.

Jim peeled off his coat and hung it on a nail, then walked into the warm office. He twirled a chair and sat down in it, arms resting on the back, chin resting on his arms. "Where's Old Man Slade?" he said.

"Dead five years, Jim. I took over from Mrs. Slade."

"You always wanted this place, eh, Meany?"

The thin one grinned. "It ain't much, but I call it home." He served up the steaming brew in huge granite cups. He sat down in his desk chair and placed the cup on the littered desk. "Seems as though you picked one helluva time to come home, James."

"It's a habit of mine, Meany."

The man nodded. "Well, I never believed you was guilty. You can bet your bottom dollar on that, James."

"Why, Meany?" Jim sipped the coffee and felt it begin its good work.

Meany shrugged. "I been around horses all my life. You get to know 'em pretty well, I'd say. Dogs, too. They ain't too different from people, come to think of it."

"How about jackasses?"

Meany grinned. "Meaning you, James? You ain't no jackass, although there ain't nothing stupid about a good jackass. Bullheaded, maybe, but not stupid. Your father was no fool, and Ben certainly ain't."

Jim looked down at the dark circle of steaming coffee. "Seems like I cost my father his ranch supply business. No one wanted to do business with Jim Murdock's father."

"Well, you got to admit Cass Crowley was his best customer," said Meany.

Jim looked up. "And when Crowley stopped doing business with him so did every other rancher in this country."

Meany nodded. "It was like one of them boykits, or something like that, where nobody wants to do business with you."

"Boycott," said Jim. "From what I hear it was more like a quarantine. First it cost me my mother. She wasn't well, and sitting around watching my father worry and get old before her eyes didn't help much."

"Well, like you said, she wasn't well."

"There wasn't anything wrong with my father's health when I left here, Meany."

Meany sipped his coffee. He eyed Jim over the lip of the big cup. "Looks like your troubles cost you your pa and your ma and made a cripple outa your brother Ben."

"Meaning I should have stayed away, eh?"

Meany shook his head. "A man has a right to live his own life the way he wants to, James."

"What about those three men up on the hill, Meany?"

Meany looked away. "Well, what about them?" he echoed.

"Who were they?"

Meany shrugged. "They called them John Does or something like that."

"They had no names?"

"Oh, they gave names all right. No one believed them anyways."

"No one?" Meany stood up and walked to the dirty window. "They just wouldn't talk. The older hombre was called Gil. The Mex answered to the handle of Orlando. The young one only answered to the name of Kid."

"He has a sister named Jessica," said Jim.

Meany turned. "You know her?"

Jim shook his head. "He spoke about her at the last. He asked Van Lassen to get word to her."

Meany spat into the filthy gaboon. "Yeah," he said.

"What do you mean?"

"You ought to know Van better'n that!"

"You mean he won't do it?"

Meany placed a thin hand on Jim's shoulder. "Didn't you know Van was ramroddin' for Cass Crowley when the old man was murdered?"

"There's a helluva lot I don't know," said Jim dryly.

"Cass Crowley was like God to Van Lassen. Maybe more. Ol' Cass was about the only rancher in the valley who could handle Van. By godfrey, he got work outa that man, too! Van seemed to appreciate the fact the old man gave him pretty much of a free rein up at the ranch. If it hadn't been for Crowley, Van would have had to leave this country."

Jim emptied his cup and held it out for Meany to fill it. "What beats me is that Murray Cullin walks out of here and lets those lynchers walk into the jail as sweet as you please. Where was the jail keeper this morning? Where were Cullin's deputies?"

"They found old Mike Curry, the jail keeper, out cold in one of the cells with a goose egg on his head. Harlan Meigs was deputy. Well, it seems as though some of the boys got him likkered up in the Ute House Bar last night. He got as far as the jail and passed out in the office. That answer your question?"

"Very neat," murmured Jim.

"Well, they did kill the old man," said Meany. "I don't cotton to lynchings, but they woulda been hung anyways, James."

Jim rolled a cigarette. *"It is not the thought of dying, hombres, that is painful, only the way of it,"* said Jim.

Meany smiled. "Say, that's pretty good! Who said that? One of them Greek philosophers, maybe?"

"Fellow by the name of Orlando," said Jim.

"Was he a philosopher?"

Jim lighted the cigarette and blew a smoke ring. He punched a lean forefinger through the ring. "You could call him that," he said.

The door swung open, letting in a blast of icy air and a swirl of dry snowflakes. A short, potbellied man shook the snow from his hat "I'll need the team, Meany," he said.

"You want the hearse too, Mr. Dakers?"

"Can't get it up that hill. I'll take the buckboard. I'll need some help. Can you get away?"

Meany shook his head.

"I can't get them down by myself and I can't lift them

into the wagon. No one wants to go with me," said Dakers. He shook his head. "I don't know why."

"Maybe the whole town is ashamed of itself," said Jim.

Dakers eyed Jim. "I don't know you," he said.

"Jim Murdock."

Dakers's lips tightened into a straight line. "Oh," he said quietly.

"You've heard of me, then, Mr. Dakers?"

The undertaker nodded. "Some," he admitted.

"More likely a lot," said Jim. He flipped his cigarette into the gaboon. "I'll go with you."

Dakers smiled. "That's very nice of you, Mr. Murdock."

"You might get into trouble with the leading citizens by associating with me, Mr. Dakers."

Dakers put on his hat. "My business is with the dead, not with the living. That's my rule, Mr. Murdock. I am a man of rules. I abide by them. Keeps a man disciplined and out of trouble. Follow a good set of rules, I say, and you'll keep out of trouble. Do you agree?"

Jim reached through the door that led into the stable and took his sheepskin from the nail. He shrugged into it and buttoned it. "We'll need something to cover the bodies," he said. "I'll get it." He walked into the stable where Meany was getting the team ready.

Dakers wet his thin lips, helped himself to a cup of coffee, and rubbed his plump jowls. "Jim Murdock," he said thoughtfully. He sipped the coffee. "Business might just pick up at that, after a poor fall season."

Jim led the team out through the front door in a swirling cloud of dry flakes. The wind cut through his thin sheepskin. He swung up into the seat and held out the reins to Dakers. The undertaker shook his head. Jim drove toward the river. There were lights on in some of the stores by this time. A number of horses stood hipshot at the racks, rumps against the biting wind, tails flying every which way. Here and there along the wide street stood men, hats pulled down over their eyebrows, shoulders hunched beneath their thick collars, hands thrust deep into side pockets, watching the buckboard rattling toward the river, and some of the men had eyes for Jim Murdock alone.

Jim halted the team at the crest of the hill and eyed the three stiff bodies swinging like grisly pendulums to and fro, twisting now and then as in some eerie sarabande, accompanied by the wild threnody of the wind and the undertone of the creaking tree limbs.

"Horrible," said Dakers.

Jim dropped to the ground. He took out his clasp knife and walked to the nearest tree.

"Those are fine ropes," said Dakers. "Can't you just untie them? They're worth a few dollars, Mr. Murdock."

Jim turned and looked at the man. Dakers flushed. "Well, there's not much profit in burying such people," he said.

"Did you get paid to bury them?"

Dakers nodded. "Mr. Hitchins stopped in this morning. Gave me a hundred dollars toward their burial. No profit, of course. I might just break even."

"I'll bet," said Jim dryly. He slashed the first rope, then whirled and caught the body of the man named Gil. He carried it to the buckboard and placed it inside. Next he cut down the Mexican and loaded him in beside Gil. For a moment be looked up at the set blue face of the kid, and then he cut him loose and carried him to the vehicle. He severed the taut nooses and threw the foul ropes into the brush.

The wind howled mournfully. It was likely the only sorrow that would be shown for these three unfortunates.

"The digging will be hard," said Dakers. "Business is always better in the early winter, but the ground is hard. Well, we do the best we can in all seasons, eh, Mr. Murdock?"

Jim climbed up into the seat and took the reins. "I wouldn't know," he said. He did not look back as he turned the team and drove down the hill, hearing

Dakers's prattle, but not listening to it. Every time the wheels hit a bump or went into a rut he heard something else—the mute, heavy protestations of the bodies in the back.

Jim drove the buckboard up behind Dakers Funeral Parlor and carried the bodies inside for the undertaker, placing them on slabs. Dakers shut the door and took off his hat. "There's no need to hold them," he said. "There will be no one here to see them, poor fellows. Swiftly, swiftly... Ashes to ashes; dust to dust, *et cetera, et cetera...*"

Jim unbuttoned his coat and felt for the makings.

"No smoking in here, Mr. Murdock," said Dakers. "Respect for the dead, you know."

Jim rolled a cigarette and lighted it. He blew a reflective cloud of smoke. "I wonder who they really were," he said, more to himself than to Dakers.

"Their full names are not known."

Jim looked at the man. "Maybe we'd better try to find out," he said.

Dakers shrugged. He felt in his pocket and brought out a limp dollar bill which he extended to Jim. "Here," he said. "For services rendered."

Jim grinned. "Don't put a strain on yourself, Mr. Dakers. Like you said, there's no profit in burying men such as these."

The dollar bill vanished like a gopher into a hole. "If there is anything I can do for you, Mr. Murdock," said Dakers.

"There is."

"Say it, Mr. Murdock."

Jim looked at the bodies. "I'd like to search them."

Dakers frowned. "Why? This is most irregular."

Jim blew a smoke ring. "Someone has to find out who they really were. As far as I can see, no one wants to do that."

Dakers turned his hat around and around in his plump hands. "I can't let you do that. Sheriff Cullin might not like it."

"He doesn't have to know," said Jim.

"I abide by a simple set of rules, Mr. Murdock."

Jim shrugged. He held out a big hand. "I'll take that dollar, then, and two more, one for each body."

Dakers frowned. "Well, it *is* highly irregular, but go ahead." He smiled a rather oily smile. "Any valuables, of course, are to be entrusted to me."

Jim shook his head. "Any valuables go to the next of kin."

"Unknown," said Dakers.

Jim flipped his cigarette into the open front of the stove. "I'll have to ask Brady Short, Alfred Hitchins, or Sheriff Cullin the correct procedure for any valuables or possessions, Mr. Dakers."

Dakers flushed again. "As you please," he said. "Excuse me, Mr. Murdock." He walked into the front of the long building and shut the door behind him, leaving Jim with the dead.

Jim lighted a Rochester lamp that hung over the marble slabs. Swiftly he went through the pockets of the three corpses. He peeled back their clothing and looked for markings of any kind, but outside of manufacturers' labels in some of the cheap clothing there were no identifying marks.

Jim drew sheets over the bodies and covered the set blue faces. He heard the front door open and close. Swiftly he gathered up the items he had found and placed them in three different pockets, thus separating them according to the body from which he had removed them. He put out the lamp and left by the back door, coming through the alleyway in time to see Dakers talking to Sheriff Cullin on the front steps of the jail. Cullin nodded and walked with the little undertaker across the street through the swirling snow toward the funeral parlor.

Jim walked past the front of the funeral parlor as the two men walked into the back room where the bodies were. He went quickly to the livery stable and got his cantle roll, emptied his saddlebags of what he required, placed the items in a feed sack, told Meany that if anyone asked for him he'd gone out to see his brother Ben, then hurried through the rear alleyway to the back entrance of the Ute House. He registered for a second-floor corner room overlooking the central part of town and went upstairs.

He closed the door of his room and dropped his gear, then walked to the window, parting the heavy curtains with his forefinger in time to see Sheriff Cullin walk toward the livery stable. Jim grinned. He was unknown to the hotel clerk, so if anyone asked for him and did not ask to see the register, he had time enough to go through the items he had taken from the bodies before Murray Cullin tracked him down.

CHAPTER FOUR

Jim peeled off his sheepskin and scaled his hat at a hook. He unbuckled his gun belt and hung it over the back of a chair, then took out the silver-mounted, double-barreled derringer he had won in a poker game in El Paso and checked both chambers. He slid it into a pants pocket. He locked the door and then turned his attention to the three little piles of dead men's relics.

The man named Gil had a left a half-bitten plug of Wine-sap, a handful of change, a lead pencil with a broken point, a filthy bandanna, and a piece of paper, spotted, wrinkled and limp, with badly written words upon it.

Deer Sarah, [read Jim] I take pencil in hand to write you these few lines. I didn't get the job with Masterson like he said he would but there is a Mex I met at Maddows who is a nice fella, who says he and I can turn a trick or two together north of here. Well I don't know but I am out of scratch and need work so I can send for you my dear Sarah. I hocked my riffle and good saddle in Maddows to a Jew who seems like he is all right for scratch, to go with the Mex who is all right for a spic I tell you Sarah. I can't always have bad luck Sarah and you know no one to home will give me a job because of the old days which are long gone and won't never come back I tell you. I will mail this letter from Ute Crossing which the spic says is a good place for work. Ha ha Sarah any place is a good place of work for me. I say goodbye now and send you my best wishes, and be patent for I will soon have good work and scratch for both of us my dear Sarah.

Gil turned the pitiful letter over. There was no address. Who was Sarah? He shrugged and placed the letter in his wallet, and left the other items on the bed.

Orlando the Mexican had left a little more than Gil. A finely figured Mexican wallet with a badly faded picture of a woman and two little children seated in front of an adobe house with *ristras* of peppers hanging down like great bunches of fruit. He turned the picture over. He could just make out the faded words "Santa Fed ..." There were a few Mexican bills in the wallet. A tobacco pouch and a few sweet Mexican cigarettes. A gilt button with the Mexican coat of arms of snake and eagle and the letter C embossed below them, likely from an army uniform. There was a worn leather box about the size of a medal box. Jim opened it. A beautiful, though worn, hunting-case watch was set in the faded green velvet. He opened the lid and looked at the dial. "American Horologe Company, Waltham, Mass.," he read. He worked a thumbnail under the back cover and snapped it open. A fine script had been engraved within. "To Teniente Teodoro... For heroic services rendered at Colonia..." read Jim. Part of the lettering had been scored through, making the names impossible to read. Jim closed the back cover and wound the watch. He pressed the repeater button and heard the expensive timepiece strike the nearest quarter hour. A helluva fine watch for a saddle bum to be carrying, but then it was likely stolen. The only other item left was a *barbiquejo* hat strap with coin-silver ornamentation.

The kid had left practically nothing. An empty bag of

Ridgewood cigarette tobacco with a curious-looking bluish stone in it. A worn handkerchief. A box of matches, Round Dome Specials, with two matches still in it. A 'dobe dollar. A hardened half bar of Pears' soap. That was it, and the name of a sister—Jessica. ...

Jim swiftly made his choices. He took the Mexican's picture, the gilt button, and the expensive watch. From the kid's possessions he took the curious-looking stone and nothing else. He could easily remember Round Dome Special matches and Pears' soap. The soap was common enough in that country; the type of matches was not.

Hard knuckles rapped on the door. "Murdock?" said a familiar voice. It was that of Murray Cullin. Jim walked softly to the gaboon and placed the button and the watch in it. He slid the picture under the edge of the marble-topped dresser and the stone under the edge of the rug.

"Murdock? You in there?"

Jim picked up the lint-specked wad of Winesap and bit off a chew. He peeled off his vest and shirt and threw them on the bed, then walked to the door and opened it.

Cullin brushed past Jim and looked about. He saw the items on the bed. "What's this?" he said.

"Must be what you're looking for," said Jim. He worked his chew into pliability.

Cullin poked through the things with a spatulate finger. "You had no business taking these things," he said.

"Why? No one around here seemed interested in who those men were."

Cullin looked around the room, glancing at the worn walnut butt of the holstered Colt. "No one knew who they were," he said. "They wouldn't give their real names."

"John Does to you, eh, Cullin?"

Cullin turned slowly and studied Jim. "What's your game, Murdock?" he said coldly.

Jim leaned against the wall and shrugged. "Someone should notify the next of kin."

"Three killers? Is it worth it?"

"Cain had relatives," said Jim. "They must have been interested even in him."

"You've got a great sense of humor, Murdock. Maybe you've even read a book in your time."

"Some," admitted Jim.

Cullin poked through the items again. "Like your brother, eh?" he said.

"Maybe even you could learn something from him, Cullin."

Cullin turned again. "Put up your hands," he said.

Jim straightened up. As he did so he spat a juicy gob into the gaboon. Cullin's practiced hands felt about Jim's hard body. "I didn't know you cared," murmured Jim.

Cullin took the derringer from Jim's pocket. "You could get into trouble with one of these stingy guns around here," said the lawman.

"Is there a local ordinance against it?"

"No." Cullin dropped it into Jim's pocket. He looked about the room again.

Jim walked over to the gaboon and spat into it again.

"Filthy habit," said Cullin.

Jim wiped his mouth. "I wasn't brought up right," he said.

"That's a damned lie," said Cullin. "You came from fine stock, Murdock."

"As the twig is bent," said Jim.

Cullin looked about the room again. "What are your plans?" he said.

"Get a bath. Change these clothes. Get some breakfast."

"Damn it, Murdock! You know what I mean!"

Jim shifted his chew. "I don't know, and if I did know, I'd be damned if I'd tell you, Cullin."

The sheriff looked down at his big hands. "Sometimes it pains me to uphold the law. There are times when I'd enjoy breaking it myself."

"Any time. Any time," murmured Jim politely.

"You never avoid trouble, do you?"

Jim leaned against the wall again. "I didn't exactly want to go with those human wolves this morning, if that's what you mean."

"That's not what I meant."

Jim shrugged. "If you mean my coming back to Ute Crossing, then I say to you that I was cleared years ago of the charge of killing Curt Crowley. It went as high as the governor and he OK'd it, Cullin. Even in the face of Cass Crowley."

Cullin's eyes narrowed. "Just what do you mean by that?"

"You know as well as I do that the governor was just as afraid of Crowley's political power in this state as most officials are."

"Does that include me?"

"You've been sheriff for a long time, Cullin."

Cullin ground a balled fist into the palm of his other hand. He walked to the bed and picked up the items there, dropping them indiscriminately into the side pockets of his coat.

"How will you know who owned those things?" said Jim. "In case anyone happens to ask for them."

Cullin walked to the door and turned. "I want no trouble from you in this county, Murdock. I have nothing but the greatest respect for Ben, like most people around Ute Crossing do, and I really believe Ben thinks he cleared you, but in my book you were never cleared. You walk quietly, mister. You walk *very* quietly." He opened the door and walked out.

Jim spat viciously into the gaboon without thinking. He locked the door and then retrieved the watch and button. He wiped them off and pocketed them.

The snow was still falling when he finished his bath and dressed in fresh clothing. He placed his hat on his head and eyed himself in the gold-flecked, tarnished mirror. "You handsome dog, you," he said with a grin. "By

God, you just walk quietly, mister, you just walk *very* quietly."

He ate well in the busy restaurant next door to the hotel, and was acutely conscious of the surreptitious glances he got from some of the other patrons. He bought half a dozen short sixes and stowed them away in his cigar case, lighting one of them at the counter before he strolled out into the open air and stood watching the falling snow beyond the wooden awning. The wide street was already an inch or more deep in snow, scored by hoof and wheel tracks. He'd have to go out and see Ben. He had mixed feelings about seeing Ben again. Ben had developed a penchant for preaching in his last letters, and Jim wasn't quite in the mood for sermonizing. "Settle down," Ben would say. "Get a nice wife. Get a steady job. Raise a family. Teach your kids the difference between right and wrong. Respect for the law."

Jim looked in the direction of the gallows hill. Nature was trying its best to hide the sight from the eyes of the people of Ute Crossing, but it could never erase the thought of what had been done there that very morning from the minds of every man, woman, and child in Ute Crossing. The ugly story would spread throughout the valley of the Ute and over the mountains with incredible speed, and the whole state would know about it before the start of the next week. This was Saturday morning. By Friday the story would have spread throughout all the neighboring states, with variations, embellishments, and changes to suit the taste and imagination of the teller.

He'd have to see Ben. Jim walked to the stable and got a fresh horse from Meany. Ben lived three miles from town in a little place he had bought after he had sold the old Murdock place south of town. There had been too many memories, he had written, and being a cripple, he could no longer handle the place. All his life now was devoted to teaching. He'd be a good teacher, thought Jim, as he guided the gray from the stable and rode west along the main stem, sheepskin collar turned up high, cigar thrust out from taut jaw, eyes far away from Ute Crossing. For some odd reason he was thinking of a girl called Jessica.

If Jim Murdock's mind was far away as he rode out of Ute Crossing that morning, there were others that were quite conscious of his physical presence in the town. Four pairs of eyes peered through the dirty, streaked windows of Baldy Victor's Grape Arbor Saloon.

"I didn't' like the way he talked to me this morning," said Barney Kessler. He hiccupped. "Him and me was amigos in the old days, all through school. I rode fence with him for Cass Crowley, too. Taught him all I know. Ridin', shootin', brandin' and roping. You seen the way he acted toward me."

Buck Grant, the man who had roped the Mexican Orlando and who had strung up the reatas to lynch the three prisoners, looked sideways at Barney. "*You* taught *him* ropin', Barney." He grinned loosely. "That's the best one I heard today."

Lyss Adams wiped his mouth and shifted his chew. "What'd Murdock have to show up today for, anyways? It was almost as though someone tipped him off to what was goin' to happen."

"You talk like a man with a hole in his head," said Baldy Victor as he wiped the bar. "Ain't no reason Jim Murdock would want to come back to witness a lynching. He come so goddamned close to one himself he wouldn't like to see another. He likely come back to see his brother."

Buck Grant turned from the window. "Yeah, but why, Baldy? Ben Murdock's been doin' a lot of talkin' around here. Drives like a madman into town in that buggy of his, lowers his wheelchair to the ground, then rolls that damned thing all over town. He wants to talk to them prisoners. He gets Murray Cullin all riled up. He sends a telegram to the governor. He tells the kids in his school them three hombres we strung up are innocent until proven guilty. That's the best I heard yet."

Van Lassen leaned his meaty belly against the bar and curled a huge hand about his glass. "He was right about that, anyways."

"You mean we done wrong?" challenged Barney. "It was you who got the idea, Lassen."

"Shut up!" said Lassen. "I get tired of hearing you run off at the mouth."

They all lined the bar. Lyss shifted his chew and spat into the gaboon. It rang with the wet impact. "All the same, what'd Murdock come back today for?" He looked at Lassen. "By God! You don't suppose he's a lawman, do you, Lass?"

Lassen's flat amber eyes studied Lyss. "So what if he is?"

"Well, we ain't got Cass Crowley around no more. Sure, we avenged him, like it says in the Bible, but he's gone now. Supposing Murdock is representing someone away up."

"Like God, maybe?" jeered Barney.

Lyss shook his head. "Like the governor, maybe?"

Buck Grant laughed. "The governor does what he's told in this state. He don't make no decisions."

Lassen looked down into his glass and then drained it. "There's another government, you know," he said quietly. "The federal government." He did not look at the others.

It was very quiet in the saloon. Boot heels struck the wooden sidewalk outside. A dog barked. Baldy passed a moist hand over his shining skull.

"That's a lotta crap," said Barney boldly. "Ain't no jury in this state would prove us guilty, like I said this morning."

"*You* said this morning," mimicked Grant.

Lassen looked into the mirror behind the bar. "I don't like this," he said slowly. "Ben Murdock is a pain in the rump, always shootin' off his mouth about rights, justice, good citizenship, and all that crap, but Jim Murdock is a fightin' man. He always was and he always will be."

"Until someone cuts him down," said Barney loudly.

It was very quiet again. They all looked at each other.

Baldy Victor rubbed his jaw. "The drinks are on me," he said. He did not look at the four men as he said it.

Jim crossed the creaking bridge that spanned Warrior Creek. The swirling water was black against the newly fallen snow. To the south was the old Murdock place on the banks of Warrior Creek. The sight of the creek brought back many old memories to Jim. Ranching had been in his blood in those days, and until he had gotten into trouble for supposedly shooting Curt Crowley, he had practically run the Murdock ranch alone, for Ben, when he wasn't talking, always had his

nose in a book and his thoughts on going to college. Well, he had finally achieved his hopes for an education —the hard way. Substituting a schoolroom for the open range and wheels for legs.

The low bridge rails were capped with snow, and the flooring of the bridge was untouched as yet by wheel or hoof tracks. The black water looked icy cold to Jim, almost as though it would freeze solid at any time.

A wraith of smoke curled up from Ben's chimney and vanished in the snow. There were no other houses anywhere near the place, which likely suited Ben fine, for he wasn't much for company except in the schoolroom, or with men like Brady Short and Alfred Hitchins, who could match Ben's intellect and his thirst for knowledge.

Jim swung down from the gray and led him into the little barn where Ben kept his team. Jim eyed the two sleek mares Ben used to pull his buggy. He wondered if Ben still drove like Jehu. Ordinarily quiet and introspective, not given to sudden words or sudden movements, Ben seemed to change when he gripped the reins. One mare would have been aplenty to pull Ben's buggy, but Ben liked two. That team must have set him back a good piece of change, particularly on a schoolteacher's salary.

Jim walked around to the front of the house and rapped on the door. "Who is it?" a familiar voice called out. "It's Jim, Ben."

There was a moment's pause, and then a chain rattled behind the door and a key turned in the lock. The door swung open and Jim saw Ben seated in his wheelchair. For a moment Jim stared. Ben was only five years older than Jim, hardly thirty-three as yet, but he seemed to have aged immensely in the seven years since Jim had seen him. His hair was almost pure gray and his face was deeply lined. He held out a thin hand to Jim and gripped it tightly. "Why didn't you tell me you were coming home, Jim?" he said quietly. "I wasn't sure I was coming, Ben."

Ben closed the door. He reached for the key in the lock, glanced uncertainly at Jim, then wheeled himself over beside the marble-topped table. A book lay open in the yellow light from an Argand lamp. "You might have let me know, Jim," said Ben.

Jim peeled off his coat and hung it and his hat on a hall tree. Ben's eyes flicked down to Jim's waist and saw the familiar bulge of holstered Colt beneath the dark coat. He narrowed his eyes.

Jim sat down and held out his cigar case to Ben. Ben shook his head. He watched Jim light up. "It didn't take you long to get into the swing of things," he said.

Jim looked through the wreathing smoke. "You heard about the lynching? I hardly had a choice, Ben."

Ben waved a hand. "I know that. You just seem to have the Devil's own luck."

Jim shrugged. "Seems as though no one will be called to account for it. Van Lassen practically defied Sheriff Cullin to do anything about it. Lassen said no jury in the state would convict them."

Ben drummed thin fingers on the table. "He's right," he said quietly. "Cass Crowley is here in death as he was here in life."

Jim inspected the end of his cigar. "There are no Crowleys left," he said.

"Cass Crowley had a host of friends," said Ben. "He was a hard man in many ways, but an honest man."

"Except in politics," said Jim.

Ben nodded. "That seemed to be an obsession with him. I never quite knew why. He had everything. Money, respect, position, and everything else most people want."

Jim leaned back in the chair. "Well, maybe Van Lassen was right when he said he'd save the taxpayers some money." He studied Ben as he spoke.

Ben flushed. "You talk like a fool!" he said hotly. "This is not justice! For hundreds of years we've struggled to have justice. Laws that punish and protect. Guilty or not, those three men had a right to the due process of law."

"To get hanged anyway," said Jim dryly.

"You've lost the point," said Ben coldly. He looked closely at Jim. "The very reason I fought to clear you is why I was fighting to help those three men, Jim. I was afraid something like this would happen. I *knew* it would happen!"

Jim relighted his cigar. "Why, Ben?"

Ben looked back at the door and then at the windows. "The evidence that was brought against those men did not satisfy me."

"It seemed to satisfy Brady Short, Alfred Hitchins, and Sheriff Cullin. Not to mention Meany Gillis and Mr. Dakers, the undertaker."

Ben leaned forward. "It was circumstantial evidence that was brought against you, Jim. Supposing I had not believed you were innocent?"

"I wouldn't be here now."

"Exactly."

"Then you think those men were innocent?"

"I do not."

"Then what's bothering you outside of the fact that the law was broken this morning?"

Ben looked again at the door.

"You want me to lock it again, Ben?" said Jim.

Ben quickly turned his head, and there was a faint trace of fear in his eyes. "No," he said.

"What's bothering you, Ben?"

Ben closed his eyes. "Make some coffee," he said.

Jim studied his brother. "You've been making trouble for yourself," he said. "You ought to know better than to stick your nose into every law case in this county. You've got no right to do that, Ben."

Ben opened his eyes. "It is the right of every good citizen."

"You're not in the classroom now, Ben."

Ben slammed his fists down on the arms of his chair. "You talk like a blind fool!" he said. "Go make that coffee before I lose my temper!"

Jim stood up and shrugged. The glass of the window just beyond his chair was suddenly shattered. Something smashed into the Argand lamp and hurled it from the table against the wall, splattering kerosene against the carpeting and the wallpaper. Ben grunted in savage pain as glass splinters lanced into his cheek. The report of a heavy rifle came echoing from somewhere across the creek.

Jim shoved his brother's wheelchair into a corner and dragged him from it. "Stay down!" he yelled. He dropped flat and bellied toward a window. The window shattered just over his head, and he winced as broken glass tinkled on the floor and struck his back and the back of his head.

Flames licked along the edge of the carpet and danced on the wooden floor, while a tiny runnel of flame worked its way along the soaked wallpaper. Jim snatched up a rug and beat out the flames. A cold wind poured into the room from the two shattered windows.

"Where's your rifle?" demanded Jim.

"I don't keep any guns," said Ben.

"That figures," said Jim dryly.

Minutes ticked past. There was no sound except the icy rushing of the snow-laden wind around the little house.

CHAPTER FIVE

Jim finished hanging rugs over the two shattered windows, nailing them to the frames, and then he walked warily outside to close the shutters. There was no sign of life in the shallow valley of the Warrior. The snow had lightened but there was still quite a bit of it, and the wind was much colder. Jim walked back inside the house and leaned his Winchester against the wall. Ben had lighted another lamp and was in the tiny kitchen making coffee. Jim dug the two slugs out of the wall. They were .44/40s, about as common a caliber as one could find in that part of the country, and throughout the West, for that matter, as they were interchangeable between rifle and pistol.

Ben rolled his chair back into the living room and placed the coffeepot on the table. "Cups in that cabinet there," he said. His face was white and taut.

Jim got the cups. "Why, Ben?" he asked.

Ben looked up. "They were after you," he said.

Jim filled the cups. "Why the double lock on the door?" he asked. "Why the look of fear in your eyes? You can't fool me, Ben. Who's been hurrahing you, and why?"

Ben measured sugar and cream into his cup. "I don't really know," he said. He looked up at Jim. "It was like the beating I got when I was fighting to clear you. I've never found out who did it."

"When did this start?"

"About the time I got interested in those three prisoners."

Jim sipped his coffee. "Seems odd," he said. "They were certainly guilty from what I've managed to learn. Were there any other suspects?"

"None."

"Maybe you should have kept your nose out of it, Ben." Jim smiled and raised a hand. "I know. Justice!"

"You're getting the idea," said Ben dryly. "I still say those shots were meant for you."

"He was a lousy shot, then," said Jim.

"Across the creek with the snow coming down? I think he did very well."

"That's because you're no rifleman, Ben. The range was hardly more than seventy-five yards, with the wind behind him and me silhouetted between the lamp and the window. I will admit I stood up just at the right time."

"All right, then! What do you think it was? Was it me or was it you they were after?"

Jim lighted a fresh cigar. "It was a warning for me," he said. He looked over the flame of the match. "You can bet your bottom dollar on that."

"What makes you so sure?"

Jim shrugged. "I didn't make myself too popular this morning. Besides, there's something else I intend to do."

"Such as?"

Jim took out the items he had taken from the bodies of the three lynched men. "Someone has to tell their people they died."

"That's not up to you."

"No one else seems much interested."

"They were tramps, Jim, Nobodies. Drifters. They saw a chance to kill Cass Crowley and they took it. They knew they'd never get away with just robbing Cass Crowley. They *had* to kill him."

Jim smiled. "Who's making up evidence now, Ben?"

Ben flushed. "All right! All right! It just doesn't make sense, your going away like this. How can you find their people, anyway? No one ever found out their real names or where they came from."

Jim eyed the little pile of possessions. "I'll try," he said.

"It might take a long time, and what profit is in it for you, Jim?"

"I've got the time," said Jim quietly. He looked at his brother. "It's my way of doing things, Ben. You've got your teaching and your interest in justice and citizenship. You cleared me, but it was me who damned near ended up on that hill with a rope around my neck in the cold light of dawn. It was me who stood up there this morning and saw those three wretches get strung up like pigs to be slaughtered."

Ben narrowed his eyes. "Go on," he said softly.

Jim looked at his brother. "The kid had a sister named Jessica," he said.

"So?"

"Someone has to tell her, Ben."

"I had hoped you'd stay here with me for awhile. Settle down. Get a nice wife. Get a steady job. Raise a family. Teach your kids the difference between right and wrong. Respect for the law."

"Oh, God," murmured Jim. I knew it, he thought. I just knew it!

Ben's jaw tightened. "I've had my say," he said.

Jim stood up and drained his cup. "I've got a room at the Ute House," he said.

"I thought you'd stay with me, Jim," said Ben in a hurt tone.

"Later, Ben. I've got some plans."

"Sure! Sure! Gambling! Booze! Women! Is that it?"

Jim couldn't help it. "What else is there?" he said. He

looked about the room. "I'll leave my rifle here and pick up a gun in town for you."

"I don't need any."

Jim shrugged. "As you will." He looked down at Ben. "These three men who were lynched. Tell me all you know about them, Ben."

Ben emptied his cup and refilled it. "They came from the south, maybe from New Mexico, about a month ago. One of them was a Mexican. They camped over on the Blue for a spell. Cullin later found traces of their camp there, and a sheepherder said they bought coffee from him. They told him they would be looking for jobs around Ute Crossing. Van Lassen was still working for Crowley then. It was him that found Crowley in his living room with three .44 slugs in the back of his head. The place had been ransacked. Lassen notified Cullin. Cullin formed three posses. One headed over Wind Pass. One headed west toward the Warrior Peak country. Cullin himself went back to the ranch with the third posse. It was Cullin alone who found the three killers hiding out near Brushy Creek. Cullin himself rounded them up. Murray Cullin has more solid guts than a brass monkey."

"So they were brought in to Ute Crossing."

Ben nodded. "There was a lot of talk going on in the saloons. Some of Crowley's riders and friends were ready to hang the three of them right then, but Murray Cullin isn't the man to be bluffed, and you can thank God for that. Brady Short suggested a change of venue, for everyone was clamoring for a trial, and you know what would have happened if a trial was held in this county."

"*I have a good idea.*"

"One of my pupils heard the shooting over on the creek when Murray rounded up the three of them. It didn't last very long. They didn't seem to be desperate men to me."

Jim nodded. He could see the three of them as though they now stood in front of him. "That's the whole story, then?"

Ben nodded. "Cullin kept a close guard over them. I suppose he was afraid of what would happen if he relaxed."

"Harlan Meigs sure relaxed last night," said Jim dryly. "The boys got him drunk as a hoot owl in the Ute House Bar last night. He was out cold in the office when the mob broke in. Old Mike Curry was laid out cold too. Maybe never had a chance to wake up."

Jim shrugged into his coat and put on his hat. "You sure you don't want a gun?"

Ben looked up. "That shot was for you, Jim. It was a warning. Why, I don't know."

"Maybe a lot of people still think I killed Curt Crowley."

Ben nodded.

"The only way they'll ever believe I'm innocent is when they find Curt's killer." Jim placed a hand on Ben's shoulder. "I'll be all right in time, Ben. Let me do what I want to do. Maybe then I'll come live with you and try to make something out of myself. After seven years I can't place myself in harness. Give me a little time, eh, Ben?"

Ben looked away. "You haven't changed much in some ways. You left here a wild, gun-flashing hellion. You don't seem wild now, and I don't know anything about your gunplay, but there is still much of the lobo in you. I had hoped for something better, Jim."

"The Mex border isn't exactly the place for peaceful pursuits, Ben. Besides, you've got a profession. You're a respected teacher. Me, I live the only way I know how. You talk about the law and justice, but all you really do is talk. No offense to you, Ben. There are some of us who have to do the dirty work, and being a lawman is accepting that kind of work. Murray Cullin will tell you the same thing."

"He still thinks you killed Curt Crowley."

"You proved I was miles away when Curt was killed."

"I proved that to the governor. I never convinced Cullin, or a lot of other people, for that matter. Curt

Crowley was popular, Jim, and he was the son of Cass Crowley. Likely if it had been anyone else around here you would have been forgiven. Then, too, you were a hellion, as I said before." Ben looked up at his younger brother. "You know, kid," he added quietly, "if I could walk and ride again, I think I'd do the same thing you are doing."

"Change of heart?"

Ben shook his head. "There is a streak within us Murdocks that calls for justice, for doing things right. I don't know whether or not you will find the people of those three men, but in the search you will learn something. Something that you will never learn here."

"I'll see you before I go, Ben."

"I hope so, Jim."

They shook hands. Jim closed the door behind him and shivered in the biting wind. The snow had stopped and the sky was a steely gray, and the cold was a living thing.

He rode slowly back into town, cigar clenched in his even white teeth, his thoughts were miles away at times, but his eyes shifted constantly, studying each snow-covered mound, clump of trees, hump of rock, any place that just might afford enough cover for a rifleman. He knew that shooting had been a warning. Someone either wanted him to forget about finding the relatives of those three dead men, or wanted him to mind his own business if he stayed in Ute Crossing. He ran quickly through his mental file. He had hardly made any new friends, or renewed old acquaintances, since he had returned to Ute Crossing.

He spent several hours in making purchases for his search and knew, without doubt, that his activities had been observed. He placed his supplies in the livery stable and went back to his room. He wasn't in the room two minutes when he knew someone had been there in his absence. The room was as neat as when he had left, but someone had been up there.

Jim stood for a long time at the window, watching the slow approach of the winter dusk. At last he lighted the lamp and took out the cheap atlas he had bought in the general store. "Maddows," he said thoughtfully. He scanned the listing of towns in this state, as well as those that bordered it to the south, finding no such place as Maddows. The man named Gil had mentioned such a place. All Jim really knew was that Gil had been at such a place and that it was south of Ute Crossing. He located the Blue, a creek high in the rough mountains southwest of Ute Crossing. The three men had camped there for a month and had said they were moving north to Ute Crossing. Jim scanned the country in the area of the Blue, but there was no Maddows. The best he could do was to start southwest to the country of the Blue and work from there. Somehow he did not want to find Three Forks and the girl named Jessica until he had first found out about the man named Gil. He had almost canceled out the Mexican. He had no great desire to return to the border country at this time.

Someone rapped on the door. It was the lone bellhop of the Ute House, with a message from Brady Short. It was imperative that Jim come and see him as quickly as possible. Jim put on hat and coat, put out the lamp, and hurried to the stable to get the gray. The wind had stopped and an icy hardness was settling over the country, unusually cold weather for that time of the year. The gray's hoofs rang on the iron-hard road as Jim rode north to where Judge Whitcomb had built his great house so many years past.

He saw the lights of the house long before he saw the house itself. Ann would be there. She had been nineteen when Jim had left Ute Crossing. An ash blonde with hazel eyes that could cut a man's heart to pieces like a Mexican *sacatripas*. It had almost been a foregone conclusion that Ann would marry Jim. The old judge hadn't been too happy about the matter. It wasn't Jim's family he had been concerned about. The Murdock name stood well in that country, and the judge had served with Sam Murdock in the volunteers during the war, down New Mexico way, and Sam Murdock had saved the judge's life at Glorieta. No, it had not been the family. Elizabeth Murdock had been a Hobbs, descendant of one of the pioneer fathers of the state. Ben had always ranked well among the young people of Ute Crossing. It had been Jim who had caused Jonas Whitcomb concern.

Now the Murdock family meant little. Elizabeth, never very strong, had died, and Sam Murdock had failed in his business and had passed on to his reward. Ben Murdock, a cripple, was still held in respect by Ute Crossing, but Jim had not gilded his own laurel wreath, if he had ever rated one. Sure, he was a fast gun, a good man with rope and branding iron, but the stigma of the brutal murder of Curt Crowley still hung about him like the dead albatross carried by the Ancient Mariner, no matter that Ben Murdock had cleared Jim's name.

He reined in the gray at the white picket fence and looked up at the familiar house with the wooden turrets, the gingerbread, the many tall windows with colored glass at the top, the wide verandas thick with crusted snow, and the swing swaying idly in the cold cat's paws of wind that crept now and then down the valley of the Ute. Jim remembered that swing. He wondered idly if it was the same one.

He led the gray into the huge barn and into a stall. There were at least a dozen other horses in the stalls. Brady Short had never been much of a rider, but he liked matched teams for his buggy, surrey, or buckboard. Jim wondered if Ann still rode as she had in the old days. The two of them had covered every mile of the valley of the Ute. Something seemed to turn in his heart as he remembered those days.

He walked up to the house and twisted the doorbell key, listening to the strident echo within the house, and the sound of it took him back a full seven years, and for a moment he almost thought he had never been away.

He saw a woman come into the hallway, and at first he thought it might be the maid. *"We have help, of course,"* Brady had said. *"It's quite too much for Ann, you know."*

He narrowed his eyes. It was Ann who was coming to the door. The door swung open, and he swiftly took off his hat. "Ann," he said with a smile.

He wasn't sure if she had changed much. Her flowing ash-blonde hair was now atop her shapely head, set with an expensive but simple comb. Her figure was just as exquisite as it had ever been, set off by a dress that certainly had never been bought in Ute Crossing. She held out a hand and flashed that lovely smile of hers, and once again his thoughts back-leaped seven long years. "Jim," she said. "It's good to see you." She tilted her head to one side. "You've changed."

"You haven't, Ann," he said.

"Come in! Come in! We've so much to talk about." She led the way into the huge living room, lighted by a huge, polished Rochester hanging lamp, and at least half a dozen Argand table lamps. A fire crackled in the fireplace. She took his old sheepskin coat and faded Stetson, Jim feeling somewhat ashamed of them the while, and placed them in the hall. He looked about the room. Hanging over the fireplace was the oil painting of Ann which almost looked as though it would come to life.

"Sit down, Jim," she said. "You may smoke if you like."

"Cigar?" he said with a sly grin.

She laughed. "I've gotten over that. Dad used to smoke them before he became bedridden and Brady, of course, is always receiving boxes of them from clients, friends, and admirers."

He glanced at her. She had slightly, ever so slightly, accented the word *admirers*. This time he managed to see through the facade of lovely memory and saw Ann Short as she really was, a twenty-six-year-old woman who still had her beauty, but with something a little glacial about it now. Jim lighted up a cigar from the humidor on a table and raised his eyebrows a little. Only in his plush days had he ever been able to afford a cigar like it.

"How is Ben?" she asked.

Jim shrugged. "Older looking. Perhaps you have not noticed it. I've seen quite a few changes in people since I've returned."

"You've changed yourself. That scar, Jim. Isn't there anything you could have done to it?"

Jim passed the tips of his fingers down the disfiguring line. "There were no stitches taken in it," he said quietly. "It was a week before I reached a doctor. The man who did it meant to mark me for life if he did not kill me."

"And him, Jim? What happened to him?"

Jim dropped his hand. "I didn't have much choice," he said.

"You killed him?"

Jim nodded.

"Death seems to hover about you, Jim."

Jim eyed her. Her face was a little flushed. He looked toward a side table, set with glass decanter and wineglasses. The firelight danced against the ruby contents of the decanter. It looked like blood.

"Wine, Jim?" she said. "I have brandy too. Scotch. Rye. Bourbon. Gin."

"Sounds like the Ute House Bar," said Jim with a smile. "Scotch too?" He raised his eyebrows.

"Make your choice."

Jim blew a puff of smoke. "I'll have what you have been drinking," he said.

She flushed a little. "I don't quite know what you mean, Jim," she said quickly.

"It's getting to be a little obvious," he said.

"You never talked like that in the old days!"

He smiled. "I had no need to. I came to see Brady at his request, Ann. It was imperative. Those were Brady's words, not mine."

She walked to the side table. "Brady had to leave," she said over his shoulder. She filled two wineglasses.

Jim studied her shapely back. "Then I wouldn't have annoyed you," he said.

"You are not annoying me," she said. She turned, and the firelight brought her smooth ivory skin to warm life. "Besides, Brady told me to tell you what he had in mind."

"So?"

She placed the wineglass on the table beside Jim's chair. She did not move, looking down at him with those lovely eyes, gold-flecked, and for a moment he almost rose to take her in his arms. "Brady said I was to warn you, Jim," she said quietly.

"About what?"

"It's dangerous for you here in Ute Crossing."

Jim sipped the wine. It was excellent port. "Did Brady tell you why? Specifically, I mean."

She sat down across from him and sipped her wine in ladylike fashion, although the queer notion came to him that if he hadn't been there she'd have tossed off a glassful like a whiskey stud downing a shot of the friendly creature.

"Brady said you had antagonized Van Lassen and some of Van's friends."

"I'm worried about that," he said.

"He also said Sheriff Cullin is keeping an eye on you."

"That would be nothing new for him, even after seven years. As he told me, I had never been cleared of the charge of killing Curt Crowley. Not in his book, as he stated it"

"He's a stickler, Brady says."

Ann emptied her glass and glanced surreptitiously at the decanter.

"I'll have another too," said Jim dryly.

She flushed again. She filled the glasses and sat down again, watching him with those great eyes of hers. A warmth, not entirely engendered by the port, crept through him.

"Why don't you leave Ute Crossing, Jim?" she asked.

"I haven't been here twenty-four hours," he said. He

grinned. "I must admit they've been eventful hours. Too eventful...."

"Where would you go if you left?" she asked.

He leaned back in his chair. "I think you know," he said. "Why are you asking me?"

She emptied half of the glass. "Some foolish notion of going to find the people of those three unfortunate men. Isn't that the idea?"

"Yes."

"What can you possibly gain by that?"

"Nothing," he said. He looked down into his glass and twirled it on its stem, watching the red port swirl high on the rim. "I wasn't thinking of gaining anything. Anything material, that is."

"Spiritual, then?"

"Perhaps."

"You have changed, then!" she said challengingly.

He looked into those eyes where a man could lose his soul. "So have you, Ann," he said.

She looked away. She knew what he meant.

Jim relighted his cigar. It was comfortable in the warm room, sipping excellent wine, smoking a top-grade cigar, feeling the heat of the fire, but strangely enough the woman made him uneasy. He suddenly wanted to leave while he still had the old picture of her in his heart.

"Brady was so concerned about you," she said. Her voice slurred a little now and then. "He said there were too many people around here who still believed you had killed Curt Crowley. He said too that Ben had made enemies for clearing you."

"Ben is still here," said Jim quietly.

"Ben has powerful friends," she said. "My husband, for one. And Sheriff Cullin likes Ben, although he won't always admit it. Alfred Hitchins thinks there is no one like Ben."

"And I have no one."

"You have Brady," she said softly. "And me..."

"I know that," he said. "I am leaving Ute Crossing,

Ann. I *am* going to look for the people of those three men. This should make everyone satisfied, but it doesn't seem to be doing quite that. What difference does it make if I do find the people of those three men? I feel that I must do it. It's as simple as that." He emptied his glass and stood up. He had a feeling that the house was empty except for Ann and himself. The wine had warmed his blood and stirred his passion.

She studied him for a moment, almost languorously, like a purebred she-cat watching an alley torn, scornful of his breeding, but interested in his obvious masculinity. "There's no need to get angry or to leave," she murmured.

"I have Brady's message," he said coldly.

She passed a slim hand across her lovely column of a neck. "It's lonely here," she said. "Brady is gone much of the time. I have little in common with the women of Ute Crossing." She lifted her eyes and looked full into his, and he knew right then and there that she was practically asking for it. A half-drunken doxy in a bordello would hardly have done it any differently.

He glanced toward the door.

"We're all alone, Jim," she said.

He did not dare look at her.

"Brady won't be back for hours, perhaps not until tomorrow."

He felt the cold sweat break out on him. Damn her! He had never been a close friend of Brady Short, but he admired the man for his ability and honesty, his education and intelligence. He knew that all he had to do was turn the lamps low, or take her by the hand. The touch of her hand would loose the floodgates within him. He had never forgotten her in those damnable seven years, nor could he drive her from his mind now.

A log fell in the fireplace. The wind whispered coldly about the great house. It was now or never!

"Stay," she murmured.

He looked at her. A spark seemed to leap the gap between them. Use your head, he thought. Keep away from her. You'll never be able to live in the valley of the Ute if you start in with her where you left off so many years ago.

"Jim?"

He had changed. She had said so. Everyone had said so. Yes, he *had* changed. "Tell Brady I thank him for his warning and advice," he said, and it seemed to him as though his voice were far away, as though someone else were talking, not Jim Murdock.

"Is that all?"

"What more do you want?" he asked cruelly.

She got up slowly. "Your coat and hat are in the hall," she said icily. "Let yourself out, please."

He walked to the door and looked back at her, and the look in her eyes struck at him like a living thing of hate.

"I was planning to spend a few weeks in Denver," she said quietly. "I will likely leave in a week or so. Brady thinks I need some city life. Some shopping. A little gaiety."

"Very thoughtful of Brady," said Jim.

"I am going alone," she said. Her face flushed. "If you happen to be up that way, Jim, I'll be at the best hotel." The last words came with a rush. She turned and walked toward the side table.

He shrugged into his coat, placed his hat on his head, looked up the wide, carpeted staircase to the darkness of the second floor, and thought of the many rooms up there. Of her room, likely exquisitely feminine, a background for the lovely creature who slept there. He could almost smell the perfume of the room, the perfume of her shapely body. He opened the door and shut it quietly behind him. The stairs squeaked beneath his weight in the bitter cold.

He led the gray from the barn and stopped in the road. Swiftly and quietly he padded back to the house and up the wide stairs. He looked into the living room. She stood with her back to him, and this time she had the decanter to her lips, her throat gulping convulsively as she swilled the good port.

Jim Murdock returned to the horse and mounted it. He rode toward Ute Crossing, and he did not look back through the thick, cold darkness to that vast mausoleum of a house that harbored a corpse of love. A love that would never live again.

CHAPTER SIX

Jim Murdock had crossed the hard-frozen Blue two days after leaving Ute Crossing. He had spent the first night in a sheepherder's abandoned shack, and the bitter, lingering cold had forced him to bring the sorrel within the shack as well, out of the freezing wind. The second night he had camped in the bottoms of an unnamed creek, with hardly an hour's uninterrupted sleep because of the cold and the distant howling of the wolves along the ridges. In those two days he had not seen another living thing, except for an occasional hawk drifting with motionless pinions against the cloudless sky like a scrap of charred paper.

He followed a faint trail down the southern slope of the foothills after leaving the Blue. The three men had camped there for a month, according to what he had learned, before heading northeast toward Ute Crossing. There was no use in looking for their campsite and the sheepherder who had told Sheriff Cullin about them. The sheepherder wouldn't be there now. The flocks would have been driven south into the lower country for the winter.

The sun came up but shed little heat over the cold world below it. It sparkled from the crusted snow and the frozen watercourses. Far down the slope, hidden in a dark fringe of trees, the sun sparkled and glinted from something else, surmounted by a hazy, drifting cloud. Smoke. Maybe a man could get a hot meal there.

Jim shifted stiffly in the saddle. Now and then he looked behind him. Always there was the feeling that someone was watching him. It was a reaction honed by his years on the border; a sixth sense that had saved his life more than once. But there was nothing behind him except the cold landscape and the glittering of the sun on the snow and ice. He would be glad to get out into the more open country to the south.

The shifting wind trailed the smoke toward him, and he began to distinguish houses, the movements of people, the faint hum of life. It was a bigger town than he had suspected. He rode slowly up the main street and a sign caught his eye. Masterson's Freight Company. A wagon yard was beside it, with light and heavy freight wagons layered with snow. From a huge corral behind the building came the bawling of a mule. Steam rose from the corral and the sheds, mingling with the smoke from the chimneys.

Jim dismounted in front of a small restaurant. A boy plodded by. "What's the name of this place, son?" asked Jim.

"Meadows," said the urchin. "Useta be Masterson's Meadows, but people jus' call it Meadows now."

Jim flipped him a dime. "Is there a hock shop here?"

The kid grinned. "You down on your luck, mister? You kin have the dime back if you are."

Jim grinned back. "No. The dime is yours."

The kid pointed up the street. "You see that buildin' down there? The one leanin' over a little like it's all tired out? That's the Jew's place. Sam buys and sells anything. Anything, I tell you!"

Jim ate in the restaurant and took the sorrel to the livery for a feed. It was almost noon when he crossed the street to the curiously leaning structure. While he had eaten he had put two and two together. Gil was a lousy speller. He had written Maddows instead of Meadows ... *Masterson's* Meadows. He had mentioned not getting a job with a man named Masterson.

Jim opened the door and walked into a weird wonderland of a vast accumulation of anything and everything he could think of. Shelving ran from floor to ceiling, crammed with all kinds of odds and ends. Boxes cluttered the floor, filled to the brims with oddments. Wires had been strung from one side of the long building to the other, and from the wires hung pots and pans, whips, harness fittings, housewares of all kinds, including a row of elegant chamber pots. The bell stopped tinkling on its big coiled spring.

"You are wanting to buy or sell, maybe?" a soft voice asked.

A derby hat seemed to rise by itself from behind a rampart of dusty sacks of feed. A wizened face studied Jim with a pair of the softest brown eyes he had ever seen outside of a doe.

"I'm looking for Sam," said Jim.

"Speaking," said the little man.

Jim walked to the rampart and looked over to see an immense rolltop desk, the pigeonholes crammed with papers, the top inches deep in forms of one kind or another. A parrot hung in a cage over the desk. "The drinks are on you, stranger!" he squawked.

"That's the story of my life," said Jim with a smile.

"You are wanting to buy? To sell? Maybe you want to buy the business? A partner I couldn't use."

Jim shook his head. "I'm afraid I'd get lost in here, Sam."

"So? I've been lost in here for ten years. What can I do for you?"

Jim shoved back his hat and felt for the makings. He offered them to Sam, and the little man shook his head. "I got a cough," said Sam. "I came west from Pittsburg to get rid of it. I should smoke? Crazy I'd be!"

Jim rolled a cigarette and lighted it. "I'm looking for information on a man named Gil," he said.

"You're a lawman?"

Jim shook his head. "He hasn't done anything," he said. He half closed his eyes. "That isn't right either."

"You are talking riddles."

Jim blew a smoke ring. "A few days ago a man by that name was lynched in Ute Crossing with two other men."

"The men what killed Mr. Crowley," said the merchant.

Jim nodded. "I found a letter in his pocket written to a woman named Sarah, but there was no address. He mentioned being here in Meadows and that he had hocked his rifle and saddle to a Jewish merchant here."

There was no expression on Sam's face.

"Do you have the rifle and saddle?" asked Jim.

"I might have."

Jim studied the little man. "There's no trouble in this for you, Sam."

"How do I know?"

"Because I tell you so."

Sam eyed the hard gray eyes, the disfiguring scar, the outthrust jaw of the big man. "I believe you," he said. He walked around the desk and brought back a Sharps-Borchardt rifle which he placed on the rampart of sacks. He went back and hauled out a good-looking saddle which he just managed to lift to a place beside the rifle.

"Can I look at them?" asked Jim.

"Be my guest," said Sam. He sat down in his swivel chair and watched Jim.

The saddle was a rim-fire hull made by Pearson of El Paso. Gil had not exaggerated when he had said he had hocked his "good saddle" in Maddows:

"A hundred-dollar saddle on a forty-dollar horse," said Sam quietly.

Jim nodded. Gil had likely worked in Texas, for the rim-fire or double-rigged hull was a favorite down that way. In this state the favorite was the Pueblo, made by either Gallup or Frazier, built more for rugged country and topping rough horses than for roping, where one had to be in and out of the saddle a lot. He had never heard Gil speak, so he couldn't tell if he had been a Lone Star stater.

The single-shot rifle was somewhat unusual, hardly the type to be carried as a saddle gun like the handy, quick-firing Winchester repeater. Jim checked the caliber. It was the government .45/70 with double-set trigger.

"A good rifle?" asked Sam.

Jim nodded.

"How much is it worth, maybe?"

Jim shrugged. "Fifteen dollars."

Sam paled a little. "I loaned him twenty-five on it. He didn't want to part with it, so I figured it was maybe worth something."

"You're all heart, Sam," said Jim.

"I know it," the little man said sadly.

"The drinks are on you, stranger!" squawked the parrot.

Jim examined the rifle. It was dented here and there, scratched quite a bit, but mechanically perfect. There were no identifying marks on it other than the maker's name and serial number.

There was a screwdriver lying on a table. Jim picked it up and removed the butt plate from the rifle. "Gil Drinkwater," he read. "Eighteen seventy-eight. Las Cruces."

"You're a clever fellow," said Sam. "In a hundred years I wouldn't have thought of that."

Jim replaced the butt plate. "Will you keep the saddle and rifle until I send for them?"

Sam shrugged. "Why not? Business is lousy. You wouldn't consider maybe buying me out?"

"Not today."

"The drinks are on you, stranger!" shrieked the parrot.

Sam stood up and watched Jim roll a cigarette. "You are maybe looking for the next of kin?"

Jim lighted up and then nodded.

"Why?"

Jim blew a smoke ring. "Someone has to do it," he said.

"He's got a wife, maybe? A family?"

"Someone named Sarah, Sam."

"A good Yiddish name."

"Did he come in here alone?" asked Jim.

"Yes."

"He was supposed to get a job with Masterson."

Sam nodded.

"Why didn't he get it?"

Sam rubbed his jaw. "About the dead I would not talk."

"Booze?"

Sam looked up. He nodded. "So drunk he was I didn't even want to take his goods, but he was desperate. You understand?"

"Yes."

Sam waved a hand. "He did not look like the kind of man who would kill an old man for money. Why, he didn't even have a gun when he left here, friend."

Jim looked up quickly from the rifle. "No belt gun?"

Sam shook his head. "I saw him ride from town with those two other fellows. A Mexican-looking fellow and a kid, a *boychik*. Someone said they were heading north to look for work. A strange trio, I thought. A drunkard, a sad-looking Mexican, and a scared-looking kid."

"You don't know anything about them?"

"No. We heard about the lynching last night. A mail carrier brought the news. A terrible thing for men to take justice into their own hands."

Jim nodded.

Sam leaned forward. "I'll keep the saddle and rifle for you. This woman. This Sarah. She has maybe no money?"

"Gil had written her that he would send for her when he had money and a job."

The sad doe eyes studied Jim. "Wait," said Sam. He vanished behind the desk. A door opened and closed. A few minutes later it opened and closed again. Sam reappeared. He handed Jim a wad of bills. "For the lady," he said.

Jim counted it. There were a hundred dollars in the wad. He whistled. "A lot of money, Sam. Maybe I'll take it and go off on a high lonesome."

The little man shrugged. "If you need a high lonesome, friend, more than Sarah needs the money, you go right ahead."

Jim grinned. "You're all right, Sam."

Sam shook his head. "It is you that is all right."

Jim walked to the door, followed by Sam. Jim turned and held out a hand.

The little man gripped it. "You will stop by on your way back, maybe? It was a pleasure doing business with you."

"The name is Murdock. Jim Murdock of Ute Crossing. I'll stop by, Sam, and let you know about Sarah. It might be a long time."

Sam smiled sadly. "What else do I have but time?"

Jim opened the door. The bell tinkled.

"The drinks are on you, stranger!" shrieked the parrot.

Sam shrugged. "He used to belong to a barkeeper. He ain't much company, but at least he talks to old Sam."

"Adios, Sam."

"Good-bye, Jim."

The bell tinkled as the door was closed behind Jim.

Jim crossed the border into New Mexico Territory at noon and camped that night in a ruined stone house in the valley of the San Juan. He reached Bernalillo four days later, put the sorrel into a freight car, and rattled down the valley of the Rio Grande to Socorro, where the railroad turned west. Then he crossed the old Jornado del

Muerto in the bright winter sunlight, ninety waterless miles to San Diego Mountain, where he took the well-traveled road into Las Cruces. He took a room in the old Amador Hotel; its rooms still had marked over the doors the names of the girls —La Luz, Maria, Esperanza, Natalia, Dorotea, Muneca, and others, twenty-three in all —who had served the officers from Fort Selden to the north and Fort Fillmore to the south in the old days. Where were they now? thought Jim. La Luz, Maria, and the others. Perhaps respectable dowagers, happily married to the young men who had patiently waited for their future brides to earn their dowries in the big bedrooms of the Amador.

Three days of questioning brought no information about Sarah. He tried first with the name Gil Drinkwater, and found that most of the bartenders remembered Gil all too well. He had been cut off many times by every one of them. Sarah? They didn't know. The only lead he got was the fact that Gil had written infrequent letters to someone in Ysleta, a few miles southeast of El Paso. Jim knew the town well, having served for a time with the Frontier Battalion of the Texas Rangers, C Company, which had its headquarters in Ysleta, but he had never known anyone by the name of Sarah Drinkwater.

A cold drizzle was turning the streets of Las Cruces into pasty, gray-white mud when he headed toward the Amador after checking out his gear, for he meant to leave the next morning for El Paso and points south. Here and there he caught glimpses of yellow light behind shuttered windows. He stopped in a doorway to light a cigar, his mind filled with thoughts, and as he raised his head and looked up he saw a man move swiftly into another deep doorway across the street. Jim winced as the match burned his fingertips. He lowered the cigar and held it behind him while he peered toward the dark doorway. There was no movement. Casually he thrust the cigar into his mouth and walked toward the next street, rounding the corner, then running as swiftly and as silently as possible to an alleyway. He darted into it, vaulted a low, crumbling adobe wall, cursing softly as his boots sank into the soft, odorous filth of someone's pigsty, then floundered across it to a gate set between two buildings. He walked swiftly toward the next street and stopped behind a sagging two-wheeled cart, peering between the rough slats so that his hat might not be silhouetted.

Boots thudded against the street, and a tall, broad-shouldered man passed the entrance of the alley. Jim padded to the mouth of the alley and looked up the narrow, twisting street. The man stood in front of a dimly lighted shop, also looking up the street. He turned as someone opened the shop door, letting a flood of yellow light into the wet street. His features were plain to be seen—a beak of a nose, a thick dragoon moustache, shaggy eyebrows that almost met over the deep-set eyes. "Lyss," said Jim to himself. There was no mistaking the man. Jim faded back into the darkness as Lyss walked toward the alley.

Jim unbuttoned his coat as an icy feeling poured through his body. He drew his Colt. A stream of cold water struck the back of his hat and flowed freely down his back. Boots squelched in the pasty mud of the street, and then the sound died away. This was no sheer coincidence, Jim thought. Lyss was looking for him, following him for some definite purpose. But why? It couldn't be a personal reason. Jim had not known the man in the old days, and he hadn't spoken to him when he had returned to Ute Crossing. But Lyss had seemed to be closer to Van Lassen than any of the other lynchers; about as close as any man could get to Lassen. Whatever Lyss had come to Las Cruces for prophesied no good to Jim Murdock.

Jim eased his way behind the cart. Boots squelched again, then stopped, then sounded again. Jim saw the wet back of Lyss's coat not two feet from him. Even as he looked, Lyss turned. Lyss opened his mouth. Jim's Colt barrel cracked alongside his head, but the heavy, wet brim of the hat saved the man from being coldcocked. Lyss staggered sideways, clawing for his Colt. He freed it. A knee came up into his groin. He grunted in agony. Once again the Colt barrel slapped at the side of his head, this time drawing blood from beneath the dark hair. Lyss swung wildly with his own Colt. The front sight traced a faint course down Jim's right cheek. Before the man could fire Jim kneed him again, and as his head came down in reflex the Colt barrel smashed across the base of his neck, driving his beak of a nose into the foul mud of the alleyway. He groaned once and lay still.

Jim padded to the mouth of the alley. No one was in sight. The shop lights were out. Jim wiped the blood from his face with the back of a hand and went back to Lyss. He rolled the man over, and wide, staring eyes looked up into his, but they did not see, nor would they ever see again.

Jim stood up, cursing softly. He had not meant to kill the man, but he knew as sure as fate that Lyss had meant to kill him. There was no time to stand there meditating about it. Perhaps Lyss had not come alone. Swiftly Jim ripped open Lyss's coat and took out his wallet. He took the bills from it, and the papers as well. He took the muddy Colt and thrust it into his coat pocket. He rolled the heavy body beneath the cart. If anyone found Lyss within the next day or so, they'd not be able to identify him, and if Jim could get clear of Las Cruces that night, it was possible he'd not be associated with the man's killing. Distasteful as his actions were, he knew he would have received the same treatment from Lyss.

Jim wiped the blood from his face again. He retreated the same way he had come. He had left word at the Amador that he would leave before dawn. There would be no one around to check what time he had left. He gathered his gear and left by the back way, walking to the stable where a hostler slept the deep sleep of the just. Jim tucked a bill into the man's shirt pocket and got the sorrel. He rode south on the El Paso road through the slanting rain. Ten miles from Las Cruces he dropped the empty wallet and the Colt into the well of an abandoned adobe. The bills he had placed in his own wallet. He ripped Lyss' papers to bits, letting the rain-laden wind scatter them through the muddy fields. He looked back through the darkness. A strange thought flitted through his mind. *Those who live by the sword ...*

CHAPTER SEVEN

Ysleta dozed a little in the bright sunlight that had followed the two-day rainstorm that had swept across lower New Mexico and West Texas. The air was fresh and clear, with a few puffs of clouds in the blue sky. The crisp ringing of a sledge upon metal came from a blacksmith's shop, mingled with the insistent braying of a mule.

The tall Yanqui rode into town on a tired, mud-splashed sorrel. There were always such horsemen on the road, and what they did or where they went was of little moment to the people of Ysleta. There was never any serious trouble in Ysleta. There was a good enough reason. A company of level-eyed, quiet-spoken gentlemen known as Texas Rangers had their headquarters there.

Now and then these tall horsemen would look back over their shoulders as though expecting to see someone following them. This, too, was not unusual. It was better, señor, for a man to mind his own business, you understand, for if the stranger did not bother you, why bother the stranger?

This stranger was not one to be trifled with or stared at, for the thin scar on his left cheek and the hardness of his gray eyes were the stamp of his breed. He was better left to his master, likely El Diablo.

Jim Murdock found Sarah's little adobe easily. In such a town everyone knew everyone else. The adobe had a neat garden in front of it, and a cat dozed on a chair in the sun. Jim tethered the sorrel to the fence and opened the creaking gate. A woman opened the blue-painted door of the adobe as Jim walked toward the house. Jim took off his hat.

She narrowed her pale blue eyes. "You've come about Gil," she said quietly.

"Mrs. Drinkwater, ma'am?" asked Jim.

She was as plain as a fence post and as gaunt as a Joshua tree, with a rather long face, almost horse-like in appearance, and the faint trace of a moustache showed on her lined upper lip. Her sparse hair was almost iron gray in color, drawn tightly back over her head. Her dress was black, with no adornment save a simple gold pin over her shallow breasts. All in all, hardly a woman a man would love, and yet the last lines of Gil's letter came back to Jim, almost as though imprinted on his mind. "*I say goodbye now and send you my best wishes, and be patent for I will soon have good work and scratch for both of us my dear Sarah.*"

"Where is he?" she asked.

Jim hesitated. "My name is Jim Murdock," he said. "From up north. Ute Crossing."

There was no recognition in her pale eyes. "What is it you have to tell me?" she asked.

She didn't know...She didn't know, but she expected the worst...

"Please come in, Mr. Murdock," she said. "It was impolite of me to keep you standing here."

The living room was sparsely furnished but neat and clean. A large sewing basket stood on a chair beside a rather ancient Howe sewing machine. "You must excuse this mess," she said with a faint smile. "You must understand that this is my place of business as well as being my home." She sat down in a rocker, straight backed, thin, worn hands folded in her lap. A plain gold wedding band showed on her left hand.

"You didn't know he was at Ute Crossing, ma'am?" asked Jim.

"The last letter I had from him came from Albuquerque," she said. "He had had a promise of a job further north. A place called Maddows, I believe."

"Meadows," said Jim. "Masterson's Meadows."

She smiled that faint, mirthless smile. "I taught Gil how to read and write," she said. "I never could teach him how to spell and punctuate."

Jim wet his lips. He looked about. This was going to be worse than he had anticipated.

"You may smoke," she said.

"Thanks, ma'am." Jim rolled a cigarette and lighted it. He drew in the smoke gratefully.

"He's dead, isn't he?" she said. She nodded. "You wouldn't have come this long distance for any other reason."

Jim nodded. "You might never have found out," he said quietly. "I thought you should know."

"How did he die, Mr. Murdock?"

This was worse than admitting Gil was dead.

"You may tell me, Mr. Murdock. I will find out someday, in any case."

"He was taken from the Ute Crossing jail by an armed mob," said Jim. He could go no further.

"Shot?" she said softly, very softly.

He twisted the brim of his hat in his big hands. "He was hanged, ma'am," he said at last. He did not dare to look at her.

"Why?" she asked.

He managed to look at her. "He and two other men murdered Cass Crowley, a prominent rancher and a political power in the state. If it had been a lesser known person Gil might still be alive with a chance for his life. Believe me, Mrs. Drinkwater, there were men in Ute

Crossing who did their best to save him and the others. The sheriff went all the way to the governor for a change of venue. It was while he was gone that the mob took justice into their own hands!"

There was a long silence. The thin hands worked a little. She was a lady, of good breeding, and she would not break down. The curious thought came into Jim's mind that she must have been a strange contrast to Gil and his rough ways. She had been educated.

"He was lynched, then?" she said suddenly in a clear voice. "My Gilbert was lynched?"

Dear God, thought Jim, *why did it have to be me that told her this news?*

"He meant to send for me," she said. "Somehow I knew he never would. That he would never come back."

Jim walked to the door and got rid of the suddenly tasteless cigarette. It was time to finish his business and leave her. There were others who had to be told. He wondered now if he could go through this experience two more times. He gently opened the thin hands and placed the badly written letter in them. "There was some money," he said.

She did not answer.

Jim took out his wallet. To the hundred Sam had given him he added the seventy-five dollars he had found in Lyss' wallet and added another hundred of his own. He placed the money on the side table beside the basket of sewing. "His saddle and rifle are up north," he said. "I can have them sent to you, if you like."

She shook her head. "Please accept them as compensation for your services."

"It's a fine saddle," he said.

"Yes. Gil wouldn't part with it for anything."

"No," lied Jim.

She looked up at Jim. "He had always been in trouble before we met in Amarillo," she said. "But those days were over. He only carried that rifle to shoot game when he needed it."

Jim studied her. "No beltgun? No six-shooter?"

She shook her head. "Gil never carried such a weapon. Not for many years."

"May I ask why?"

"Gil drank a lot. Years ago he accidentally killed his best friend in a drunken shooting match." She looked away. "Gil was a crack shot. When he was sober he'd win shooting matches with that rifle of his. He and his friend were shooting tin cups from each other's heads. Gil missed. He was exonerated, but he never carried a six-shooter again, and would only carry a single-shot rifle. It was a sort of taboo for him to have more than one cartridge. If he had stayed away from drink it would have been all right." She smiled. "I altered that."

"You stopped his drinking, then?" he asked.

She looked up. "Yes. They said I couldn't do it. He was a fine man when he wasn't drinking, Mr. Murdock." She narrowed her eyes. "Was he drinking up north?"

"No," lied Jim.

She stood up. "You want to leave," she said. "I don't blame you." She walked with him to the door. "How did Mr. Crowley die?"

"Shot through the back of the head. Three bullets. Forty-four caliber. Pistol bullets. They say each of the murderers had one empty shell in his six-gun when they were captured."

She placed a hand on his arm. "Then it was not Gil who was guilty," she said firmly. "He never carried such a weapon."

Gil Drinkwater had not been carrying a belt gun when he had been in Meadows. According to Sam, Gil didn't have any weapon at all, at least no gun of any kind. He could have picked up another, or borrowed one from the Mexican or the kid, who had been with him when Crowley was murdered.

"They did take care of his body?" she asked.

He nodded. "One of the leading citizens of the town paid for the burials," he said.

"Perhaps someday I will come and see his grave," she said.

"Perhaps you'd like to have his body brought down here," he said.

"No. He had no one who cared about him beyond me."

"*I can't always have bad luck Sarah and you know no one to home will give me a job because of the old days which are long gone and won't never come back I tell you...*"

She looked up into his face. "Let him stay with the two men with whom he died," she said. "They will have something in common, at least. They will be together. Good-bye, Mr. Murdock. It was kind and generous of you to let me know."

He walked to the gate without looking back and untied the sorrel. He mounted and rode swiftly away.

He was gone half an hour before she looked at the money for the first time, and she knew in her heart of hearts that Gil Drinkwater had never left her *that* much money.

———

IT WAS Sergeant Les Gilson of C Company, Frontier Battalion, Texas Rangers, who gave Jim a possible tip-off on where the people of the man named Orlando might be found. Gilson's strong, tobacco-stained fingers poked through Orlando's relics. "This button is from a Mex Army uniform," he said. He checked the inside of the watch as Jim had done. "Looks like a presentation watch for some kind of service. Won by a Teniente Teodoro something or the other. At Colonia someplace or another. There are a lot of *colonias* in Mexico, Jim."

Jim turned over the faded picture. "San Fed..." he said.

Gilson nodded. "Possibly San Fedro or San Federico."

"You know of such a place?"

Gilson pulled down a detailed roller map of the

border country, and then one of the State of Chihuahua in northern Mexico. He studied it for a moment. "Let me see that watch again," he said. He opened it and took a powerful magnifying glass from a drawer, studying the engraved script that had been scored through. "Eighteen seventy-two," he said at last.

Jim nodded. "Just as I suspected," he said. "The Mex must have stolen it. He was too young to have earned such an award that many years ago as a *teniente* in the Mexican Army."

Gilson snapped shut the watch. "About 1872 there was a helluva big Apache raid down into Chihuahua. A small force of Mexican soldiers fought them to a standstill and defeated them. There weren't many Apaches left alive after the fracas, and hardly enough soldiers left to bury the dead." He eyed the map. "The little *placita* where the Mexes held off the Apaches was abandoned by the people who had lived there because of the curse on it."

Jim rolled a cigarette and handed the makings to Gilson.

Gilson fashioned a smoke and lighted it. "By God!" he said. "That place was called Colonia Federico!"

Jim took the cigarette from his mouth. "You're sure about that, Les?"

The ranger nodded. "It's down near Laguna de Haros. There's nothing left down there now, Jim, except mounded graves and ruined dobes. I passed through that country some years ago on an undercover scout. You're wasting your time going down there."

Jim gathered together the relics of the man named Orlando. "It's enough of a lead to warrant a little time down there."

Gilson shook his head. "Beats the hell out of me," he said. "You were one helluva fine ranger, Jim, although I always did say you thought too much, too deep."

Jim grinned. "My mother used to say that about me." He gripped the sergeant's hand. "Much obliged, Les. I've found the kin of one of those poor men. I feel it is an obligation to find the others."

Les flipped his cigarette butt into a gaboon. "Where'd you find the first of them?" he asked.

Jim looked Les full in the eyes. "It doesn't really matter, does it, Les?"

Les shook his head. "I understand," he said.

The ranger watched Jim leave the headquarters building and lead the tired sorrel toward a livery stable. "Four hundred miles to tell the kin of a murdered man that he has died. Now he's riding south more than a hundred miles to do it again, *if* he can find the kin of the second murderer. I still think you think too much and too deep, Jim Murdock, but it's your life, and I know better than to tell you different."

———

JIM CROSSED the Rio Grande on a flatboat ferry to Zaragoza the day after he reached Ysleta, riding a chunky dappled gray he had traded the crippled sorrel for, plus twenty-five in cash. He had no desire to stay too long in Ysleta. There was extradition between New Mexico and Texas, of course, but none between those places and Mexico. They would have found the body of Lyss by now, and the law in Las Cruces and Dona Ana County might be more than passing interested in the man who had left the Hotel Amador in the dark of a rainy night to head south toward the border. He had registered under his own name, of course, for he had had no reason not to. If he had known he was being tailed by Lyss he would have registered under an assumed name. The damage had been done, however. The dark streets of towns along the border and near the border quite frequently yielded dead men staring at the cold dawn sky with eyes that did not see, stripped of wallets and other valuables.

One thought ran constantly through his mind. Sam had said Gil Drinkwater had not carried a belt gun or rifle when he had left Meadows. That in itself meant little, for it would have been easy enough for Gil to pick up a six-gun. It was the deep sincerity of the woman Sarah, who had told him that Gil would not carry a six-shooter, which stuck in his stubborn craw. Yet Cass Crowley had died with three .44 slugs in the back of his head, which also meant little, for the shooting could have been done by one of the killers with either a rifle or a six-shooter. But the three killers had been found armed with six-guns, *and an empty cartridge case in each weapon!*

Now and then Jim would turn in his saddle and look back north as he rode, as if it might help him to penetrate the minor mystery of a man who would not carry a six-gun because of a terrible accident in his past. *"Then it was not Gil who was guilty,"* she had said firmly. *"He never carried such a weapon."*

He took the stagecoach from Villa Palmito, after selling the gray for the fare, and arrived two days later in Chihuahua at dusk. If he could find out Orlando's last name, he might possibly be able to trace the man. As it was, it took him almost a week to get the information he wanted about the siege of Colonia Federico by the Apaches, and the stout defense of the Mexican soldiers led by a Teniente Teodoro Abeyta, who, severely wounded, had been forced to retire from the army. There was no mention of anyone called Orlando, and no information about a place called San Federico in the State of Chihuahua.

He walked through the plaza his last night in Chihuahua City, ignoring the shrill-voiced boys pimping for their teenage sisters, listening instead to a deep-toned church bell which seemed to call to him. He lighted a cigar and walked slowly toward the church, watching the mantilla-clad heads of the women converging on the church. There was a small building beside the church, and an aged padre stood there, enjoying the crispness of the night air.

"Good evening to you, father," said Jim.

"And to you, my son," said the old padre. "Can I be of help to you?"

"I am looking for a place called San Federico," said Jim.

"There are likely many San Federicos." The padre smiled. "Have you no clue to locate it approximately?"

"None, except that it might be near a place called Lagunade Haros. There was a place called Colonia Federico there some years ago, now abandoned."

The padre looked at him intently. "Yes, it comes to me now! The people there thought there was a curse upon the place. They moved, bag and baggage, as you Americans say, to another place, far to the west."

"But where, padre?"

The father held out his hands, palms upward, and shrugged his rounded shoulders. "Beyond the Sierra Vallecillos, it is said."

"Perhaps in the State of Sonora?"

"It is possible, my son." He eyed Jim. "Why do you ask?"

"There are possibly people there who would like to know of the death of a son, a father, a brother. I know nothing of the dead man except that his given name was Orlando, and that someone he knew, possibly relatives, a wife and children, perhaps, lived in a place that could either be San Fedro or San Federico."

"You know only his given name? It is a very common one."

Jim shrugged. "Perhaps it is Orlando Abeyta. There is a possible connection between this man I knew and a Teniente Teodoro Abeyta."

"Ah," said the padre in a soft voice. "Abeyta! That is better. There was an Orlando Abeyta I once knew."

"Here in this city?"

The padre nodded. "Yes, but that was many years ago." He studied Jim. "How did this man die, señor?"

"Does it matter?"

"To me it does. You see, I was once the teacher of a young man named Orlando Abeyta."

The bell stopped ringing. It was very quiet in the dark street except for the low voices in the church.

"How did he die, señor?" repeated the padre. "Not badly, I hope."

"He died like a man, padre. As he said at the last: '*It is not the thought of dying that is painful, only the way of it.*'" Jim looked steadily at the padre. "He was hanged for murder in the States, padre. You will tell no one?"

The padre's face was set and white, as though someone had struck him across it. "Hanged?" he said in a weak voice. "Orlando Abeyta hanged for murder? But this is impossible!"

"I swear it is true, padre."

"No, it cannot be. He was such a gentle lad. Brave in his own way. Not a hero like his elder brother, of course, but then Orlando had never wanted to be a soldier. Had he been stronger in spirit he would have resisted all efforts to make him a soldier, except for being a soldier of God. Tell me about him, señor."

Jim quickly told his tragic story. "He was a brave man," he concluded.

"Why did you take this task upon yourself? What did this man mean to you?" asked the padre.

Jim glanced at the church. "Perhaps it is a form of penance. Perhaps an unspoken vow. I don't really know. Something made me come."

"God moves in inscrutable ways, my son."

"You do not know if he was married and had a family?"

"He once told me he would never marry."

Jim took out the faded picture and lighted a match so that the padre could see the woman and the two little children. The padre shook his head. "I believe his elder brother was married. Yes! I remember now! She was a beautiful young woman. Much younger than her husband. Somewhat older than Orlando." The padre studied the picture again. "I cannot tell. It is too faded. There is one thing I do know, and that is that Orlando Abeyta was in love when he was very young, but that it was an unrequited love."

Jim replaced the picture in his wallet. "It is said that Teniente Abeyta was severely wounded at Colonia Federico and was forced to retire because of his wounds. Perhaps, if I could find him, I could tell him of his brother's death."

"All those people moved west, my son, into the Sierra Vallecillos. The Abeytas had lived near Laguna de Haros for many generations. There are few people, if any, living there now."

Jim blew a reflective puff of smoke from his cigar. "Then my best bet is to head west into the Sierra Vallecillos to try and find the relatives of Orlando Abeyta."

"Do you know that country?"

"I've heard of it," said Jim dryly.

"It is almost impassable in places. Infested with outlaws, wild animals, marauding Apaches and Yaquis."

"It is something I have to do, padre."

The padre nodded. "I will say prayers for the soul of Orlando Abeyta," he said.

"He died a condemned man, padre. At least he was condemned by the people who hanged him."

"Do you believe he was guilty?"

"All the available evidence indicates that he was."

The padre shrugged. "It is impossible for me to believe that he would murder a man. Continue on your quest, my son. I will say prayers for you as well."

Jim smiled. "Likely I'll need them. Good night, padre. Thanks!"

The old man watched the tall Americano walk away, cigar at a jaunty angle, booted feet striking the street steadily, arms swinging by his sides. "Yes," said the padre softly. "You will need prayers, my son. Many prayers. Go with God!" He walked into the dimly lighted church. It would be well to begin right away.

The streets were dark except for an occasional lamp flaring in the cold wind. It would be a cold, hard journey to the west into the wild country of the Sierra Vallecillos, many areas of which were marked "impassable" or "unknown," the home of the wild ones, animals, white and red men, all as wild as the country.

He was within a block of his shabby hotel when something seemed to warn him. He crossed to the other side of the dark street and worked his way toward the hotel. Two men stood on the corner in the biting wind, looking at the hotel, dark except for faint lamplight in one or two windows and in the little, dusty lobby where the clerk dozed in one of the rundown chairs.

Jim watched the two men. One of them nodded his head. He scraped a match against the nearest wall and lighted a cigarette, and in the dancing flare of the match flame Jim saw a face he knew from Ute Crossing. It was the man named Slim. The match flickered out.

Jim stepped back into a deep doorway and eased his Colt in its sheath. Once again an icy feeling surged through him, as it had that wet night in Las, Cruces when he had recognized Lyss. He was a long way from Las Cruces, where Lyss had likely been buried by now. He was a much longer distance from Ute Crossing. But it wasn't too far for men from Ute Crossing to follow Jim clear down into Chihuahua.

He had registered in the Amador Hotel in Cruces under his own name, so they would know for sure he had been that far south. He had left no written record of his presence in El Paso or in Ysleta, but Sarah Drinkwater and Sergeant Les Gilson had known he had been there, a week or more ago. It would have been logical enough for anyone following him to have crossed the Rio Grande into Zaragoza to ask a few questions. Perhaps someone there would remember the tall Americano with the knife scar on his left cheek. They might have worked as far south as Villa Palmito and learned there that he had taken the stagecoach to Chihuahua City. They might have arrived a few days behind him. They weren't just standing on that windy street corner speculating on where he was staying. They damned well knew!

He waited until he had a chance to slip back down the street. It took him only a few minutes to get to the run-down livery stable where he had left the coyote dun he had bought. Most of his gear was locked up in the storeroom of the stable. A handful of centavos was enough to send a hostler back to the hotel via the back way to get the rest of Jim's gear.

The wind shifted, blowing strongly from the northwest, as Jim left the city and rode through the darkness toward Gran Morelos.

CHAPTER EIGHT

"Colonia Federico," said the gray-haired Mexican. He shoved back his heavy felt steeplehat and looked at Jim Murdock. "Why would one want to come here, señor?"

Jim hooked a leg about the pommel of his saddle, rolled a cigarette, and passed the makings to the old man. His eyes were busy taking in the long-abandoned site of the *colonia*. "One comes because one has a reason, Augustin," he said quietly. He lighted the cigarette and blew a puff of smoke that was taken away by the cold wind blowing from the north across the site of the old settlement.

"There is nothing here but ruin," said the old man. He deftly fashioned a cigarette, twisted the tip together, and accepted a light from Jim. *"Gracias,"* he said.

"Por nada," said Jim.

Augustin waved a brown, veinous old hand. "The bat and the owl, the lizard and the snake, live here. No humans will live here. It is an accursed place, señor."

"It is all in the mind, old man."

The sloe eyes of the Mexican studied Jim. "That is not so," he said quietly. "You yourself, perhaps, live under a curse?"

"Why do you ask?"

"Why would one come here? There is something in your eyes. Your voice. The way you say and do things. A man who, perhaps, has a dog riding upon his back. A thing he must do? There are those under a curse who must wander on and on until the curse is lifted."

"And if it is not?"

Augustin shrugged. "Perhaps the señor knows that better than I do."

"Come, old man, let us see this place."

Augustin looked up at the sky. "It is almost dusk," he said.

"There will be an early moon."

The Mexican shook his head. "There is no need to guide you, Señor Murdock. I will make the camp beyond this ridge. There is a water hole there. I will make the food."

Jim smiled. "One is not afraid?"

"Who? Me? I am not afraid, señor!"

Jim held his hands out, palms upward, smiled and shrugged. "I was but jesting, Augustin."

The old man smiled faintly. He tugged at his heavy gray moustache. "You have, perhaps, a cross? A Bible?"

Jim shook his head.

Augustin handed him a rosary. "Keep it in your hand," he said. "Señor, do not stay there after dark..." He turned his mule and led the pack mule up the ridge and was soon out of sight.

Jim hefted the rosary in his hand. He smiled and slipped it into his coat pocket.

The old man was right. Colonia Federico was now little more than a dusty name upon the empty landscape, soon to be completely forgotten. The home of the owl, the bat, the lizard, and the snake. There seemed to be little pattern in the humps of sand, gravel, and eroded adobe bricks that had once been houses, cantinas, shops, a small barracks and, of course, a church. Jim led the dun into the smoothly swept plaza, kept neat and tidy by the wind. By half closing his eyes he could visualize this little *placita* sleeping in the bright, hot suns of the summers, bowed beneath the bitter winter winds. Beyond the *placita* ruins he saw the vast, shallow bowl of the long-dry Laguna de Haros, which might fill up for a time during the heavy rains, or when the snow melted, although there would not be very many heavy snows.

Here it was that Teniente Teodoro Abeyta, with forty men, had held the *placita* against all the assaults of a combined force of Apaches and Yaquis, hundreds in number, it was said, who had been on their way south to strike at the gates of Parral, or perhaps even those of Durango itself. They had had no great interest in Colonia Federico save that they needed fresh meat, and there were many mules in those days at the *colonia,* and the flesh of mules is sweet to an Apache or a Yaqui. Perhaps the alcalde could have dealt peacefully with the fierce warriors, the tigers of the mountains and deserts. It had been done before. The quixotic minds of the marauders might have let them take the mules and spare the inhabitants, as a sort of tribute to the fierceness and the power of the Apaches and their cousins the Yaquis. They might even have ignored the barefooted, shakoed infantrymen of Teniente Abeyta's company. This, too, had been done before. Likely the warriors were better armed than the little brown men whom they usually scorned.

But if the Apaches and the Yaquis were tigers of the mountains and deserts, there was also a tiger who had been sleeping in Colonia Federico. A man, an officer of the Mexican Army, whose blood was as proud and fierce as that of the warriors. A soldier whose fierce independence had caused his senior officer to practically bury him in Colonia Federico. His exile had done nothing to curb the spirit of Teodoro Abeyta.

No one knew to this day what had caused the spark to leap the gap from Mexican to Apache, but in the cold light of the early dawn, with the plaza filled with warriors, bands of white paint across their fierce noses and high cheekbones, the *ridehb'keh,* the thick-soled, button-toed, thigh-length moccasins on their muscular legs, strong hands resting on rifle or lance, the spark had leaped. In the first few minutes of confused shooting Teniente Abeyta lost nine men, the Apaches six. The Apache and the Yaqui do not like hand-to-hand fighting. Their methods are those of the guerilla—the rifle shot from the mesquite, the ambush in the narrow pass, the killing of men before they have a chance to kill, then the leisurely knife and war-club work on the screaming wounded who see their deaths on the impassive brown faces of the warriors. Here, in the plaza, they had lost six good warriors. Perhaps if they had been fighting better troops, like those of the famous Indian-fighting Sixth Mexican Infantry, they might have taken their losses and retreated, for after all, they had killed more Mexicans than the Mexicans had killed warriors. But they did not retreat, and in the vicious infighting through the narrow streets of the *placita,* the Mexicans, led by Abeyta, drove the screaming warriors out to the naked land between the *placita* and the lagoon, which in those days was filled with water. Abeyta drove them out, but the price was high ... too high, for he lost eight more men.

The blood madness came over Mexican and warrior. For two days they fought with the *heshke,* the "killing craze" upon them all—the infantrymen behind their battered walls, the warriors working in close, using every scrap of cover to sharpshoot any head that appeared. Abeyta kept the frightened women and children behind the thick walls of the church. He armed every man and boy in the *placita.* He leavened the frightened civilians with his best fighting men. He was himself worth ten men.

When the warriors thought Abeyta was defeated, they charged into the plaza once more to meet Abeyta and the few men he had left. A blast of gunfire came from the church. The women and children, and the walking wounded caught the bucks in the flank with a hail of lead, and Abeyta then led his few soldiers into the melee of screaming bucks, firing a volley, then charging in with needle bayonets. Rifle butts smashed into the warriors, and when the rifles were shattered the Mexicans, masters of the knife, stayed to fight until the Apaches and Yaquis had enough. The warriors fled, although their numbers were still far greater than those of the enemy. Only a handful of the soldiers remained alive, and from beneath a heap of the contorted dead they dragged out the body of Teniente Teodoro Abeyta, riddled with wounds, more dead than alive.

———

THE SUN WAS DYING in a welter of rose and gold in the west, and then swiftly it was gone, and as swiftly came the beginning of the night cold. In the quick rush of the darkness Jim Murdock saw the many mounded graves between the ruins of the *placita* and the empty *laguna*. He led the dun toward the graves, and as he walked the eeriness of the place suddenly came upon him. He turned and looked back, but there was nothing to see. Yet many men had died there in bloody violence, and a curse was upon this place.

There would be an early moon. Augustin would have made the camp and would have beans and tortillas ready. The old man had seemed glad to leave his granddaughter's comfortable casa in Gran Morelos to guide Jim to the west. It had been said of Augustin Galeras in the cantinas of Gran Morelos that he was *muy hombre*, still much of the man, despite his many years, and no one, señor, knew the country to the west better than he, unless perhaps it was the coyote or the eagle.

Jim sat down on a rock and smoked, listening to the wind sweeping across the desert to the north, hard at work tidying up the already immaculate and sterile neatness of Colonia Federico, or what had been Colonia Federico. With its phobia for neatness, the wind would in time sweep Colonia Federico into its immense dustpan, and thence into the great dustbin of limbo, whence no human could ever return, even in memory. It made a big man feel damned insignificant. The desert and the mountains have a way of doing just that.

In the first faint light of the rising moon that silver-washed the low hills to the east, Jim walked about among the mounded graves. There were many of them, but most of them would be of people who had died before the great fight there. To one side, separated by a shallow ditch, he found a group of graves with a marker set among them, a yellowish-white stone set upon a rock base, cemented together. The new moon shone full upon the face of the rock and the inscription cut thereon, although wind and sharp-edged dust, rain, and snow had softened the words and partially erased some of them.

Jim shoved back his hat and studied the inscription, his lips moving silently until he got the gist of it, and then he read it aloud for the bat, the owl, the lizard, and the snake to hear, for there wasn't any other living thing to listen.

To the exalted memory of the Third Company, Fourth Provisional Regiment, of the Army of the glorious Republic of Mexico: these brave men did their duty at Colonia Federico in the face of hundreds of Apaches and Yaquis, and decisively defeated them despite the great disparity in numbers. Here are inscribed the names of the honored dead and the few living men of the Third Company, who under the command of Teniente Teodoro Abeyta wrote in heroic blood a page of Mexican history. Honor to them! Learn here a lesson, you who read this: Learn that only men who do their duty are entitled to be honored on such a monument as this. To the coward: Slink silently away! Your curse is that you will always wander, but you will never escape the memory of what you did here at Colonia Federico!

Jim slowly rolled a cigarette. The monument was unusual. The "heroic" dead and the "heroic" living had indeed been honored, although few would travel to this abandoned place to read the glorious words, and the memory of man is short even when he can read the wording on such monuments. What was unusual was that there was a thrusting reference to cowardice. The cowardice of a number of men, perhaps, but more likely of one. Jim lighted the cigarette and blew a reflective puff of smoke. He hadn't expected to learn much at Colonia Federico, but Augustin had said it was only a few miles out of the way on the route to Santo Tomas in the sierra to the west.

The moonlight was beginning to flood the desert. Far across the cold wastes came the faint howling of a coyote, greeting the pallid beauty of the new moon.

Jim sat there beside the eroding monument for a long time. Bits and pieces were fitting into the puzzle that had been the fatalistic Mexican known as Orlando Abeyta. A brave man who had died ingloriously with a drunkard and a frightened boy. *"He was such a gentle lad. Brave in his own way. Not a hero like his elder brother, of course, but then Orlando had never wanted to be a soldier. Had he been stronger in spirit he would have resisted all efforts to make him a soldier, except for being a soldier of God."* Jim whirled and was on his feet, fingertips brushing the worn butt of his Colt, before he realized the voice had been only in his mind. And yet it had seemed at the moment that someone, the old padre, had spoken to Jim as he had spoken to him that night in Chihuahua City, when they had talked about Orlando Abeyta, the boy who had wanted to be a priest.

The searching wind shifted, rattling bits of gravel against the monument. The moon shone upon the ruins of Colonia Federico in an eerie silvery light, etching sharp shadows from the few walls that still stood free from the harsh embrace of the desert that was again taking over the country.

Was it indeed Orlando Abeyta, the condemned and

executed murderer, who had been the coward of Colonia Federico? But his brother had been the hero of Colonia Federico. Jim withdrew the fine presentation watch from his pocket. He opened the back cover and eyed the faint inscription in the clear light of the moon. His lips wordlessly shaped the inscription. "To Teniente Teodoro ... For heroic services rendered at Colonia ..." He closed the back of the case and pressed the repeater button. The soft, sweet chime struck six o'clock.

The dun had strayed. Jim could hardly blame him. It had been a long day's ride to Colonia Federico across rough, cold country. He stowed away the watch and walked past the dead *placeta,* heading for the ridge. There was nothing more to be learned from the place.

He slowly walked up the ridge, his thoughts miles away. A horse nickered. He turned toward the sound. A movement in the scant brush of a hollow drew him to it. He saw a horse, and his eyes narrowed. It wasn't the dun. It was a clay-bank, saddled and with pommel and cantle packs as well as filled saddlebags. He looked about. There would be no tracks on that hard ground. The horse nickered again, and when Jim turned to look at him he saw another horse further up the draw. A black, saddled and with cantle and pommel packs. Both horses had been tethered to the tough brush.

He whirled at another sound and saw the dun trotting up the slope toward the other horses. One of them whinnied. Jim met the dun and led him far down the slope into a deep arroyo, tethered him, and then unsheathed his Winchester, levering a .44/40 into the chamber. He removed his spurs and padded up the ridge again, falling belly flat on the near side of the crest, dropping his hat behind him as he wormed his way up to the top of the ridge and thrust his head between two clumps of growth to peer down the far side. The moonlight glinted from the calm surface of the water hole. A thread of smoke arose from the embers of a fire set in a ring of smoke-blackened rocks. Here and there lay packs and other gear.

Three men stood there in the bright moonlight, two of them tall men, Americans, no doubt, with pistols in their hands, looking at Augustin Galeras, who stood there hatless, his white hair clear and sharp in the moonlight, and a trickle of blood glistening on his brown face as it crept from his scalp to his lined jaw.

The wind shifted and blew toward Jim from the trio of motionless men. "Where is he, greaser?" said one of the men.

"I do not know of whom you speak, señor," said Augustin.

"The big gringo! Murdock! You left Gran Morelos with him three days ago! Where is that scar-faced son of a bitch?"

Jim wet his lips. The voice was that of the man named Slim, and further, there was no mistaking his build and height, for the man was a good four inches taller than Jim's six feet even.

"Talk, damn you!" said the other man.

Jim knew him too. It was the man named Jules, another member of the lynching party.

"He has gone north," said Augustin at last. A hard hand slapped the Mexican's white head back and forth until he swayed on his feet.

"You talk, by God," said Slim, "or we'll toast your dirty feet over them coals! Where did he go? What's he aimin' to do?"

Jim stood up and Augustin saw him, but the Mexican's face did not betray what he had seen. Jim walked softly down the ridge, rifle at hip level, hammer back, fingertip pressing lightly against trigger, taking up the slack. If Slim and Jules saw him or heard him, they could kill Augustin before Jim could open fire for fear of hitting the old man.

"He has gone to Temosachic," said Augustin in a quavering voice.

"Where is that?" demanded Slim.

Jim was fifty yards away now, still too far to open fire.

"In the Sierra Vallecillos, not far from Laguna de Bavicora. He goes there to talk about mining."

Slim's hard hand slashed across Augustin's face, and bright droplets of blood glistened in the moonlight as they flew from the Mexican's slack mouth. "You lie!" yelled Slim. "That bastard ain't no miner! He's looking for someone's kin, ain't he? Name of Orlando or somethin'! Ain't he?"

Jim was twenty-five feet away now. His left boot kicked a stone. "Drop!" yelled Jim to Augustin. As the old man hit the ground the two Americans whirled. Jim fired once into Jules' lean gut, and the two-hundred-grain slug doubled the man up and drove him back against Slim as though a mule had kicked him. Jim had jumped sideways as soon as he had fired, slamming the Winchester lever up and down and firing the instant the lever closed home. Slim cursed. He shoved the falling Jules aside and slapped out two rounds. Something plucked at Jim's left sleeve. He reloaded and charged directly toward the cursing man slamming out round after round. Slim went down on one knee, game, though wounded, and raised his six-shooter for his last shot. Echoes slammed back and forth between the ridges.

Augustin rolled to his feet like a cat, and something glittered in his hand as he closed in on Slim. Slim turned and struggled to his feet. The old man was in under the smoking six-shooter and the knife sank deep into Slim's hard-muscled gut, and then, with a terrible, wrenching pull across the belly and down into the soft groin, a figure seven stroke, Augustin finished the job.

Slim dropped the hot six-shooter, clutching his opened belly. He looked at Jim with terrible, staring eyes. Jim raised the rifle and fired once, right between the eyes, and Slim fell at Augustin's feet and lay still. Slowly the moon-whitened ground beneath him began to turn black from the soaking of the flood of blood.

The echoes died, fleeing off into the grim silence of

the watching hills. The stench of acrid smoke hung in the draw between the moon-washed ridges.

Augustin bent on one knee and calmly wiped the bloody knife on Slim's coat. He stood up and looked at Jim. "I did not tell them," he said proudly.

"You did well, old one," said Jim quietly.

Augustin sheathed the blade. He spat on the two bodies.

Jim wiped the cold sweat from his face. It had been a near thing.

"Why do they seek you, Jaime?" asked the old man. He studied Jim with narrowed eyes.

"I have done nothing to them," said Jim. "It seems to be something that they helped do to others that makes such men follow me." He looked about. "This is a bad thing. The killing of two Americanos here in your country."

Augustin picked up his sweat-stained old hat. He looked sideways at Jim. "Who is to know?" he said softly. He smiled. "As I said before: Only the bat and the owl, the lizard and the snake, live here."

"You said something else, old man," said Jim.

"Eh?"

Jim looked at him. "It is an accursed place..."

"That is true." Augustin looked at the fire. "The meal is ready." He laughed. "They did not touch my beans or tortillas, Jaime."

"You would eat here?" asked Jim.

Augustin walked to the fire and pulled free the black-ened clay pot of beans. He looked back at Jim, his great eyes peering beneath his wide, upturned hat brim. "Those two will not share our food," he said. "There is more than enough for two of us, but not enough for four. Come! Eat! We will get rid of them and hide them so not even God can find their bodies. So, then, what is to fear? *Los muertos no hablan...*"

Jim nodded. The dead do not speak. It was enough.

They would have killed Jim and the old man as well if they had had the chance.

There was moonlight aplenty for the ride west, after the bodies had been buried and the gear hidden. There were no brands on the two horses. Augustin picketed them lightly not far from the water hole. In time they would break free, but by then Jim and his guide would be many miles into the looming mountains.

They took the dim trail toward Santo Tomas in the last hours of the cold moonlight. Jim looked back at the dreary, godforsaken site of Colonia Federico. He had left three dead men behind him on his quest for the kin of the three men who had been hanged at Ute Crossing. Perhaps a poetic justice, for he was almost sure that there had been much more behind those lynchings than just the outraged feelings of the hard men of the valley of the Ute. Something dark and evil, so evil he did not want to think about it. Not yet, anyway; not that night, for a certainty.

As they entered the first gateway into the quiet hills a coyote broke voice far in the lonely distance.

CHAPTER NINE

The high peaks of the Sierra Madre were snow-clad, serene and distant, as though belonging to another world. Always they looked down impassively into the terribly deep barrancas and the timbered mesas, covered with spruce and pine and red-hued madronas. They seemed not to notice the antlike creatures that walked upon two legs or rode upon larger antlike creatures with four legs. These antlike beings came and went during the centuries on some meaningless business of their own, and although they changed over the years, they were always the same to the peaks of the Sierra Madre.

For days and then weeks Jim Murdock had waited in a tiny village in a valley far below those stupendous mountains, while old Augustin Galeras struggled with life and death. In the weeks that the old man and Jim had worked their way upward into the mountains, Jim had grown to like, then to respect, and then to love the old man. He would never return to Gran Morelos. Jim knew that and Augustin knew that. A bad fall from his mule had broken many of his ribs. He had broken ribs before, but then he had been a much younger man. Still, as he had always done, he fought, but this time he fought against the one enemy who could never be defeated by man.

The old year had slipped away with hardly a murmur into the past. The mountains didn't care. The simple mountain people seemed to care less. This was a world far removed from dates and places. How could one feel important with those mountains watching him with half-lidded eyes all day?

They buried old Augustin in a grave punched out of resisting earth on a shelf that overlooked the brawling stream, with a good view of the great peaks. Jim Murdock had wanted to leave then, but a great norther had swept across the Sierra Vallecillos and carried with it a weight of snow that recapped the peaks, bringing the white mantles lower than anyone living in the village could ever remember, even old Santiago Esquivel, of whom it was said that he had lived in those mountains longer than the Devil himself. The snow choked the narrow passes and filled the canyons and barrancas, until, Body of God, it seemed as though no one would ever again get in or out of the lonely, almost forgotten valley.

Yet, no one really wanted to leave, and cared less about anyone coming into the valley. Even the big gringo, the gaunt man with the scar upon his face, and the big brown hands that carved such wonderful toys for the boys and girls, seemed to care little. If there was anything broken in the village, he fixed it. If a horse, a goat, or a burro became ill, he knew how to treat it, and he even could treat the human sick with the little store of medicines he carried with him.

He kept his two well-oiled guns in their worn sheaths in the little hut he had shared with the old man before the old man had died. The simple villagers would surreptitiously eye that disfiguring scar on the Americano's face, the stubborn set of the strong jaw, and those steady, penetrating eyes, eyes so light in color, to the villagers, at least, that they seemed almost disfiguring. Those eyes could be as hard as granite, and yet when the Americano helped the sick or comforted a child, they would soften marvelously. They had seen him use that heavy rifle to bring down deer and bear at incredible ranges.

In the third month of the new year the big Americano rode from the village on the soft trails, guided by a silent mozo, a tribeless Tarahumare who spoke no English and very little Spanish but who knew those mountains as few other men did. Yet, not even the mozo had heard of San Federico, and not even old Santiago Esquivel himself had heard of it.

The mozo parted company with Jim at the junction of the Rio Yaqui and the Rio Moctezuma and faded away into the mountains. In two weeks he had not spoken a word to Jim.

Jim had been away from Ute Crossing for many months now. He was on a long, long trail to which there seemed to be no ending. He could not quit. *"There are those under a curse who must wander on and on until the curse is lifted."* Those had been the wise words of old Augustin Galeras to Jim Murdock. Since the deaths of Slim and Jules, Jim had heard nothing about Ute Crossing before the mountain trails had been blocked, stopping even the hardy monthly mail runner. Nothing. It had been as though he had moved into another world once he and the old man had left Santo Tomas.

The days faded into weeks, and the mountain world grew warm as Jim patiently worked his way through the mountains as far west as La Colorado on the road to Hermosillo, as far south as the Sierra Baroyeca, thence east into the Rio Mayo country, then back again to the Sierra Baroyeca, to Esperanza, and up the Rio Yaqui to Tecoripa and the—north to Nacozari and Bacoachi, thence south again and east to the wild Rio Escondido. There *was* no San Federico. There never *had* been a San Federico. Perhaps there never *would* be a San Federico, señor. *Quién sabe?* Who knows? The phrase echoed in his ears in the lonely camps and in the little *placitas* and mining camps, on the twisting trails and beside the calm waters of the *lagunas*. The spring had shifted into the early summer, and still he had progressed no further than he had been when he had entered those great mountains with old Augustin Galeras so many months ago and had paid the blood price for the passage with the life of the old man. Stranger than the unknown San Federico was the complete lack of knowledge of the name of Abeyta. It seemed as though that name had never been known in those wild and forbidding mountains.

With the coming of the summer came dark news. The Chiricahua Apaches had raided down as far as Casa Blanca. The notorious Streeter Gang of half-breeds, pure quill Apaches, and renegade whites had struck in the vicinity of Fronteras. Bandits haunted the roads between the border and Hermosillo and ranged as far east as the San Miguel. Hard times, hard times indeed, señor, had come to Sonora.

Not far from Magdalena was a good spring where Jim Murdock, the gringo with the curse upon him, would camp when he was in that vicinity, resting his horse and his pack burro, letting them get fat again, although no amount of food or resting would layer fat upon the tall Americano's muscular body, gaunt from too many months on the trail that had no ending.

He approached the spring one early summer evening, an unlit Mexican cigar stuck in the corner of his mouth, the dust of the trail thick upon his animals, his clothing, and his own tanned flesh. He had seen smoke rising from the spring area on his slow climb up toward the spring from the desert-like country below. He was within a quarter of a mile of the spring when he noticed that the smoke had thickened, and the shifting breeze of the oncoming darkness brought with it the smell of burning cloth and something else he recognized, and as he recognized it, he dropped from his horse, slapped it on the rump, and jerked his Winchester from its saddle scabbard as he did so.

He drifted like a cloud shadow across the dry ground

and into the shelter of rocks and scrub trees. The wind shifted again, and he was positive of the odor that came with it. Burning flesh.... There was only one possible source for *that* odor. It was a favorite device of Apaches and Yaquis to use fire on their victims.

The horse had led the docile pack burro into the shelter of the trees down the slope, unseen if anyone looked down from the spring area. Jim worked his way through the trees and tumbled boulders until he could belly forward to overlook the spring. Years ago someone had built a rock house there, but now the roof had partially tumbled in and one of the walls had collapsed. The spring was beyond the house in a great cup of sun-bleached rocks. The thickening smoke rose from a fire at the edge of the rocks where a man, a Mexican by his clothing, lay sprawled on his back across the coals, his arms outflung and his face a red mask of blood. Beyond him lay another man, more likely a big boy, doubled up, with a dark stain on the back of his shirt. A mule, tethered to a tree, was fighting the rope that tied him to the tree.

Jim wet his dry lips, studying the scene with slitted eyes. There were others down there somewhere. He was sure of it. He looked back over his shoulder to make sure he wasn't being flanked. There was no one there.

Suddenly a woman screamed, and Jim's head snapped around. He raised his rifle. She had come staggering out from the old house, holding rags of clothing about her almost naked body, running across the empty ground toward the spring. A man stood up from among the rocks, his steeple-crowned hat on the back of his head, a grin on his brown face, and his arms outstretched to catch this ripe plum of femininity. She darted sideways and ran down the slope. Two more men appeared from the brush, grinning at her, their white teeth in sharp contrast to their dusty moustaches and dark skins. One of them snatched at her rags, and as she pulled away she stood there trembling, mother-naked, trying to cover her full breasts with her arms, while the three men roared with drunken laughter.

Jim slid down the slope. They were too busy to see him. The woman turned again and ran in the direction of the rocktangle just below Jim. He dropped into a cup thick with brush. Something buzzed dryly, and he smashed down the metal-shod butt of the rifle on the ugly, flat, triangular head of a rattlesnake. The thick, powerful body wound itself about his left leg.

Another man came from the house, staggering a little in his drunkenness and eagerness as he ran toward the desperate woman. Her great dark eyes saw the face in the brush.

"Bandidos!" she screamed.

There was no time for Jim to deliberate now. He'd have to take her word for it. In any case they meant little good toward the naked woman, and the two bodies mutely testified to their profession.

Jim fired once. The two men who stood together dashed back into the brush. The man at the spring raised a rifle. Jim fired twice. The Mexican was slammed back over the rocks and his rifle exploded as he fell, sending a whining slug up into the blue. The rifle shot echoes thundered against the hill slopes and ran along the mountain face to die in the distance, but they were closely pursued by others.

Jim hurdled the rocks at his feet, pushing the screaming woman back into the brush. The writhing snake tripped him. He fell headlong, thrusting forward his rifle as he did so, and the snake saved his life, for slashing lead cut the air where Jim had been standing. He rolled over and fired into the brush where the pair of bandits had vanished, aiming at the gun flashes and puffs of smoke. A man screamed and fell thrashing down the slope, rolling over and over until he fell from a low cliff to crash into the thick brush below.

A bullet smashed into Jim's right boot heel, tearing it off, numbing his lower leg. Another plucked his hat from his head. He fired into the brush again. The Mexican stood up and fired at a fifty-foot range. Jim grunted as the slug smashed into his left shoulder. He fired a round from the rifle with his right hand and then dropped the weapon. He swayed up to his feet, pulling free his Colt. Three times the six-shooter slammed back into his hand, and the Mexican fell backward in death, dropping his smoking rifle.

The big gringo swayed on his feet, his eyes wide with shock. The hot blood ran down inside his shirt and undershirt. He turned slowly to look at the remaining bandit. The Colt fell from Jim's hand.

The Mexican stood there, head and shoulders bent forward, looking at Jim with his one eye, for the other was a puckered hole in his seamed brown face. The Mexican slowly sheathed his nickel-plated pistol and swiftly drew his *sacatripas*. This gringo would have to be gutted like a chicken for what he had done. No easy, swift death for him.

The woman screamed again, the echoes flying down the now strangely quiet hillside.

The Mexican tested the razor edge of his curved knife with his thumb. He walked slowly toward Jim, his one eye like an amber marble, unblinking as the stare of a basilisk. He faded in and out of Jim's sight like a chimera.

The Mexican was within ten feet of Jim when Jim went down, clawing at his belly with both hands in what seemed to be intense pain. The Mexican laughed. He closed in and thrust down with the knife.

The silver-mounted derringer in Jim's right hand spat flame and smoke. The soft-nosed .41 slug caught the Mexican low in the guts. As he fell he drove the knife at Jim's contorted face, and the razor edge ripped across Jim's right cheek to match the scar on the other side. Jim fired the second barrel of the stingy gun. The slug smashed into the bandit's mouth and up into his brain. He fell heavily across Jim.

Then it was very quiet. Jim lay with his blood-masked

face against the harsh ground. His left arm and shoulder were completely numbed. The waves of excruciating pain would come after the shock of the impact died away. Slowly he raised his right hand to his slashed face, and he winced as he felt the torn lips of the wound.

The bandit's body was rolled off him. Jim turned his face upward to look at the woman. She was still naked. Her eyes were wide in fear and compassion for the big gringo who had come out of nowhere to save her from multiple rape and possible murder. She was not young, but not very old either, and her body was that of a much younger woman, firm-fleshed and luscious. Jim closed his eyes. Waves of faintness swept over him. He felt his face strike the ground once more.

The last thing he remembered was soft hands working on him, ripping away shirt and undershirt, stanching the big hole in his shoulder, washing the wound in his face and binding it, and all the time she worked on him he was acutely conscious that her warm, full breasts touched him constantly, and once his hand touched the velvet smoothness of a full thigh. After that there was nothing but limbo.

CHAPTER TEN

He came out of the fever very slowly. There were times when he was aware of movements, voices, actions, and then he would drift off into that vague, hazy land where nothing was ever very clear, and where, at times, he was sure he was dreaming. But gradually he grew aware of other things. Of deft, sure hands bathing him and shaving him. Of soft flesh pressing against him as he was moved about. Once he opened his eyes to see a thick tress of dark hair just above his face, and the faint fragrance of perfume mingled with that of warm, feminine flesh came to him, and then he was gone again.

He opened his eyes one day and did not move. Above him was a corbeled, whitewashed ceiling. He moved only his eyes. To his right were two deep-set windows, and through them came sunlight, shifting as though it came through the moving branches of trees. In one corner was a neat beehive fireplace. A massive chest of drawers stood against a wall, and a crucifix hung above it. There were several wall niches with Indian-faced *santos* within them. The bed in which he lay was massive also. He looked down at his arms lying atop the neat spread, and at his hands. He was stunned as he saw his hands. Once strong and brown, they were now white and lifeless looking, and the hairs seemed to stand alone, like the charred trunks of trees left when fire has swept a mesa.

Birds twittered beyond the windows. He heard the faint braying of a burro. The wind shifted, and an unseen windmill began to hum its busy song. Then clearest of all came the heady, pleasing laughter of children at play.

He closed his eyes. Weakness filled his limbs, and for a moment he thought he was going to drift off into limbo again, but by a conscious effort of his will he held himself in the land of the living. Memories came slowly back to him, piece by puzzling piece, and he fitted them together like a child, by patient trial and error. There had been a day of hazy sunshine. No, it had been late afternoon, closing swiftly onto dusk. There had been the smoke of a campfire. No, a house. No, the house had long been abandoned. Smoke... Smoke? It had been smoke, but not from a house, but from a fire where clothing, leather, and flesh had burned in an acrid, sweetish-smelling combination. For a long time, he lay thinking. There had been some shooting. He thought hard. Men had died there in the hazy sunlight and the drifting smoke of the fire and the gun muzzles. Who had died, and why?

He slowly dragged his right hand over to his left shoulder where a dull, nagging ache persisted, like the beginning of an abscessed tooth. His shoulder was neatly bandaged. He had been wounded, then. He remembered that. Slowly, like a snake uncoiling in its den after the sleep of winter, his right hand touched his chin and then passed up to his right cheek where something lay on the taut skin like a thick-bodied worm. His questing fingers touched the hard granulation of a newly healed wound.

Jim wet his dry lips. His mind drifted again. Again he drove it back to its task. Then, with startling clarity, he saw her, naked, screaming, wide-eyed with pain and sheer terror, running across the ground toward him. "Mother of the Devil!" he yelled in a hoarse, cracked voice. "The woman! *What happened to the woman?*"

Soft footfalls sounded outside the room, and the thick door swung back on gently creaking hinges. She stood there framed in the wide doorway, dark, thick hair plaited in a heavy coil which crossed a smooth white shoulder exposed by the low, wide neck of the white blouse she wore, and rested high on a full breast, like a kitten asleep. Her full skirt fell from her smoothly rounded hips, and beneath the embroidered edge of the skirt he saw the tiniest of feet, bare except for huaraches. It was her eyes that held him fascinated. Like those of a fawn, but full of a compassion and a life no fawn had ever exhibited.

She crossed herself. *"Con el favor de Dios,"* she said in a soft, almost husky voice. "With the favor of God you are with us again, Señor Murdock."

She came beside the bed and placed a soft, smooth little hand on his forehead. She smiled. "Yes," she said with delight. "Everyone will be so pleased."

He looked up at her, wincing a little as the muscles drew in his shoulder. "You know who I am," he said. "Who are you?"

"You do not remember?"

He narrowed his eyes. "The woman at the spring!" he said. "Yes! I remember now."

She reddened and looked away. "I am Rafaela Velarde," she said.

"Your servant, Senorita Velarde," he said.

She straightened the spread. "Senora Velarde," she corrected him.

"I am sorry for that, senora," he said with a smile.

"You Americans," she said with a flirt of her lovely head.

He looked about the room. "How long have I been here?"

She tilted her head to one side and counted on the tips of her slim fingers. "Five, no six!" she said.

He eyed her narrowly. "Days?"

"Weeks, Señor Murdock."

He closed his eyes again. It was impossible.

"The doctor said the bullet might have been poisoned."

"There was much fever, then?"

She placed her hand on his forehead again, and he looked up at her. "It was very close," she said quietly. "The doctor said you had the strength of a dozen men and the stubbornness of a mule."

Jim smiled. "I think he knows me pretty well."

"Would you like a mirror?"

"Yes, please."

She brought it to him and held it in front of his face. A stranger stared back at him with deep-set gray eyes. A gaunt death's-head of a face. A thin white scar traced a course down his hollow left cheek, and on the other cheek was a twisted reddish scar. He shook his head. "He did a neat job," he said.

She took away the mirror. "When you have strength you will feel and look better. I will get some soup." She placed the mirror on the wardrobe and walked to the door, gently swaying hips intriguing Jim. He *must* be recovering.

"Where am I?" he asked.

She turned and smiled. "San Federico," she said, and then she was gone, closing the door behind her.

The children laughed again. The mule brayed. The windmill hummed on and on.

"San Federico?" said Jim. He shook his head. *"San Federico?"* He rested his head on the pillow. "Well, I'll be double-dipped in a vat of fresh manure!"

He shifted in the bed, and slowly worked himself up into a semi-sitting position. "Rafaela," he said softly. He remembered all too clearly now. He remembered that lush body, exposed to the hot, lusting eyes of those two-legged animals at the spring. He remembered, too, when she had come to him to help him, forgetting her nakedness in her efforts to stanch his wounds. He might very well have died except for her. "Six weeks," he whispered.

He shook his head. With all his months of searching he had not found San Federico, only to find it by sheer luck. The hard way, he thought.

The sun had gone when she returned with a tray. She lighted candles as Jim watched her. Everything she did she did with an effortless grace. He ate slowly as she busied her, self about the room. "I have been looking for San Federico for a long time," he said.

"It has been here a long time," she said.

He finished his soup and leaned back against a pillow. She rolled a cigarette for him and placed it between his lips, then lighted it, leaning close, so close that he did not dare look down, for he knew that her blouse would be hanging free from her body. She straightened up and rolled herself a cigarette. She lighted it and blew a puff of smoke.

"There was a Colonia Federico beyond the mountains," he said at last. "I was told the people who had lived there had left that place because of a curse and had come beyond the Sierra Vallecillos to make a new home, a place to be called San Federico. That was all I knew. Strange that I have spent so many weeks on the trail in Sonora, and yet no one knew of this place. Not a word from anyone. Not a trace, and then to find it this way, or rather, to have it find me."

She studied him closely. "Did you not think of looking elsewhere for San Federico?"

"No," he said. "Beyond the Sierra Vallecillos. That was what I was told. But no one knew for sure."

She took the cigarette from her full lips. "It is very simple," she said. "You are not in Sonora, Señor Murdock, but in Arizona Territory, in your United States of America." She laughed at the surprised look on his face. "The people of Colonia Federico did come west of the Sierra Vallecillos to find a new home. It was too wild, too dangerous, because of the Apaches and Yaquis. The people scattered. Some of them drifted west to Hermosillo and Guaymas, or into the mining country. My husband and I came to Arizona for better medical care because of his wounds, and because he had a cousin who was an American citizen. My husband died."

There was a flicker of interest in Jim's eyes.

She ground out the cigarette butt in a dish and looked sideways at him. "He was my first husband," she said quietly. "I married his cousin a year ago. Señor Velarde. The owner of Rancho San Federico. I think you must already know the name of my first husband."

He narrowed his brows and stared uncomprehendingly at her.

"He was Teniente Teodoro Abeyta," she said. "The hero of Colonia Federico."

"How did you know I knew about him?"

She shrugged. "We were on our way here when the bandits struck. I did not know who you were when I had you brought here, north of the border. It was necessary, you understand, to identify you. We looked through your things. I found a picture of myself taken some years ago with my two children. There was a watch, too. I knew it well. It had been presented to my husband for his heroism at Colonia Federico. I have not seen that watch for many years. Where did you get it?"

Jim rolled another cigarette and lighted it. He eyed her through the thin cloud of smoke that drifted toward the open window. How much did she know? Was it possible that she knew Orlando Abeyta had died a felon's death far north of Rancho San Federico?

"There was some question about you having the watch," she added. "But, for what you did at the spring, we forgave anything else."

"I did not steal it," he said.

"I never believed that you did," she said. She sat down on the edge of the bed and studied him closely with those lovely eyes of hers. Something else came back to Jim. Something the priest had said about Orlando Abeyta. *He once told me he would never marry. Orlando Abeyta was in love when he was very young, but it was an unre-*

quited love. A piece of the puzzle slipped suddenly into place. Rafaela was older than Orlando would have been, perhaps not by very much, but these Mexican women married very young. A coward, a boy who had wanted to be a priest, sensitive and proud, who had become a soldier, not by choice, perhaps because he had deeply loved the woman who had married his elder brother, an officer and a hero.

"Where is he?" she asked softly.

Jim looked at the tip of his cigarette.

"Is he dead?"

Jim nodded.

"He was a friend of yours? Is that why you came to find us?"

Jim looked at her. "He was not my friend," he said. Could he tell her how Orlando had died?

She stood up and paced back and forth. "Something terrible happened to him," she said. "I know."

The wind had shifted. It blew in through the window. The candles guttered and flared, casting her shadow on the whitewashed wall. She stopped pacing and looked directly at Jim. "How did he die? Why have you come here to tell us?"

Jim fingered his new face scar. "Who was the coward of Colonia Federico?" he countered.

"How did you know about that?"

He shrugged. "I know," he said quietly. He looked up at her. "It was Orlando, wasn't it?"

"It was not his fault! He was no coward. There are many kinds of cowards. In his own way he was a brave man. It was a label they placed on him."

"Why did they do it?" he asked.

She wet her full lips and looked away. "It was after the fight. There were many wounded. The ground was stained with blood. Men were screaming in their pain. There was no doctor at Colonia Federico." Her voice died away.

"Go on," he said gently.

She caught her breath. "There were only a few soldiers left standing on their feet. My husband was badly wounded. He was wounded, but he was an officer and a soldier of Mexico. He gave orders to kill the enemy wounded. It was the custom. There was never any quarter given or asked for in that type of warfare. You understand?"

Jim nodded. "I have experienced such warfare," he said.

"Orlando was thought to have been killed or wounded. It was not so. He had hidden himself away so that he would not kill. My husband found out about it. In front of the people of Colonia Federico and the few soldiers left alive he gave Orlando a direct order to kill the enemy wounded. Orlando must do it alone to redeem himself." She laughed bitterly.

"He did not do it?" asked Jim.

She shook her head. "It was not within that gentle boy to kill like that, or any other way..."

"I can guess what happened to him," he said.

She nodded. "They shaved his head, stripped his buttons from him, and drummed him from the ranks."

"Because he could not kill."

"Yes," she said. She took the makings and rolled a cigarette. She looked at Jim over the flare of the match. "How did he die?"

"Bravely."

"But why?" she said.

He could at least tell a little lie. "There was a gunfight. A man was killed. It was thought that Orlando had killed this man. His friends shot down Orlando. Before he died he gave me those things you found."

She walked to the window and turned her back toward Jim. Her lovely shoulders shook a little. "Was there anything he said?" she asked.

The wind seemed to die away and it was very quiet, as though the oncoming night too wanted to hear what Jim Murdock had to say.

"Rafaela," said Jim. "That was what he said."

"There are many women named Rafaela," she said huskily.

"Perhaps. But that is what he said."

Her shoulders drooped a little. "It was I who gave him the watch," she said, without turning.

"A little cruelty, perhaps?"

She shook her head. "He wanted it."

"And the picture?"

"I did not know he had it."

Jim wet his dry lips. This was more painful than his healing wounds.

She turned slowly. "Would you like to see the children?" she said.

"Very much. Your husband as well."

She took the tray and walked to the door, looking back over her shoulder at him. "He is in Tucson on business," she said. "He will not be back for at least a week. Two days ago a package came from him for you. Medicines. Don Federico Velarde, my husband, is a fine man, and a good stepfather to my children."

"Federico again?" His eyes held hers. *He will be gone at least a week,* thought Jim.

She nodded. 'There was a *cura* here at one time, many years ago, long before the Americans took Arizona from my people. This was a holy place, but it fell upon evil times. My husband's grandfather took it over and named this place after his patron saint, Saint Federico. After that, each eldest son has taken that name. You must rest now."

The door closed behind her. Jim slowly fashioned another cigarette. There was something in the woman that cried out to him, but why he did not know. She had been married twice, and surely both husbands had been good to her, and she had probably loved Teodoro. Jim wet the end of the paper and thumbed the paper together. He snapped a match on his thumbnail and lighted the cigarette. But she had been loved by the ill-fated Orlando and she had wanted to know his last words. Had she loved him too? What kind of woman was this? He closed his eyes. *"Don Federico Velarde, my husband, is a fine man, and a good stepfather to my children."* He opened his eyes and blew a smoke ring. "He will not be back for at least a week," he said aloud.

The wind shifted. A shutter banged. A draft of air swirled in through the open windows and played with the guttering candles.

Jim felt his wounded shoulder. It would be some time before he could ride. Until that time, he would be a guest in the casa of Don Federico Velarde.

The door opened and Rafaela brought in her two children. There was Teodoro, a grave-faced faced boy of perhaps twelve, and little Teresa, perhaps seven or eight years of age. Teresa was formed from the same pattern as her mother, with mischievous eyes and a flirtatious look. Teodoro? Once, the boy looked quickly sideways at Jim, and for an instant, the blinking of an eye, perhaps, Jim thought he saw the face of Orlando Abeyta.

When they were gone, Jim lay there for a long time staring up at the dim ceiling. He had to leave this place. He had done what he had set out to do. He had told Orlando's kin of his death. He had found out what kind of man Orlando Abeyta had been. It had taken many months. It would soon be time for him to ride north, back to his own country, to find Three Forks and a girl named Jessica. Then it would all be over, and he'd be able to sleep well once again, and the dog would be off his back. So far it had not been an easy task, nor were his problems over. He dropped off to sleep, and as he did so the oval face of Rafaela appeared to him, and there were other things as well. Things that disturbed his sleep as it had not been disturbed for many months.

THE SIXTH DAY after Jim's return to the world of the living he had spent outside in the bright sunshine of late summer, watching the children at play, looking at the purple haze over the hills, listening to the distant bawling of the cattle, and also to the voice of Rafaela as she gave orders to her servants. The doctor had visited Jim twice in that time. All Jim needed now was rest and good food. The doctor had done all he could do. The doctor, and Rafaela, thought Jim. *Rafaela*. She was rarely out of his mind.

That night they dined together in the huge, low-ceilinged dining room of the sprawling hacienda, after the children had gone to bed, and if Rafaela Velarde had not known she had made a conquest prior to that dinner, she must surely have known it then.

They sat together a long time in the moonlight of the patio, talking of Orlando and of Teodoro, of Colonia Federico, which was well remembered by Rafaela. She remembered, too, the old padre who had given Jim his first real lead in his search for the kin of Orlando Abeyta.

Later, in his room, with the dying moonlight silvering patches of the polished floor, Jim paced back and forth, smoking, his arm in a sling to ease his shoulder, thinking of Rafaela until he thought he must be going mad.

It took a long time for him to sleep. He did not know when he dropped off, but the scene that came before him in his sleep occurred some hours before the coming of the dawn. He saw those damned trees of hell standing on the cold, windswept ridge. He saw the bitter fruit of men's sudden madness swinging like grisly pendulums in the eerie grip of the whining wind, and he shouted aloud in his terror.

He opened his eyes to feel the icy sweat covering his naked flesh, and his body shook like aspen leaves. He closed his eyes and turned his head desperately from side to side to shake the awful dregs of the nightmare from his mind. The room was pitch-dark when he opened his eyes. Then the door swung open to reveal Rafaela standing there in her thin gown, a candle in her hand and fear upon her lovely face. Fear, not for herself, but for Jim Murdock. She came quickly to him and sat on the edge of the bed, holding the candle in her free hand as she stroked his wet brow. He slid his right arm about her slender waist and looked up at her face. For a long, long moment they looked into each other's eyes, forgetting why he had cried out and why she had come. She bent close to him. The candle fell to the floor and extinguished itself, and she was in his arms, lips pressing hotly against his mouth while his free hand roved her soft, warm body.

Now was the time. There was nothing, no one, to hold them back from each other, from what both of them had known in their own minds for days. They were on the very edge of complete surrender to each other. Then they seemed suspended, balanced in time, as though it were really nonexistent, and a moment later her hot lips parted from his and she drew back her long dark hair from his face and naked chest. His right arm fell away from her. Slowly she sat up and pulled her filmy gown about her shoulders. Another moment or two drifted slowly past. A cold, searching wind crept in through the windows and chilled the two of them.

"Good night, Jaime," she whispered.

"Good night, Rafaela," he said huskily.

She walked slowly to the door, half expecting him to call her back and knowing she could not refuse him, while he wanted to call her back and knew in full conscience that he could not.

"I am leaving in the morning," he said at last.

She nodded her head and then closed the door behind her.

He lay there for a long time until the inner fires waned and then sank into a dim glow, leaving a thick layer of ashes on the deep-seated passion within him. There seemed no longer a great haste to leave the rancho and travel north on the last part of his self-imposed mission. As he had left a part of himself on the grim gallows hill back in Ute Crossing that cold morning when three men had been lynched, so he had also left a part of himself when old Augustin Galeras had died in the Sierra Vallecillos. The deaths of Lyss, Slim, Jules, and the four *bandidos* meant nothing to Jim, for he had killed in such fashion before, but the deaths of the others had affected him deeply.

Something was driving him on and on. Perhaps he was seeking himself. Loneliness had become part and parcel of his life. Perhaps he needed someone to share his thoughts and plans. It might be that this was assuming far more importance in his mind than it merited, but what else was there for a man to do in an effort to achieve wholeness?

He knew there was deadly danger for him up north. Lyss had died in a muddy alley in Las Cruces and Slim and Jules had died near Colonia Federico for some deep, dark reason that had something to do with the hanging of those three men in Ute Crossing. Someone wanted Jim Murdock permanently out of the way; Perhaps they had lost track of him, thought him dead in the Sierra Madre. It would be easy to stay in the south and avoid the prospect of sudden, violent death if he returned north.

He opened his eyes and stared at the dim ceiling. "Jessica," he said. He knew he had to go.

CHAPTER ELEVEN

The summer was dying as the tall, gaunt man, his set face marked for life with two scars, rode slowly north from the border country, gathering his strength as he rode, camping out at times in the lonely canyons beside chuckling streams, lingering there for days, only to saddle up and ride on again. Patagonia saw him, and Sonoita, and he lingered for days in brawling Tombstone, quietly walking the streets of the toughest town in the West. He bothered no one and no one bothered him. They knew the stamp and quality of his breed. Such men were better left alone. His drift took him north to Benson, and then by train to Lordsburg, in New Mexico Territory. He dallied for a time in Silver City, finding the food passable, the liquor good, his luck at the tables better than it had ever been, and the company of a little, dark-eyed Cajun girl gradually dulled the sharp edge of his memories of Rafaela Velarde.

In Albuquerque an ex-army surgeon he had known along the border inspected his shoulder and pronounced it well again. The hollows had filled out in his face and the sun, wind, rain, and good air had made him seem like the old Jim Murdock. The real wounds were invisible.

It was easy, far too easy, to try to avoid the inevitable.

He turned away from the valley of the Rio Grande at Bernalillo and rode northwesterly at a steady pace for days through the lonely, windswept country until he reached the San Juan. It occurred to him only then that he was really heading for Meadows to see a little man in a derby hat who bought and sold anything and everything. Fella by the name of Sam. *"You will stop by on your way back, maybe? It was a pleasure doing business with you."* Jim grinned.

The leaves had turned when he reached Meadows. The country was a glory of scarlet, purple, and gold, with a haziness always in the distance. He could see the wolf-fanged mountains to the north that held Ute Crossing in their grasp, and the highest peak of them all, Warrior Peak, was just visible, tipped with a golden cap from the rays of the sinking sun. He was getting close to home, if one could still call it that.

Meadows dozed in the bright, clear sunlight. The air had a thin and brittle quality to it. The cottonwoods along the street were like yellow flames. A blacksmith's hammer beat a steady, metallic song that echoed against the low hills just beyond the town.

Jim dismounted and tethered the dun. He slapped the dust from his trail clothing. The building where Sam held forth in solitary splendor seemed to lean just a little more from the perpendicular. Jim opened the door. The bell tinkled rustily. He walked slowly between the piles of dusty boxes, a vast mausoleum of the unused and useless, waiting for someone who might, just *might,* mind you, have use for them. Their hope was as dead as the dusty air of the gloomy cavern in which they waited.

The bell stopped tinkling.

"You are wanting to buy or sell, maybe?" a soft voice asked out of nowhere, like a disembodied spirit trying to establish contact with the world of the living. A derby hat seemed to rise by itself from behind a rampart of dusty feed sacks.

"Hello, Sam," said Jim.

Sam studied Jim. "Mr. Murdock," he said quietly. "It has been a long time. You have changed."

Jim instinctively touched the scar on his right cheek.

Sam held up a hand. "No, it is not that. Not that alone, my friend. It is something else. I cannot put my hand on it."

Jim nodded. "I know what you mean," he said.

"The drinks are on you, stranger!" shrieked the parrot.

Jim grinned. He took out his cigar case and opened it, holding it out to Sam. "I know," said Jim. "You came west from Pittsburg because you had a cough. You should smoke? Crazy you'd be!"

Sam smiled. "It is good to see you in such a mood," he said. "It has not been easy for you. Tell me! You found, maybe, the woman Sarah?"

Jim nodded. "I left her the money you gave me, Sam."

"Good!" Sam tilted his head to one side. "You want to talk, maybe, about it?"

Jim shook his head.

"You found, maybe, the others you were looking for?"

"I didn't say I was looking for any others."

"You didn't have to, Jim."

"I found the kin of the Mexican who was hanged."

"But the kin of the boy, you did not find them?"

"That is why I came back, Sam." Jim bit the end from a cigar and held a match to the tip.

Sam rubbed his cheek. "Maybe you should have stayed down south."

"Why?"

"After you left for the south there was a man who came looking for you. A big man. Such a nose he had! A big, thick moustache. Eyebrows like raveled rope above his eyes. a mean-looking character, Jim. I was afraid from him. I told him you had gone to Albuquerque. But nothing more, Jim! I swear!"

Jim blew out the match. "He won't be coming back," he said quietly.

Sam shivered. "There were two more men some time after he was gone."

"One of them tall and slim with sandy hair? The other dark, very dark, broad-shouldered, and had a slight limp? Names of Jules and Slim?"

Sam smiled weakly. "They won't be back either?"

"No." Jim blew a smoke ring. "Were there any others?"

"None that I saw or talked to, Jim. But I heard there was two men here a month or so after the second two left. They hung around drinking and then went south."

"Any names?"

"One of them was called Barney. The other I do not know. Like I said, Jim, I didn't see them or talk to them, and I didn't want to. But there is something else, my friend. Something you should know. About your brother."

Jim took the cigar from his mouth. "Ben?"

"Yes. You did not know?"

"Know what?" asked Jim quietly.

Sam looked away. He took off his faded derby and turned the brim around and around in his thin hands. "It is a terrible thing to tell a friend," said Sam softly.

"Tell me, Sam," said Jim in a harsh voice.

Sam looked directly at Jim. "He is dead, my friend."

"How did he die?"

"It was not long after you left. We heard the story here in little bits and pieces. It was said he drove his buggy very fast."

"He did," agreed Jim.

"They found the team still drawing the front wheels. They searched back along the road. The rest of the buggy they found in the creek near his house." Sam stopped and wet his dry lips. He swallowed. "Your brother was a cripple? No?"

Jim nodded. He could plainly see Warrior Creek and the black water against the newly fallen snow as he had last seen it. The creek wasn't deep but it ran very fast, and the water would be icy cold.

Sam rubbed his thin throat. "They found him in the spring. Very strange, too, for his body was found on the bank on the ranch that used to belong to your family, Jim. Like maybe he had come home. No one knew where you were."

It was very quiet in the big store. Even the parrot had stopped rustling, preening, and squawking in his cage.

Jim shook his head. "He was a man of principle, Sam. A man who fought for justice. It was almost an obsession with him."

"Such things are not obsessions," said the little man. "If they are, then more of us should maybe be obsessed." He eyed Jim. "He was, maybe, the only one of your family left?"

"Yes."

"It is a lonely thing for a man to have no family. I know."

Jim relighted his cigar. It wasn't in him to accept sympathy. Much as he might want it, he always avoided it. To him it was a mark of weakness, and yet he knew not why he felt that way. He was like a lobo or a wild dog who would crawl away to lick his own wounds without benefit of sympathy. Would it be that way the rest of his life?

"You are going north again?" asked Sam.

"Yes."

Sam shrugged. "You are like a man who courts death."

"There are things a man has to do."

"He does not have to seek his own self-destruction."

"You talk like a preacher."

Sam smiled. "A rabbi! You will stay a few days? There is room here for you."

"Here?"

"Come and see."

Sam led the way into the back of the immensely long store. He opened a door and ushered Jim into a surprising room. Books lined two of the walls. A polished piano stood against one wall. Pictures graced the walls here and there. A fine Navajo rug was on the floor.

"You surprise me, Sam," said Jim.

"This is my hideout, Jim. Days I spend in the front. Nights and Sundays here, reading my good friends the books."

"You have no real friends here, Sam?"

Sam shook his head. He glanced sideways at Jim. "I have been waiting. Maybe I have found such a friend."

Jim blew a ring of smoke and punched a lean finger through it. "A gunman? A killer? Me? Not me, Sam. I'm not your style."

Sam busied himself with a dusty wine bottle. "Not the guns and the killings, Jim. It is something else. We make a strange pair, but we are friends, and you know it."

Jim nodded.

Sam filled two glasses and handed one to Jim. "While you are here, stay with me, Jim. I know you have to go. Maybe if I was in your boots I would do the same thing. Who is to say?"

They touched the glasses together. The wine was delicious. In a little while the two of them began to talk of many things, far removed from violent death and dusty merchandise, and when the dusk came, and Sam locked up the store and turned to the big range in his kitchen to fashion a meal, Jim knew that the utile man was right. Sam had found a friend.

When Jim left his new friend, Sam came to the door of the store with him. "You will maybe let me know how you make out?" he asked.

Jim checked his saddle girth. "If I can't, someone else will," he said dryly.

"Do not talk like that, my friend. Find this Jessica. Tell her of her brother."

"She likely already knows the story, Sam."

"Even so, she would like to hear it, maybe, from a man who has spent so many months of his time to tell the kin of those three unfortunate men."

Jim turned and stuck out a big hand. Sam gripped it "When this is all over and you are at peace," said Sam, "what do you plan to do?"

"Get a little ranch. Hunt and fish. Read a few books."

"You will do this alone?"

"Probably."

Sam hesitated. "When I first met you I said a partner I didn't need. Maybe, when you look for this ranch, you could use some cash. A partner, maybe?"

"You, Sam?"

Sam nodded. He looked back at the leaning building. "Of this place I am sick."

"I'll consider the offer, Sam."

Sam turned. "Maybe I could be a Yiddisher cowboy, hey?"

Jim grinned as he mounted. "Adios, Sam." He rode west along the wide street, then turned in his saddle. "Hey, Sam!" he called out. "If we have a Yiddisher cowboy we'd have to have kosher cows!"

The little man was still laughing when Jim turned off from the street and took the road north out of Meadows. The smile vanished from Sam's face. He opened the door and walked inside. The bell tinkled. "Shut up!" snapped Sam at the bell.

"The drinks are on you, stranger!" squawked the parrot "You too!" shouted Sam. He vanished into his hideout.

For a man carrying a message of death, and wondering in the back of his mind what further violence lay in store for him, there was deep enjoyment in Jim Murdock as he worked his way through the mountain approaches that bright morning. He was going home, for better or for worse. It had been a long time. A long, dusty, deadly trail from Ute Crossing to Las Cruces, Chihuahua City, Colonia Federico, and Rancho San Federico, and now he was nearing the end.

A fine, needlelike drizzle was falling on the valley, slanting down from the great range of mountains to the east drifting across the thick timber at the bases of the heights, and stippling the leaden surface of the river. The rain had darkened the false-fronted wooden buildings of the town and was puddling in the hollows and ruts of the road. Hip-shot horses stood patiently at the racks in front of the stores and the saloons, mostly the saloons. The harder rains, the gully washers and fence lifters, would come later, forecasting the bitter winter. It was getting along toward that time.

A chain of sheet lightning zigzagged across the streaming sky and forked into a bluff. A low rumble of drums came from the thunder gods. The rain came down harder and harder until the bluffs were hidden from sight.

A lone horseman crossed the wooden bridge that spanned the rushing river, hunched into his slicker collar, hat pulled low over his eyes, a tiny spark of flame showing from the cigarette he cupped in his hand. He looked at the high, warped front of a store. "Three Forks General Mercantile Company," he read. Jim kneed the horse toward the nearest rack and swung down into the thick mud. He unstrapped a poncho from the cantle and hung it over the horse. He stepped up onto the sagging wooden sidewalk and found himself looking directly at a dirty-windowed saloon. "Well, fancy that," he said with a tired smile. It had been a three-day ride through the mountains.

He walked into the saloon and rested an elbow on the end of the bar. The bar was pretty well lined. Four men played poker at a rear table. A swamper was listlessly mopping up the water from a leak in the roof. There wasn't much talking. It wasn't talking weather. Just drinking weather.

"Rye," said Jim to the bartender.

Bottle and glass were placed in front of Jim. The bartender was a melancholy-looking soul with an uneasy Adam's apple. One of his eyes, slightly larger than the other, seemed to wander off on a mission of its own now and then, to be brought back only by a conscious effort. "Long ride?" said the bar critter.

"Passable," said Jim. He filled the glass.

"From the north?"

"South."

No one looked at Jim. Saddle tramps were a dime a dozen in the Three Forks country.

"Looking for work?" said the bar critter.

Jim tossed down the drink. "Not exactly," he said.

The man wiped the zinc-topped bar. "Well, you are or you ain't," he said. "Temple Smeed is looking for teamsters."

"Out of my line," said Jim. He felt the rye hit his cold guts and explode. His face suddenly felt warm.

"Buck Witty is looking for riders."

Jim eyed the man. "You run the employment agency here?" he asked with a smile.

"No. Sort of a hobby of mine, mister." The sad eyes studied Jim and the two scars, the hard set of the jaw, the gray eyes that seemed to make a man a little too uncomfortable to stare at very long. He had known all along that this wasn't any teamster or line rider. No, and not a livery hand, and certainly not a townsman. Gambler? No. Gunfighter...

Jim refilled the glass. "I'm looking for a girl named Jessica," he said quietly.

A broad-shouldered, bearded man laughed. "Hell!" he said explosively. "Who ain't?"

Jim looked at him. "You know her?" he asked.

"No."

"I wasn't talking to you, mister," said Jim evenly.

Hard dark' eyes peered into Jim's eyes, and what the bearded man saw he did not like. "Sorry," he said. "I thought it was funny at the time. No offense, mister."

"Forget it," said Jim. "Pour yourself a drink."

The man nodded. He wanted no part of this lobo.

The bartender leaned on the bar. "Girl by the name of Jessica lives up the North Fork," he said. "Jessica Lyle.

Lives by herself except for one hand." He grinned. "She shoots as good as any man too, mister."

"Lives alone? No people?"

The bartender shrugged. "She had a brother named Jesse. They was twins. No, there ain't no one out there but her and old Jonas."

Jim downed his second drink. The cold was leaving his body. "What happened to her brother?"

The bartender rubbed industriously at an imaginary spot on the zinc while his wandering eye moved back and forth. "What do you want to know for?" he asked quietly.

A gray-faced man halfway up the bar looked at Jim. "Tell him, Les," he said. "Go on. Tell him. I'd like to see the look on his face."

The saloon was suddenly very quiet. The poker players were watching Jim. The swamper was leaning on his mop handle doing the same thing. Every man at the bar except a drunken fool at the end was looking at Jim. The drunk was looking into his empty whiskey glass. It was all that really seemed to interest him.

Les took a final swipe at the imaginary spot. He looked directly at Jim, and for once his loose eye was steady. "The kid was lynched over to Ute Crossing a little less than a year ago," he said. "Lynched for murder."

There was no expression on Jim's face. "I know," he said.

The gray-faced man's hand tightened about his shot glass. "No one bothered to tell the girl," he said bitterly. "No one told her until the whole damned town knew about it from the Denver newspapers. It was too late then to remember she got delivery of the same newspaper. Someone should have broken the news to her before that."

"Take it easy, Kyle," said the bartender.

"The sons of bitches," said Kyle. "That kid never killed no one. His sister has more guts in her little finger than he had in his whole body. There was only the two of them, and some of the bastards around here used to chase after Jessica, and the kid couldn't do anything about it. They drove that boy outa here."

Les rubbed his thin throat. "Well, anyways, there ain't no one bothers her now," he said.

A short, red-faced man nodded. "Beats the hell outa me how she keeps that place a-goin'," he said. "My missus told me to go over and give her a hand. She says to me: 'No thanks, *Mr.* Watts, I kin take care of myself and my property.' I felt like a damned jackass about it. She don't want nothin' to do with nobody, I tell you."

"Cute trick, too," said a grinning cowpoke. "One time I was hunting strays over on the North Fork. I stops to pass the time of day. Well, maybe I did get too fresh. I crossed the North Fork two jumps and a holler ahead of a .44/40 slug."

The gray-faced man looked at him. "You let her alone, Kelly," he said thinly.

Kelly shoved back his glass. "What for, Kyle? You got a brand on her? She turned you down half a dozen times, from what I hear."

Kyle turned and looked at him. "You got a big mouth, Kelly," he said softly.

Les walked to the middle of the bar. "Drinks on the house," he said. "Sam! Get to leaning on that mop handle! Jerry! Stick some nickels in the piano! You boys at the table want fresh drinks!"

The man named Kyle emptied his glass, wiped his mouth with the back of a hand, and looked at Jim. "What business you got with Jessica Lyle?" he demanded.

"That's my business," said Jim.

Kelly whistled softly. "Now it's you with the big mouth, Kyle," he said.

"Something about her brother?" said Kyle.

Jim emptied his glass and shoved it back. He paid for the drinks. He felt inside his coat for his cigar case, withdrew a long nine, lighted it, and fanned out the match.

"Well?" said Kyle. He stood a little way back from the bar.

Les leaned forward. "One more remark out of you, Kyle," he said quietly, "and I'll cut you off. You know Marshal Craig will back me up. He's had a bellyful of your trouble-making lately."

Kyle wet his lips. He turned back to the bar. He wasn't so damned sure at that that he wanted trouble with the tall, scar-faced man at the end of the bar. There was plenty of time to find out what business he had with Jessica Lyle.

Les looked at Jim. "Cross back over the bridge," he said. "Take the first road to the right. Follow it about five miles to the North Fork. You can't miss it. There's a plank bridge there. The other side of the bridge is Jessica Lyle's property."

"Watch out she don't come a-shootin'!" said Kelly. "Hawww!"

Jim walked to the door, feeling the eyes of every man in the place, except likely the drunk at the end of the bar, boring a hole into his back.

"You never did tell us your name," said Les.

Jim turned a little. "Murdock," he said. "Jim Murdock." He closed the door behind him.

The drunk slowly raised his head. Just as slowly he looked toward the door; Suddenly it seemed as though he wasn't drunk at all. He paid his tab and put on his slicker. "What time does the company telegraph office close, Les?" he asked.

"Half an hour, Monk."

Monk walked slowly to the door, peered out into the dimness, and saw Jim riding toward the bridge. Monk stepped out onto the boardwalk and hurried up the street toward the telegraph office. It had been a long, long time ago that he had been told to keep an eye out for a tall, scar-faced man named Murdock. Jim Murdock...

CHAPTER TWELVE

The fall rain had thinned out to a misty drizzle when Jim Murdock reached the sagging bridge across the North Fork. Now and then eerie lightning flashes illuminated the dusk and silvered the falling rain. The North Fork was bank-full and already beginning to lap over the rotten planking of the bridge. The structure creaked and groaned in the current. The bloated body of a drowned calf swirled lazily in an eddy on the far side of the stream. There was nothing to be seen beyond the bridge except the dripping woods, dark and secretive, parted by the narrow road, just wide enough for a wagon, which vanished into the dimness. No sign of a house, a cabin, or a shed. Not a sight of an animal *or* a fence. Nothing but the dark, dripping woods, a rusted mailbox on a tilted post, and the leaden-colored waters of the stream.

Jim rolled a quirly and lighted it, flipping the match into the water. Words came back to him: *"She shoots as good as any man too, mister... That kid never killed no one. His sister has more guts in her little finger than he had in his whole body... She don't want nothin' to do with nobody, I tell you... I crossed the North Fork two jumps and a holler ahead of a .44/40 slug... Watch out she don't come a-shootin!"*

Jim tapped his side pocket. He could feel the hard lump of the bluish-looking stone within it. It was all he had brought those hundreds of miles and after so many months to give to a girl who had lost her twin brother; likely, according to the barflies in the local saloon, the only near kin she had had around Three Forks.

"By God," said Jim. "What the hell is the matter with me? I didn't come all this distance to be scared of a female gun toter!" He grinned, his saturnine face lighted momentarily by the flare of the cigarette tip as he took a drag. "All the same, I'd rather face a bee-stung she-bear with cubs than a gal wearin' pants and making Winchester music around my ears. You can't shoot back. All you can do is cut stick for the *Ho* and hope you reach the brush on the far side ahead of a .44/40 slug, like the man in the saloon said. He was laughing then. He wasn't laughing when she was helping him make up his mind he ought to leave."

He touched the horse with his heels and rode slowly out on the creaking bridge, nervously eyeing that swirling water which had risen higher even as he had watched it. He reached the far side and looked back. "By God," he said. "I won't try that bridge until the North Fork goes down, gun-totin' woman and all!"

The way through the woods was an uneasy way for Jim. Wasn't likely she'd be squatting there in the brush cuddling that damned Winchester of hers, looking for fair game. Not with the rain and the darkness coming on. Still ...

He had ridden almost a mile and half through the woods when at last he saw them thinning out as the light-ning lanced across the sky and struck into a towering, naked butte that dominated the landscape like a brooding giant He drew rein at the edge of the woods and waited for the next eerie flash. When it came he saw a wide meadow-land area stretching beyond the woods, bisected by the road. To the right he thought he caught a glimpse of some cattle bedded down in the edge of the woods. Here and there on the meadowland were outcroppings of lichened rocks, like dislocated bones thrust up against the surface flesh of the earth. The ground at the far end of the open area sloped upward, and the road climbed it and vanished on the far side. There was nothing else to do but traverse that open area, hoping that Jessica Lyle wasn't out prowling with her trusty Winchester.

It was fully dark when he reached the far side. A dilapidated barbed-wire fence stretched on either side of the road, and the remains of a Texas gate had been hauled to one side to clear the road. He rode down the far side of the rise, and then suddenly, when he least expected it, he saw a faint yellowish glow of light beyond a motte of wind-swaying trees. He halted the tired horse and began to roll a cigarette, then thought better of it. A lighted match or the glow of a cigarette could be seen etched against the darkness, giving just enough target and time to slam out a round or two.

He rode slowly forward, then dismounted, and led the dun on. A man on a horse is too big a target. He tethered the dun to a shattered tree, and for a moment his hand lingered on the wet buttstock of his saddle gun, and then he shook his head. A flash of lingering lightning revealed a well-built house of peeled logs, set on a knoll. Light showed from two windows at the side of the house and from one in front. There were other buildings beyond the house. Sheds and a big barn, slightly the worse for wear, a fallen-in log building and a dark-looking structure, likely a bunkhouse. Jim whistled softly. This had been a nice spread at one time.

A dog barked suddenly from an outbuilding. Jim watched the house. The dog barked again and again. Likely he was penned in or chained. The wind shifted and brought the bittersweet odor of wood smoke to Jim. It brought something else as well, the lovely odor of cooking food. He could have sworn mere were fresh-baked rolls or bread, and maybe even a pie or two. He remembered then that he had not eaten all day, except for a few scraps of trail rations around noon.

A dark shape moved near one of the outbuildings. Too low for a man or woman. The dog barked, and Jim knew what the shape was, but it didn't move any closer. He had been right about the animal being chained. Something moved between the light and the window in one of the lighted rooms. The wind brought the sound of a closing door to him. Then he saw someone standing on the edge of the rear porch.

"Hello, the house!" yelled Jim.

The dog slammed against his chain, barking and growling in turns.

Jim walked slowly forward, hands at shoulder level. "You there!" he called out. "I've come to see Miss Lyle on business! Are you Miss Lyle?"

The figure moved. "Not likely," said a man.

"You must be Jonas, then."

"You know a lot about this place, don't you?"

"Damn it! All I know is that Miss Lyle lives here and that my slicker is leaking in this rain! Water running down my sleeves!"

The man laughed. "Then put your hands down, mister! Who are you? What do you want?"

"The name is Murdock! Jim Murdock! I've come to see Miss Lyle." Jim lowered his hands, cursing softly as he felt the water soak the sleeves of his shirt and coat.

Jim waited. He narrowed his eyes. He had the damnedest feeling that someone else was watching him. He saw the man turn his head a little as though someone had spoken to him, and then he nodded. "Bring on your cayuse," said Jonas. "Put him in the barn there. I'll get a lantern."

By the time Jim reached the barn the man was coming from the house with the lantern. He was a short bench-legged man who walked with a slight limp. He grinned at Jim from as homely a face as Jim had ever experienced, but his eyes were squirrel-bright and seemingly friendly. He didn't have on a slicker or a coat, and there was no belt gun at his narrow waist. His face was wrinkled like a dried apple, and it was difficult to tell how old he was, perhaps fifty-five or sixty years of age. His eyes, at least, were still young.

Jim led the dun into the barn. He looked at Jonas. "All right to unsaddle?"

"Why not?"

Jim grinned. "I didn't know what kind of reception I'd get around here."

"Sho! Well, you can't expect a man to go all the way back from where he come from on a night like this."

Jim unsaddled the dun and rubbed him down, covered him with a worn blanket he found in a stall, and fed him. "Times a little hard around here?" he said conversationally as he picked up his saddlebags and cantle roll.

"Not so's you'd notice it. Nice country around here. Good stock. Plenty of water and grazing."

"I noticed that." Jim looked about the cavernous barn. Half a dozen streams of water came down from the roof at the rear of the structure. "Plenty of water..."

"Well, we ain't exactly in business right now."

Jim looked at him. "I heard Miss Lyle would run off anyone in pants."

"She never run me off. 'Course, I'm too damned old to bother much with fillies now. Been a confirmed bachelor all my life, anyways. I never give the name Barlow to no filly. Saves time, money, and trouble, with the accent on trouble." Jonas lifted the lantern from a box. "I sleep in the bunkhouse. Kinda lonely with all them bunks empty there, but I use the foreman's room. There are two bunks in there."

Jim followed the short man through the wet darkness to the sagging bunkhouse. Jonas hung the lantern on a hook in the room. "You can clean up if you like. Supper will be ready in an hour."

Jim nodded. "Does she know I'm here?"

"You joshing? Mister, that gal don't miss a thing."

Jonas felt for the makings and rolled a cigarette. He tossed the makings to Jim. "You can start a fire in the stove there and dry out." He lighted the cigarette and fanned out the match. "Where you from, Murdock?"

Jim smiled as he peeled off his slicker, coat, and shirt. "Anywhere and everywhere." He rolled a cigarette and lighted it.

"Colorado man?"

"Originally."

Jonas walked to the door. He looked back. "Ute Crossing, maybe?" he asked quietly.

"I was born in the valley of the Ute."

"Been there lately?"

"Almost a year ago."

The wind shifted and rattled the windowpanes. A cold draft crept through a broken pane and swirled the cigarette smoke about the room.

"Maybe last November, mister?"

Jim looked at the little man. "You're asking a helluva lot of questions, aren't you, mister?"

For a second the bright eyes hardened. "Sorry, Murdock. It really ain't none of my business, is it?"

"You're getting the general idea, Barlow."

Jonas nodded. He closed the door behind him. Jim heard his boots squelch in the mud, and then the sound died away. He heard a door slam.

Jim started a fire and hung his clothing near it. He examined the puckered bullet hole in his shoulder. The cold had made his shoulder a little stiff. He heated water and then washed and shaved. He studied himself in the cracked, gold-flecked mirror. "My God," he breathed. "I look like the devil's twin brother."

He dressed in dry, clean clothing and tied a string tie about his corded neck. He reached for his gun belt and then stopped. He rubbed his jaw. Wasn't exactly polite to walk into a house and sit down to supper carrying a six-gun at your hip. On the other hand, he remembered too well the reputation the young woman had for dealing with men. He satisfied himself with placing his double-barreled derringer in his coat pocket. Maybe the characters in the saloon had been building up a stack about Jessica Lyle, the sharpshooting gal of Three Forks. He grinned. He must have walked into a real setup on that rainy afternoon. He'd be willing to bet they were still laughing into their tanglefoot.

Still, Jessica must know who he was, as Jonas had. Maybe the story of his mission to find the kinfolk of the three dead men had passed through that country. Maybe she was just wondering why it had taken the most part of a year for him to reach Three Forks. He'd have to explain that one. He was sorry for her without even meeting her. He had been sorry for her ever since he had seen the kid die with a hemp necktie cutting off his young life. He was sorrier still that she had learned about his death in clear, cold print in a three-day-old newspaper deposited in that rusty mailbox on the banks of the North Fork.

Jim turned out the lantern and opened the door. The rain was hardly more than a thick mist now. He walked toward the house, the lights warm and cheery through the darkness and mistiness. He stepped up onto the rear porch and flipped away his cigarette. He rapped on the door.

Jonas opened the door. "Almost in time," he said. "Go on in, Murdock. Miss Lyle is waiting for you in the living room." He glanced over his shoulder, then came closer to Jim. "Take it easy on her. She ain't forgot a thing about the kid's death."

Jim wiped his feet and took off his hat. He crossed the brightly lighted kitchen, eyeing a row of fresh-built pies as he did so. The little man, or Jessica, was a prime cook.

He entered the big living room. A fire crackled in the cavernous fieldstone fireplace. A woman, slim as a birch, stood beside the fire, looking down into it. Jim cleared his throat. For a moment she stood there, and then she turned and looked directly at him, and it was like a shade from the other world for the brief span of a second or two, for she was an identical twin, as much as a woman can be twin to a man and not show masculinity, and yet in a way the kid had been more feminine in his appearance. He remembered all too well the sick, ghastly look on the boy's face before he had died. He remembered as well the set blue face of the boy when Jim had cut him down.

"Mr. Murdock," she said quietly. Her voice was much like her brother's had been, as Jim could recall, but there was a firmness in it, a resolution, that the kid had lacked. But then, maybe most any man would have lacked resolution and firmness if he knew he had only minutes before he was to be lynched.

"Miss Lyle," said Jim. He bent his head.

"Jonas said you came from Ute Crossing."

She knew where Jim came from, and it hadn't been Jonas who had told her. This much Jim knew. "I was born in the valley of the Ute," he said quietly. "I returned there almost a year ago after an absence of seven years. I spent only a short time there before leaving for New Mexico and Mexico."

There was a long pause. Jim narrowed his eyes. His impression of her was quite different from that which he had expected, even before the jokesters had ribbed him in the saloon in Three Forks.

"Jonas said you told him you had business with me," she said.

"It can wait until after supper, if you like."

"No," she said. She looked directly at him, and pretty as she was, all blue eyes, fine blonde hair and smooth skin, soft, full mouth, he had the uncanny feeling she was indeed the expert markswoman she was said to be.

How does one tell a lovely young woman that one was an unwilling witness to the lynching of her brother?

"Well, Mr. Murdock?"

"I think you know why I am here," he said quietly. "I think you know who I am, and that I witnessed the death of your brother Jesse. The story about that terrible day must have spread clear through this country not long after it happened."

"It came to me by newspaper," she said. "It was the first knowledge I had of his death. In later editions of the paper I learned of a man named Murdock who left Ute Crossing shortly after the lynchings. It was said that he knew a great deal more about those lynchings than he had let on."

It was suddenly too quiet in that big room. Jim had the uneasy knowledge too that Jonas was not rattling around in the kitchen, and that he was not far behind Jim, maybe with a scatter-gun in his hands, or a cocked six-gun. He dropped his left hand into his coat pocket.

"Don't move, mister," said a dry voice a few feet behind him.

"I wasn't reaching for a hideout gun," said Jim. "Can I draw out my hand?"

Jessica nodded to Jonas.

Jim breathed easier as he withdrew his hand. He held out the Ridgewood tobacco sack with the stone in it. "This was about all I found of value in his clothing," he said.

She came to him and took the sack, her cool fingers touching his calloused hand. She opened the sack and emptied the stone into her left palm. For a moment she stared at the stone, and then she quickly turned away. Her shoulders shook a little.

"I'm sorry, ma'am," said Jim.

"You damned fool," hissed Jonas.

"It took you a long time," said Jessica at last.

Jim smiled. "It wasn't intentional," he said dryly.

She turned slowly. "You must be mad to come here."

Jim's eyes narrowed. "Why? Someone had to come and tell you. I am sorry you learned by other means. They told me about it in town."

"Who told you?"

"Man by the name of Kyle."

Her face tightened. "Chris Kyle," she said. She looked

past Jim at Jonas. "Did Mr. Kyle, or any of the other *men* of Three Forks, tell you about me?"

Jim grinned. "They said you were right handy with a Winchester."

"You can copper that bet," said Jonas.

"I've had to build up that reputation," she said. 'I'm not sorry for it."

"Can you have the little man take that gun out of my back?" said Jim. "What crime have I committed?"

She walked to the fireplace and held the stone up between her and the firelight, which caught and reflected the hidden glow of the semiprecious gem. "You were one of the men who murdered my brother," she said.

"That's a damned lie!" Jim said harshly.

"Take it easy!" snapped Jonas.

"Would I have come here into this damned trap if I had been one of those murderers?" said Jim. "What kind of fool do you take me for?"

"He might have a point there," said Jonas.

"You don't know everything I know, Jonas," said Jessica. "There was a man here last spring looking for you, Mr. Murdock. He came to this ranch. He was a deputy sheriff from Ute Crossing. He had a warrant for your arrest"

"On what charge?"

"Being part of that gang of lynchers. Stealing from the bodies of the dead."

"Well, I'll be double-damned," said Jim. "Begging your pardon, ma'am." He studied her. "Did he give his name?"

She nodded. "Meigs. Harlan Meigs."

"The man who was dead drunk the morning they took your brother and those other two men from the Ute Crossing jail."

"By God," said Jonas. "We never heard that one before!"

"Did he say that any of the others had been appre-hended?" asked Jim.

"Most of them were unknowns."

"That's the biggest lie yet," said Jim angrily. "Every one of those men was well known in Ute Crossing!"

"None of their names were in the papers."

"No one would state that they had been in on it, that's why!" said Jim. "You don't know that town!"

"I know it well enough," she said bitterly.

"I'm beginning to see a little light coming through my thick skull. For some reason I'm not wanted back in Ute Crossing. It seems to me that someone tried to lay a trap for me here. A young woman whose brother was lynched, an expert riflewoman who supposedly had a habit of shooting first and asking questions afterward. Very neat. Perhaps if I hadn't managed to reach this place under cover of bad weather I'd have been shot when I put foot on your land."

"I wish I knew what you were talking about," said Jessica.

"Look," he said patiently. "Would it make sense for me to come here if I felt guilty for your brother's death? What logical reason would I have for coming here at all?"

"I have been wondering about that," she admitted. "A few months ago I might have shot you on sight. Now I don't know what to think."

"I have a suggestion," said Jim.

"Yes?"

"If you're as hungry as I am, I give my word I won't give you any trouble. There's a derringer in my right coat pocket, Jonas, but I won't reach for it. Take it out. Good! Now you can both sit at the other end of the table with six-guns beside your plates. The only weapons I want are a knife and a fork."

Jonas began to laugh. Even Jessica had a faint smile on her lovely face. "I guess we can afford to give a condemned man a good meal," she said.

"Ma'am," said Jim seriously, "I'm almost as good a talker as I am an eater. Let me tell you why I came here, and why it took me so long. About the time we ruin one of those pies out there you'll either believe me, or you can give me five minutes' start for the North Fork."

She nodded. Then she reached inside the bodice of her dress and withdrew a slender chain. She held it away from her breasts, and Jim saw a twin stone to the one he had brought from Ute Crossing, taken from the pocket of a dead boy to give to his twin sister. "We found these stones together when we were very young," she said softly. "Jesse always said they'd be good luck for us. He was wrong about that."

"Maybe he meant as long as you stayed together," said Jim.

She held the two stones side by side. "I never quite thought of it that way, Mr. Murdock," she said.

CHAPTER THIRTEEN

Jim Murdock led his horse up the narrow, twisting trail, following Jessica Lyle as she guided him up atop the great butte that seemed almost to hang over the North Fork far, far below, a glinting, sparkling stream that dashed across the stones in its shallow bed. The heavy rains of the past week had stopped at last, and the runoff was almost gone, although the ground was still soft with the soaking it had received. It was nice country, as Jonas had said. Plenty of water and grazing, but hardly any stock.

She rounded a turn in the trail and vanished. Jim slowly led the dun around the outthrust shoulder of the butte into a tangled jungle of scrub trees and brush that choked a great gash in the living rock, affording a shallow layer of earth for the tenacious roots of the growths. He climbed up a steep slope and then suddenly, as though someone had dropped the walls of the room, he found himself standing in the open, on naked, lichened rock, with a cool breeze sweeping about him, drying the sweat on his face. He looked about and whistled softly.

She turned and smiled. "It's worth the climb, isn't it, Jim?" she said. She pushed back her hat and let it drop to her back, hanging from the barbiquejo strap. The vagrant breeze toyed coyly with her fine hair. "You can smoke if you like."

He shoved back his own hat, watching her instead of the magnificent western view that seemed to extend all the way into Utah. He rolled a cigarette and lighted it. She was right. The view alone was worth the whole ranch that lay below the butte, neatly encompassed by the North Fork, but the view wouldn't bring in the beans and bacon.

The sky was dotted with white cloud puffs that drifted, one after the other, like leaves on a stream, toward the west, while their fleeting shadows raced along the terrain below, up. heights and down deep into the canyons, in a race that could never be lost or won. The air had a lift to it that hit a man's lungs and made him feel ten feet high.

He looked down at the ranch. A wraith of smoke drifted up from the big log house. The sun glinted from the windows. It was a good spread. There was timber to spare. A man could set up a sawmill and do some business. There was plenty of land for cattle. Water in plenty. Jim eyed the stream. Probably alive with trout. He smiled at the thought.

She sat down on a rock and wrapped her arms about her knees, tilting her head to one side to study him. "What's tickling you?" she asked.

"Nothing much. I was thinking there might be trout in that stream."

"There are. My father fished quite a bit. My mother sometimes said he fished too much, but then she never attempted to stop him. He was English and talked a lot at times about the fine fishing in Scotland."

"An educated man, no doubt."

"Yes. He had taught school in England, and later here in America. He was a college professor when he came west for his health, met my mother, and bought this place."

Jim blew a smoke ring. "A good rancher?"

She shrugged. "He got by. He liked his books. Mother was the real ramrod around here, but the two of them were happy." She smiled. "I'm more like her, I suppose."

"And Jesse?"

She looked away. "He was a great deal like Father. Sensitive, moody, more interested in books than in ranching. Father always said I should have been the male."

Jim shook his head. "What a terrible waste that would have been."

She flushed prettily. "I never wanted to be a man."

"Thank God for that," he said fervently.

"Mother didn't live long after Father passed on. As different as they were in many ways, they still seemed to have a great deal in common. Jesse had been planning to go to college, but when they were gone we found we had just enough money to hold onto the place. This is a hard country. A woman can't very well run a ranch, although my mother seemed to do rather well at it, but then she had Father there to back her up. As refined and educated as he was, he was no coward. It didn't take the local men long to find that out. After the two of them passed away there was no choice for Jesse. He had to stay here and try to run the place." Her voice died away.

Jim remembered the bitter voice of Chris Kyle. *"There was only the two of them, and some of the bastards around here used to chase after Jessica, and the kid couldn't do anything about it. They drove that boy outa here."*

She looked out across the great span of country to the west. "Jesse said he had to leave. To find himself. I knew he never would. That is, he wouldn't find himself like the others. If Jesse had been raised in a city, he would have risen to be a success. He couldn't adapt himself to this kind of life. Oh, I know what you're thinking! Why couldn't he adapt himself? You'd like this country and this ranch and everything about it if you had been raised here. Jesse was a loner. His only fault was that he was different. *So different. ...*"

"And he never carried a gun?"

She shook her head. "I had to learn to shoot for the two of us. My father was an excellent shot, and my mother handled a gun as well as most ranch women. Jesse would have nothing to do with them." She looked at Jim. "He never shot anything in his life. The other boys used to haze him because he watched birds and animals rather than shoot them."

There was a long silence during which both of them were occupied with their own thoughts. Jim rolled another cigarette. "I'll be leaving in a day or two," he said quietly.

"To go back to Ute Crossing?"

"Yes."

"You can't bring Jesse back," she said.

"There's more to it than that, Jessica."

"The principle of the thing? You sound like my father now."

"Don't you agree with him?"

She looked away. "Someone is trying to kill you, Jim. Don't go back."

"I have to," he said. "I don't know whether Gil Drinkwater, Orlando Abeyta, and Jesse Lyle actually murdered Cass Crowley, and I know I can't bring the three of them back, but from what I have learned I find it difficult to believe those three men did it. I nearly lost my own life on that same gallows hill because of circumstantial evidence, and I am beginning to believe that the circumstantial evidence against them was fixed. Jessica, those three men were lynched to cover up the real murderer or murderers. I mean to find out who actually did it, and to clear the names of Gil, Orlando, and Jesse."

"Does it really matter now?"

"It does to me." He smiled thinly. "I never got along too well with my own brother. I respected him, but I couldn't ever think like he could. I was the wild one."

She stood up. "So? A man who takes a full year out of his own life, rides hundreds of miles, and is trailed by men who would kill him if they could. A man who *had* to tell the kinfolk of those three lynched men their last words and actions. You are more like your brother than you'll admit."

She led the way down the steep, twisting trail, and there was no time to talk or look at the view. It took them the better part of an hour to reach the talus slope at the foot of the gaunt butte and then cross that into the cool shade of the trees. It was unseasonably warm weather, but the snow would be flying before too long, perhaps to block the passes to the east. Jim would have to leave before that time.

The North Fork rushed through the thick timber, drowning out all other sound. Jim led the horses to water. He turned to look at Jessica. The flat, whip-like crack of a rifle sounded above the rushing of the stream. Just as the rifle was fired Jim's dun tossed its head between Jim and the oncoming bullet. The dun died on its feet and fell heavily against Jim. He leaped clear of the horse and drove a shoulder against Jessica, felling her across a mossy log that lay on the damp ground. An instant later the rifle flatted off again, raising canyon echoes. The slug whipped within inches of Jim's head. He dived for cover as the slug slapped into a tree.

Then it was peaceful again. The stream rushed on. The clear waters were stained pink from the blood of the dun. Jessica's bay had taken off through the woods like the Devil beating tanbark. Jim studied the woods across the stream. Shafts of sunlight came slantingly through the timber and made spotlights on the ground. The rest of the woods were in shadow. There was neither sight nor sound of anyone. Whoever the ambusher was, he had either pulled leather out of there, or was waiting for another shot. Only by the grace of God had the dun raised his head to intercept that deadly slug.

Jessica lay flat, her soft cheek pressed against the grass. "Why?" she whispered.

"Quién sabe?" he said. His rifle was under the horse, pressed into the bottom of the shallow stream. It was too

far for pistol range, and Jessica's bay had carried off her rifle.

Jim lay flat, peering across the stream from under the brim of his hat. He knew the slug had been meant for him. Jessica had been beyond a thick-boled tree. Besides, who would want to kill her? This was a question that was easier to answer in reference to Jim Murdock, but even so, it gave him an eerie feeling to know that they, whoever *they* were, had not given up on him. There was no one in Three Forks who would want to kill him. No, whoever it was had come from Ute Crossing. Who had notified them that Jim Murdock had returned from the dead to finish his self-imposed mission?

Jim bellied along the ground until he was in thick brush beyond a bend in the stream. He waded quickly across the stream and lay flat in brush on the far side. He drew his Colt and cocked it, inching his way across the ground until he could see the area where the ambusher should be if he had not left. There was no one in sight, no movement, no thickened shadow. Then he felt earth tremors beneath him, and he knew that a horse was being ridden swiftly away from the stream area. He stood up behind a tree and studied the area for five minutes until he was sure there was no one there.

Jim walked toward the place where the rifleman had waited. He looked across the stream and saw a thick tree trunk which had fallen long ago. Behind it he saw half a dozen cigarette butts, and twin depressions in the ground where boot toes had dug in. Jim knelt and then lay flat behind the log. Whoever had waited there must have known there was but one trail from the talus slope through the woods to the stream. He had known something else, that Jessica and Jim had been up on the butte. It had been a close thing; too damned close.

There was no other evidence except the crushed cigarette butts and the marks left by the ambusher. That and the dead dun staining the clear waters with his life's blood. It had been a good saddle horse, one of the best he had ridden since he had left Ute Crossing seemingly so long ago.

He waded across the stream and beckoned to Jessica. "Who knew we were going up on the butte?" he asked.

"Only Jonas."

He rubbed his scarred face. "Yeah," he said. He looked back across that peaceful-looking stream. "How well can you trust him?" he asked.

"It wasn't him," she said quickly.

"He might have told someone we were up there."

"No, Jim," she said firmly.

He looked at her and knew she was right.

"Now maybe you'll reconsider about going back to Ute Crossing," she said.

He did not answer. He caught Jessica's bay and then roped the dead dun, pulling it with the bay until he could get saddle and rifle from the dead animal. They rode double back to the ranch as the late afternoon sun slanted down into the huge canyon. The sun was gone when they reached the ranch, and a cold breeze drifted down the canyon.

"Goin' to be a hard winter," said Jonas from the porch. "Got lots of work to do before then. Sure could use a hand or two around here, Miss Jessica."

"No," she said.

"We can't keep on tryin' to keep this place up." Jonas glanced casually at Jim as Jim led the horse to the barn. "Where's the dun?"

Jessica told the little man. His face grew dark. "Dry-gulching! Bad enough they run off the stock and pester you without that going on."

"It wasn't meant for me," she said. "Whoever it was, he meant to kill Jim, Jonas."

"If he goes back to Ute Crossing he oughta have his head examined before it gets a bullet in it and spoils it."

"He's going," she said simply. "I can't stop him."

Jonas looked at the lovely young woman. "All the more reason he oughta have that head of his examined."

She flushed as she walked into the kitchen. "He must go," she said. She walked to the inner door and looked back. "Oh, Jonas! It isn't important anymore! Can't he understand that?"

Jonas shook his head. "You can't turn a man like him away from what he thinks he has to do."

"They'll kill him, Jonas!"

Jonas poked up the stove. He looked at her. "It takes a heap of killin' to get a man like Jim Murdock, and from the looks of him, he can do a mess of killin' himself if he has to."

The darkness had filled the canyon when Jim returned from the barn. He eyed the lighted windows. It reminded him of the time he had been fired upon when he had been sitting in Ben's little house outside of Ute Crossing. He had never learned who had fired on him then either. He could hear Jonas singing "The Sago Lily" in the kitchen and got a scent of the evening meal. Something held him back. He stopped in the thick shadows beside an outbuilding, watching Jonas pass back and forth in front of the windows, a fair target for even a middling rifle shot.

He narrowed his eyes, probing into the darkness. The wind was seeping down the canyon, carrying man scent away from the dog Jonas kept chained at night in one of the outbuildings.

Something held him back from walking to the house. If he opened that kitchen door he'd be sharply silhouetted in light. There was the wariness of the wild animal in Jim Murdock. Ben had hit it on the head when he had said that Jim still had much of the lobo in him. Jim drifted through the darkness, a lean, scar-faced ghost of a man. He crouched and crossed to the front porch of the house. Jessica was in her room. There was no light in the living room. He crawled to the front door and softly opened it, wriggling inside. The door to the kitchen was closed, and no light showed except a thin crack at the bottom of the door. He walked softly to the door and tapped on it, stepping aside when Jonas opened it. "What the hell!" said the little man.

Jim drew him into the dark living room. "I smell something out there in the darkness," said Jim.

"Like what?"

"Like the son of a bitch who tried to kill me this afternoon."

"You see him? Hear him?"

"No."

"Then how the hell do you know he's there?"

Jim drew the little man close and looked into his wizened face, and the sight of that scarred mask Jim wore for a face shook Jonas more than he'd care to admit. "I *know!*" said Jim softly. He released the little man. "Tell Jessica to act like nothing is going on. You keep up your usual work. Is there a rifle in the house?"

"Mine. I'll get it. Best damned saddle gun I ever had."

Jim drifted out into the thick, pre-moon darkness, working his way into the timber a hundred yards in front of the brightly lighted house. He took to the ground and inched along until he was well into the timber. Now and then he would stop and raise his head, testing the windy darkness with his senses. The wind shifted and brought the bittersweet odor of wood smoke to him, mingled with the good aroma of food.

Half an hour drifted past on the moaning wind.

Jim lay behind a rock outcropping. Maybe he was a fool.

There was a sudden flare of light not thirty feet away from Jim. A hand cupped a match to a cigarette, softly illuminating a hard-looking face. Then the match went out, and all Jim could see was the alternate lighting and darkening of the face as the man drew in on the cigarette. Damned fool! He was so sure of himself. Jim recognized him from somewhere, but he wasn't sure where. Ute Crossing? No. Meadows? No. He lay flat and cudgeled his memory. Then it came to him. This was the drunk he had seen in the saloon the day he had arrived at Three Forks!

Jim rubbed his scarred face. The rifle was at his side, half-cocked, and he could drive a .44/40 slug into the man before he'd hear the shot. He heard the man move. The cigarette was ground out. Softly, ever so softly, like a hunting cat, the man moved through the motte toward the house, until he was fifty yards from it. He held a rifle in his hands. He was so interested in the house that he never saw the man standing behind the tree fifty feet behind him, watching his every move, nor did he realize his shoulders and head were etched against the darkness by the light from the windows.

Jim looked beyond the man. Jonas was still moving back and forth. He saw Jessica come into the room. She was still wearing her hat. It was difficult to see that she was a woman from that distance. Suddenly the dog barked. The man raised his rifle, moved it a little, and tilted his head to get a sight.

"Drop that rifle!" snapped Jim.

The man swung and the rifle spat flame and smoke toward Jim. The bullet almost touched Jim's right cheek. He fired from the hip. The big slug smashed into the man's chest. He grunted, spun about, dropped the rifle, and fell heavily. The twin rifle reports slammed back and forth in the canyon and then fled muttering to die away. The wind whipped a tendril of acrid-smelling smoke across Jim's face.

The lights blinked out in the house. The dog went wild.

Jim walked forward, then knelt beside the man. He snapped a match on his thumbnail and held it over the man's face. A pair of staring, sightless eyes looked up into his. Jim fanned out the match. A door slammed up at the house. Someone ran across the porch and toward Jim.

"Jim! Jim!" cried Jessica. "*Jim!*"

"It's all right," he called out.

She was in his arms with such a force that she staggered him. He dropped the rifle and held her close.

Jonas trotted through the darkness with a six-gun in his hand. "You all right, Jim?" he called.

"Yes, Jonas."

Jonas knelt beside the dead man and lighted a match. He whistled softly. "Monk!" he said.

"You know him?" asked Jim.

Jonas shrugged. "I've seen him around. He's a drifter. No one knows where he came from. He always seemed to have a dollar in his pocket. He'd come and go for long periods of time. Why would he want to kill you?"

Jim looked down at the dead man. "Someone hired him to do it. The only time I ever saw him was in the saloon in Three Forks. The one where Les is the barkeeper."

Jonas stood up. "He got his orders from somewhere. Ute Crossing, likely."

"But from who?"

"There's the question," said Jonas.

Jim nodded. "He didn't have time to go back there. Maybe someone came here to tell him what to do."

Jonas looked at Jim. "There's a company telegraph line between here and Ute Crossing."

"That might be the answer."

Jonas nodded. "Ben Cole is the operator. He'd have a record of any messages sent."

"Can we get a look at those records?"

Jonas grinned. "I can. Ben and I served together in the war. First Colorado Volunteers. Ben would do anything for me." Jonas looked down at Monk. "What about him?"

An idea had drifted into Jim's mind. Monk was about his size, build, and coloring. "A dead man can move around for a time without being expected," he said.

Jonas stared at him. "You gone loco?"

"Not yet. I have hopes. You go into Three Forks in the morning and find out what, if any, message Monk sent out. Keep your mouth shut about this. Find out where Monk is supposed to be. When you get back I'll tell you what I plan to do."

They carried Monk to an outbuilding and covered his stiffening body. Jessica was waiting for them in the house. "Jim," she said pleadingly. "Must you go back to Ute Crossing?"

"Yes."

"I won't let you go."

The look in his eyes silenced her even before his words. "I'm going, Jessica," he said flatly.

"We never did get to eat," said Jonas.

"After a killing?" said Jessica.

"Far's I'm concerned, Miss Jessica," said Jonas, "it's like a celebration when you kill a dry-gulcher."

"Amen," said Jim.

CHAPTER FOURTEEN

Jonas was back by noon of the next day with a wagon-load of supplies, and a nose full of news. Jim helped him unload the wagon. "Monk sent a telegram the day you got to Three Forks," said the little man. "Got there just when Ben was closing the office. Message was sent to Ute Crossing. *'Consignment arrived,'* it read, *'please advise disposition.'* The next day there was a reply from Ute Crossing. *'Dispose of merchandise as previously directed,'* it read."

Jim slid a box of canned goods onto a storeroom shelf and wiped the sweat from his face. "Who had signed it?" he asked.

"It was from a Ute Valley Mercantile Company. Signed by a man named Alfred Hitchins."

Jim turned slowly, and his eyes were like twin lances boring into Jonas' eyes. "Alfred Hitchins?" he said softly.

"That was the name. You know him?"

Jim nodded. "I know him," he said. He seemed to see the round, smooth face of the man in the reflection of a can of peaches. Peaches thick in syrup. Alfred Hitchins, for all his good works, had always been a little too syrupy to suit Jim. The Reverend Matthew Jarvis was next to

God in Ute Crossing, and Alfred Hitchins was next to the reverend.

"What do you aim to do?"

Jim lifted a sack of flour and placed it on a shelf. "Saddle a horse, Jonas," he said over his shoulder.

"For you?"

"For you, amigo. Go back to town. Send this wire to Alfred Hitchins, Ute Valley Mercantile Company: 'Merchandise disposed of as ordered.' Sign it 'Monk.'"

They finished unloading the supplies, rolled cigarettes, and lighted them. Jonas eyed Jim. "You're taking a hell of a risk," he said.

"No worse than if I had gone back there without doing it."

Jonas grinned. "It's a prime idea," he said. "If you're right in your hunch they'll think you're dead."

Jim nodded. "That's why I wanted to save Monk. What did you find out about him?"

"Les told me he had left for Utah some days ago, and said he wouldn't likely be back until spring, if he came back at all."

"*Bueno!* We'll dress him in some of my old clothes and plant him"

"You mean bury him?"

Jim shook his head. "Put him where he'll be sure to be found. On the other side of town."

"Hell! That ain't so bright! They can see he ain't you."

Jim blew a smoke ring. "Dead body lying out in the woods gets the face eaten away first, doesn't it?"

"We can't take a chance they will eat it."

Jim looked at him. "A man could fake it, couldn't he?"

Jonas swallowed. "Yeah. A dirty job, Jim."

Jim spat. "It would have been a helluva lot dirtier job if he had killed me that day at the river, or if he had killed Jessica by mistake last night."

"I get your point. Leave it to me. There's only one thing, Jim. People in town know you came out here."

"They don't know I stayed here."

"Still looks bad for us."

Jim shrugged. "Shoot one round out of a pistol. Here, take mine and I'll take Monk's. It's a good one. Better than mine. Put the pistol in his hand, or near it."

"Suicide, eh?"

"You're getting brighter every minute, Jonas."

"What happens when you come back? If you do come back?"

"They made a mistake in identifying the body, is all."

Jonas flipped away his cigarette. "It might work at that, Jim."

Jim grinned like a lobo. "It will work long enough for me to do my job in Ute Crossing." He rubbed his scarred face. "By God," he added. "Alfred Hitchins! Who would have believed it?"

He said good-bye to Jessica at dusk that same day. Jonas had told him of a trail over the butte that would take him to the foot of the pass which he could cross that night. There would be a moon. The weather was making up, hinting at more rain. He could be across the pass by dawn with a bit of luck, hole up on the other side during daylight hours, then move on during the night. In three to four days he could be in Ute Crossing.

He kissed Jessica and drew her close.

"You'll come back?" she asked.

"Yes."

She looked up at him. "Maybe you'll want to stay in Ute Crossing," she said quietly.

Jim shook his head. "Never. There's nothing there for me now. My brother is gone. When my job is done I'll be back."

He kissed her again and swung up on the chunky roan Jonas had selected for him. "Adios," he said. He touched the horse with his spurs and rode off into the windy darkness.

"*Vaya con Dios,*" she said.

The wind shifted, moaning down the valley, and

bringing with it a hint of the cold rain to follow before the dawn.

"He'll be back," said Jonas.

She did not answer. She walked to the house and entered it. Jonas rolled a cigarette. He lighted it. "He has to come back, God," he said softly. "For her... "

———

THE RAIN HAD STARTED the dawn of the day Jim reached the eastern entrance of the pass. Warrior Peak, towering high to his left, had a skullcap of snow on it. In a matter of weeks, perhaps, the first snows of the season would fall. He rode through the dark, wet nights, holing up in the daytime under the tarp Jonas had given him, drinking coffee and smoking, trying to fit together the pieces of the puzzle he had blundered into by becoming an unwilling witness to a triple lynching. The enigma was Alfred Hitchins. "Deacon" Hitchins... the man who had helped Ben Murdock get his education after he had been crippled in his fight to clear Jim of murder charges. The man who had fought against public opinion to get Ben his job as schoolteacher in Ute Crossing, and who had won his fight. A man respected by one and all for his business ability, his civic pride, and his support of the local church. A man said to be as close to God as a man could be within reason. "Jesus wept," he had said when he had seen the lynchers take those three men up the gallows hill.

The rain was a fine, misty drizzle when Jim Murdock passed his brother's house on the banks of roaring Warrior Creek. The place was nothing but a blackened shell dimly seen through the mist. Warrior Creek swirled blackly beneath the creaking bridge. It was here that Ben had gone to his death over the low rail into the dark, cold waters, not to be found until the spring, on land that had once belonged to the Murdocks.

There was only one man he could go to in Ute

Crossing and be sure of secrecy. Meany Gillis. It was well after midnight when he entered the town. Here and there along the main street he could see watery-looking yellow light as a saloon or two remained in business. One of them was the Grape Arbor.

There was a light in one of the rear windows of the Ute Valley Mercantile Company. Jim looked at it thoughtfully as he kneed the tired roan into an alleyway and then led him toward the rear of Slade's Livery Stable, where Meanwell Gillis held sway. Meany lived in a set of rooms built into the livery stable, a little strong-smelling, but comfortable and cozy, and besides, as Meany had always said, he preferred the company of horses and dogs to that of many people.

The alleyway was empty and dark. Jim walked around the side of the big frame building and tapped on the window of Meany's bedroom. The window was up a few inches. "Meany!" called Jim.

Bedsprings squeaked. "Who's that?" said Meany in a frightened voice.

"Jim. Jim Murdock."

"Oh, my God! You've come back from the dead! You always was a restless sort. I didn't think you was that restless." Jim grinned. "Meany," he said softly. "It was a dodge. A trick to throw them off the trail."

Feet padded on the floor, and Meany's familiar, homely face appeared, white as a sheet. "Lemme touch you, Jim," he said. "Just to make sure." A thin hand felt Jim's arm. "Keno!"

"Open up the back door and let me get my horse inside."

Meany opened the back door. He peered up and down the alleyway. "Anyone see you?"

"No."

The door swung shut and was barred. "You hungry, Jim?"

"No. But cold as ice."

"I got something to take care of that. Take care of your hoss."

Jim came into Meany's little combination kitchen and sitting room after he had unsaddled and rubbed down the roan. The liveryman had drawn the curtains and pulled down the shade. He handed Jim a tumbler full of spirits. "You got guts comin' back here," he said.

Jim sipped the whiskey. "How'd you find out I was dead?"

"The story was all over town a few days ago. I don't know where it started. That's the second time it came around."

"When was the first time?"

Meany shrugged. "Damned near a year ago. They said you was killed down in Mexico somewheres."

Jim touched the scar on his right cheek. "I damned near was. Anyone miss Lyss, Slim, and Jules around here?"

Meany stared at Jim. His jaw dropped. "You!" he said.

Jim smiled thinly. "It was them or me, Meany."

"Wasn't nothing said about them. They was just supposed to have left. Rumor come that Lyss was murdered by bandits in Las Cruces, and Slim and Jules disappeared in Chihuahua or somewheres. They meant to kill you then?"

Jim nodded. "Why did they come after me? Who sent them, Meany?"

Meany poured a drink. He was pale again. "Jesus God," he mumbled. "Three hardcases if there ever was any. You took care of all *three* of them?"

"Two of them. I had a little help with the third."

Meany sat down heavily. He drained his glass. "Thank God you was always a friend of mine, James."

Jim leaned forward. "A man was ordered to kill me at Three Forks a few days ago, Meany. The order came from Ute Crossing."

Meany wiped his mouth. "Who sent it?"

"I think it was sent by Alfred Hitchins."

Meany was less surprised than Jim thought he should

be. "I never liked that sanctimonious son of a bitch," he said. "Never could stand a man who's always telling you how honest he is. You sure about that?"

Jim told him of the cryptic telegraph messages.

"Sounds logical," said Meany.

"But why?" said Jim.

Meany swirled the liquor in his glass. "Beats the hell out of me," he said. "There is one thing I do know. 'Bout a year or so ago before you came back, he was having financial trouble. Rumor had it he was in hock for quite a bit. Someone had a big note on him and was hounding him for the money."

"Like who?" said Jim.

Meany looked into his glass. "Cass Crowley," he said. He looked up at Jim. "After them three drifters killed Cass, Hitchins seemed to be doing all right again."

"The note would have been found in Crowley's papers," said Jim. "Hitchins would have been forced to pay the estate."

"If they found the note," said Meany. "Far's I know, it never was found. Hitchins denied there ever had been a loan."

"Seems to me it would have been a big break for him if Cass Crowley had died."

Meany looked up again. *"Murdered,"* he said.

"By three drifters. One of them a drunk who wouldn't carry a six-gun and was supposedly unarmed when he came to the valley of the Ute. A Mexican who had wanted to be a priest and was afraid of firearms. A frightened, sensitive kid who likely fell in with the other two because they thought the same way he did."

"What are you driving at? You mean them three who was hung?"

Jim nodded. "It has taken me a year to find out about them, Meany. If those three men killed Crowley, it was certainly out of character."

"Then who done it if they didn't?"

Jim stood up and drained his glass. "That's exactly why I came back to Ute Crossing," he said.

Meany shivered. "I don't envy you."

Jim picked up his hat. "Keep your mouth shut about me," he said. "Can you put me up here at night?"

"Sure thing! Where you goin' now?"

Jim smiled. "Looks like Al Hitchins is working late."

Meany spat into the gaboon. "He always is. Got a Bible in one hand and his cashbox in the other."

"Is Van Lassen still around town?"

Meany nodded. "Don't ever seem to work, but always has dinero. Beats me how he does it."

Jim flipped his cigarette butt into the gaboon. "I wonder," he said quietly. He left the room, followed by Meany. He passed a dusty buggy and stopped suddenly to look at it.

"Yes," said Meany from behind Jim. "It's Ben's." He placed a hand on the dashboard. "I had it hauled here. Kept it for you, Jim, in case you wanted it."

Jim looked back at him. "Thanks. You keep it, Meany. I have no use for it."

"When you get back, providing someone don't put a slug into you, I'll tell you something about that buggy."

Jim nodded. He let himself out into the drizzle and heard Meany close the door behind him and drop the bar. He padded through the pasty mud, cutting swiftly across the cross streets. Ute Crossing was quiet beneath the cold drizzle. The faint thudding of a mechanical piano came from the Grape Arbor as Jim passed behind it. He reached the rear of the Ute Valley Mercantile Company. The light was still on in the rear office. Jim peered into the rain-streaked window. A man was seated at a rolltop desk, hard at work on some papers. There was no mistaking the plump back of the merchant and the bald spot at the back of his head.

Jim gently tried the back door, but it was locked. He walked along the other side of the building until he found a warped window. He forced a piece of wood under the sash and pried upward. The lock snapped. He eased up the window and stepped inside. He could see a faint streak of light from the rear of the long building. Cautiously he worked his way past piles of sacks and ranks of boxed goods until he found himself in the aisle that led to the offices in the rear of the establishment. He paused, listening to the rain drumming on the tin roof. There was neither sound nor sign of anyone else in the place besides Hitchins.

Jim walked softly to the rear hall that opened to offices on either side. Hitchins did a big business. It was the same type of business Jim's father had successfully run until Jim's trouble with the law. An odd thought came to Jim. Al Hitchins had been small potatoes in this line of work until Jim's father's business had failed because of people talking. It was only after his father had failed that Hitchins had gained prominence in the business. He had taken over the lucrative Crowley account, one of the mainstays of the Murdock business. Maybe it had been Hitchins himself who had started the talk against Jim's father. People listened to Alfred Hitchins.

Jim walked softly into the hallway and stood in the open door of Hitchins' private office. The merchant's pen scratched on. Jim studied him. It wasn't going to be easy to beard Al Hitchins in his own den. It seemed ridiculous to suspect this godly man of having anything to do with ordering a killer to get rid of a man who stood in the way. It was loco, and yet...

Hitchins stopped writing. He raised his head. He sat still for a moment or two, then shook his head and started writing again. Jim stood there, boring a hole in the bald spot at the back of Hitchins' head with his cold eyes. Hitchins stopped writing again. He sat there for another moment, and then he slowly turned his head, to see an apparition standing in the doorway. A tall, gaunt man, scarred on both lean cheeks, with granite-hard eyes looking at him with an unblinking stare. Hitchins sharply drew in his breath. His face went fish belly white. Slowly he extended a hand toward Jim and shook his eyes. "For the love of God," he husked. "Go away! I didn't want to do it! Go away! I'll forswear my God if you'll go away!"

Jim did not move. He tried not to blink.

Hitchins began to tremble. His mouth opened and closed. "They made me do it! They told me I was in it as deep as they were! I had to do it! Don't you understand? All I wanted was that note from Cass Crowley. That was all! I didn't want to put a bullet into his head!" He stood up and held out both hands, as though to ward off the cold, basilisk stare of the man he was sure had come back from the dead. Then he shook spasmodically. He fell to his knees. His head jerked and he cried out in savage pain, gripping his left side. He fell heavily and stared at Jim with unblinking eyes. Spittle drooled from his slack, mouth.

Jim walked toward him. "Who made you do it?" he asked.

The man tried to speak. His breathing was sharp and erratic.

"Talk, damn you!" said Jim.

"They said I *had* to put a bullet into his head! All three of us did it! It was a pact with the Devil!"

"Who were the other two?" demanded Jim.

Hitchins' eyes widened. "You're alive," he whispered.

Jim nodded. "Tell me," he said.

Hitchins raised his head and suddenly it fell again. He stiffened, then relaxed, and his eyes still looked at Jim, but they did not see him. They would never see anything on earth again.

Jim stood up. "Score one," he said quietly. All he knew now was that the three men who had been lynched had not killed Cass Crowley, but who had been the other two men who had put bullets into the rancher's head? He rubbed his newest scar and looked down at Hitchins. God had dealt out his own kind of justice to this man. It was just as well. Jim wanted no more blood on his own hands. Justice, yes, but not blood... No one would know Jim had been there.

They would find Hitchins in the morning, dead of a heart attack. The whole town would mourn. Likely his two partners in murder would breathe more freely. Hitchins had probably been the weak link in the chain. They would breathe more freely, but they did not know that retribution was stalking the wet streets of Ute Crossing in the guise of a man who was thought to be dead of a dry-gulcher's bullet.

Jim left the same way he had come, lowering the window against the rain. He padded into the alleyway. His work was done for this night, at least. He heard the thudding of the mechanical piano in the Grape Arbor as he neared it, and then the sound stopped. Jim stopped beside a rear window. A man was walking toward the mechanical piano, flipping a coin into the air and catching it again. Beyond him were the hunched backs of other men at the long bar. The man reached out with the coin to insert it in the piano slot. He stared at the rain-streaked window and saw a lean, scarred face staring at him, and then it was gone. Barney Kessler's eyes widened. The coin fell to the floor from nerveless fingers and rolled under the piano. Barney turned on his heel and ran to the bar and filled a glass, which he downed in one gulp. Van Lassen looked at Barney. "What the hell is the matter with you?" he said sarcastically. "You see a ghost?"

Barney slowly wiped his mouth. His eyes were glassy with tanglefoot and fear. "I don't know," he said slowly. *"I don't know...."*

Baldy Victor grinned. "Oughta cut you off, Barney," he said.

Buck Grant spat into the filthy gaboon. "Who was it you seen, Barney?" he asked.

Barney refilled the glass. "I'll swear to Christ it was Jim Murdock! Them eyes! The scars!"

Van grinned. "Jim Murdock had only one scar," he

said. He drew a thick finger down the left side of his face. "There!"

Buck laughed. "Maybe Monk give him another one," he said. "Afore he died, that is."

Baldy studied Barney. "Maybe he did see something," he said curiously. He walked around the end of the bar and peered through the window. He unbarred and opened the back door and peered up and down the muddy alleyway, with the rain sleeting down, cold and penetrating. He grinned, and then the grin faded. He felt something in the atmosphere, something that sent a crawling chill through him. He closed and barred the door, picked up Barney's coin, and dropped it into the piano slot. The piano began to thud out a tune. Baldy walked back to the bar.

"Well?" said Lassen.

"Nothing," said Baldy. But for the rest of the night he kept shifting his eyes toward that back door when he was sure no one was watching him.

CHAPTER FIFTEEN

Jim Murdock knelt in the damp straw that covered the livery stable floor, holding a lantern while Meany Gillis, underneath Ben Murdock's buggy, pointed out something to Jim. "The team was found at the edge of town still pulling the front wheels, Jim," said Meany. "The rest of the buggy was found in the creek. The rail had been busted as it went through. I pulled out the buggy body and rear wheels and had it hauled here. I already had the tram and the front wheels. I had a little free time one day, so I started work on it. I noticed marks on the wood around where the kingbolt goes through. Like someone had been sawing or filing. Then I finds the upper part of the kingbolt still in its socket. It was a good sound bolt, Jim, but it was in two pieces, and all I had was the upper piece."

"It broke, and caused the accident?"

Meany shook his head. He reached up inside the buggy and handed Jim the upper part of a kingbolt. "Take a good look at it," he said.

Jim held it close to the lantern. A cold feeling came over him as he saw file marks on the bolt.

Meany crawled out. "I went back to the bridge and found this." He handed Jim the rest of the bolt. Jim studied it. It had file marks on it, and at one edge was a slightly raised lip of metal as though the bolt had been filed almost through, leaving just enough so that the strain on it would eventually snap it off.

Meany wiped his hands. "You know how fast Ben drove. Likely he come out of his gate and turned hard, hit the bridge at a good clip, and the bolt busted right there. Talk about timing!"

Jim looked up. "But why, Meany?"

Meany held out his hands, palms upward. "After you left Ben did a lot of talking about those three men that got lynched. He was talking about justice before they got lynched. Looks like you put a head on his suspicions, or whatever they were. Ben might have been on to something at that.

Anyways, he was drowned before he could do anything about it. A week or so later his house goes up in flames. People said drifters had been bunking there and accidentally set it afire."

"Maybe there was something in there that might have pinned the guilt on whoever killed Cass Crowley."

"Mebbe," said the liveryman. "Whatever *might* have been there is gone now. No one will ever know now."

Jim rolled a cigarette and lighted it. He fanned out the match. "You're wrong there," he said. "I told you Hitchins was in on it. He implied there were two others. They're likely still around here, Meany. I won't stop until I find out who they were. This is a personal thing now. They murdered Cass Crowley and they murdered my brother. That type never stops killing to cover up, and the first killing is the hardest After that they get easier and easier."

"Hard to figure out why they killed Cass," said Meany.

"We know why Hitchins was in on it. Money was his real god. Cass could have ruined Hitchins. Maybe money had something to do with the others as well."

Meany led the way to his rooms and poured two

glasses of whiskey. "Maybe not," he said quietly. "Cass was in a lot of things. Finance, politics, and anything else he had a mind to get into. Cass liked power of any kind. You know damned well there never was an appointment in this county he wasn't behind, one way or another."

"You can say that about the whole state," said Jim dryly.

Meany sipped his drink. "If Cass stood in Al Hitchins' way, maybe the other two hombres what killed him felt the same way he did. Cass was as tough as whang leather when you crossed him. Many a coming man run into old Cass when he wasn't feelin' too well, said the wrong thing, and ruined his whole career. Just like that!"

"Just like that," repeated Jim. "Like who?" he added.

Meany laughed. "Well, they can be numbered by the dozens. I run into trouble with him once and was lucky enough to get off the hook." He grinned. "One time I took a repaired surrey out to Brady Short's place. I went up to the house to get paid and heard Brady sounding off to his wife. He was cutting ol' Cass to ribbons, being as how ol' Cass wasn't there. Seems like Brady had been counting on Cass to back him up politically. Brady could hardly get anywheres without Cass backing his play. You know the old story. The 'boy wonder" of the Ute Valley. Marries old Whitcomb's daughter, getting a nice piece of change in the process, plus that cliff dwelling of a house. By God, he's ambitious, and his wife is worse, or so they say."

"Take it easy, Meany," said Jim quietly. He swirled the liquor in his glass and then looked up at the liveryman. "When did all this take place, Meany?"

Meany looked at the ceiling and closed one eye. "About a year and a half ago. No! It was less than that. It was late summer of last year."

"Just before those three men were arrested for the killing of Cass Crowley."

"Yeah." Meany stared at Jim. "You mean?"

Jim finished his drink. "I don't know," he said. "Who would have suspected Alfred Hitchins?"

"Who indeed?" echoed Meany.

Something came back to Jim. The night he had gone out to Brady Short's house at the lawyer's request, only to find that the man was gone, Ann was in her cups and willing to play games with Jim. She had practically thrown herself at him. An icy, evil feeling crept through him. She was ambitious. Meany himself had just said that. She'd get behind a man and drive him on. Supposing she had been grooming Brady for big things and the fool had antagonized the one man in the county he had to have behind him to win political success. She had warned Jim to leave the country. Brady Short had never intended to be at the house when Jim arrived, or perhaps he had been in the house, keeping out of the way while he let his lovely wife bargain with Jim, using her lush body as bait. If a man was making love to Ann Short he'd damned well forget anything else he had in mind at the time.

Meany filled the glasses. He looked at Jim. "You're sure talkative tonight, James."

Jim took the refilled glass. The whiskey had no effect on him. Ann's last cast of the dice had been the blunt invitation to Jim to visit her in Denver. "Did Mrs. Short go to Denver last fall, Meany?" he asked. Meany would know. Nothing much went on in the valley of the Ute without Meany knowing about it.

Meany laughed. "Hell, no! She's hardly been outa that house. They say she's always on a high lonesome up there while Brady's chasin' around doing his political maneuvers. Sits up most of the night, they say, dozing in a chair, with a wine decanter next to her. When it's empty she gets another, and another..."

"Every night?" asked Jim.

"Just about."

Jim emptied his glass. "Let me have a horse," he said.

"This late?"

Jim stood up. "I haven't much time," he said.

"You've done enough tonight."

Jim shook his head. "If I'm not back by daylight I'll hide out in the hills. I don't want to be seen. Not yet..."

The streets of Ute Crossing were empty as Jim Murdock rode north out of town, heading into the slanting rain. The last time he had passed that way the road had been iron hard in the grip of the winter's first freeze. That time was close again.

This time he did not see lights in the huge house until he was close to it. The shades had been drawn in the sitting room that opened off the huge parlor where he had last talked to Ann Short, but he saw thin lines of light about the edges of the shades. There were no other lights on in the house. He tethered the horse to the picket fence and softly opened the gate. He walked to the front steps and softly padded to the side window of the sitting room. Through the narrow slit at the side of the shade he could see into the room. A woman sat in an armchair, facing a dying fire in the grate. A decanter stood on the little table beside her, and even as he looked he saw her fill a glass with wine.

He walked to the parlor windows. One of them was open a few inches. He eased it up and stepped inside, careless of the mud that stained the thick carpeting. He walked into the wide hallway and looked up the stairway. The house was dark and quiet. Jim crossed the parlor and softly slid back the sliding door that separated parlor from sitting room. The woman did not move.

Jim walked forward a little. "Ann," he said softly.

For a moment she did not move, and then slowly she turned to look at him. Shock fled across her flushed face, and then she smiled, although there was no mirth in her great eyes. "I knew they'd never kill you," she said.

"You're not surprised to see me, then?"

She shrugged. "Why should I be?" She glanced at the wine decanter. "I don't get surprised at anything anymore, Jim."

She had changed, even in the space of one year. Her

face was flushed looking, and not from the bloom of health. Her once clear eyes had a slightly glassy look to them, and her hands trembled a little until she clasped them firmly in her lap.

"Where's Brady?" he said.

She laughed. "Out on his political maneuvers. Likely in one of the back rooms of the Ute House with one of the high-class doxys who ply their business there."

"Not Brady," he said dryly.

She sipped her wine. "Brady likes his women from the gutter," she said. "They give him what he wants. I won't."

She was almost stinking drunk. She wouldn't care what she said. "Did you ever go to Denver?" he asked.

She shook her lovely head. "I had no reason to go after you left," she said.

"You really wanted me to meet you there?"

A log snapped in the fireplace, and a little cloud of ashes drifted out onto the carpet She laughed softly. "No," she said. "Does that sting your ego, Jim? Your man's ego?"

"Not really," he said. "Whose idea was it?"

She emptied her glass and refilled it. "I think you already know," she said.

"I want to be sure."

She nodded. "It was him. He was scared to death of you. I told him to kill you or have you killed. He's yellow."

"You would have done what you told him to do if you were in his position?"

She looked at him with thoughtful eyes. "Why not?" she said coldly. "He should have known he'd never side-track you. If you had that man's legal mind and his appearance, with your guts and me to back you up you'd have been governor someday. He lost his nerve. He could have gone a long way. I agreed to ask you to meet me in Denver just to help him." She wrinkled her nose and shook her head. "Making a whore out of myself to help him. Putting myself at your feet after you walked out on me." She hiccupped.

"That's a switch," he murmured. "You never intended to marry me, Ann. You had bigger game in mind."

"Go to hell," she said.

"Was Brady mixed up in the killing of Cass Crowley?"

"Ask him," she said shortly. "He's standing right behind you."

Jim turned slowly. Brady Short stood in the doorway wearing a wet slicker, his hat dark with rainwater. His face was pasty white beneath its tan. A nickel-plated, short-barreled Colt was in his right hand, pointing at Jim's guts. His handsome face was set and there was haunting fear in his dark eyes. "What are you doing here?" he said in a low voice.

"Just a social call, Brady."

"At two o'clock in the morning?"

Jim smiled. "My, my! Is it that late?"

"Why didn't you stay away?" asked the lawyer. "Why did. you have to come back, grinning like a death's-head at the feast?"

"You did your best to keep me away," said Jim. He glanced at Ann. "In more ways than one. The game is up, Brady."

"What do you know? What can you prove?"

Jim smiled. "Al Hitchins told me the whole story," he said.

The shot struck home. Brady stared at Jim. "He doesn't know anything," he said.

"He said you forced him into the deal. That he was in it as deep as you were. That Cass Crowley had turned against you, and that you knew damned well you'd never get anywhere in this state politically without Cass backing up your play. You had to kill him, Brady, or your career was shot, just as Al Hitchins had to be in on the deal to keep from being ruined financially."

"For God's sake!" said Brady. "You devil! No one outside of the three of us knew that!"

Ann stood up and began to fill her glass. "You'd better kill him, Brady," she said. "It's your only chance."

The lawyer's finger tightened on the trigger. Jim wet his dry lips. Did he have a chance to draw and shoot before Brady got up his nerve?

"Go on, Brady," taunted Ann. "Show us you're a man! He's all that stands in your way. You helped kill Cass Crowley. The first one is the easiest one. Go on!"

"Shut your drunken mouth," said her husband.

She laughed. "One little press of that trigger and you're on your way again. Who can prove otherwise? You're a lawyer. You know I can't testify against you. I'll even help you, Brady. I'll say he came in here drunk and tried to rape me. This is your last chance, you fool!"

He drew in a deep breath and raised the pistol. For a moment he looked into Jim's eyes, and then his gaze wavered. He raised the pistol again. The empty wine decanter was hurled past Jim, and it struck Brady's gun arm. The pistol exploded, driving a slug into the floor at Jim's feet. He ran forward through the swirling smoke to grapple with Brady. Brady swung the smoking pistol up and down, cutting viciously at Jim's head. Jim deflected the blow with his forearm, but the gun still struck his face, staggering him. Brady whirled and ran. The front door was opened and then slammed. Feet thudded on the gravel walk, and a moment later the thudding of hoofs came back to the two people in the sitting room.

Jim wiped the blood from his face. He turned to look at her. "Why?" he said.

She shrugged. "I couldn't live with him any longer, Jim," she said. "I wanted to see if he had the guts to kill you."

"Thanks," he said dryly.

"How far can he get?"

Jim held out his hands, palms upward. "Brady Short is too well known to get very far. He'll run and keep on running, but someday they'll find him. He'll live a hell on earth until they do find him. Who is the third man, Ann?"

She walked to a side table and picked up a full wine decanter. "I saved your life tonight," she said over her shoulder. "Isn't that enough?"

"No."

She turned. "If I told you I didn't know would you believe me?"

He studied her. "Yes."

"You're walking a thin line, Jim. There are men in Ute Crossing who have sworn to kill you. You were nearly killed tonight. Get out of town and keep going, Jim."

"I can't do that."

She filled her wineglass and studied the ruby contents. "I didn't think you would. Good luck, Jim."

"I'm sorry about Brady," he said.

"I'm not."

He turned on a heel and walked from that house and he knew he'd never enter it again or see her again. He closed the front door and walked to his horse through the cold, drifting rain. He mounted and rode south toward Ute Crossing. "Score two," he said to the night.

She had parted the curtains to see him ride off. "*If you had had that man's legal mind and his appearance, with your guts and me to back you up you'd have been governor someday.*" She drew the curtains and walked back to her chair, moved the wine decanter a little closer, and stared unseeingly into the dying fire.

CHAPTER SIXTEEN

The wind shifted just before dawn and carried the train off with it. With the coming of daylight, the wind died away altogether, and left a drifting mist in the bottoms of the Ute that seeped through the streets of Ute Crossing.

Jim awoke to Meany's shaking hand and low voice. "Rise and shine," said the liveryman. "It's nigh nine o'clock. Murray Cullin just came into town and is at the jail."

Jim rolled over on the cot and looked up at Meany. "How's the weather?"

Meany rubbed a hand over the fogged panes of window glass. "Never seen the like of it in many a year. You can hardly see acrost the street."

"Suits me," said Jim. He sat up and accepted a cup of Arbuckle's from Meany.

"This fog won't stop a bullet, James."

"They have to see me to shoot at me."

"You sure no one else outside of Al Hitchins, Brady and Ann Short has seen you?"

Jim grinned. "Barney Kessler saw me, or thinks he saw me."

Meany spat. "Him? He's usually so full of booze he

ain't never quite sure of what he does see, less'n it's another drink. Now, if that had been Van Lassen, he would have come right through that window glass after you."

"Have you seen him in town?"

"Every day, just about. Beats me how he can loaf and drink most all day without working."

"I wonder," said Jim. He drained his cup.

"Usually shows up at the Grape Arbor as soon as Baldy Victor opens up at ten o'clock. Him, Barney Kessler, and Buck Grant."

Jim pulled on his pants and then his boots. "Al Hitchins saw me, but he's dead. Brady Short is still running."

"What about his missus?"

"She could have let him kill me. She doesn't care anything anymore about Brady. Right now she's playing the wine jug. She doesn't care about *anything.*"

"All the same, you'd better stop playin' a lone hand. You ain't killed anyone yet, but you keep foolin' around and you will. Murray Cullin never accepted the fact you was cleared of killin' young Crowley. Best thing for you to do is go see him, explain everything, and let him settle this business. Cass Crowley was like a brother to him. Besides, Murray Cullin is the law in this county, and you know damned well he is. He won't sleep or eat until he rounds up Brady Short. He never had much use for Brady Short, anyways."

Jim nodded. He was tired. Mentally and physically he felt the great strain that had been on him this past year. Murray Cullin really had nothing on Jim except the fact that he still believed Jim was guilty of the killing of Curt Crowley, but he was still lawman enough to know he had to have definite proof, not just suspicions.

Jim washed out in the stable, shivering in the damp cold. Winter was closing in. He dressed slowly, fortified himself with another cup of coffee and then peered through the fogged window. The drifting mist was almost opaque, swirling slowly through the seemingly deserted streets. Now and then the sound of voices came to him, magnified by the fog. He left the stable by the rear door and walked softly to the street, right about where he had stood almost a year ago to witness the mob breaking into the jail. It was almost nine-thirty. He looked quickly up and down the street and then crossed it swiftly, angling toward the ugly, slab-sided two-story building where Murray Cullin held forth when he wasn't out on other business.

Jim stepped into the deep-set doorway and opened one of the two double doors, letting himself into the hallway that led past the sheriff's office to the bullpen and the cells. The place seemed empty of life. The narrow staircase that led up to the county offices was to his left. He peered up the staircase. There were no lights up there, and then he remembered that county employees worked only part time and never on Saturdays.

He looked back over his shoulder and then opened the door of the sheriff's office. The tall, broad-shouldered lawman was seated in front of the big stove, warming his hands. A coffeepot sat atop the stove with a wisp of steam coming from the spout. Murray Cullin turned his swivel chair slowly as Jim walked toward the desk. "Murdock," he said coldly. "Come to give yourself up?"

Jim shook his head. "I have information as to who actually killed Cass Crowley," he said.

"A likely story. Those three men who were lynched here last year did the job and you know it, Murdock."

"Not me. Will you listen to me, Cullin?"

"Why not? Sit down. When you're done we'll do a little more talking about *you.*"

Jim sat down across the desk from the lawman. "Three men were responsible for the murder of Crowley."

"I know that! The three that were strung up."

"No! None of those three men could possibly have

murdered him. It's taken me almost a year to track down their kin. Cullin, you've got to believe me on that score."

"All right," said Cullen patiently. He dropped his hands from the desk and leaned back in his chair. "Shoot! What three men were responsible for killing Crowley?"

"I know of only two of them, Sheriff. Alfred Hitchins and Brady Short are two of them."

Cullin narrowed his eyes. "By God!" he said. "Have you been drinking? Are you out of your mind?"

"No. I can prove what I say."

"Al Hitchins was found dead of a heart attack in his office early this morning when his chief clerk came to work. Accusing a dead man of murder is an old dodge, Murdock. In any case, slandering the name of a godly man like Hitchins will get you nowhere. What's your game, Murdock?"

"I said I knew two of them," said Jim quietly. "The second man is Brady Short, and he's not dead, Cullin. He's running like a coyote."

Cullin smiled faintly. "Great," he said. "You come in here and tell me you know two of the three murderers of Cass Crowley. Then you name a man who is dead and can't answer for himself, and accuse another who doesn't happen to be around."

"The fact that Short is on the run should make you suspicious."

Cullin waved a hand. "Brady Short is on the move quite a bit."

"His wife can tell you that he admitted killing Crowley."

"A wife's testimony has no weight against her husband."

Jim began to feel uncomfortable. He should have known better. Cullin wouldn't give Jim an inch.

Cullin eyed Jim speculatively. "Just for a laugh," he said. "Tell me why men like Short and Hitchins would want to kill Cass Crowley?"

"Hitchins was into Cass for a large sum of money. Payment of that debt would have ruined Hitchins."

"Go on," said the sheriff. "What about Brady Short?"

Jim felt for the makings and began to roll a cigarette. He lighted it and eyed Cullin through the wreathing smoke. "Cass had turned against Short. Short knew he'd never get anywhere politically without the support of Crowley. It is as simple as that."

"You've given me two good reasons, in your opinion, why Hitchins and Short wanted to get rid of Cass Crowley. That leaves the third man. Who is he? Why should he want to kill Crowley?"

"He must have been the ringleader. Neither of those two men had the guts to think up a plan like that and carry it through. They must have been sure of their hand. So sure. ... By God! Brady Short tried his damnedest to stop that lynching and he knew all along he'd never stop them, nor did he want them to stop. Al Hitchins did the same thing."

"And the third man?"

It was very quiet in the office. Not a sound came from the fog-shrouded streets or from anywhere in the big building. Jim looked into the cold, hard eyes of Murray Cullin. *Then he knew.* Where had Cullin been when he should have been protecting those three innocent men? Off on a wild chase to get a change of venue from the governor, while his deputy was dead drunk and unable to stop the mob.

"Well, Murdock?" said the sheriff softly, very softly.

"You!" said Jim. He took the cigarette from his lips.

Something double-clicked beneath the big desk. "I've got a six-gun pointed at the pit of your belly," said Cullin. *"Don't you move!"*

"I wasn't thinking of it," said Jim quietly. "But why you, Cullin? By God, you had me completely fooled!"

The lawman's eyes narrowed. "I've hated Cass Crowley's guts for years," he said thinly. "He married the girl I loved. He got me over a barrel years ago and I lost my ranch to him. He tried to compensate by getting me the sheriff's job in this county, and I did the best I could with it. You'll have to admit that, Murdock."

"Granted," said Jim.

Cullin leaned forward. "He began to needle me about the death of his son. He wanted the killer brought to justice. He wouldn't let up on me, Murdock! I was sure it was you. A lot of people were positive it was you until that damned brother of yours got you cleared. I began to hate Crowley as I never hated anyone before, and he knew it! It was only a matter of time before he changed from backing me at elections to someone else. He could make or break anyone in this county, and a lot of men in this state as well. I had to get rid of him!"

"So you rigged an arrest of those three drifters and brought them in. Why didn't you kill them then, Cullin? *Los muertos no hablan.*"

"They didn't have a chance. I wasn't sure that I would be unsuspected. It was Brady Short who thought up the lynching deal. It was Al Hitchins who agreed to pay off Van Lassen and the boys. You've got to admit it worked."

"Almost," said Jim quietly.

Cullin laughed softly. "Almost? I can kill you here and now and cover up. Al Hitchins can't talk. I can find Brady Short and shut his mouth as well, one way or another, Murdock. One way or another. You see, I hold all the aces."

The coal fell in the stove. A wagon rattled by in the street. A dog barked in the distance.

Jim dropped his cigarette into the gaboon and slowly rolled another. "I left a letter with a friend of mine," he said quietly. "In it I have written everything I know. There's enough evidence in that letter to fully incriminate Hitchins and Short, but not you, Cullin. However, by piecing things together, and making an official inquiry, I think the governor may soon learn who the third man was who was in on the deal."

"You're lying!"

"Am I? Did you think I was a big enough fool to come back to Ute Crossing with a price on my head? I knew the odds, Cullin."

Cullin sat there for a long time, and then slowly he raised his right hand and placed the cocked pistol on the desk. "I might have known," he said huskily.

Jim lighted the cigarette and eyed Cullin over the flare of the match. "Who rigged my brother's buggy for that last ride, Cullin?" he asked.

"I don't know."

Jim fanned out the match. "It would be the sort of dirty work Barney Kessler would do."

Cullin wet his dry lips. "It was him and Van Lassen. Barney filed the kingbolt. Van waited on this side of the bridge until he saw Ben come out of the drive and head for the bridge. Van timed it to ride onto the bridge at the same time Ben rode out on it. Van slammed his horse against the side of the buggy. I guess you know the rest."

Jim stood up and waited. Cullin stared at the cocked pistol on his desk. "Get out of here," he said, without raising his head. "I've got work to do."

Jim closed the door behind him. He was in the street when he heard the muffled sound of the shot from the sheriff's office. "Score three," he said.

He looked through the wreathing mist toward the Grape Arbor. Down the street the clock atop Al Hitchins' Ute Valley Mercantile Company began to strike the hour. "Next time I ever get in a mess like this," said Jim to himself, "I'll be damned sure I do write such a letter." The clock rang for the tenth time.

Jim unbuttoned his coat. He walked slowly across the street. A man was walking toward the Grape Arbor. The man stopped to light a cigar, and when he looked up he saw the lean, scarred face of a man he knew well. Too well...

"Buck Grant," said Jim softly. "Where are your drinking amigos?"

"I don't know, Murdock."

"You're lying. Don't try to call out to them."

Buck slowly took the cigar from his mouth. "I had nothing to do with killing your brother," he said. He glanced sideways at the saloon and opened his mouth to yell a warning. The heavy barrel of a Colt slammed alongside his skull and dropped him on the boardwalk. Jim stepped over him, looked up and down the street, then sheathed the Colt. He pushed through the swinging door.

A man leaned on the bar watching Baldy Victor removing the cork from a fresh bottle of rye. Another man stood in front of the mechanical piano idly flipping a coin in the air as he eyed the selections. Baldy looked toward the door and his jaw sagged. Van Lassen turned slowly. "Barney!" he said over his shoulder. Barney turned as Jim walked toward Van Lassen. His eyes widened.

Baldy stepped back against the back bar and glanced nervously from side to side. "Oh, my God," he husked.

"Have you been drinking, Lassen?" asked Jim quietly.

"What the hell is it to you?"

"I want no advantages."

"I haven't had a drink yet, Murdock. I will when I'm through with you."

"You know why I'm here?"

"You don't have to write it out, Murdock."

Barney wet his loose lips. His face seemed to go in and out of focus. "I ain't done nothing, Jim," he said.

"Nothing but a little filing, eh, Barney?"

Van Lassen smiled thinly. "It was him that done it," he said.

"Who drove his horse against the side of the buggy?"

Van jumped sideways from the bar, clawing for his Colt. Jim gripped the brim of his hat with his left hand and scaled it at Van's flushed face. The gunman flinched. Jim jumped to one side and fired at Barney Kessler as the man fumbled for his Colt. The first slug caught Barney in the guts, dumping him forward. The second slug caught him in the top of the skull, and the third smashed into the piano. It tinkled erratically into life.

Van Lassen fired. The slug whipped past Jim's face and shattered the back bar mirror, cascading shards of glass down on Baldy Victor, flat on his face on the duckboards. Jim fired once, jumped to one side, and fired again. Van opened his mouth in squared fashion like a Greek tragic mask as the two slugs thudded into his chest. He fell heavily and lay still beneath the wreathing gun smoke while the piano ground steadily away.

Jim picked up his hat and placed it on his head. Slowly and mechanically he opened the loading gate of his Colt and began to load the hot cylinder. He could hear men shouting and calling out in the foggy street.

Baldy's head showed above the bar. "My God," he said. "No more than three minutes by the clock!"

Jim looked at him. "Was it self-defense, Baldy?"

"Absolutely! I'll swear to that!"

"They were your friends, Baldy."

Baldy brushed broken glass from the bar. "Hellsfire," he said. "They drove away more business than they brought."

Jim walked to the door and out into the foggy street. No one stopped him. He walked to the livery stable. He asked Meany Gillis to go to the general store on an errand for him. When Meany got back with the purchases, Jim had saddled the roan. He shook hands with Meany. "If the law wants me," he said, "you can tell them where to find me."

He mounted and rode east on the wide street. The wind was rising and the fog was being driven away. In a matter of minutes, the wind had begun to hone a bitter edge to itself. It drove up the valley of the Ute, thrashing the trees and whipping the fog to tatters and then into nothingness.

Jim rode up the gallows hill. He dismounted and took a spade from the cantle. Slowly and deliberately he dug a hole at the base of the first of the three great trees that stood there. By the time he had dug a hole at the base of each of the trees the wind had cleared the valley of fog. People down in the streets of Ute Crossing could see him moving about on the gaunt hill.

He placed a can of Kepauno Giant Blasting Powder in each of the holes and carefully fused each one of them, then tamped in the earth. He lighted a short six, sucked it into life, and touched its end to each of the fuses. Then he mounted the dun. He was almost at the bottom of the hill when the first explosion came, followed rapidly by the others. Clods and dirt flew through the air, and the harsh echoes slammed back and forth between the valley walls and were lost in the windy distance. The trees thudded heavily to the wet ground.

He had a long ride to the west through bitter weather, but he'd make Three Forks before the passes were closed. He would be there in the spring if the law came looking for him.

He had a feeling it never would. As far as Jim Murdock was concerned he'd never ride east of Warrior Peak again.

It was almost time for the first snow of the year. There was a different feeling in the wind. A driving gust of it struck Jim's face like stinging, sharp-edged grit, and it wasn't until he reached the bottom of the slope that he realized that it wasn't grit at all, but the harsh reality of the first snowfall of the year.

TAKE A LOOK AT RIO DESPERADO AND TOP GUN

Two Full Length Western Novels

Spur and Owen Wister Award winner Gordon D. Shirreffs spins tales of adventure in the old west that are heart-pounding and invigorating. Two of those tales are found in this volume, for your enjoyment.

In *Rio Desperado*, Burke Dane sets out to avenge the unlawful lynching of his half-brother. The further he goes, the more entangled he becomes in a web of lies and deceit. His desire for vengeance is tempered and strengthened when he finds himself a hunted man, on the run for his very life. He'll get justice, though, no matter the price...

In *Top Gun*, Dade Averill was fed up with being a gunslick. Before getting locked into the path he'd been on for years, he'd wanted more out of life than the clothes on his back and the pair of silver-inlaid Colts on his hips.

When an old friend pleaded for his help to fight off a bunch of killers, he wanted no part of it but couldn't simply turn his back. He knew what he had to do, simply because he was the best. There was no rest for the weary, and no resting place for a top gun—except the final one.

"Shirreffs' work is a mastery of pacing and tough, gritty prose." – James Reasoner

AVAILABLE NOW

ABOUT THE AUTHOR

Gordon D. Shirreffs published more than 80 western novels, 20 of them juvenile books, and John Wayne bought his book title, Rio Bravo, during the 1950s for a motion picture, which Shirreffs said constituted *"the most money I ever earned for two words."* Four of his novels were adapted to motion pictures, and he wrote a Playhouse 90 and the Boots and Saddles TV series pilot in 1957.

A former pulp magazine writer, he survived the transition to western novels without undue trauma, earning the admiration of his peers along the way. The novelist saw life a bit cynically from the edge of his funny bone and described himself as looking like a slightly parboiled owl. Despite his multifarious quips, he was dead serious about the writing profession.

Gordon D. Shirreffs was the 1995 recipient of the Owen Wister Award, given by the Western Writers of America for "a living individual who has made an outstanding contribution to the American West."

He passed in 1996.

www.ingramcontent.com/pod-product-compliance
Lightning Source LLC
Chambersburg PA
CBHW011343010726
47493CB00011B/2937